LAND OF PROMISE

Edward shaded his eyes and stared into the blue distance. He could just make out the high staff that rose above Fort Sackville, a dot of color fluttering at its tip. "*Ma foi!*" he breathed. "Closer!" He could not believe what his eyes had seen.

"What is it, Edward?" He heard Abby's soft voice for the first time in more than an hour.

"The flag! Can you make it out from here?"

Ned's shout almost made the canoe jump. "By thunder, it's a Virginia flag! The Union Jack's gone! Look at it, green and red! The fort's fallen to the Yankees!"

"*Allons y!*" Edward leaned into his paddle. "Come on, let's go!"

WHITEWATER DYNASTY CONTINUES!

WHITEWATER DYNASTY: HUDSON! (1304, $2.95)
by Helen Lee Poole
Amidst America's vast wilderness of forests and waterways, Indians and trappers, a beautiful New England girl and a handsome French adventurer meet. And the romance that follows is just the beginning, the foundation . . . of the great WHITEWATER DYNASTY.

WHITEWATER DYNASTY: OHIO! (1290, $2.95)
by Helen Lee Poole
As Edward and Abby watched the beautiful Ohio River flow into the Spanish lands hundreds of miles away they felt their destiny flow with it. For Edward would be the first merchant of the river—and Abby, part of the legendary empire yet to be created!

WHITEWATER DYNASTY: CUMBERLAND! (974, $2.95)
by Helen Lee Poole
Journeying into the Virginia and Carolina country—through the horror of Indian attacks to the passion of new-found love—the second generation of the Forny family continues a tradition in creating an Empire, and in building an American dream. . . .

WHITEWATER DYNASTY: WABASH! (1293, $3.50)
by Helen Lee Poole
The American Revolution has begun, and Edward Forny's love for Abby must be tested—when he travels alone to the Wabash River to open up trade to the soldiers. By forging a new frontier, he will secure his family's future for generations to come, an unforgettable WHITEWATER DYNASTY!

WHITEWATER DYNASTY
THE WABASH

HELEN LEE POOLE

ZEBRA BOOKS
KENSINGTON PUBLISHING CORP.

ZEBRA BOOKS

are published by

KENSINGTON PUBLISHING CORP.
475 Park Avenue South
New York, N.Y. 10016

Copyright © 1983 by Helen Lee Poole

All rights reserved. No part of this book may be reproduced in any form or by any means without the prior written consent of the Publisher, excepting brief quotes used in reviews.

First printing: December, 1983

Printed in the United States of America

To
Hilda & Jerry Jones
of
Richmond, Virginia

I

Marie Forny felt as bewildered by the unsettling changes in her own body and mind as she was by the talk she heard of the tumultuous events of the great world somewhere east of the settlement here at Fort Pitt. The adults spoke uneasily and sometimes fearfully of Concord and Lexington, which she finally understood as the names of towns in Massachusetts Colony — wherever that was. Her mother and father seemed as concerned about them as every other adult, even the redcoated soldiers she overheard. "*Demme!* Them buggers as shot our lads who was just doin' their work for the king should 'ave their backsides branded with the broad arrow. Criminals they are — and no more!"

Right now as she looked out the window on the road between the cabins that led to Ligonier, she heard Edward's grave comment to her mother. "Abby, *j'ai peur de la guerre!*"

"I think I fear war too, unless calm tongues on both sides speak up. But this has been building for some time — ten or twenty years."

War? It was the first time Marie had heard that word spoken. She started to turn from the window to ask a question but just then a group of boys raced about the corner of a cabin in a melee of whirling bodies, shouting incoherently as each tried to strike a ball with the stick he carried. It was nearly spring and the rains had melted winter's snow but the ground had not yet dried. The mud was cold but the boys did not seem to mind. Their bare feet plunged ankle deep in it. One lad slipped, tried to catch his balance but fell.

Marie could not help but laugh as he jumped up, the whole front of him a dripping blue-black from chin to bare ankles. The whole group raced on by the cabin, right under her window, and disappeared. But their shouts trailed behind them like smoke shredded and thinned by the wind.

"*Ma foi!* You laugh at fighting and war!" Edward's sharp voice wheeled her about.

"Not war . . . boys," Abby explained. She smiled at her daughter and then her husband. "They are much, much more important at Marie's age."

"Were they to you?"

"There's much I haven't told you about the years before we met, my dear. But . . . like mother, like daughter."

"Minx!"

The soft, rich chuckle in her father's voice was like pure gold, Marie thought and then, suddenly, she wondered about her mother. Had Abby also been all sixes and sevens with herself? It couldn't be! Surely at fifteen, with sixteen almost a year in the future, Marie's emotions, thoughts and body were different from all others past and present — perhaps the future too. Maybe other people are like other people, but no one is like Marie Forny, she felt certain.

Her attention returned to the window and her restless eyes searched as far as the last cabins.

Every door was closed against the sharp bite of chill in the air that not even the bright sun could quite dispel. Like the mud, she thought, frozen in hard cutting ridges at night but turning mushy and gooey evey day.

As abruptly as the shouting, swirling gang of boys had disappeared around one side of the cabin they reappeared around the other, this time racing away from her, sticks flailing, ball bouncing one moment, stuck fast in blue-black muck the next. She watched them and puzzled why they had suddenly become such fascinating mysteries. She could name and had played with every one of them, singly or in a melee such as they formed now, her shouts as loud as any, her elbows and feet as quick to strike and kick.

Yet at unexpected moments such as this, they became almost strangers, peculiar creatures, a species apart from the rest of humanity; her girlfriends, the grown folks, her father and mother, or even herself. Especially herself. She looked down along her body. It was properly covered to the ankles by a dress of gray, broken at intervals on bodice and skirt by stripes of black. It was not the usual frontier linsey-woolsey, for Edward had bought it in far-off Philadelphia — the only one of its kind in Pitt.

Now she was hardly aware of the dress but of the body it covered. Her mind pictured it as clearly as though she stood stark naked. It had once been arrow-straight and somewhat angular, like Henry's. Now and then through the years she had accidentally seen Henry without clothing. She still had occasional glimpses though he had moved to another bedroom a few years back. Sometimes she had spied on him through a crack in his doorframe, holding her breath at the temerity of her forbidden act, ears and nerves keened for the least sound, ready to silently flee.

Both of them had changed; Henry the lesser of the two. He remained basically all bone and muscle. His face had lost its round, fleshy little-boy look, becoming more and more handsome, his hair growing longer, curlier and turning jet black like Edward's. The greatest change in him had been in the size of the things between his legs.

"He's all on the outside," she marvelled time and again to herself, "while I'm all on the inside." Except for her second mouth and pair of lips down there. Her girlfriends at Pitt shared her curiosity. In the room of one or another of the young damsels, the door closed against intrusion, they tried to resolve the questions bandied back and forth. None of them as yet knew for certain, many of the "answers" were sheer guess or folklore. Now and then solid fact emerged and almost always from Carrie Ryan, the oldest.

"You say boys have little sausages a-dangling down there." Her lips curled in contempt of her friends' ignorance. "Well, let me tell you, that little sausage can grow long and hard and stand 'most straight up."

"Why?" Marie demanded.

Carrie touched her dress atop her groin and then rubbed her hand slow and deep into her crotch. "So it goes in here — inside you — that's why. He works it in and out and it feels good."

"How do you know?" another asked breathlessly.

Carrie scornfully tossed her head. Her long hair swung wildly. "How do you reckon I know?"

"You mean? . . ."

"What else? When you kids git older like me, you'll be doing it, too."

After that Marie watched the boys with a confused mixture of fear, deeper curiosity and the first stirrings of desire. Her attention did not center on any one of the striplings. She saw them only as a group, only as "boys," but the word now had many deeper, confusing connotations.

Abby tried to explain to her daughter, and Marie could not have had a better teacher. Marie had been warned in advance of the changes her body would experience during the next two or three years and so she accepted them as normal to every girl growing into womanhood instead of as freakish things that happened only to her and set her shamefully apart from her kind.

Also in those two or three years, events — like her body — changed tremendously in the great world beyond the settlement and even at Pitt itself. The British soldiers suddenly packed up and marched away, north along the Allegheny. Rumor from travellers headed down the Ohio had it that England's forces west of the mountains would be concentrated in two posts, one at Detroit and the other at Niagara. The Indian tribes, fiercely loyal to the "Great Father Across the Waters," would be sufficient to hold this nearly empty wilderness empire for the crown.

Then newspapers from Philadelphia and far-distant New York confirmed the rumors and talk. The newspapers had passed from hand to hand westward and by the time they came to Pitt, they had been reduced to one creased, soiled and sometimes torn sheet. Occasionally an issue would be nailed to the inner wall of the single tavern in the town. Neither Marie nor Abby ever saw it, since proper ladies never entered the hostels. But Edward did and reported the news.

Word was also carried each day by the constant stream of settlers who came along the eastern road or up from the south along the Monongahela. In this way even Marie heard how the initial skirmishes had turned into a siege of Boston-town. There had been a battle at Bunker Hill. She wondered if it was like the hills around Pittsburg: high, steep, covered with trees and underbrush, and laced with black coal that could be burned in fireplaces and crude iron that blacksmiths used.

Soon after the soldiers left, the settlers began to examine the abandoned post. They approached it cautiously as though expecting the usual harsh challenge of a guard or the curt, snapped order of an officer not to trespass on the king's property. No redcoat with musket and bayonet barred the open stockade gate to check them and the settlers became bolder. Marie clung to Abby's hand as the crowd followed Edward and half a dozen of the leading townsmen into the compound. Marie looked curiously about, first at the row of low log huts built against one stockade wall. Though empty, their silence seemed somehow threatening. "Sojers' quarters," someone in the crowd said. "Over there be the officers'. Ye can bet yer eyes them dandies always had the best."

Another row of cabins, these much larger and obviously more comfortable, lined a second wall. Marie then saw the remaining walls were also lined with storage sheds, smithies and workshops. She saw ladders leading to high platforms from which the soldiers could fire between the pointed stakes that formed the walls onto any advancing enemy force. She saw the painted mast in the center of the compound. It looked strangely naked and she wondered why until suddenly she knew it had been the flagpole. Each morning the Union Jack had been raised to its top as a bugle sounded and muskets volleyed a salute and each night it had been lowered with the same ritual.

The settlers milled about the abandoned post, in and out of the cabins and storage huts, aimlessly crisscrossing the compound. Few of them noticed Edward moving to the flagpole where he stood and critically judged the frame of mind of his neighbors. He finally stopped a roving courier and asked for the man's heavy hunting knife. He struck the bare pole with its massive handle. The repeated raps finally brought him full attention.

His voice carried over the crowd. "The king's troops are gone — and for good."

"Thank God for that! They ain't gonna lord over us no more," someone gleefully shouted.

"*Eh, bien!* True enough. But we are left with no defense and no protection."

Absalom Cooper, the settlement's furniture maker, answered, "We can always take care of ourselves, I figure."

"How?" Edward demanded.

"Why, fight when we have to. I ain't forgot how to use my Kaintuck rifle."

"Nor me!" a dozen men said almost as one.

"And lose your hair to the first big war party?"

Absalom bristled and truculently approached Edward. The a-borning quarrel between the two men attracted the inquisitive crowd. They immediately became the center of attention. Marie edged closer to her father and Abby stood directly behind her. Absalom stood almost as tall as Edward and his leathery, deep-wrinkled face had pulled tight, chin jutted and hard as though daring Edward to take a swing at it. His brown eyes turned dark and angry.

"Ye doubt what I can do? . . . or what near' ever' other man in the settlement can?"

"No."

"Then what in hell so you mean? Ain't none of us cowards, but ye be saying that?"

"I am saying every one of you is brave, an excellent shot, a fighter to the last breath, *mon ami*. But what holds you together so that you fight as one, eh? The Indians have chiefs and war leaders. It is certain they will be down upon us — mayhap soon. Then there are the swarms of people coming to settle in the western lands."

He pointed through the open gate to the village cabins and the road from the east that would bring the hordes of newcomers.

"The king's law forbids them to enter this country, but has it stopped them? They come, defying the king. The soldiers could not stop them though they tried. Now, with the royal law thrown off, we will see thousands each year. They'll sweep right over us. There will be thieves and murderers among them. They will pillage and burn us if they do not fear us, eh?"

Absalom studied Edward, hard eyes locking with his. Then, slowly, he lost his angry stiffness. His shoulders sagged as he rubbed his chin. He looked about at his close-pressing companions.

"Ye might have the right on it, Forny, but how do we make 'em fear us?"

"Become a town and take over the stockade. Have a

militia armed and ready. Have riflemen manning the firing platforms and make sure the travellers see 'em day after day. We stand as one then, not single men who can be cut down one at a time when it pleases the cutthroats. Let us hold a meeting here and now. Have the matter decided and so be ready for red war party or white bandits."

A murmur of assent swept the crowd like a sighing of a strong breeze. Someone called, "Forny, you lead us. You have a warehouse here and stand to lose the most."

Edward held up his arms, spread wide, but he shook his head. "You all stand to lose unless we have some temporary law and order, some organization strong enough to keep all of us safe until regular authority — British or Yankee — can take control. You can depend on it, one or the other will be back. I can't be around all the time and you need someone like that. I'm always out on the rivers or deep in the mountains. I'll lead the first meeting but one of you who farms or works each day right here at Pitt is what you need — say, Absalom Cooper."

Absalom's jaw fell. He started to object but the settlers' eagerness to be about the business of organization swept him along. Both Marie and Abby were astounded by the speed with which the milling crowd became a decorous meeting. The men pressed forward to make a tight circle about Edward while the women faded to the rear, mere onlookers, that being the proper role and custom for the female.

Edward sent his clerk to the warehouse to fetch paper, feather quills and a bottle of ink with which to record the decisions to be made. The first was a change of name of the place from Fort Pitt to Pittsburg, this as the end result of some heated discussion on other proposed names. That proved to be the hardest problem, for every man and woman present had come from some colony town to the east — Maine, New York, New Jersey — where the town organization and meeting was well known, many of them organized long ago when the first Englishmen arrived.

Marie listened and looked on with fascination, marvelling at the ease with which Edward manipulated all those clamoring men. She stole a glance at Abby. Her mother shared her pride as he began to list the officials the town should have and received agreement. Finally, names flew back and forth for councilmen. Time began to drag as argument succeeded argument.

Marie turned away, working a path back to the open stockade gate. The street of silent cabins stood before her as empty of interest now as the meeting had become. She heard constant shouts behind her and knew the arguments continued back there. She petulantly thought they could end it with one sensible act — leave it all to her father, allow him to rule the town.

She angrily tossed her head and her auburn hair swirled about her shoulders. She spoke to the silent, unheeding cabins. "He'd be the very, very best they could ever get!"

"Who would be?"

The voice came from her left. She wheeled about, startled. A boy of her own age, maybe a year or two older, stood between two of the buildings. She had an impression of blue eyes in an oval, tanned face, of the typical frontier long shirt caught up at a slender waist by a wide belt. Then suddenly he laughed at her.

She drew up stiffly, shoulders back, fists clenched and asked in a freezing voice, "Am I all *that* funny?"

His grin widened. "It's the way you look, all surprised

and flustered. Like you thought an Injun had jumped out at you."

"Well! There ain't much difference a-tween you and an Injun, is there?"

"I always thought there was. Anyhow, my daddy told me so."

"And who's your daddy?"

"Absalom Cooper. Don't tell me you ain't heard of him or seen me before. I been living here five-six years. You're bound to've seen me playing stickball with my friends — that is, when Daddy ain't teaching me sums or having me learn his trade of making furniture and such."

"Cooper!" She lost her anger and looked back into the fort compound. "Why they just named him to the new town council and they're voting now if he be head councilman."

It was the boy's turn to show surprise. "Councilman? My daddy?"

"Head one at that. I heard some call it 'mayor.' "

"I stayed away figuring it'd be all palaver and nothing more. I best go see."

He started to run to the main gate. She called after him. "Hey!"

He stopped short. "What ye want? I gotta see how Daddy comes out."

"What's your name?"

"Ned — Ned Cooper."

He raced off the next instant. Marie looked after him, now of half a mind to return to the meeting. He disappeared through the gate and she knew he had plunged into the press of settlers about Edward. Oh, let it go! she thought and wheeled about to continue her aimless stroll down the dirt street. She thought of the group of boys

17

who shouted and raced by her home, not one face outstanding, just "boys" about whom she was curious — a pack, something like animals, though maybe more important.

She heard his voice, ". . . living here five-six years . . . bound to've seen me playing stickball with my friends." But she hadn't seen him — until just a few moments ago. That is, really *seen* him.

For the first time an individual stood apart from the pack. He had a face distinct from all the others. He had a name — Ned Cooper. The rest remained faces and figures moving in a meaningless blur by the window.

She stopped, turned back and stared at the distant gate. Something had happened, judging from the shout that suddenly arose. She started back to the fort. She had to make sure that some boy at long last had a face, a shape and . . . somehow a meaning. Ned Cooper . . . he was handsome and had a nice voice even though he had laughed at her.

She puzzled about the strange, warm feeling throughout her body.

II

Marie eased up to the fringe of the crowd, uncertain that a girl should be present among grownups engaged in business as serious as converting a mere settlement into a new town. She received only an occasional curious flick of a glance. She moved with more assurance then, mingling with the women and young girls who still remained in the background. The women might have much to say to their husbands later in the privacy of their own homes. But in public they covertly expressed their thoughts in swift, meaningful exchanges of looks, an occasional thinning of lips or angry but discreet lift of chins.

Marie paid the women scant attention. Her father no longer presided, but had lost himself in the milling crowd. Absalom Cooper had taken his place. He rubbed his chin, looked almost wildly from man to man, astonished by his election, bewildered by friends who pressed close about him pumping his hand, slapping him on the back. His rounded, constantly moving eyes seemed baffled, begging someone, anyone! to resolve his dilemma, to give him a hint of what to do.

Though Marie had a fleeting touch of understanding, she dismissed it with the heedless callousness of the very young. She wanted to see Ned Cooper, to study him as best she could from a distance. In all this crowd, he would never, never notice her interest. That would embarrass her though she didn't know why. She had a few fleeting glimpses of him in the sea of shifting bodies. It wasn't very satisfactory — except that they confirmed her impression that he was a handsome boy. That peculiar warmth flooded her body again and again.

Later that afternoon, she once more stood at the window overlooking the street. The boys would play stickball again. They had to! She had to make certain Ned Cooper was different than the others. He would surely stand out — bold and handsome.

Without warning, as usual, the boys swept from between the buildings and swirled, shouting and laughing, by Marie's window and out of sight. But Ned had not been among them! A second later she understood that he probably was with his father and mother talking about the afternoon's surprising turn of events. Henry spoke so close behind her that she jumped.

"Mooning over the boys again, Sis? You spend most of your time at the window looking at them."

"I do not!"

"Every day. I've noticed it. What about this afternoon at the meeting?"

"I wasn't the only girl there!"

Henry's grin widened as he teased her. His voice held no malice, but still his perception infuriated her. He touched the tip of her chin with his finger. "But you were the only one who watched Ned Cooper all the time."

She stamped her foot, hands doubling into fists. She almost shouted, "Oh, shut up!"

"Marie! Henry!" Abby spoke sharply, looking up from the pots hanging from cranes over the flames in the fireplace. "We'll have no quarrels."

Brother and sister spoke contritely with nearly one voice. "Yes, Mother."

Abby stood with her hands on her hips, piercing eyes sharp and steady. She could look more Indian than white in such moments. "What is all this about, pray?"

Henry scraped the edge of his shoe along the floor and he looked abashed. "Nothing, Mother. I was just teasing Sis about Ned Cooper."

"Absalom's son? Why?"

Marie angrily interrupted. "He thinks I've gone mushy about him. It's not true."

Abby studied Marie for a long time then said quietly, "Henry, you've heard Marie. You must be wrong."

She managed to meet her brother's skeptical look though she felt her cheeks grow warm. He finally shrugged. "I guess I might be, Mother. Sorry, Sis."

Just then the boys slipped around a corner of the cabin and it was all Marie could do to keep from looking at them. But she succeeded. Henry walked to the door. "I'm going to the warehouse. Father or Dean Smith might have something for me to do."

Abby returned to her cooking and Marie fidgeted a moment and then looked out the window. Quiet filled the big room long enough that Marie felt the strained time had passed. She heard a small noise behind her and knew Abby had placed her heavy stirring spoon on the table.

Her mother spoke quietly.

"Perhaps you haven't gone mushy about Ned Cooper but I take it he does catch your eyes."

Marie slowly turned, expecting to meet with vexation. But Abby had a soft smile and her dark eyes were filled with understanding. Marie could not avoid an answer.

"I . . . well, I just saw him — really saw him — today. I didn't even know his name. He was just one of the boys always playing along the street."

Abby walked in her graceful Indian way to the big work table and sat down on the bench. She pulled a bowl of vegetables to her and slid another beside her as she patted the bench. "Help me peel and cut the vegetables, honey. I think you and I need girl talk."

Marie reluctantly complied. She worked silently. Abby began to describe her girlhood in Westover, the Connecticut village where she had lived so long ago. Marie became interested and also thankful that her mother had forgotten Ned Cooper. She listened to stories of her grandmother, killed by an Indian arrow in the raid that finally destroyed Westover. Abby spoke of Daniel Williams, the young man to whom she was betrothed and had been so near to marrying.

Abby sighed. "But he was killed in the same raid and by the same Onondagas who killed Mother. I was their prisoner . . . Corn Dancer's prisoner."

Abby seldom spoke of those days but when she did, Marie listened in fascination. Surely no woman had ever lived as adventurous and romantic a life as her mother's! Marie said as much but Abby answered flatly, "Don't be such a ninny! Many and many a woman in these western reaches have met with dangers over and over again. I never talk of mine except to you or Edward or Henry, just as the other women say nothing but to their own families. That's why you never hear of them."

So Marie remained silent and listened. Long vanished Westover came to life again and Daniel Williams courted Abby Brewster but they had to wait for one of the circuit rider's capricious visits to be married. Marie comfortably listened as she worked the vegetables. Abby's story took an unexpected turn today.

She said dreamily, "I've not thought of my other swains in a long, long time."

"Other! . . . Mother, you mean Daniel wasn't the only one?"

"Of course I do." Abby tossed her head with a smile. For an instant she became a girl as young or younger than Marie. "I've been told I was a very pretty maiden. Heaven knows, I believed it myself! The boys noticed me — all of them. If one didn't, I'm a bit ashamed to confess this late in life, I *made* him notice me."

Marie impulsively squeezed her mother's wrist. "I'll bet there were very few who didn't."

"Very few indeed! But the point I'm trying to make is that I noticed boys . . . particular ones." She made a sound somewhere between a laugh and a sigh. "I can't remember several. . . . Some stay in my mind — like Obed Blake or Darius Stone or Jedediah White. Either way, remembered or forgotten, I loved each and every one of them. I *knew* my devotion would last a lifetime."

Marie looked askance. "But . . . none did?"

"I think your father's name is Edward. He's from France, not Connecticut colony. The forever, ever love came along at last. It always does. All before then were just crushes. I was really in love with love, not the boy of the moment. To be honest, *ma cherie,* I was also quite a bit in love with myself, with all sorts of fancies. I was the beautiful damsel whose love was pure and steadfast. I was positive I would die if my lover turned to someone else because he knew he could depend on my love, always and always."

She laughed again. "Of course, *he* more than likely didn't know he was in love with me or could depend on me. Somehow, I never told him. More than likely, by the time I might have spoken, it didn't matter. I was deeply in love with someone else."

Marie gasped. This was a part of Abby's life she had never heard of before. Abby was the essence of steadfastness, stability and certainty. *She* wouldn't flit carelessly from boy to boy, lover to lover! Abby didn't notice. She busily peeled a huge potato, her eyes distant, her fingers automatically but skillfully handling the knife, her thoughts obviously buried in her past.

"This was all when I was your age, or maybe it started when I was a bit younger. I remember at first that boys were, well, just boys. Then I suddenly noticed one especially and all the others somehow became fuzzy. Oh! How madly I loved Obed Blake . . . for a while. Then the others, some for a longer time and some for shorter. But love them I did. Yes, indeed!"

Marie narrowed her vision to the vegetable in her hand. She didn't see Abby's covert, sidelong look. Why, Mother had the same thing I'm living through right now! She could hear in her mind the noise of the daily stickball game down the village street, whirling around the cabins. She knew every player by name and all about him, but nevertheless one face blended in with the others.

Until now — Ned Cooper. Just like Mother said. All of a sudden one of them stood out, became different, separate. He had a handsome face and a strong young body, worthy of every bit of her devotion. He loved her as she loved him, only Ned didn't know it yet.

Marie lifted her head, her eyes flashed and her face darkened with anger. She turned to her mother to make fierce denial. Ned Cooper was no crush! She met Abby's knowing eyes and knew how cruel it would be to tell her she was wrong. Times had changed and modern girls could really tell true love from a passing fancy. But how could she tell Abby she was now becoming an old woman and out of date?

She didn't have to. Abby suddenly swung the talk to another subject. "Speaking of the Coopers, Ned's father has heard talk from the east. We think we know why the British left so suddenly. Edward agrees with him."

"Oh?" Marie asked with scant interest. What could be more important than Ned?

"The war against the crown. It's called the Revolution of late and that's just exactly what it is — a revolt. The British have too few soldiers scattered in too many small posts in this western country. So they're putting all their strength in two main forts — one at Detroit, the other at Niagara. But maybe you're too young to be interested."

The implied accusation stung. "Mother! I'm not too young. Don't you think I care about what's going on?"

"I should hope so, darling. Edward says the English have decided to let the Indian tribes fight for them. They'll send war parties everywhere from the lakes to the north to the Spanish Floridas to the south. Before long, no Yankee clearing or settlement will be safe. We can expect attacks even here — or on Boone's settlement and Harrodsburg in Kentucky. That leaves the British free to fight wholly in the colonies."

"Why do the Indians hate us and fight for the English?"

"Because we Yankees keep coming over the mountains to settle on Indian lands. The king ordered a stop to movement out here but no one paid any attention. Now we're paying for it. The Indians hate us. We didn't obey the order of the Great Father Across the Waters and he is their friend."

For as long as Marie could remember she had seen the immigrants passing by the fort. Sometimes the redcoated soldiers had stopped them but King George's ministers in England issued edicts impossible to enforce. The immense land west of the Appalachians to the Spanish holdings along the Mississippi was empty of all but Indians. It was composed of fertile farm country, of never-ending stands of timber — oak, hickory, chestnut — of brooks, streams, rivers and lakes where fish abounded in such numbers that they would supply millions and millions of people forever and ever. There were endless miles of grasslands, open pasture as suitable for a farmer's cattle as it was for the innumerable buffalo the Indians hunted. Bear and venison supplied an overflowing larder of meat.

No colonial farmer with half a brain in his noodle, as Marie had often heard it said, could turn his back on all that richness. So they came from the east, some boldly along the roads and trails from Philadelpha to Fort Pitt. Others came down the Allegheny and the Monongahela, sweeping by on clumsy rafts piled high with lashed-down supplies and farming tools as well as human cargoes of women and children. Marie often wondered what magic or faith kept them from drowning. No one she knew could answer that question.

She had once heard a circuit rider preach under a tree to

the Pitt settlers. He had vividly described the ancient plague of flies the Lord God had long ago visited upon the Egyptians. Edward had dryly remarked that the Yankees were a modern plague upon the Ohio country. No wonder the English had such stout allies in the tribes or the Yankees such implacable foes.

Just then Edward and Henry came from the warehouse and the discussion, thankfully, ended.

Late that evening, after supper, made up in part of the vegetables she and Abby had just peeled and prepared, all of them talked lazily before the fireplace of the gossip of the settlement and about the scant bits of real news the few travellers of the day had brought to Pitt. Then Marie and Abby scrubbed the copper pots and pans until they gleamed in the candlelight while Edward and Henry banked the fire so only a few embers glowed deep in the pile of gray ashes.

All of them dispersed to their rooms for the night. The Forny cabin was by far the largest in the settlement, having not only the typical long and wide main room with a loft above, but also wings forming bedrooms for Abby and Edward, for Henry and Marie and even a small storeroom for household supplies. The cabin was a mark of Edward's increasing wealth and worth as a trader on the rivers.

Marie closed the door behind her as she entered her room and, shielding the candle in its holder from the vagrant air currents, walked to a small table placed just under a mirror against one wall. Absalom Cooper had made it, a handsome piece of furniture with a smooth, varnished top. Marie had no doubt at all but that Ned had worked on it under his father's critical eye.

She thought of Ned with a deep sigh of romantic yearning as she loosened her hair and pulled her dress up over her head. She sat down before the mirror and began combing her hair. The candle flame flickered now and then and the mirror had imperfections that distorted her lips, eyes and jaw as she chanced to move her head. Still and all, she assured herself, she looked on a very pretty face and surely Ned should be attracted.

A naughty thought slipped into her mind and she sat quite still, looking at her image. Maybe she needed more than just a pretty face if Carrie Ryan's superior wisdom was to be trusted. Marie slowly lifted her hands to the straps of her camisole and pulled the garment off her shoulders. Her smooth upper chest bared then, slowly, the darker line of her cleavage. She looked fascinated as she lowered the garment and the upper curves of her breasts appeared. With an abrupt, decisive and almost savage jerk, she exposed herself to the waist.

She critically studied her image. "I don't have such bad tits, do I?"

She answered herself after a moment. "No, they're not bad at all. Maybe sort of nice and soft. Could be bigger, though. Lots bigger."

Carrie had told the circle of girls that boys liked pink-red nipples, the kind that stuck out. "They want to nibble and suck 'em. If a girl ain't got no tits with nipples like that, she's gonna have a mean time catching a fella."

Marie frowned as she leaned forward and her breasts did not make nice cones like Abby's. Of course, Abby's were larger, rounder. After all, she was a grown woman and Marie was just beginning to sprout. Marie laughed at herself even as she continued her critical examination. Ned Cooper would never in the world think about Abby as Marie wanted him to think about her!

She started to lift her hands, blushed and dropped them with an impulse to turn away from the mirror. But she couldn't. Her train of thought, mingled with sudden hot desire, would not allow her. She closed her eyes and clearly saw Ned in her imagination. She held tightly to the image as her hands rose again and slowly cupped about her breasts. The tips of her index fingers touched her nipples, rotated slightly. She felt the nipples grow taut and then her cupped hands lifted her breasts.

Oh, if those hands were only Ned's! Those fingers only his!

Suddenly shame swept over her. She blew out the candle and the room plunged into darkness. She swiftly finished her undressing and jumped into bed. The room was pitch black. She could see nothing.

But she could almost feel Ned at the edge of the bed, standing tall and looking down upon her with the same desire she felt for him.

III

Edward Forny's knowing, sharp eyes travelled over the lashed and covered cargo in the huge trade canoe but could find nothing wrong with the way it had been loaded. It would not shift in even the most swift and dangerous river current and so tip the craft over without warning. His two French-Canadian *voyageurs* nervously awaited his judgment, smiled and sighed with relief when he spoke.

"*C'est bien, mes amis.* How about our possibles?"

He referred to smaller packs of personal belongings each man, including himself, must of necessity bring along on the voyage down the Ohio. Justin and Luc indicated the bundles neatly placed and anchored beside the hulking main cargo of trade goods. A long Kentucky rifle gleamed beside each pack, lashed so that a quick jerk would free the weapon. The lidded firing pans and the high-curled hammers bearing flints were covered by waterproof, protective skins that could be snatched away as swiftly as the rifle lashings.

The long, wide canoe's keel made a deep groove in the sandy bank of the Allegheny and the far end, projecting into the main current, tended to sway with it, threatening to break away from the strong hands that held the craft captive. Many of the settlement people had come along with Abby, Marie and Henry to see him off. The business of beginning a nearly normal river trip had the trappings of a major voyage.

It was that "nearly normal" Edward knew that had caused the unusual gathering. These were not wholly normal times, now that war definitely raged in the east and cast its sinister shadow as far west as the Spanish posts on the Mississippi. Red foes of the Yankees had already struck at several isolated farms, leaving dead bodies and burning structures behind them. This was uppermost in Abby's mind, and Edward tried to soothe her.

"*Ma cherie!* For how many years have the Indians on the rivers known me? They think of me as Canadian if not French and they think of me as one who brings them the white man's goods and tools they can get nowhere else. I will be all right."

"I wish I could be sure. They might shoot first and look later — when it's too late."

He laughed but it was gentle, not mocking. "Do I hear my Onandaga wife, Strong Woman, talk about poor Indian eyesight? There is no need to worry just for the sake of worry, eh?"

"No," she reluctantly agreed. "That would be foolish. But there are white men out there who use the war as an excuse to murder and rob. David Williamson and his band are of that kind."

He lifted her chin with a long finger and smiled into her eyes. "You make too much of it. Would that band of thieves be as at home as we on the swift river currents? No, we would leave them far behind."

"There's treachery on land, through the whole country. Many out there are still loyal to the English king and they hate everyone else enough to kill."

"*C'est aussi vrai ici*," he answered. "It's also true that here there are men counted Tory, though, for the most part, they keep their opinions to themselves."

"Because most here are patriots and a Tory who would talk or do any act to help King George would be strung up in a minute. But they do as they please out along the river. Besides, why do you go when the whole land's a-boil?"

He pointed to the huge lashed pack in the canoe. "*Le bon Dieu* knows when we can get more trade goods out of Philadelphia or New York while armies march back and forth and fight battles. I have just enough now to open a post at Vincennes in the Wabash country. Captain Busseron commands there and he knows me. The way is clear but can easily be closed at any time by this plagued war."

She flared. "You don't sound like a patriot!"

He laughed. "I leave that to my good wife. I'm considered neutral French, what with all my *courieur du bois* and *voyageur* along the rivers."

"Best not let the Yankees catch you. Busseron may be French but he commands Vincennes for the British."

Edward shook his head in wonder as he looked deep into her worried eyes. He swept his arm about her waist and pulled her close, pressing his body hard against hers. He felt her responding pressure as he gave her a full and lingering kiss. His voice held a tender note that instantly touched her heart.

"*M'amoureuse,* you and I met in the midst of Indian as well as French and British threat. We lived for years in danger from Pontiac's warriors and Simon Girty's treachery. It was our love that brought us through. *Ma foi!* It can surely be with us on another trip down the river and return!"

She leaned back in his arms, frowning up at him and then smiled in surrender. "It will . . . but on your way, before I change my mind!"

He embraced Marie and then Henry, giving the boy added instruction. "Work daily in the warehouse with Dean Smith. I have plans for you when I return so you must know the goods we sell and the goods and peltry we buy."

He jumped into the canoe. Justin and Luc pushed it out until the current truly caught it, then they swung up and into the craft. Their paddle blades flashed in the sun as they swept out beyond the stockade to the point where the Allegheny became lost in the Ohio.

They pulled into the northern bank to establish a camp of sorts while the sun was still an hour or more high in the west. By the time it had fully set and twilight swept down the river, they had built a fire, caught fish and Edward bagged a deer that foolishly grew too curious. They set guard turns then rolled up in Indian blankets to sleep.

They continued the journey the next day. Edward loved this great river, as did Abby, who had made several trips with him along it. To round one of its sweeping curves meant encountering another breathtaking vista of a wide, silvery water highway bordered on either side by beautiful trees and bushes. High hills often lifted precipitous peaks above the foliage and often, without warning, trees gave way to carpets of grass a mile or more long and sometimes rolling even further back from the river. Birds often darted in erratic flight above the travellers' heads. Just before noon, Justin made a sudden call and pointed to the southern sky. They instantly pulled to the bank and watched in wonder as thousands on thousands of passenger pigeons darkened the sky in one immense flock.

Justic and Luc blindly fired up into the cloud and two birds fell into the river with jarring splashes. Edward shouted an order to stop and Justin stared uncomprehendingly. "But there are millions of them, Edouard! This is one of many flocks. If we had shotguns we could bag many more. What harm is done when we take a few for our evening meal?"

"Millions of the birds," Edward answered, "but how many Justins and Lucs are there scattered on farms and settlements? Each kills just a few — oh, only just a few — and what does it matter? A few hundred a day, maybe more or less. Keep that up day after day and how long will it take to kill off all the birds, eh?"

"No fear of that. They will last forever."

"*Tu n'as pas raison,*" Edward snapped. "You are very, very wrong. They will last less than a century."

Justin shrugged disbelief and Edward knew it would be futile to continue. He grumpily allowed them to retrieve the dead birds. They pulled to the bank. Edward built a small fire while Justin and Luc plucked and cleaned the birds down at the river. Edward wheeeled about when he heard a rifle blast. Two more birds fell as the *voyageurs* lowered their weapons. He roundly cursed them, then realized it did no good. They shrugged, apologized as good *employes* should, but they exchanged knowing glances. Obviously, Edward had some kind of craziness about killing a few birds. Not long afterwards Edward wondered if that might be true as he nibbled delicious meat off a small bone.

Late in the afternoon they again watched for a good camping spot but more than an hour passed before the high, unbroken cliffs at water's edge ended on the Kentucky side of the stream. Soon after, Edward saw a smooth, cleared beach. They angled across the current. Justin and Luc jumped out into ankle deep water and pulled the canoe high up on smooth sand.

This time Edward fished while the two men set rabbit traps for the evening meal. They ate as dusk turned into full night. Fireflies began their lovely, erratic dance out over the water and Edward heard the low, sharp cry of bats as, nearly invisible, they swooped and soared in hungry search for insects. Edward's eyes grew heavy and before long he and Luc slept on the warm, smooth sand while Justin kept watch, his back against a thick, sturdy tree.

Edward had the last sentry watch of the night and it was he who witnessed the delicate, magical birth of the day. Huge, invisible cosmic fingers snuffed out the stars one by one until at last the black sky had but a single guardian. So slowly did first light seep in that Edward hardly noticed. There was no more than a faint lessening of the pitch black of the forest lining the river banks. Gradually Edward saw the final star pale as tenuous, unreal light seeped into the sky, flowing almost like water into the crevices of solid black. The light strengthened and Edward watched a faint tint permeate it, a peculiar, delicate pink and rose glow.

This time of the day always fascinated him. He was glad Luc and Justin slept soundly, leaving the magic for him alone. The constantly changing colors of dawn, the increasing strength of light spread further and further over the sky. Totally overwhelmed, night disappeared as though at the snap of a finger. Edward thought he heard the brazen blast of victorious trumpets as the eastern sky broke apart under the assault of streams of golden light, heralds of the rising sun.

His rapture shattered as a strange guttural voice said, "You meet day like Shawnee."

Edward's fingers tightened on his rifle. He had to fight a dangerous, instinctive impulse to whip it up to his shoulder. He half turned his head to look along the river bank to the west, the glory to the east forgotten. An Indian in the barbaric trappings of a war chief stood so close that Edward could amost touch him. Justin and Luc awoke and cried out in terror. More Indians stood in a towering ring about them. Like their chief, they held rifles, flint hammers pulled back to strike sparks into powder pans.

"*Ne faites marcher!*" Edward called a warning. He need not have wasted breath. Neither man intended to move a muscle. They lay terrified, certain they would be murdered within seconds. Edward said to the chief, "They only look like men. Do you take women's scalps?"

"Me Two Drums. No take bounty for Yankee hair," he said proudly.

"Bounty? For scalps? *Mon Dieu*, who pays?"

"Redcoat chief at Detroit pay — man, squaw, papoose, no mind. He pay."

"Hamilton?"

"That one." Two Drums nodded. His warriors confiscated the *voyageurs'* rifles then sat in an ominous, silent ring about them. Two Drums sat down cross-legged before Edward. He placed his rifle beside him and, from long Indian trading experience, Edward knew the man wanted to parley, not battle.

"How can I help Two Drums? I have trade goods in the canoe."

The Indian's eyes lighted. "No trade, though gifts maybe. After talk, huh?"

"*Mais oui* . . . talk about what?"

"You . . . me . . . all Indians . . . all French."

"*Tiens.*" Edward pointed to the sun now well above the trees and swept his arm westward. "All day talk."

Two Drums studied Edward closely, eyes sharp and direct. Edward bore the long scrutiny, aware of Indian suspicion and thinking. Two Drums abruptly broke the silence, pointing eastward toward Pitt.

"British . . . Yankee exchange war belts."

He alluded to the specially designed, beaded wampum belt that tribes exchanged to signify war between them. Edward didn't explain the white man had no such custom. A paper bearing a pompous declaration of war could be equally destructive. He merely nodded.

"But that British-Yankee fight." Two Drums stabbed a finger at Edward. "You French. You trade. You not fight, no?"

"I don't fight . . . yet. Might have to later. Not now."

"But Indian fight — Shawnee, Seneca, Cherokee, Choctaw, all fight Yankee for British brothers. Yankee come moon after moon, year after year. Take our hunting grounds. Burn our towns. Murder our people . . . almost all Lenni Lenape."

He referred to the wanton destruction of the unarmed,

Christian Delaware Indians at the Moravian Mission in Gnadenhutten. The deed had spread a wave of horror among Yankee and British alike along the frontier. Edward could not suppress his own slight shudder. Two Drums' eyes lighted.

"Yankee do that. So tribes hate. The Great Father Across the Waters try keep hunting grounds for Indian. Now he ask Indian take up hatchet for him. We fight for him."

"I don't — nor for Yankees."

"So all tribes do not fight French. Our friends. From the time of our fathers' fathers we friends."

"My friend?"

"Your friend. British friend. I come say you safe from Indian wherever you go."

"Vincennes, Fort Stanwick."

"British post. British man there. Also French man who is chief for British."

"Lieutenant Governor Abbot," Edward nodded. "He has returned to Canada, I have heard. Capt. Francois de Busseron commands there now."

"Good friends," Two Drums nodded. "You good friend. All French good friends. My warriors see you go along river. Two Drums afraid maybe you think Indian fight you."

"And you've paid this visit to let me know you're not? *Fort bien, mon ami.* That is very good."

"No tribe fight French trader. You come . . . go . . . anywhere. No fight. No hurt. Two Drums' tongue is tongue for all tribes."

"*Parbleu!* you deserve gifts."

IV

When the canoe bearing her father and his *voyageurs* sped out of sight around the first bend of the Ohio, Marie heard her mother sigh with resignation. The girl thought she detected fear in the sound, but Abby showed no visible sign of it. Mother kept it well hidden. Even so, Marie put her arm about her.

"He'll be safe, Mother."

Henry blurted proudly, "Of course he will! If anyone can take care of himself, it's Edward Forny! Everyone knows that!"

"Of course they do." Abby hugged them both. "I'm not worried about him . . . really. It's just the lonesome time while he's gone." She held them tightly when she turned to the village. "There's enough to do, what with the house to keep and sewing and mending. We girls will be busy. Henry, you have Dean Smith to obey instead of your father. Dean will teach you a deal of the business while he's at it."

Marie hardly heard her. Ned Cooper moved out of the crowd and she had eyes only for him. He gave her a bashful smile but swiftly turned away. She wanted to stomp her foot there and then but petulance would invite Abby's attention.

"Ned Cooper's a fine looking boy, I'd say. What think you, Daughter?"

Marie caught her breath in confusion. "Why . . . I'd . . . I never noticed."

"Then you're a blind young lady. Surely every other girl in the village has. Don't you like him?"

Marie turned scarlet and she stammered, "I — of course I do. But he's like all the others, isn't he?"

"Is he?" Abby asked knowingly. Her fingers pressed slightly into Marie's shoulder. "No need to come to the house right away. Give me time to set your tasks for you."

Henry had already walked away to the warehouse and now Abby abruptly left Marie not knowing what to do. Ned looked back over his shoulder just then and saw her alone. He stopped, slowly turned. His eyes met hers, flickered away, and instantly flicked back. He awkwardly rubbed his hands along his legs, smoothed his long frontier shirt down under his wide belt.

"Howdy," he mumbled.

"Good morning," she replied and waited. He appeared even more uncomfortable. She hurriedly sought for something to talk about. "It's sure a beautiful day. The sky's real blue, isn't it?"

"Yeah. Sure is."

Her adoring eyes drank him in. So handsome! Beautiful! But if he would only . . . ah! She understood. He de-

42

liberately restrained himself from sweeping her into his arms. No matter how much he loved her, the dull folk of the settlement would never understand their ethereal, unspoken romance. It was on much too high a plane. She read the plea for understanding deep in his eyes.

A princess should not allow her prince to look like an oaf to all these dullards! "My girlfriends are waiting for me. It's been good to see you, Master Ned."

His hands made a convulsive move and for an ecstatic moment she thought, defying all proprieties, he would truly bless her with a small touch of his fingers. But she read distress in his blush. He choked over a few words.

"It's good . . . see you . . . Miss Forny."

"Marie," she corrected, smiled and strolled daintily around him, moving slowly for she knew he wanted to look at her as long as possible. Certainly she wanted him to.

She continued toward Carrie Ryan's cabin. Although she did not look back, she could feel him watching her with despairing longing. The sensation brought on that peculiar warmth throughout her body she had come to know of late. It must be pure and holy love. It had to be! She angled toward Carrie's house, daring a glance over her shoulder. Sure enough. He had not taken a single step.

Jenny Ryan, Carrie's mother, opened the door to Marie's knock. The girls were gathered near the fireplace at the far end of the long room. They chattered like wild birds as they carded great piles of cleaned wool that Carrie's spinning wheel transformed into an endless line of yarn. Marie paused to look through a window onto the street. Ned Cooper had disappeared.

There was a dove cotelike fluttering as the girls made

room for Marie in the circle. She started working with the others and the conversation, as usual, turned to settlement gossip. There was little that hadn't already long since worn thin so, also as usual, boys became the focus of their attention.

Jenny Ryan's work had brought her close to the circle of girls. She listened a moment, shook her head in mock despair, and cut in on the chatter.

"Ther's more'n boys in the world." She immediately faced a battery of disbelieving, questioning eyes. "Why, there's a heap going on. We be fighting the British. Carrie, ye heard Paw talk about that thing called the Declaration of Independence. We be a free nation now."

"Ye mean when Paw sort of stood up tall-like reciting like a schoolmaster: When in the course of human something or other?"

"That's it."

"Pshaw! Ain't nothing but grownup meaning to that!" Carrie said half defiantly. "It ain't nothing a passel of girls like us has anything to do with."

"Ye best git your wits about ye — every one of ye. They'll be sojers here at Pitt afore long — either Yankee or Lobsterback. There'll be fighting, mind ye. Ye could grow up and git married as Pennsylvanians or Virginians rather'n British." Her voice dropped ominously. "Any one of us or any one of our loved ones could lose life and hair to Injuns as fight for the British. Oh, it has a heap to do with all of ye."

The girls completely silenced, she walked off in triumph. Marie felt a chill wave of fear at her prophecy. She recalled half-heard remarks Edward and Abby had exchanged about the news coming over the mountains. Like her friends she had not given any of the grownup talk real importance.

Beulah Day softly cleared her throat and spoke in a whisper. "My! Oh my! Your Maw's crotchety, Carrie."

"Like all the grownups lately, Boo," Carrie answered in another whisper.

Marie said underbreath, "Might be she's right."

"Shoo!" Sabina Jackson made the word sound like a low hiss. "No mind to us 'til we grow up or 'til sojers march in. Maybe not even then." Her eyes sparkled as she looked about. "Why, they'll be new ones to flirt with!"

"Never thought of that," Carrie admitted with a cautious look beyond the circle toward her mother. She smiled, adding, "They'll be as easy to cozzen as any boy around here — easier, 'cause they won't have known us."

Boo Day spoke up. "There's already a new one in the settlement. Handsome, too."

"Ye mean Ike Ilam," Carrie nodded. "Handsome he is, but a whole lot more. Watch out for him. He be quick to find a way into your pantaloons, than'n."

"How you know?" Sabina demanded.

Carrie made certain her mother was well out of earshot. She cupped one of her breasts and her lips grew red and moist. "First I saw him, he was a-staring at this'n, then at the other one and then he looked me up and down like he could see right through my skirt."

Marie sucked in her breath. "What'd you do?"

"Ho! I was just as bold as him. Asked him if he liked what he was lookin' at. He tried to scare me figuring I'd run if he answered."

"Did he?" Boo drew back in shock at Carrie's lustful

reply.

"He said lookin' wasn't enough to be sure it was good. His pants was perking out and I knowed he meant it. So . . ."

Her voice trailed off into suggestive silence, her lips slack. She cupped her breast again. "I pushed this'n out at him so he could plain see the size of it. Right then and there I thought he'd bust his britches! He said we oughta take a walk along the river where we'd be alone."

"Did ye?" Sabina demanded. "Did he . . . you know . . . did he?"

"Yup, we did — and he did. He could hardly wait 'til we was behind a thick clump of bushes up the Allegheny. He had me flat on me back, me legs spread. He whipped that thing out." Carrie stopped, eyes distant, and she said in an awed whisper, "Ain't never seen one so big. I ain't never been as deep-full of man. All the other boys is just toddlers compared to him. I've had him twice since then and —"

She broke off as Marie suddenly arose. "You leavin' us?"

Marie dared not look at Carrie for fear of showing her disgust and disbelief. She muttered, "I'm late for chores at home."

It took all her powers to dutifully make her thanks to Mistress Ryan in a normal voice and manage to walk without betraying her anger. Listening to Carrie Ryan, Marie suddenly realized that the girl lied for the most part. Oh, maybe she did fool around and flaunt herself. Maybe now and then a boy touched her or made smutty remarks. It might even be that, way backs somewhere, she and a boy had showed themselves to one another.

But the rest was made up of all the dirt that must be in Carrie's mind. That story she had just told about Ike Ilam? Poo! Carrie wanted everyone to think she was all grown up and wise, actually knowing from experience the whispered, mysterious things that women and men did when they were alone.

Listening to the salacious tale about the newcomer, Ike Ilam, Marie realized Carrie made up the same sort of story about every boy in the settlement. That must include Ned Cooper, though as yet Carrie had not mentioned him. But as sure as sure she would. Ned was not that way — not ever! He was noble and clean and strong, a prince that only the Princess Marie could love. That horrible Carrie Ryan! Marie vowed she'd never go back again.

She pulled up short when a tall boy came around the corner of a cabin. He also halted in surprise but quickly regained his composure. Ike Ilam in the flesh confronted her. She had an impression of tanned, sharp, handsome features before her eyes dropped to his trousers. She saw no sign of the instant "perking" Carrie described. Of course, the skirt of his long, coarse wilderness shirt hid the most vital part.

"Why, howdy, missy." He pulled off his wide brimmed hat. "We ain't met afore, me being new here. I'm Ike Ilam at your pleasure, missy."

His slightly narrow coal black eyes did not look right through her skirt as Carrie had said, nor did they dwell on her breasts for more than a second. His hair, hanging to his shoulders and tangled above his high forehead, was as dark as his eyes. His lean cheeks formed long planes, from jawbone to eyes. His neck was a trifle long though not thin. His torso was muscled and powerful as were his long legs and arms. Why, she thought, here's a boy I could've been taken with had I seen him before Ned!

"Howdy, Master Ilam. I'm Marie Forny."

One of his brows crookedly lifted. He really did have a devilish appearance. It was gone in an instant and the note of awe in his voice pleased her.

"Why, ye must be related to Edward Forny, missy!"

"I'm his daughter. Who be your folk?"

"Nothing so important as the Fornys. Paw 'n' me are just plain horse traders. We brought a few nags out this way, hearing Pitt settlement could use work or riding animals. Maw's been dead since I was a lickety-kid hardly more'n a hand high. My aunts and uncles raised me, if'n ye can all it that."

He's nothing at all like Carrie told us! He's really nice and polite. She felt more certain of herself . . . and of him. So she smiled. "Oh, I'd say your kinfolk did a fair job of bringing you up. But where do you stay? There ain't any empty cabins."

The jerk of his thumb over his shoulder indicated the Monongahela. "We're campin' in the woods by the river over there. If things work out like Paw hopes, we'll likely raise a cabin and a barn and stable, and build a rail pen for the critters."

"What's your paw's name?"

"Jeptha, but most call him Jep. He likes it."

"My pleasure to me you, Master Ilam. Folks about here can use horses, what with plowing and all. They'll make ye welcome. So will my father when he comes back." She moved around him to continue on her way. Ned Cooper stepped out of his cabin door but pulled up short when he saw her with a strange boy.

Ilam moved just enough to block her way. Though his

smile had widened, there was a peculiar quirk to his lips and his black eyes subtly changed. She didn't like them. Maybe Carrie was right about him.

"Mistress . . . Marie, maybe you 'n' me could take a walk someday soon." His eyes made a quick sweep of the river and woods beyond her. "Mighty pretty country for you to show me. I'd like that considerable."

Ned walked slowly toward them and the contrast between her prince and this oaf pushing himself at her became instantly apparent.

"*I* wouldn't like it, Master Ilam."

"Ho, now! How can you tell? You ain't walked with me yet."

Her chin lifted in disdain and her hands balled into small fists on her hips. Her words fairly scorched from her lips.

"I don't intend to — ever." She looked beyond him, smiled and raised her voice. "Morning, Ned. Be your paw keeping you busy?"

"Like always, Marie."

"So that's how it is?" Ike asked in a low voice.

She answered clearly. "That's how it is. Don't forget it."

All of them jumped when a volley of rifle shots sounded beyond the empty fort stockade. They stood immobilized by surprise. Marie judged the firing had come from across the Monongahela, just at the point where it merged into the Ohio. Cabin doors banged open. Men and women flooded into the street, the men armed. Absalom Cooper hastily rammed powder and shot down the long barrel of his weapon.

Marie recalled what Edward had predicted. The post would not remain unoccupied by soldiers for long —

Yankee or British, and either could mean trouble and war. Another rifle volley sounded and then many voices at a distance called a loud "Halooooo!"

V

Edward relieved Justin's constant labor with the canoe paddle as the long trading craft fought and bucked the Wabash River current. They had left the Ohio many miles back, although some in these parts said that this smaller stream was really the Ohio. All those many miles of magnificent bends and forest scapes were only a tributary. Hah! Edward thought as his muscles rippled along his bare back to the steady rhythm of the paddle, *les imbeciles* have no concept of the truth of the matter.

He had stripped off his shirt, for the sun was warm and he longed to feel it on his body. His rifle lay ready beside him. A single tug would loosen the knot that held it and the weapon could flash, roar and spit flame and lead in less than a second. He had noticed a smaller stream flowing into the Wabash some distance ahead. A small canoe shot out of it a split second before Justin called his warning.

The two Indians were equally quick to see Edward and with amazing skill in the fast current swung the canoe so that its high prow offered a narrow, difficult target. Edward snapped loose the knot, swung the rifle to his lap, at the same time whipping the paddle out of the water.

He called out in Seneca, "Peace! We trade, not fight."

He lifted his arm high, palm out in the sign of peace. After a tense interval a red arm raised in acknowledgment, then sun flashed on paddles as the Indians approached. He spoke to Justin and Luc in a low voice that would not carry across the water. "Keep your rifles out of sight but ready, eh?"

"*Tiens*," they replied in a single voice.

The Indians bore down upon them. Edward could see their necklaces of claws, the clan markings on their chests and arms. They were as strange to him as the arrangement of their coarse hair and the feather each warrior sported. They must be of an interior tribe that seldom came to the Ohio. However, they obviously understood the Seneca tongue. He used the Indian word for tribe when he asked his question.

"What people are you?"

"Kickapoo — rulers of all this land."

He thought many tribes might dispute the statement but his voice and face reflected only respect. "Who has not heard of the Kickapoo? Great warriors and hunters."

The Indians' faces grew haughty, their eyes disdainful. They maneuvered their craft alongside.

"You — who you? British? Yankee?"

"French . . . Canadian. I come to Wabash country for trade. I give you hatchet, knife, needles, cloth — for furs, eh?"

"You come to Kickapoo towns?"

"Where are they?"

The Indian pointed back to the tributary from which they had emerged into the Wabash. Edward later would learn that the smaller stream was called, at least by the British and local settlers, the Vermilion.

"Two-three day east. You come now?"

"First smoke pipe with British chief at Vincennes and build place where I stay. Maybe better you bring furs there, eh?" He saw their faint frowns and quick exchange of look. He spoke swiftly. "No, I'll come to your towns . . . say in one-two moons?"

Their faces cleared and they nodded, repeating his one-two moons phrase. Then with a sudden flick of paddles they caught the Wabash current and raced away south. Edward watched them for a moment over his shoulder and then resumed paddling. They had obviously not wanted to go to Vincennes and Edward wondered why. He shrugged in Gallic resignation. *Le bon Dieu* would give the answer in due time.

The country through which the Wabash wound looked rich but treacherous to Edward. Time and again he saw marks to the west indicating flooding year after year. As a result the earth was dark and mucky, and high grass grew as far as the eye could see. To the east, however, he saw many high, smooth hills, crowned with trees of every size. But the hills seemed unnatural, as though man-made in some long ago time. If settlers ever came to this country, Edward thought, they would be forced to erect their dwellings on the hills. But he had no doubt the lowlands would raise any kind of crop, probably as lush as the grass that now grew so high and wild, bending and swaying with the slightest breeze to make beautiful green shadowy waves.

Several days later, late in the morning, Edward sat atop the huge pack of trade goods, his attention always forward to the next bend of the river. He became impatient to see the place he had tentatively chosen for this second trading station in the Ohio country. From all he had heard through *voyageurs,* Indians and returning travellers, the town and its fort should exactly meet his needs. But — *qui sait!* — who would know until it was in sight.

He met with disappointment several times when they rounded a bend only to find more open river ahead, more miles of hard paddling against a strong current. Always, he'd hope, *this* curve would be the last, that once around *this* bend, they'd finally see the place.

They slowly entered yet another turn and worked along it at an agonizing snail's pace. Suddenly there it was! He straightened with a spasmodic bunching of muscles. His eyes rounded, his jaw fell. Then he closed his mouth with a snap and jerked his hat off his head. His triumphant yell echoed back from the high hill upon which a low, stout log fort dominated the Wabash.

Lower down the slope, but still high above the river, stood the houses and streets of the town of Vincennes. Ah, but the French must have prospered here! He saw a few stone houses, as outstanding among the frame and log structures as castles of the nobility. He had an impression of well kept gardens, splashes of color here and there indicating flowers, probably hollyhocks. A long length of the riverbank had been smoothed and sloped to form a landing beach lined with a dozen or more canoes, a flatboat and a raft. The houses stood whitewashed behind high picket fences lining the street.

His attention shifted to the sturdy log walls and stockade of Fort Sackville, the remaining seat of British power in the Ohio country now that Fort Pitt had been abandoned. In his eagerness to drink in all of Vincennes and its fort, he had forgotten paddle and canoe until Justin urgently spoke.

"Monsieur, we lose way!"

It startled Edward into awareness of the river as well as of the town. They had lost at least three canoe lengths. He nodded his thanks to Justin and bent to the paddle with a smile. *Ma foi!* His instincts had proven right. The big trade craft surged forward, splitting the current with a small white wave under the prow.

Sharp eyes in the settlement ahead had obviously long since spotted them, perhaps from the moment they had rounded the last bend back there. He saw people emerge from the houses and saunter to the landing to meet him. Movement at the fort above caught his eye and he saw three figures emerge from the stockade gate and slowly walk down the steep slope to the river.

By the time the canoe angled toward the landing across the current while still fighting it, thirty or forty people awaited them. Edward saw two men in uniform, one in British red with gold trim. The other man wore a long coat, white shirt with ruffled lace collar and a cavalier's hat with a rakish plume. He bore the insignia of a captain in His French Majesty's Canadian troops and the golden cord loop of a royal citation. Edward thought it strange to see English and French soldiers, obviously officials, strolling side by side when, less than two decades before, their nations had been locked in bloody combat.

The canoe came into shallow water. Justin and Luc jumped over the side, the river curling about their ankles. They pulled the craft up on the bank. Edward stepped to dry land and faced the two men. He then became aware of half a dozen red-jacketed men bearing muskets. They looked suspiciously French to be British soldiers.

The man in the red coat with gold trim spoke in a clipped, dry voice. "Who are you, sir? And from where do you come?"

"Edward Forny, from Fort Pitt."

"Pitt! Yankee? Rebel?"

"Neither. French trader hoping to ply my business here, should the lieutenant governor approve."

"I am lieutenant governor Abbot, sir. This is Capt. Francois de Busseron, commanding his Majesty's troops here at Fort Sackville."

Edward touched his forehead in somewhat of a salute and acknowledgment. From the corner of his eye he saw the crowd of curious men and women just behind the two officials and their soldiers. He pointed to the canoe's cargo.

"Trade goods, milord," he said to Abbot, "and of some value. My men can stand guard if need be, but I'm hopeful there is an empty house or cabin of use until I can build a store of my own."

Captain Busseron abruptly asked, "*Etes-vous Francais, monsieur?*"

"French? *Oui* . . . Gascon. *Et vous?*"

"Montreal. But my parentage is Picard."

"Gascony and Picardy — both far across the waters," Edward smiled desolately, "and, for me, long ago. Ah, but we are here and now in this new land."

"Once New France," Busseron added.

Abbot sniffed but with no real rancor. "Which is now King George's America."

Edward bit back his thought that King George was well along toward losing total rule. He brought them back to the problem at hand. "Do I have permission to land and start trading? Is there a cabin empty?"

Abbot gave the Frenchman a questioning look. "You will be in sole charge tomorrow or the day after, Francois. So what say you?"

Busseron's brows drew down and he looked troubled, uncertain, absently smoothing his long, waxed mustache. He subtly shifted his weight as though avoiding an invisible blow, then shrugged. "Eh, but you are still in charge. I would not intrude."

"Make him welcome if you like, Francois," Abbot spoke with a touch of asperity. "Be your own master a day or two ahead of time. No one will mind."

"Very well, milord." Busseron looked around at the assembled villagers. "Where is Madame Rodare?"

"It is her baking day," someone volunteered. "She dared not leave her fireplace."

"*Peste!* But she owns an empty cabin. Perhaps she will rent it for a time to Monsieur Forny?"

Edward spoke up. "I'll ask her, Captain."

"*Oui*, that would be best."

Again, Edward sensed the man's dislike of making decisions on his own. Edward spoke to Justin and Luc. "Stay here. I will seek out Madame . . . Rodaré, is it?"

Abbot nodded, then dismissed the problem with a slight gesture. "It can wait, Mr. Forny. Come up to the post. I have some excellent claret to make you welcome as well as to wash the river miles from your mind. We can exchange news, eh?"

Soon after, Edward sat at ease in the governor's office within the fort. The back wall was all solid logs with no break of window or door, since it formed part of the high stockade walls of the fort itself. But light streamed into the windows of the far wall and through the door, open upon the small parade ground with its flagpole. It reminded Edward of Pitt, standard British construction for the frontier.

When it came to news, Edward had the most to offer. He told of the British evacuation of Fort Pitt, thinking that surely a lieutenant governor would have explanation for it. Abbot's sallow face only darkened with anger as his frown deepened.

"Damned Yankee rebels! We'll have 'em all hanging from gibbets before this thing is over. How many loyal to the king are at the settlement or along the Ohio?"

"It's hard to say but I should guess not as many as you'd like. Say ten out of every hundred."

"And rebels? Neutrals?"

"Neutrals would be about as many as the loyalists. The remainder rebels. But almost all the Indian tribes count the king as their Great Father Across the Water."

Abbot smacked his palm down in triumph on his chair arm. "Ah! As I assured Governor Hamilton! Thank God, the ministry rid us of that fool, Amherst! D'ye know he wanted to stop all gifts to the tribes? Said they were just savage scum that needed to be cuffed about, not bribed, to learn who ruled this western country!"

Edward nodded. "Pontiac's rebellion made —"

"Amherst!" Abbot roared. "He brought that on. Since he was hauled back to England by his heels, we've repaired the damage. The bloody colonials helped us no end when they poured over the mountains like a thousand rivers from York Colony to Georgia, killing every Indian they sighted, be he man, woman or child. When the greedy bastards grabbed tribal lands, the gave us redskinned allies by the thousands — even a million, for all we know."

"You have the truth of it, milord."

"Indeed I do! So we need no post we can't defend like Pitt. Let the blasted rebels take it and be surrounded in siege like Pontiac's. They have no Colonel Bouquet to rescue them?"

Edward shrugged, glanced at Busseron. The captain intently watched Abbot as though he received orders. *Entendez-vous,* Edward? Do you understand? That is exactly what this uncertain soldier does! He learns his duty and does not ask the questions of an *imbecile,* eh?

Busseron quite unwittingly and almost instantly confirmed Edward's thought. He rubbed his hands together and smiled, his voice rich with unctuous flattery as he placed his finger knowingly beside his nose in a Gallic gesture.

"We are quite strong here, milord. Our Indian friends are all about us should we need them. We have outposts like Cahokia and Kaskaskia along the Mississippi to guard the water route to the lakes and also to watch the slippery Spaniards in St. Louis. You can safely go to Detroit to confer with Governor Hamilton."

Busseron sat rigidly in his chair like a soldier and struck his chest with his fist. "You can depend upon it, milord."

"Of course," Abbot said dryly. "But we talk politics, rebellion and treachery while the good claret waits our attention."

He lifted his glass to Edward. "To your successful enterprise, Mr. Forny."

"*Merci* . . . and to your health . . . and yours, Captain." The glasses emptied by the toast, Edward suggested, "Perhaps your Madame Rodare has finished her baking?"

"Francois?" Abbot asked.

"I should think so. I shall send for her."

"I would prefer to go to her," Edward said. "She would then feel free of authority and pressure. Tell me where I can find her."

Busseron pointed through the open door down the hill to the settlement. "Follow the first street north to its end, monsieur. Hers will be the stone house with the tall sunflowers along the wall."

"And the empty cabin?"

"A little further along, but across the way. It is the last structure on the street."

"*Eh bien.*" Edward arose. "I will find and speak to the good dame. *En passant*, how does it happen she has two houses?"

Abbot chuckled. "The cabin can hardly be called a house. Her husband lived there until he married Mathilde and, being frugal French, moved in with her and made the cabin a storage place for his furs."

"He is *courieur?*"

"Was . . . he fooled around with one too many squaws at long last and took a Kickapoo arrow from the woman's man. Treacherous bastards, those Kickapoo."

"And thieves," Busseron added. "We ran them off and they dare not show their faces any more. Not that Laurant Rodare wasn't just as bad. She is well rid of him and no one was happier when the news came. Had she not been a widow she would not have made so bad a bargain, but she hungered for a man."

"*Ciel!* Vincennes is as scandalous as Paris!"

Abbot laughed. "If it was as large, it would be even more. Ye can depend on it. I have often remarked to

Francois that it is difficult for a Frenchman to keep his tool in his pants."

"True of the lady's first husband?" Edward asked.

"Not that anyone has ever heard. He kept himself too busy fleecing the Spanish traders along the Mississippi. Raoul LaPlace built the house where Mathilde lives and he died in it. I have heard some sort of devil's bug ate up most of his insides."

Turning all that information over in his mind, Edward wondered what sort of woman he would meet as he went down the slope to the village and turned northward along the street as he had been directed. Big-boned, broadly-built and strong-willed like most peasant women, he thought. Or maybe thin, wiry, ugly and tough as an old leather shoe as they become out here in the wilderness. In either case, she's sure to have a wart on the end of her nose, or a mole sporting an aureole of black hairs on her face. It simply must be one or the other. He laughed at his sardonic fantasies.

He came to the stone house with the sunflowers but gave it only a quick study as he looked ahead for the cabin. There it sat — and his interest quickened. It looked stout and large enough. The good Madame Rodare had kept it in excellent shape. Two large windows that looked out upon the street had been boarded up and the stout plank door was closed and barred.

He slowly walked about the structure. There were two windows in the rear, also boarded, and at one end protruding stone and a high chimney above it marked a fireplace. He could readily picture the interior: one large room, loft above it, topped by a high-peaked shake roof. The *courieur* who had built it used more care than the average of his kind because he trapped and traded peltry for himself and not for some *patron*. So they needed more protection once they came off the racks where they were stretched, scraped and cleaned.

Returning to the front door, Edward considered the village, the landing, the location of this cabin in relation to his needs. It would be best if he had a place closer to the river. Ah, but that can be built, he thought. There must be carpenters here who can do it while I explore the river and its tributaries. I can temporarily move my trade cargo from the canoe to this safer place.

He looked back to the stone house with the sunflowers and then up the hill to the fort. He became aware again of the neat, painted houses, the gardens, the flowers. This was far better than Pitt crowded as it was on the narrowing point of land between the converging rivers. Abby would like it. Marie and Henry might miss their friends but Edward already had plans to take his son to the Watauga country and keep him busy for a time. There must be a few girls Marie's age here, so she would not be lonely for long.

"*Que diable!* Let's face the wart or the mole."

He crossed the road, walked up the short, neat path and tapped on the front door. He waited, looking around at the yard. There was no answer. He looked at the solid planks of the door and this time used his fist. He waited again but no answer. He sighed with irritable resignation and turned away. He took but three or four steps toward the street when a woman spoke behind him in a clear musical voice.

" 'Allo monsieur. You seek me?"

He turned around, sucked in his breath. The woman stood in the doorway. He saw no blemish at all on her rather long, oval face. Her skin was a pearly translucent white and her well spaced eyes a misty blue, direct and sparkling. Her high, broad forehead was crowned by luminous black hair neatly combed and brushed back over her head and caught in a soft roll at the nape of her neck.

Edward remained transfixed, his stunned gaze drinking her in. She stood tall, almost large, forming an unforgettable picture in the black frame of the open doorway behind her. For all her size, there was nothing out of proportion about her from wide shoulders to ample bosom and the suggestion of long legs hidden by the folds of her gray dress, the wide skirt ending just at the ankles.

This is such a woman as men dream about, flashed through his mind . . . how few of them . . . and afar out here in this wild country! Her clear voice cut through his thoughts. She smiled, revealing perfect teeth. He realized her mouth was a bit long, but the lips were red and invitingly soft.

"Monsieur?"

He made a low choking sound, stuttered a word or two, then found his voice. He slowly approached her, almost as though he suddenly moved in the presence of a goddess.

"Madame Rodare?" he ventured to ask her.

"*Oui*. Can I do aught for you?"

His thought screamed in his head. "Can you? Ah, *bon Dieu!*"

VI

The green and red banner of Virginia Colony flew atop Fort Pitt's flagpole, and forty Virginia militia men occupied quarters once filled by the king's regular soldiers. Homespun black and gray replaced scarlet uniforms and white clay belts; tricorn hats sporting cockades of leafy tree twigs replaced royal high, black-faced helmets. Long Kentucky rifles whose deadly accuracy had destroyed Braddock's troops replaced smooth-bore British muskets.

The advent of the troops threw the whole settlement into such turmoil that sometimes Marie had difficulty even thinking of Ned Cooper. Edward Forny's prophecy that troops of one sort or another would occupy the fort had come true but who would have thought of the Virginia rebels against the crown? Abby wondered.

Tatum Long, the commander of the militia, resolved the puzzle in his conference with Absalom Cooper held within minutes after the Virginians had canoed across the river. The whole of the settlement had been witness, Marie and Abby among the press of people.

"Be ye here to defend us?" Absalom demanded.

"Aye, and also to occupy Virginia land along the Monongahela and Ohio. It's rightfully ours. Lord Dunsmore laid claim to all this under the Royal Charter granted Virginia. The British garrison here did not dispute him when he drove out the Shawnee two years ago."

Marie thought Captain Long to be quite handsome, though he was not very tall and really somewhat stocky. But he had a full, deep voice that set her a-tingle and no knight of old had such challenge in his step. Abby decided he had a bit too much swagger.

"Aye," Absalom answered, "and then Lord Dunsmore withdrew until he made sure the governor in Philadelphia would treat with him."

"The governor — Philadelphia!" Long snorted contemptuously. "Quakers! And what have *they* ever done for folks on the frontier?"

"Given us powder and shot on occasion."

"Grudgingly, sir. They sent no soldiers when the French and Indians burned and killed."

"They are a people of peace."

"Aye, that they are — and it's very safe for them to be so, a couple of hundred miles away from tomahawks and scalping knives. Their mighty Lord Penn protected them before the king and his ministers. But what about now, when the king's rule is thrown aside? Do they send you soldiers — or even powder and shot?"

"They can't," Absalom replied reasonably, "what with Lord Howe's army occupying the city and his brother's war fleet on the doorstep in the Delaware River."

"They wouldn't even if they could. Ye know it and so

do your good folk behind you. Would ye have our protection under Virginia's flag . . . or none at all?''

"Touche!" Abby mentally used Edward's phrase for the neat trap. Long impatiently and haughtily awaited an answer. Absalom grinned wryly when he heard the murmur of his friends behind him.

"Your choice ben't none at all, lad."

"Lad? Captain, sir!"

"Sorry . . . Captain. No offense. Just a matter of age between us. But I do hear your country and Pennsylvania have agreed that them surveyors will run their line clean out here to the Ohio."

"And Mason and Dixon will place Pitt in Virginia's control."

"Might be, might not. But, shoo! Let's leave it rest until the survey's finished. Right now, you and your men are welcome. I don't doubt we can rassle up some good, warming Monongahela whiskey for all — and there be quarters a-plenty inside the stockade for every manjack with ye. Be ye of mind for it?"

Long eyed Absalom as though fearing a hidden trap in the invitation. Absalom met his probing eyes, held them until Long slowly released his defiance and swagger.

"Aye, the liquor'd be warming to me and my men after all our marching. Besides, I'm getting ideas about them blasted Quakers as might do us both some good."

"And what would it concern?"

"The powder and shot ye've mentioned they've sent to Pitt now and then."

"Ye be daft! They send it rarely and grudgingly. They'd not give an ounce of either did they know Virginia soldiers was here."

"Ah, but suppose they didn't? Or suppose I moved

back across the river into Virginia country and ye could say we'd take the fort, what with no powder and shot for the defenders? Let's talk on it. Haven't ye heard all's fair in love and war!"

"God's bones," Absalom exploded. "Ye're already here and we be helpless. What need we of powder and shot — or what argument to git it?"

Marie gasped at how swiftly Long's handsome face turned hard and cruel. He suddenly looked like a white savage. Menace vibrated in every word.

"Argument? The very best. Look at your people around you. I can drive them out into the wilderness before the day's over. That'd please my governor, making more room for Virginians. But was ye armed, and had powder and shot for your rifles, I'd have second thoughts about risking battle. It can go either way."

Absalom choked back his anger, recognizing his basic helplessness. He turned on his heel and said shortly, "Let's talk on it at my house. Your men camp here in the post."

He stalked off leaving Long to give orders as he pleased. The crowd of settlers also stirred and slowly, almost aimlessly, moved through the open stockade gates out into the settlement. Marie and Abby, close together, allowed themselves to be swept out of the compound.

Ned Cooper suddenly appeared. He saw Marie but only gave her a hurried, fleeting smile. His lack of attention annoyed her.

"Ben't ye speaking to me?"

He stopped. He threw a distressed look toward his home and then back at Marie. "My father . . . and Cap'n Long . . . Paw'll be expecting me to fetch 'n' carry when they meet. He'll be looking for me."

Ned hurried off, leaving Marie to frown after him. Abby watched her with just a hint of reproof that was also in her voice. "The lad can't help himself, ye can see it with half an eye."

"He could be civil," Marie snapped and then added contritely "I don't mean to speak mean to you, Mother."

"But how about Master Cooper? Will ye make it up to him later?"

"Yes."

But Marie was really not so certain. Her prince had become no more than a boy frightened by his father's scolding! All her sighs, romantic dreams and fantasies were only just that — nothing. He had somehow wronged her. Even worse, she felt foolish and embarrassed by her own idiocies. A spark of reason touched her: He's just a boy, hardly older than me. I never told him my thoughts, so he can't understand. Then reason fled as her anger returned. She didn't know who she hated more — Ned Cooper or herself.

Nor had she fully decided the next morning. She was early about the house chores, Abby as busy as she. Now and then Marie looked out a window, always toward the Cooper house. She saw smoke curling from its chimney and once she saw Bernice, Absalom's wife, sweeping off the wide, wooden stoop before the cabin door. Ned himself did not appear and she grew more and more irritated with him. At least, she thought, he might find some way to send her a sign he knew she existed!

"Quit mooning, girl!" Abby broke in on her thoughts. "Bring in the day's water from the well."

"Henry's supposed to help me!"

"He will as soon as he's finished cutting wood for the fireplace. You can make a start on it, anyhow." Abby's voice lost its sharpness. "Mayhap you'll see your young man on one of your trips to the well."

Marie brightened and picked up one of the heavy wooden buckets beside the cabin's water barrel. She knew only too well how much the bucket would weigh when filled. She often felt her arm would be pulled from her shoulder or that she would be permanently pulled to one side like a cripple before this daily chore was finished. She truly needed Henry's help and wondered what she would do if her brother ever left the settlement. This morning, Abby's suggestion that she might have a chance to see Ned offered a little compensation.

She strolled rather than walked to the town well, its high sweep like a gaunt arm against the sky. She expectantly eyed the Cooper cabin but Ned appeared neither at the window nor in the doorway. Her lips thinned though she hardly knew it.

She swung the well sweep around and dropped its bucket in a plunging fall to splash in the water many feet down. She exerted all her strength on the ponderous stone counterweight to lift the filled bucket to the well rim, then to swing it over to pour out into her own. She sighed in exasperation as she started to carry the heavy load back to her cabin. It pulled her to one side, straining her arm.

Just then the Cooper cabin door flew open. Marie thudded the bucket to the ground and a dollop of water splashed onto her skirt. Absalom appeared first, then Captain Long and at long last Ned. He and his father were cloaked and booted for travel! Ned saw her, said a word to his father and took a plunging step toward her.

"Ned!" Absalom's voice held a whip-crack snap. "There's no time to lalligag. Come along. We have to hitch the wagon and load our possibles for the trip. The sooner we start, the more miles we'll cover by nightfall."

Ned gave Marie a long, despairing look and dutifully turned away. She watched him trot after his father while Captain Long walked to the fort.

Well! Ned could at least have said a word . . . or something!

She hadn't heard him approach but Ike Ilam stood at her side. His eyes, so black and fathomless, met hers and bored into her. She noticed they were never really still, but constantly, minutely shifting. His brow quirked high, giving his handsome face that devil-be-damned cast she had found so titillating and she knew the warmth of his smile was meant only for her.

"Ben't that water a heavy load? Seems to me some feller shoulda been helping ye with it."

Her eyes flicked beyond him in time to see Ned disappear into the Cooper stable. The door slammed shut, the sound carrying to her. She answered in a flat voice.

"Some fellows just pay no mind."

"Some maybe . . . not me . . . especially if'n I had a pretty girl like you." He laughed before she could take umbrage. "Why I'm no more'n taking a load ye shouldn't be carrying."

He picked up the bucket, his sudden movement graceful and supple. She thought, he's like some of father's *courieur* who move with the grace, speed and silence of a prowling cougar. He stood straight again and bobbed his head toward her cabin.

"Best ye lead the way and open the door for me. I've seen your folks but I ain't met any of 'em yet. They might take it amiss —"

"Of course!" She caught herself up. "Mother will be glad you're helping until my brother can."

Abby turned from the fireplace when they entered, intending to speak to Marie. She stared in surprise at Ike then her questioning eyes cut to her daughter.

"This is Ike Ilam, Mother. He's helping me with the water."

Abby wiped her hands on her apron as she recovered from surprise. "I hope you've thanked him properly."

"She certainly has, ma'am. Where you want this dumped?" He shifted his load to his other hand and arm.

"Oh, I'm sorry. There." She indicated the house barrel and, still somewhat off balance, said, "Then sit ye down, Master . . . Ilam, is it?"

"Yes, ma'am, but there ain't no 'Master.' Nothing like that. Just plain Ike." He emptied the water and peered into the barrel. "You're gonna need several more buckets, ma'am. It's a mite heavy load for a slip of a girl like your daughter."

"Mast — Ike Ilam," Abby answered. "I thank you for helping Marie but that gives you little right to question our ways."

Ike hastily protested. "Oh, no ma'am. Not like that at all."

Abby refused to be silenced. "Here, all of us have tasks — my husband, my son and Marie. Normally, Henry would be helping her and he will be as soon as he brings in —"

At that moment Henry kicked open the outer door and entered with a heaping armload of chopped wood. He dumped it with a clatter on the floor in a corner beside the fireplace. He brushed bark and splinters from his sleeve.

"Ilam! What brings you here?"

"I gave your sister a hand with her water bucket." He looked from Henry to Abby and exploded, "God's sake!

You act like I scalped her or something!"

"I'm sorry," Abby said quickly. "We don't intend any rudeness —"

"But Mother!" Marie flared. "That's exactly what you're doing. Ike, I apologize for them."

He walked to the door. His black eyes blazed as he looked first at Abby and then at Henry, but they softened when he turned to Marie.

"No mind. It's a pleasure helping ye. I'll take myself off now."

"But —"

Abby's single word brought Ike's attention back to her. She sucked in her breath. Concentrated hate glazed out of his shifting eyes. He swung to Henry, who instantly bristled, hands clenching into fists. Ike opened the door before a word could be spoken.

"Good day to ye and that's the last fair word ye'll ever have from me."

The door slammed behind him so hard that it shook the cabin. The three stood frozen. Marie first regained use of her mind and muscles and took a step to follow after him. Abby's sharp command pulled her up.

"Leave it be. The harm's done now."

"It can be mended," Marie protested.

"Not with that one. He's the kind that nurses a-hate."

"How do you know so much about him? He's newly come to Pitt. I've seen him but once or twice and he's been nice and polite to me! Like helping me with that water bucket."

Henry looked out the window to the street. He spoke over his shoulder. "Makes no difference. He's nowhere in sight."

"Can you blame him? If I was Ike Ilam, I wouldn't

ever again set foot inside this house. I doubt if he'll even speak to me and —"

"That would be best, Sis." He met Marie's disbelieving, angry eyes. "What do you know about him?"

"What do *you?*"

"Yes, what *do* you know?" Abby echoed the question, then sighed. "I wish Edward was back! Why do we have our first serious family quarrel while he's busy miles away down the river! Let's get it settled before he returns — here and now. What do you know about Ike Ilam?"

"His paw is Jep Ilam, a horse trader from somewhere down in the Virginia or Carolina hills."

"That's an honest trade, isn't it?" Marie demanded.

"Of course," Abby said, "if he's an honest trader."

"That's it, Maw," Henry spoke painfully to Marie. "Sis, I don't want to hurt you but Jep Ilam don't set well with our neighbors. He's already tried to make some sharp deals."

"I don't believe it. Why, he's only just set up his horse pens and stables and —"

"Some of his nags sickened on the drive up here. He tried to push them off as good plow beasts, or fit to pull a wagon or carriage. That's not honest."

"You're just taking say-so from others."

"Sis, I've been out to his pens. He's building a stable and house in the woods about five miles down the Monongahela. It's like he doesn't want anything to do with the settlement. The few times he's come to the warehouse for staples and goods he's made it clear he's not neighborly."

"No reason he should be, the way we've treated him and his."

"You talk like Ike has put some evil spell on you, Sis

". . . and I don't doubt but what he could. You'd be better off setting your bonnet for Ned. The Coopers are more our kind. Honest, at least."

"Ned Cooper! Foo!"

"What's happened?" Abby asked sharply. "Just a day or two ago you were mooning about him."

Marie tossed her head again. "That was before I found out he runs off at anyone's beck and call and I can lump it if I don't like it. Well, I don't like it. He simply left this morning. I saw him go."

"With his father," Henry said. "Absalom's not 'anyone,' is he? Did you give Ned a chance to explain?"

"He was as close to me as you are, Henry Forny. He coulda said something. But he jumped when his paw snapped his fingers and trotted like a puppy to their lean-to."

"Where they hitched their wagon and took off for Philadelphia to try to get the Quakers to help us out here when we face Indians as well as the Virginians. Did you know that?"

Marie flushed. She hadn't known but she should have been able to guess it from all the discussion she had overheard with Captain Long. She flounced around, intending to go to her room rather than admit her fault.

"Marie!" Abby halted her in midstride. "We've had quite enough of this vexation. It's ending this very minute. Do you understand? You, Henry? It's all because of this Ike Ilam and I can't say I like him very much myself."

She looked from her son to her daughter, hesitated and then made her decision. "Marie, you will not see him until Edward returns."

"But it's all right to see Ned Cooper, I take it?"

Abby had to keep tight control to prevent slapping her

daughter. What in God's name had come over the girl! She managed to keep her voice level.

"Nor Ned Cooper. Get to your room and stay there. Henry and I will finish bringing in the well water."

Marie wanted to slam the door when she entered her room but Abby's temper stood at the boiling point. It surprised and frightened her. Mother had always been so understanding and kind! She started toward her window but instead threw herself on the bed. She buried her face in the pillow to muffle her sobs. Couldn't anyone understand her? She wondered if she understood herself. Was she only a scatter-brained girl so boy-crazy that she had completely lost her wits?

Her bitterness turned from her own wrongs to those of Ike Ilam. She cupped her chin on her fisted hands as she looked out on the trees climbing the far slopes of the Allegheny. She didn't see them clearly for Ike's angry eyes and drawn face intervened. A new anguish crept over her . . . for him.

Ike, not she, was the one all of them had needlessly and cruelly wronged. Everyone should make amends to him . . . but they certainly would not! Well — she would. But she had been ordered not to see him. She considered the dilemma and, bit by bit, found a solution.

She wouldn't see Ike — deliberately. But if she chanced to walk or roam where he would accidentally come upon her, could she be blamed? It took but a few seconds to decide she could not. She lifted her head. Her eyes gleamed and her chin firmed. She struck the bed with her fist.

So be it!

VII

Late in the afternoon after Edward had gone down into the village to find a suitable cabin for his business, he dined in the fort with Captain Busseron, his wife, and Governor Abbot, who would leave for Detroit the next day. There had been the usual formal ceremonies of the evening gun and hauling down the British flag as the sun sank lower and lower in the west. Then he had joined his hosts over glasses of wine. He curiously watched Aspasie, the young, nubile Negro slave, as she served them. He had seen very few of these bondaged folk in Canada, one or two who accompanied their masters as they moved westward through Fort Pitt along the Ohio.

He listened to Madame Busseron's voice and watched her gestures and expressions as she gave the girl an occasional order. He detected none of the arrogance he had often heard in the harsh, sadistic tones of slave owners. Madame Busseron treated Aspasie as she would a daughter who needed instruction in household tasks such as starching and ironing the captain's snow white shirt lace. Once when Aspasie left the room, Edward made a cautious comment.

"She's an attractive girl. I find a black skin can be beautiful."

Madame Busseron chuckled. "*Sur ma parole!* So does every *courieur* and *voyageur!* Even more beautiful than the red squaws they live with out in the forest or here in town. I'd free her in a second except I'm certain she'd become like the squaws — dirty, overworked and constantly pregnant."

"How did you happen to come by her, madame?"

"Two years ago, I went with the captain on a duty visit to Detroit. Governor Hamilton wanted to see for himself that Milord Abbot had appointed an acceptable assistant."

Abbot spoke with dry annoyance. "Colonel Hamilton is a stickler for royal regulations. He found Captain Busseron quite acceptable, so the journey was for nothing."

"Not quite — considering Aspasie. She was owned by an old hag with enough money to make her a Grande Dame of sorts. She had a son who looked more scarecrow than human but who considered himself quite handsome. None of the Detroit girls would so much as look at him so he used Aspasie as his harlot, when he wasn't lashing her for some fault his mother found with her. He also used the lash if she couldn't work him up to an erection — a miracle for him! *En tout ça* I bought her. And also, in any case, I think of her as something of a daughter rather than a slave. Eventually, I hope the right time will come to free her."

Captain Busseron shrugged. "In the meantime, she

keeps my clothing and uniform acceptable for a commander of Fort Sackville. But tell me, monsieur, how did you find the good Madame Rodare?"

"Overwhelming. You should have warned me!"

"That one!" Madame chuckled. "She'll have you in her bed at the bat of an eyelid."

"Remind me not to blink," Edward answered. "In fact, she suggested I might find her cooking as good as any along the Wabash."

"And you still chose mine and Aspasie's!" Madame exclaimed, patted his shoulder as she left the room to help prepare dinner.

"I not only find it excellent enough to doubt Madame Rodare, but also expedient. Of course, I pleaded I must arrange for Justin and Luc to move into the cabin to guard my trade goods. Until then, they must remain with the canoe on the riverbank and I must see to their safety."

"She's wilderness-wise enough to disbelieve you, monsieur. I can hardly blame her. *Ma foi!* What is the harm in having a woman when she offers herself?"

"As I have said," Abbot spoke up, "no Frenchman can keep his tool in his pants. There seems to be some sort of natural law involved."

After an excellent dinner, there was brandy and Abbot had a cigar. He soon excused himself, wanting to get in extra hours sleep in preparation for the start of his long journey at the crack of dawn. Soon after, Madame Busseron called Aspasie to help her retire, so Edward and Busseron were left alone. Edward heard the tramp of booted feet above his head as sentries moved about in the high blockhouse with its rifle posts. Sackville boasted four of them, one on each corner so that every approach to the post could be defended.

In the village below, lamplights snuffed out one by one and the very air seemed to grow softer, the stars became brighter and more profuse. With Abbot gone, Edward and Busseron swung from English to French without realizing it. The captain proved willing enough to answer Edward's friendly but probing questions.

"Yes, I fought under the Royal Lillies of France — one campaign against the Lions of Castille after my father bought my ensign's commission. The de Busserons are of the lesser gentry of Picardy but still influential enough in that province. There was loot a-plenty to be had in Spain. I bought my lieutenant's commission."

"What pulled you from Europe to America?"

"Ambition along with a promotion and more pay if I accepted service in New France. Few regular officers wanted to come to the wilds. It would prevent them from any chance at court duty where they might favorably gain the king's eyes and favor."

"Did they also make certain you were forgotten?"

Busseron chuckled. "At Versailles, yes . . . very much so. You see, my friend, I have never had illusions, certainly never the one that I'd go very far in the royal troops without money to pave the way. But New France . . . a captaincy without the cost of a single sou . . . a raise in pay besides! Ah, it was time to seek fresh pastures and chance opened the gates of one for me — an officer of the governor's guard at Montreal." He sighed. "It lasted such a short time! Until the British General Wolfe defeated and killed our General Montcalm at Quebec and the Crosses of St. George and St. Andrew replaced the Lillies of King Louis."

"Eh, but I have the thought the evil bird of bad luck only brushed you with the tip of its wing."

"True — then once more, luck. The Province — ah, no, it was really a kingdom — of New France included a million miles of wilderness. Regular British officers of the king's regiments were as loath to accept duty in some log and dirt fort as French officers to leave Paris. I had been captured with many other Canadians, but, having been given my parole, I was free within Montreal. I became friendly with one Major Blandon who had the ear of the new British governor. I was approached. Would I renounce my allegiance to King Louis and become a colonial militia officer for King George? I would be given duty somewhere in the wilderness with sufficient pay to live comfortably, support a wife if I so desired — so long as I obeyed the orders of any crown official officer placed over me. There was a plump, saucy little Canadian — Madame, you understand."

"So you are stationed here."

"And quite content, as you see. That is, so long as the lines of command are clear and I know to whom I report and who takes my orders."

"Governor Abbot is leaving. You'll be alone."

"Ah, but Governor Hamilton remains in Detroit. I have met with his approval so nothing is really disturbed."

Edward thought, this is the key to the man and explains his lack of advancement. He was born first to obey and then to command. He probably can't think of any loyalty higher than his immediate superior, who receives the same blind obedience Busseron expects of his men. Busseron lifted the wine bottle to pour another drink but Edward refused with a laugh.

"No, Captain. I had best turn my attention from good wine to the care of my good men."

"You should have moved them into the cabin off the Ouabache landing."

"Ouabache?"

"The Piankeshaw Indians name it so. But Ouabache or Wabash, it is a dark and lonely place to be until the moon comes up. Ah, then you think you are in a dream rather than a place."

"*Tiens,* I look forward to the experience."

His eyes adjusted to the soft spring darkness. The hundreds of stars above cast a light of sorts. The path was wide and clear so it did not take Edward long to come to the landing. Justin and Luc arose from the shadow of the canoe while he was yet some yards away and their sharp, alert challenge pleased him. He had made a wise choice in them.

He had brought a leather flagon of wine from the fort and the *voyageurs* took it with gratitude. When he asked about food, Luc said they had already eaten. He grinned across the small fire they had built in the lea of the trade canoe.

"Madame Rodare came down to the landing, vexed that you have not yet rented her cabin and moved us into it." His grin broadened. "I think she was also vexed that you were not here."

"That one will cause us trouble," Edward growled.

"Eh, but of the best kind. She is very much woman. So you will rent a cabin from her? It will be our post here?"

"We talked of rental at her house. It is just across the way from the cabin. We came to no final decision."

"She acted as though you had. Certainly there is no other vacant place in the village."

"How do you know?"

"We have spoken to many who came down to see us,

the newcomers to Vincennes. We learned there is but the one place. Best take it, Edward, or plan to live in this canoe or camp in the woods. Neither would speak well of Forny along the river.''

Luc had the right of it. They finished the flagon, banked the fire, and Edward rolled up in a blanket beside his men. He looked up at the stars. He thought of Abby and wondered if Henry or Marie was giving her any trouble back at Fort Pitt. She would be able to handle it. There was no one like Abby.

Nor like Mathilde Rodare. Disturbed, he rolled onto his side and tried to find sleep. But he kept seeing her magnificent figure, her inviting smile. He tried to cast her out of his mind but couldn't. At last, with a grunt of irritation, he sat up and, his knees pulled up to his chin, the blanket still around him, watched the play of the starlight on the waters of the Wabash.

Sleep persistently eluded him for hours but was finally partially captured only to escape once more, so that he came wide awake several times in the night. When dawn came, Edward felt he had sand in his eyes, his head ached and he was tired and grumpy. He found a secluded spot many yards upstream where he could strip off his clothing and dive into the river. He heard the fort's morning gun while still splashing in the water. He knew the whole settlement was awake and well about its business when he returned to the canoe to have breakfast with Justin and Luc. That finished, he came to his feet.

"I'll see about the cabin," he told Justin.

"*Bien*," Luc spoke up. "Then perhaps we sleep under a roof tonight?"

Edward reluctantly nodded. "I'll see to it."

When he came to the end of the street, he saw the door

to the stone building lined with hollyhocks stood open as though in silent invitation. He glanced ahead at the stout cabin. If he wanted to establish a second post here, he would be a fool to reject it . . . and so he took the walk to the open door.

As he rapped on the planks, he could look through the open doorway down a long hallway, its wooden floor waxed and polished, onto a second closed door that must open on the small garden in the rear that he had glimpsed from the street. He received no answer so he rapped again.

"*J'y vais!*" a clear, lilting voice answered from somewhere deep within the house.

Edward could not arrest his increased anticipation. He warned himself to remain detached and calm. After all, Madame Rodare was just another woman with whom he would trade as he had been trading with many other pioneer women along the river. He looked over his shoulder to remind himself that he had come to rent a cabin, no more.

"*Ah, je suis enchanté!*" She stood at hardly more than an arm's length before him.

"No, madame, *I* am delighted."

"*Entrez, monsieur, s'il vous plait,*" she invited.

"I would talk with you about the cabin over there."

"Of course. I had hoped you would come." She made a welcoming gesture. "But, as I said, come in." She saw his hesitation and laughed, the sound sending renewed currents along his spine. "Ah, monsieur, everyone knows Madame Rodare is most proper and discreet, a businesswoman, not one to create gossip. Or does that worry you?"

"No, of course not."

"Then, come, we will complete our business."

She led the way along the hall ahead of him with a sway of back and hips that made him breathe a little faster. Caution told him to walk away from her and the house — fast. But his eyes and senses fed his desires no matter how he tried to push them out of his mind.

She turned off the corridor into a perfectly proper and safe room containing only chairs placed about a small table. Two whitewashed walls were broken by heavy dark armoires, a window broke a third and a long, low bench covered with ornate covers and cushions the fourth.

She indicated the table and he sat down. She took a seat opposite him. He only then realized that as she had walked down the hall before him, she had loosened the two top buttons on her dress. He saw the upper curves of milk white mounds and the darker beginning of a deep cleavage. He could not help but stare. She acted completely unconcerned.

"How will you use my cabin, monsieur?"

He found his voice. "Warehouse, furs, trade goods. Mayhap a store for cloth, needles, pins — such things as the good folk of Vincennes might need."

Her face lit with pleasure and he saw dancing lights deep in the velvet of her eyes. "Ah, how we have needed something like that! We must always wait for a chance river peddler or for one of our own to make a trip to St. Louis or Pittsburg. Of course, there is the Portuguese, Francis Vigo, who lives several miles to the north."

In her animation she leaned toward Edward. The neck of her dress gaped wider and he now looked on a goodly portion of the inner curve of her breasts. A trifle more! his desires clamored. A trifle more and the nipples will appear. Ah, they will be superb!

She unexpectedly sat erect and the illicit exposure vanished, covered by her smooth dress. He swiftly looked up. She could not completely hide her knowing, expectant look though she instantly lowered her eyes.

What Gascon who had once dallied with the coquettes of Toulouse, Bordeaux and Versailles would not recognize the signs? Compared to the little vixens Edward had known so many, many years ago in France, Madame Rodare was much too crude and obvious. But how much finesse could be expected in a village of *voyageurs* on the banks of the Ouabache? Madame Rodare at least had a basic knowledge of men and some skills in enticement.

She had given him a glimpse of the rewards of victory but now hid and forbade them unless he was the man she obviously believed him to be. She covered her play with another question about the cabin.

"Will you be living there, monsieur? Or perhaps your men? . . . mayhap all of you?"

"How can I know?" he managed to ask. "We go where trading is to be done — up the Wabash, the Ohio. Along the rivers — anywhere and everywhere. But what is the difference how many? I want the use of the cabin for my business."

"But you? . . . sometimes you will be there alone?"

He nodded, met and held her eyes. "That will be of importance, madame?"

"*Je m'appelle* Mathilde. I have told you."

"And I am Edward if that pleases you."

"It does. Very much. Your presence would make me feel safer. I would really like to know there is a protector across the road. It could make a difference in the rent, a small savings?"

"A man? . . . for safety? Surely you have enough men around Vincennes —"

"Not like you, Edward. Would I be such bad company if I could give you —"

She fumbled at her buttons. The last one opened. She jerked her dress apart and stood up. Her full, white breasts fairly burst out at him — rich, delectable, the nipples pink and upstanding. She came around the table, bent to him. The alabaster mounds quivered deliciously before his eyes. She slid her hands under their curves and lifted them to his lips, whispered a low, ecstatic moan as she pulled his head against the yielding flesh and guided a nipple to his lips.

He forgot everything but the taste and feel of her. He managed to struggle to his feet. She jerked the dress from her shoulders and it fell about her waist. With nimble moves so fast her fingers seemed to blur, she loosened her skirt and stepped out of it. She stood naked. He drank her in with his eyes from narrow waist to ample hips to smooth flat stomach, the black thatch of hair between her legs through which he traced her second mouth.

She looked at him and gave a gasp of delight. He looked down and saw his trousers straining against his erection. She pushed herself against it, then fumbled and freed it. Her warm fingers held it, making small strokes that set him afire.

"*Quelle baton!*" she panted. "My God, the bedroom!"

VIII

Marie finished the ironing Abby had laid out for her, then gingerly and carefully placed the hot, heavy metal iron on the stone apron of the fireplace. Abby worked on mending under a window and looked up as she turned slightly to get more light.

"Finished so soon, honey?"

"Almost. Things have to be put away."

She lifted the stack of smoothly finished shirts and blouses and placed them neatly on the shelves of a cupboard. A plank across the table had served as her ironing board and she leaned it against the wall on the far side of the fireplace.

Abby made an angry sound under her breath because the thread would not slide through the needle's eye, then she moistened the thread in her mouth and tried again, successfully this time. She talked without looking up.

"You've been working steady all day and here it is

mid-afternoon. I bet you'd like to get out and walk around or visit with your girlfriends."

"It would be nice if there's nothing more to be done."

"Oh, there's always work, but for once it can wait . . . or Henry can handle it. He'll be back from the warehouse soon since Dean doesn't spend the long hours Edward does." She sighed. "I wish he'd return soon."

"So do I, Mother."

"Ah, but we don't know what problems he's met at this Vincennes town. He's so anxious to establish a second post there."

Marie walked to the window and looked out on the empty street. She spoke over her shoulder. "Will we stay here or go to this new place?"

"The new one, I think. Edward has always wanted us near him and he plans to leave Dean in charge here." She caught herself up. "But begone with you, honey! I'll bet Sabina or Boo or Carrie will have boys to talk about. Too bad your Ned had to go with Absalom to Philadelphia. You'll be anxious for him to get back."

Marie thought angrily, I will not! If he can't properly tell his sweetheart he'll think of her all the time he's gone, he doesn't deserve one. Abby was too busy with her own concerns to notice that Marie had not replied. Marie scowled out on the street, her irritation mounting as she thought of the way Ike Ilam had been treated, as well as Henry's scathing assessment and Abby's order to avoid him.

"I'm going out," Marie said abruptly.

"Have fun with the girls."

"I don't know if I'll see them. I feel more like taking a walk."

"Be careful, honey. Don't stray too far from the fort."

"There's been so sign of Indians."

"When you don't see them, be wary. I learned that from the Onondaga. Besides, the new Virginia militiamen could be wandering about looking for trouble."

"Shooo! I'll not be giving them any!"

"But they might give you some. Heaven knows when last they had the company of girls, especially any as pretty as you."

"Thanks, Mother, but don't worry about me."

She closed the cabin door behind her and looked toward the fort. The gate stood wide and she saw several of the Virginia soldiers moving aimlessly about the compound. Though none paid any attention to her, she felt safer as she turned away to stroll slowly along the road to the Monongahela riverbank.

For a long time, she watched the rippling current flow by as though eager to mingle with the Allegheny and swell that broad, watery highway into the heart of the west, the Ohio. She pitched pebbles one at a time into the water, the splashes hardly noticeable in the choppy, hurrying stream.

She looked north along the tree and shrub choked bank, the narrow road snaking a way through the tangle. Ike Ilam would be up that way. Marie brushed her hands, then smoothed them along her waist. She looked back. She could see but two of the settlement cabins and the high, solid logs of the stockade walls.

She remembered her thought, "I won't try to see him but if I should happen to be walking nowhere in particular and he chanced to come on me, it would not be planned or deliberate."

The narrow road beckoned. She would walk along it — not for very far. She gave the settlement a last, careful search and then set her feet to the path. She soon entered the aisle formed by the bushes and trees. No one could see her now. Her pace quickened and she felt a faint quiver of forbidden adventure.

For a time she could see only green walls to either side and then the sandy, open path ahead. Then she emerged from the thicket onto an unbroken, smooth carpet of grass. The river curved eastward here. She saw the trees on the slopes across the stream, impenetrable and growing right to the water's edge. But on the near bank, her side, the way was open, peaceful and empty. Many yards ahead, bushes once more made a green wall that could hide anything from house to man . . . of skulking Indian. She shivered faintly and pushed aside the thought.

She walked out onto the open sward and was half across it when she stopped short. She thought she saw a movement of bushes over there and the picture of ambushers came vividly to mind. She stood poised, nearly paralyzed by fear, but ready for flight.

Bushes thrashed wildly and Ike Ilam stepped out. He instantly stopped and Marie knew he was as surprised as she. He recovered quickly and came toward her in long strides, scanning the high green wall around the glade and then searching across the river. He halted directly before her.

"What in hell be ye doing out here alone?"

She blazed angrily. "Don't speak to me that way!"

Contrition touched him. "Sorry, but ye've done a foolish thing and I fear for ye. Injuns is likely to be anywhere at any time these days. Your scalp would bring 'em a pretty penny up in Detroit."

"Selling scalps?"

"Sure, that fine British governor takes all they bring

him and no questions. He ain't called the "Hair Buyer" for nothing. Ain't ye heard there's a war atween Redcoat and Yankee?"

Now it was her turn to be repentant. "Yes, I've heard but I didn't think it had come this close."

"It's everywhere along the rivers and through the wilderness. But ye ain't said why ye be out here."

She lowered her eyes and scraped the edge of her moccasin in the grass. "Looking for you."

"Me! For God's sake, why?"

"My folks didn't treat you good after what you did for me — toting that water. I figured to make up for it somehow."

He studied her and once more she noticed his eyes constantly and swiftly shifted. When he smiled, his lean face became handsome, the lift of his brow roguish.

"Well, now! That's mighty handsome of ye! How do ye figure to do it?"

She could not help her baffled look. She really hadn't thought that far and had no answer to the unexpected question. "Why . . . why . . . just say 'Thank you,' I reckon."

He stood very close and she had to slightly tilt her head to see his face. "Ain't that pretty small onions for all that walking out here?"

"But . . . but . . . what else? . . ."

"How about this?"

He moved so quickly she had no chance to know what he intended to do, let alone stop him. He kissed her full on the lips and stepped back ready to ward off a blow. But she could only stand round-eyed, trying to sort out the new sensations and emotions that flooded through her.

He laughed. "Ain't ye never been kissed afore?"

"Not by a . . . not like that."

"Well! What ye know! Cherry, eh?"

"What's that . . . cherry?"

Something flicked in his eyes, gone in a split second. "Why, your lips be red as cherries and just as sweet."

"You say such nice things, Ike."

"You deserve it, Marie." He grew even bolder. "But ye ain't been really kissed, like ye oughta be."

"How's that?"

"Like this."

His arms whipped around her shoulders. She only had time for a single gasp, choked off as his lips pressed fiercely hard on her mouth and he held her tight against him. She raised her arms to lever him away but, instead, dropped them and surrendered to the feel of his lithe, muscular body, his entwining arm. For a moment she became aware of a strange pressure against her groin, but he stepped back and away, his chest lifting and falling in a rapid rhythm. He turned his back to her. He seemed to make some adjustment to his trousers but she couldn't be certain. Before she could collect her wits he again faced her.

"I know I shouldn't have done that," he said in a husky voice. "But don't be mad at me. You standing there so pretty and all, ye drove my wits right out of my head."

She gasped and gulped air. The sound of her own voice surprised her. "I . . . ain't mad. That is, I don't think I am. I never heard that's what boys do to girls."

"Don't ye tell your maw! It'd set her meaner'n ever against me."

"I won't." Her chin lifted defiantly. "I do what I please with whoever I please most times. Mother don't rule me every minute of the day."

"Fine . . . though I know she'd be no different than other folks 'round here that think we Ilams ain't good enough for 'em."

"You're good enough for me, Ike."

"Then you'll meet with me again, soon?"

"Of course. But we have to be careful. Like you said, my family —"

"We'd both catch blazing what-for," he cut in with a nod. "They'd probably lock ye up and try to run me 'n' Paw outa the settlement. He'd not take it easy-like, but fight back, believe me. That'd lead to more trouble — all for nothing. 'Cause you 'n' me wouldn't do anything mean, would we?"

"Of course not! But maybe we'd best not stir things up. Just leave one another alone."

"Little girl, I just couldn't stand the idea of never seeing you again. I figure you're of the same mind." He hurried on. "We're just made for one another, you 'n' me! We won't ever git a chance to love one another like boys love girls . . . or even grown women love grown men, would we?"

"No. . . ." She looked mystified. "How you mean about loving one another like others do . . . or grown women and men?"

"Cain't tell you. Only show ye when we meet again." He looked around. "But not out here. Too close to our horse pens and stables. How about somewhere up along the Allegheny? They'd not be looking for us together out that way."

"But how will I know when to meet you?"

"Easy. I'll first fool around the fort gate and then wander along the Allegheny slow-like so ye'll have a chance to see me from your house. I'll keep going right to the woods where no one can see me. Then I'll wait."

"Suppose I don't see you?"

He lifted and dropped his shoulders. "Then it cain't be helped. I'll wait until I'm sure you ain't coming and try it another day. Now be ye gitting home and watch for me."

He kissed her squarely on the lips once more but did not pull her to him. He grinned and turned her about, away from him. She gasped when his hand landed with a smack against her buttock.

"Head for home. Watch for me."

The light blow propelled her forward a stumbling step or two. She caught her balance, turned, but Ike imperiously waved her on, though he grinned and his voice held mock anger.

"I mean it. Git ye gone!"

He watched her as she crossed the grass and, with a final backward look, plunged into the woods and disappeared. He did not move but continued to eye the swaying bushes that closed behind her. He sucked in his cheeks, then smacked his lips.

"Cherry! Real cherry — and with all them soft curves and that round, unused bottom." He pulled down his brow in an angry frown. "Won't them hightee Fornys be taken down a peg or two when I have her flat on her back and loving ever' inch of it!"

Marie hurried along the trail, slowing only when she broke through to see the Monongahela again and the settlement cabins in the distance. She sighed, a deep and ecstatic sound, then touched her lips and felt an electric tingle where his hand had smacked her.

"He's so exciting! So wonderful!" she thought.

IX

Edward Forny had become a man filled with guilt. He felt certain it plainly showed on his face, in his voice, in his actions. In her bed, Mathilde Rodare had turned into a seething, moaning and twisting sexual animal, almost completely draining him. When he finally left her house, the keys to the cabin in his pocket, he could not help but look swiftly about.

Despite his certainty that all Vincennes waited and watched just outside, he saw no one, heard no accusing jibes or curses. The only faint sound was a distant, toneless whistle. Far down the street he saw an old man wielding a hoe in a garden patch. Edward looked up the slope to the log walls and corner blockhouses of the fort. No, he had best wait until his blood stopped racing and he could be more certain of himself before sharp and knowing eyes.

He walked wearily along the street to the main river

path, turned down its slope to his trade canoe. Justin and Luc lolled at ease, basking in the sun, but they jumped to their feet when they saw Edward approach. They waited expectantly but Edward read their attentiveness as sly probing. He couldn't check his irritable, sharp question.

"Eh, and what do you think you see?"

Their eager smiles vanished. They looked crestfallen and puzzled. Luc spread his hands. "Have we done something wrong?"

"You have anger," Justin said in a hurt voice. "Is there something we should be doing?"

Edward shook his head. "*Non! Non! Je suis sujet aux lubins.*"

"Crotchety! You? *Pourquoi?*" Luc blurted.

"Yes, why?" Justin repeated. "Didn't you rent the cabin from the good Madame Rodare?"

"*Oui,* that is done." He offered a lame explanation for his mood and for the undue length of time he knew he had spent in Mathilde's house. "She drives a hard bargain."

"Ah, that one . . . she would," Luc nodded and smiled knowingly. "But so do you, monsieur. I wager you brought her down."

"I did," Edward answered wryly.

"When do we move in?"

"Whenever we like."

"*Tiens!* Then why not now?"

Indeed, Henry thought, why not? With Justin and Luc right at hand, Mathilde would doubtlessly leave him alone, at least for the time being. He gave the order and his men eagerly loosened the knots of thick rope lashed about the cargo's canvas covering.

The work proceeded without interruption from Mathilde, although other *habitants* of the village proffered actual help while many more gave advice. By noon, everything from trade goods to blankets, supplies, powder and shot had been transferred to the cabin. As Edward surmised, Mathilde did not leave her house, though once he caught a glimpse of her at a window.

They broke off work for a short rest and something to eat. Luc built up a fire for cooking while Justin rummaged in the pile of supplies to bring out a dumpy jug, its mouth stoppered with a corncob plug.

"We have no wine, so this fire of the devil will have to do."

Edward consoled them. "I have seen vines, so there must be grapes of some sort in the settlement."

"*Merci à Dieu*, whatever kind they are," Justin breathed. "It is a miracle to find more than trees and Indians this deep in the wilderness. You are wise to think of this place, Edward."

He thought of Mathilde and answered dryly, "Let me first make sure, eh?"

"In any case," Justin grinned, "we will find more than squirrels and rabbits. There are vegetables and I've smelled the odor of good bread a-cooking, the first since Pitt."

Edward laughed. "*C'est bien, mon ami*. This afternoon you will scout about the town and barter for all this fine food, eh?"

"*Certainment mon Capitain*. And you?"

"I visit the fort and the good de Busseron to learn more of the country 'round about."

When he climbed the hill and approached Fort Sackville's open main gate, a redcoat sentry presented his musket in a salute, a military courtesy that surprised Edward. "Captain de Busseron says you're free to go and come as ye like, Mr. Forny."

"Are you a regular British soldier?"

"Nay, militia. But the captain likes to think we're full-fledged soldiers out here. I don't know where he found enough uniforms to dress the garrison."

"Soldiers have a way of 'finding' things," Edward chuckled. "It has been that way in all times in all countries."

"Ye have the right on that, Mr. Forny. I've done some of it myself."

"Is the captain busy?"

"No more or less than any other day. Gibault showed up again this morning and the Papist-Jesuit's with him now."

Edward could not wholly hide the distasteful quirk of his lips. The wilderness people were mostly descended from Scotch and English dissenters who less than a century ago had fought to keep Bonnie Prince Charlie from returning and destroying the freedom they had gained at the expense of so much blood. If only the Stuart kings had been reasonable about religion, Edward sighed, this intolerance would never have been born. But history, or destiny, followed some arcane plan — *le bon Dieu* knew what!

When he entered the fort compound, Madame Busseron looked out the door of her husband's office-cabin. "Monsieur Forny! We have hoped to see you. *Bienvenue!*"

"Nay, you are the welcome sight, madame. It is always my pleasure to see such loveliness."

"*Flatteuer!* We have someone you should meet. In fact, *two* someones." She laughed. "Do not look so confused! Solve the riddle for yourself. *Entrez!*"

But before entering, he bowed over Madame's hand and kissed it. She giggled, caught herself.

"Eh, but you're lucky the captain is not a jealous man! Someday that might get you killed."

"It has not yet and I've known many delights — but none so *charmante* as your own."

On first entering the cabin, he saw a tall, proud and aloof Indian. The man wore the trappings of a chief and his dress was that of the Piankeshaw. De Busseron arose from his seat behind his desk.

"*Mon ami,* meet Tobacco's son. He is sometimes called the Grand Door of the Wabash."

Edward asked in rapid French, "Where in the world did he get *that* name?"

De Busseron replied just as rapidly, "Who knows where these heathen find their names! Something that frightened their mothers or something their fathers saw at the moment the bastard was dropped. They are always talking about voices in the air or what the birds are singing and what bats and butterflies have to tell us."

He swung from the patois of Picardy to that of Canada, and Tobacco's son instantly showed understanding.

"This is Edward Forny. He has come to Vincennes to trade with Indian as well as white man."

The tall Indian's eyes brightened and he lost his formal stiffness. "There has long been word of Edward Forny along the Ohio. He is friend to all the tribes — the Seneca, the Miami, the Shawnee. Even the Cherokee have heard of him."

"Do you know Two Drums?" Edward asked.

"I know him. Sometimes we are enemies. Sometimes we are allies."

"Depending on who's fighting who." Edward smiled.

"Two Drums talked to me not long ago. He said all the tribes would be friends of the French traders no matter what comes in this new war. Will this be true of Tobacco's Son and the Piankeshaw?"

"It will be peace between us."

"And between the Piankeshaw and the British?"

Grand Door's eyes hooded, instantly secretive. "We are far from war."

Edward's encircling gesture included the room and the whole of the post. "Far from war — and you stand in a British fort?"

"Piankeshaw think of friendship, not warpath . . . British, Yankee . . . anyone."

"*Par bonheur* only. It will be my luck — and that will not last long. Sooner or later Yankee or Britisher will make you choose."

De Busseron's rapid French blocked Grand Door's answer. "The utter gall of that red bastard and his tribe! So long as we control Sackville, he and his tribe will live under our rule. If not, we'll drive them out of the country."

Edward thought of the untold miles of forest, warpaths, hunting trails and rivers lacing the country. De Busseron spoke in idle, boastful anger. Grand Door's people had only to scatter at the first sign of attack, gather at some appointed spot and Piankeshaw life would continue as though nothing had happened.

The captain turned haughtily to the Indian and resumed the Canadian patois. "The Great Father Across the Waters accepts your friendship but will not divide it with the Yankee. You and I will speak of this later. Now, Monsieur Forny and I have business at my home."

Grand Door nodded loftily and stalked out of the office with the proud air of a conqueror. De Busseron glared after him, spat and repeated, "*Le Batard!*"

During the exchange with Grand Door, Madame Busseron disappeared. The captain, banishing his anger, explained, "Madame has gone up to the house to get out wine for us, and for dinner later. We have a guest you should meet and know. He will be of great help to you in the Wabash country and also along the lower reaches of the Ohio, even up the Mississippi above St. Louis. He's known by every trader, tribe and trapper through all this country. If he says a good word for you, your future trading is assured — a bad word and all will be closed."

"*Tonnerre!* Who is this man of power?"

"See for yourself, *mon ami*. Come and meet him."

De Busseron linked his arm in Edward's as they left the office and strolled across the parade ground to the officer's home, so situated that the front door gave a view of the fort's gate, the path down to the river and the houses of the town below. It was here that Edward had first met Lieutenant Governor Abbot and had looked on the Wabash flooded with moonlight.

Madame again met him at the door with a welcoming smile and stepped aside as de Busseron, with a flourish, waved Edward in. As he entered, a man in a black soutane arose from a chair. De Busseron made the introduction.

"Father, this is Edward Forny of whom I spoke. He is king of traders along the Ohio. Edward, meet Father Pierre Gibault."

Edward realized his swift impression of height must have been of an inner thing of spirit rather than an outer thing of body. The man was actually frail, considering the robust standards of the wilderness, but Edward perceived resilience in the flowing, graceful move of the man's arm as he raised his hand in an automatic motion of blessing. Gibault's face was lean, narrowed, pared down to sunken cheeks, hard bony jaw, deep set dark eyes and high forehead. His voice emerged in a deep rumble from his narrow chest.

"Forny — that sounds suspiciously French."

"It is, Father. I came from Gascony and bore the name de Fournet in France and for a brief time in Canada."

"Ah, Canada! I am of Montreal, attended seminary there. You spent but a brief time? Why did you leave?"

Edward hesitated, then smiled crookedly. "If you must know, Father, a royal *lettre de cachet* bearing my name followed me. I had the bad judgment to dally with a powerful ancient noble's much too young and tender lady."

Gibault frowned. "This is not the time or place for a confession, my son. I hold chapel here in Vincennes."

"This is not a confession. I intended no more than an answer to your question. I came to these parts when France fought England. Twenty years ago a Frenchman had short shrift among colonists loyal to King George instead of the fifteenth Louis."

"The times have changed," Gibault said. "You can change it back if you wish."

"I have not thought on it. Besides, Forny is now well known from Pitt westward and I doubt if my wife would care for the change."

"Not of the faith?"

"No, unhappily."

Gibault puckered his lips as though he tasted sour fruit. But instantly his eyes cleared, the frown vanished and he shrugged as though to say, "So much for my duty."

De Busseron said quickly, "You will honor me in the billiard room, Father? Monsieur Forny, do you play the game? . . . Good! Would you join us?"

The three men went into another room, almost wholly filled by a huge billiard table, convenient seats about the walls and a rack holding five or six slightly crooked cue sticks. The ivory white ball and two red ones had been placed for a game. This was de Busseron's pride and joy. He had bought all the items in New Orleans and had them shipped to Fort Sackville. Edward wondered how many weeks or months it had taken. He thought of the torture of muscles in unknown backs, arms and legs to pole, paddle, portage, load, unload and unload again and again the table on carts, wagons, perhaps even some Indian travois. It was unthinkable! He touched the smooth green felt over the table's hard slate and dutifully thunked a cue on the floor to verify his readiness.

Father Gibault had the honor of the first play. As the game continued, Edward learned more and more of the priest who had a keen eye and an uncanny control of his cue, scoring point after point. Edward and the captain found themselves hard pressed to give Gibault respectable competition.

As they played and talked, Edward became more and more impressed by Gibault's accomplishments. He had travelled, alone for the most part, from below the Ohio into the Spanish lands beyond the Mississippi and northward to the lakes.

"They are really inland seas," Gibault said, "an amazing example of God's handiwork."

"I agree, Father. I have been on two of them, even canoed across the lake of the Eries with a Huron girl escaping from the Iroquois."

"A Huron! She ran from the enemy right into the hands of another, the Erie."

"I know, and they killed Spotted Doe before my eyes

and damn near killed me. My wife-to-be rescued me. But we speak of you, Father, and your work."

"Not mine, but God's. I bring light to the Indian people of whatever tribe, wherever I find them. After ten years most of them know me as well as I have come to know most of the country from marching back and forth across it. Now and then I'm lucky to come on a new farm being hacked out of the wilderness with axe or broken with hoe and plow. I've blessed some, worked with most and buried quite a few without their scalps — man, woman and child."

"And I've traded with the same kind. They're fools to strike out alone from the settlements — at least as far in the woods as they do."

"Someone must always be first, my son. They are the little fingers and tentacles of civilization, I believe. If one is killed, another takes his place. Someday all this land will be towns and farms with roads instead of trails."

"*Vraiment*. The tribes fight a losing battle."

"Best call it a war that started before you and I were born and will last long after we are dead."

Time passed faster than any of them realized. They were surprised when Aspasie came with a lamp and Madame's orders to prepare for dinner. Wine also waited their pleasure before the meal. Shortly after dinner, Edward sat at ease with Madame, the captain and Father Gibault, watching through the door and distant gate the last glow of light on the Wabash.

The contour of the land once more forcefully struck Edward. He called the attention of the others to it.

"*Regardez la riviere*. The west bank is low, while here, on the east, even the village is high above the water and the fort is a veritable mountain."

Father Gibault nodded. "If there are heavy rains for two days steady in the summer, it floods down there. In the early spring, when the winter snows melt, water is everywhere over there as far as you can see. It is hip deep, sometimes chest deep."

De Busseron added, "The Yankees call it 'bottom land.'"

"I have canoed across it," Gibault continued, "for a hundred miles and more. Now and then there's a small hummock of dry land suitable for camping. When all the snow has melted — poof! — it is a rich, black muck that dries out until the next melting. The crops are unbelievable."

"Strange one bank should be so high and the other so low."

"A natural thing here," Gibault explained. "But south of us, the high banks look as if they are mounds."

"Indian work?" Edward asked.

"Open Door will tell you the Indians believe they were made by ancient demons who vanished long ago. Certainly, no present day tribe builds them."

Interesting, Edward thought, but of no real moment or importance. He idly studied the "bottom land" across the Wabash, unaware that it would play a major role in his destiny.

A few hours later, he reluctantly took his leave of the pleasant company, thanked the sentry who opened the closed fort gate for him and continued down the step path, turning off onto the street leading to his new headquarters. He would awaken Justin and Luc, he thought, but they would soon be sound asleep again.

As he walked by, he gave Mathilde's house a swift scrutiny. No light showed through any of its windows so he knew she would be sound asleep. He didn't know whether he was pleased or disappointed. By the time he turned in the walk to his rented cabin, he decided to be pleased. Wisdom told him so. Vivid memories called up burning desires. Best put them behind, he told himself, before they led to trouble.

He lifted the latch, opened the door and stepped in. He faced complete darkness and heard no sound. It puzzled him, because both Justin and Luc had the instant alertness of the wild. Their lives had depended upon it too often. Edward strained to hear a slight movement, a grunt, a sleepy sigh . . . nothing.

"Justin?" he spoke softly. "Luc?"

He heard a slight stirring near the fireplace and he knew relief. Nothing was amiss. They had simply made their pallets close to their supper fire. An ember made a finite red glow for a second and died. But, *mon Dieu*, how deeply they slept.

He cautiously moved through the darkness, sliding moccasined feet along the floor boards. His toe suddenly struck the edge of a pallet. He squatted down and felt blindly about. Was this bedding his? Where in the name of a hundred devils were Justin and Luc!

His blindly groping fingers touched a body. "*Peste!* Speak up! Luc!"

The person on the pallet moved. Fingers touched his wrist, fiercely wrapped around it. Those were slender fingers! Long! Not a man's!

"Edouard? *Mon etalon!*"

Stud? Stud? It was a woman's voice. Soft arms snaked around him and pulled him down. Mathilde's hungry lips found his face, his ears, cheeks, mouth and covered them with kisses.

X

Marie uncontrollably jerked when Henry spoke directly behind her. "Has the Allegheny changed? Or something along it? You spend tedious time just staring at it."

She swung around, fearful that in some way he had discerned the arrangement she had made with Ike Ilam through some act on her part. Her brother's gaze held curiosity with no hint of suspicion.

"I just like to watch it, that's all. Is there anything wrong with that?"

"No." He cast a curious, sweeping look out the window. "No, but the Allegheny has been there all our lives. You've paid it little heed . . . except for the past two weeks or so. I wonder why all of a sudden you watch it every chance you get . . . like you expect to see someone canoeing down it."

"Why should I? Who would I know that'd come from

the woods or the lake of the Erie?"

"That fashes me for sure."

Just then she glimpsed Ike strolling slowly, idly along the bank as though he had just emerged from the entry-gate of the fort. She whipped away from the window and walked into the room, carelessly.

"Mayhap just mooning. Girls get spells like that. But you wouldn't know."

"Reckon not, Sis."

He turned from the window with her and she managed to suppress her sigh of relief. She must plan to join Ike but she had ample time. Unexplained eagerness might prove as suspicious as unexplained window gazing. Judging from Ike's slow pace, he had a good half hour in which to loiter. Henry stretched and yawned so she knew he had cast the incident out of his mind, this time. However, it would certainly crop up again stronger than ever if she persisted in looking out the window.

The street door opened and Abby came in. She swung her light, knitted shawl off her shoulders and dropped it on a settle. She talked all the while she moved about the room.

"I've been with Dean Smith at the warehouse and then Letty came over."

"What'd his wife want?" Henry asked.

"Gossip, mostly — but also news. Late papers have come from the east and a sheet is pasted on the tavern wall. Dean read it."

"Who wins the war?" Henry quickly demanded. "The colonies? Or the king?"

"It swings back and forth across the Jersies and in the Carolinas. The real news is that the Continental Congress has sent an ambassador to France — and he's also a purchasing agent for us."

"Fine, but what can he purchase for us without money?" Henry scoffed.

"More news there. Robert Morris, a Jew from Philadelphia, I think — is using his own wealth and that of his business and merchant friends to finance the Congress."

"Oh, I didn't know." Henry sounded crestfallen. "Thank God for him! But who is the ambassador?"

"Also from Philadelphia. He's been a printer there for years. More'n that, it's said he's a scientist, an inventor. They say he devised the lightning rod they're beginning to put on barns and houses back east. He's also made a thing of cast iron and metal called a stove to burn wood indoors. Before long nobody'll really need a fireplace."

"What's his name? Has anyone but Americans ever heard of him?"

"Dean says he's known all over Europe by all kinds of brainy men. Every one of 'em writes him letters or sends him scientific papers. Until we started fighting the king, he was in England and even the king wanted to meet him."

Becoming aware of the passing of time and of Ike undoubtedly deep in the woods waiting for her, Marie impatiently stamped her foot. "And just who is this terrific person?"

"Benjamin Franklin," Abby answered, pointing to a small dog-eared pamphlet hanging from a wall peg by a cord. "We've had his *Poor Richard's Almanac* every year for at least the past ten."

Marie edged toward the street door. Henry didn't notice and Abby continued her eager recital of the news. "Dean heard the French are taking an interest in us."

"The French! Why should they?"

111

She answered Henry's scornful question in a tone that bordered on the superior. "Young man, keep in touch with what goes on in the world! The French and English have been at one another's throats for centuries. They are at war again, one that extends from India to Europe. The French Louis still smarts from his last defeat. Why, this very spot where we stand was once part of his realm."

Marie came to the door but dared no more since, for the moment, Abby faced her. But she swung to Henry. She laughed at him, then frowned. "Edward would wonder at how slow you are, Henry. A trader's mind must be quick and sharp. If the French can help the colonies fight King George, the English will have less men, ships and arms to use against Louis. That is precisely one of the reasons our Mr. Franklin is in Paris, or Versailles, or wherever the French king holds his court."

Marie achieved the door, lifted the latch. Abby continued to lecture Henry. Marie eased out the door and closed it but waited a moment or two before she turned to look along the street. She caught a glimpse of Boo Day disappearing into Carrie Ryan's cabin and the door closing. But no one else moved along the street. It seemed unlikely that anyone would chance to see her if she hurried along the rear of the line of cabins. Clearly, Abby and Henry had not noticed her absence. Satisfied, she hurried off.

She plunged into the bushes and under the low boughs of the nearby forest trees before she halted to reconnoitter the village. Satisfied, she turned once more to the woods. Pulse pounding and heart singing, she darted along the glades. Ike simply must be somewhere close! She had no sign or glimpse of him. Discouraged, she stopped, peering this way and that. She jumped when his chuckle sounded right at hand.

"Hey! Little lady, be ye lookin' for someone?"

He stepped from behind a tree not ten feet from her. Sunlight trickling through the leaves above made an alternating golden and soft dark green pattern on him, so that he appeared even taller, more handsome and slim than she had ever seen him.

She covered her discomfiture with a flirtatious toss of her head. "Who would I see in the woods when there's a-plenty boys in the village?"

His dark brow lifted and his lips curled in that crooked, delightful way that so enchanted her. "Who? Would ye say maybe Ike Ilam?"

Her face became serious and her eyes soft. She breathed her answer. "Of course."

"Then come ye here."

He held out his arms. Her reason departed, leaving her with only desire, need, and something hitherto unknown but golden. It quite took her breath away. She almost threw herself at him. His arms enwrapped her as she lifted her face to kiss and be kissed. Her groin and stomach flamed. Her heart joyfully skipped and fluttered.

His tongue parted her lips and darted in and out of her mouth. Her eyes flew open in amazement and shock. As though he read her reaction, he ended the kiss, drew back his head to look deep into her eyes. He still held her close as he examined her. He spoke in an understanding whisper.

"Sho, now! Ye be new to the ways of kissing and loving and such."

Her face grew scarlet. She could feel the heat of it. She answered in an apologetic voice but suddenly grew proud. "Think ye I give myself carelessly? Ye be the first. Is aught wrong with that?"

"Wrong? Hell, no! It's perfect. Ye come without any crazy ideas and ye can be taught easy. Ye want I should do it?"

Far back in her mind reason sent a slight, instinctive warning. In her agitation she could not understand it, let along heed it. Her words fairly burst from her lips.

"Yes. Oh, yes!"

"All right. We start now."

He moved his arms from about her and placed his hands beneath her hair at the nape of her neck. His fingers moved in a slow, light massage, and the touch electrified her. Her eyes rounded in surprise and Ike's smile grew wider, more confident.

"I can tell ye sure like that! How about this?"

His hands slid slowly, gently, down her neck to her shoulders, along them to her arms and then back to her neck. He repeated the motion several times and then his hands stopped just under her chin. She felt a tug but, wholly wrapped in sensation, she did not realize what he did until the second tug came, then a third fumbling of his fingers. He unbuttoned her blouse!

"NO!"

Her fingers taloned about his wrists and she tried to pull his hands away. He wouldn't permit it, his stronger muscles dominating. But he stopped further assault on her buttons.

"Little lady, I ain't aimin' to hurt ye. I love ye too much. Seems like ye'd love me enough to know I mean no harm for ye."

"But . . . but . . ."

She stopped her struggling but still clamped his wrists. He put his lips to her ears and kissed the lobes. His whisper was tender, intimate, thrilling.

"Ye be woman, little lady Marie, and ye have a woman's body. It'll be fair to see and they's no shame in ye showin' it to someone ye love. Honest, there ain't no shame. Ask them girls ye be with so many times."

His hands moved back to her bare neck, just under her chin. His tender smile striking deep into her eyes made her feel faint. His hands once more moved, this time down the column of her neck along her tingling flesh to slide within her blouse. She gasped as he touched a folded strip of cloth she always wrapped tightly about her breasts.

"Now that ain't right, honey! Hiding them pretty, tender knockers."

"Kn-kn-knockers?"

His fingers made a single, hard pull, jerking the cloth below her breasts. The white spheres stood wholly revealed, pink nipples erect, soft flesh quivering. He avidly drank them in with a searing look. Marie could not move, completely in shock. Her numbed mind cried out that this was all wrong, evil, but she was hypnotized as she heard rabbits were before snakes. Her mind registered his movements and hers as though viewing them impersonally from a vast distance. His voice sounded equally as far away. She vaguely wondered why that girl down there — Marie — had not protected herself, could not even move. What did that boy — Ike — say?

"Knockers . . . tits . . . like you got. I ain't never seen any so pretty, by God! But, here, ye be scared. No need. We ain't gonna do no more today. Ye need slow and easy teaching, that ye do."

He fully buttoned her blouse, placed his hands firmly on her shoulders and gave them a reassuring squeeze.

"There's always tomorrow, or the next day or the one after that. Git yourself home but keep a look for me wandering along by the river and into the woods."

"I — I don't think we should meet anymore."

He laughed. "Don't bother your lovely noodle about it. You'll know when you want another lesson. Now . . . home with ye."

For a week she forced Ike out of her mind and avoided looking out the window on the river. She sought the company of the girls who, for a time, gave her protection from the continuing urges of her body and the thrust of unwanted desires. With agonizing slowness she was finally able to look at the window as casually as she would a chair or the fireplace. She listened to the girls without substituting Ike's image for whatever boy Carrie, Sabina or Boo chanced to discuss.

It was a false peace. She did not understand she fought the most powerful of human drives, the necessity of one sex to find completion in the other. Her monthly period also distracted her and Abby. It kept them busy cutting up threadbare strips of cloth and the unpleasant later task of thoroughly cleaning them for the next time. One day, in the midst of the job, Abby startled her, with a laughing remark.

"Well, at least we know you're not with child."

"Mother!"

Abby looked up, her eyes suddenly sharp and penetrating. Then she affectionately touched her daughter's arm. "Don't be so shocked, child! The eternal curse comes to every woman."

"I know . . . but . . . you don't think I. . ."

"Of course not!"

Abby's confidence banished the tidal wave of guilt

threatening to sweep over Marie. Her mother's unwitting suggestion of danger strengthened her decision to avoid Ike . . . always. Abby's next remark took Marie's mind from Ike.

"I hope Edward hasn't met with trouble in Vincennes. It seems to me he should have been home long since. Or maybe I'm just a worrisome wife."

Now Marie exuded confidence. "You're not, Mother. You just need to see him. If something had happened, we would have heard of it within a day or two as well known as Father is along the rivers."

The cloud left Abby's face. "You're right, of course. It's just these troublesome times and the way the British stir up the Indians against the Yankees that makes me afraid."

"They won't touch Father. They need him as much as every farmer or settlement. Maybe even more. How far would they have to go to sell their furs to buy supplies and that horrible firewater they drink?"

"Edward does not deal in whiskey with the Indians, Marie. He believes it makes them killing, mindless beasts."

"I know. But they use Father's coins to get it."

"If he had his way, the whiskey traders would all be driven out." Abby sadly shook her head. "An impossible task, that."

"I suppose so."

For a long time after, Marie clung to the illogical conclusion that their conversation actually brought Edward home because at mid-morning the next day, Henry burst into the cabin with a shout.

"Father's here! He's just to the fork of the river. We'll just have time to meet him when he lands on the Allegheny bank."

Marie, Abby and Henry had to force their way through the crowd gathered at the riverbank. Just as they broke free, Edward shot the canoe into the shallows and vaulted over the gunnel into foot-deep water, greeting everyone with a shout. He elbowed neighbors aside in his plunge to Abby. He swung her around in a bear hug and his lips cut off her little squeal of delight. He saw Marie and Henry.

"*Mon Dieu!* I have returned to heaven!"

XI

Marie and Henry didn't need so much as a word or a glance from Abby and Edward. They knew what to do once the welcoming crowd had been dispelled from the cabin. Henry suddenly remembered Dean needed him at the storehouse and Marie recalled she had promised Boo Day she'd be with the girls that afternoon. Abby's grateful eyes spoke more loudly than any voice, and her close hug revealed delight behind her concern.

"Are you sure Jenny Ryan can stand all the chattering you girls will do?"

"Of course, Mother!" Marie could not help adding with a sly smile, "Have fun."

All the Ryan family as well as the girls understood Marie's presence. She was sure Dean Smith knew why Henry surprisingly sought extra work at the storehouse. In a village so small as Pittsburg, any little happening became enlarged, momentous, a matter to be discussed and considered from all angles. So when a person of so much importance as Edward Forny returned, a buzzing of conjecture filled every cabin. Marie found the speculation particularly rampant among the girls. Being Edward's daughter, she instantly became the target of questions.

Marie expected it and was not overly bothered. She airily answered those questions that did not probe too deeply into family matters. Gradually curiosity was sated. Then, without warning, the conversation took an appalling turn. Carrie Ryan's sly, feline question came like a blow to the stomach.

"How do you like Ike Ilam?"

"Ike! Why . . . how should I find him?"

"I don't know. Ain't ye been with him of late?"

"Who's told you that!"

Carrie's foxy air vanished in uncertainty. "Ain't no one really told me anything. They've been whispers goin' about. Maybe I chanced to hear some of them."

"Then drop it," Marie snapped, "and pass the word to whoever is spreading gossip. Has anyone seen me with him?"

She held her breath until Carrie reluctantly answered, "Not that I've been told."

"Then it be best all tongues stop clacking."

Carrie silenced, the conversation went on to other topics. However, the sharp exchange had a dampening effect. The talk began to die down as Marie caught several covert, askance looks from the girls. She finally rose and looked around.

"I best be returning home . . . unless there's some more gossip ye have to tell about me and Ike Ilam. Or mayhap Carrie has some new tale of her own. There've been planty of them afore now."

Out in the street again, she walked thoughtfully, almost fearfully toward home. How in the world had talk about her and Ike started! They had been quite careful not to be seen together. She could find no answer. Fear touched her with a cold hand. What if the whispers came to Abby? And, now, Edward? Oh, Lord! Henry! He'd probably be the first to hear them. By the time she reached home, she knew quite well that it would be some time before she joined Ike in the woods . . . if ever! But a small, dark and niggling voice within cast a faint shadow on that decision. She put the thought out of her mind and firmly opened the door.

Father and Mother sat in easy chairs that Absalom Cooper had made years before. Henry occupied a third. The three looked around at her entrance and Henry grinned.

"Sis, would ye believe they already have plans for me?"

"*Pourquois pas?*" Edward demanded. "In this place and time you are considered a man grown, so why not?"

"Our menfolk no more than come home," Abby said to Marie, "than they plan to be gone again. Is there no way to tie them down?"

"Leave?" Marie demanded. "But you've just returned from that place — Vincennes? That's it. Is that where you're taking Henry?"

"I have no need for him there as yet. I'm taking him to the Watauga where things are suddenly happening." He placed his hand on Henry's shoulder. "Settlers are moving up out of the Waxhaws in the Carolinas as well as Watauga itself."

At first it sounded involved and confused but Marie finally made some sense of it. The magnet of the empty, rich and wooded lands west of the mountains had as great a pull on people of the southern colonies as on those directly east and north of Pittsburg. A few men organized large bands of land-hungry emigrants. Marie heard strange new names such as Daniel Boone, someone called Henderson and also a Judge Robertson.

"*Attendez*," Edward continued. "They all converge on a place called Cumberland Gap. Henry and I will go there. Then I'll stay with Messieurs Boone and Henderson while Henry goes with Robertson down a river strange to us — the Cumberland. We are in trade with the new settlements along that stream even as they are established. We will also have posts in the Kentucky country where Boone and Henderson will build their stockades. *Ma foi!* This is a rare and lucky doing for us, not likely to be repeated. We must take advantage of it."

Abby's expression showed she agreed no matter how reluctantly. Marie sensed that all had been fully decided but she still needed clarification.

"What about Vincennes? Is it to be forgotten?"

"Not at all, *ma petite*. I return to that business as soon as I see Henry well started on his own." Edward laughed at her and squeezed Abby's hand. "Eh, my two beauties must tire of Pitt. Are you so very anxious to be on the Wabash?"

Abby answered cautiously, "Edward, is aught amiss there?"

"Amiss? *Tonnerre!* What could be amiss?"

"Well — it's British, not Yankee and —"

"But the commandant is from Picardy by way of Canada so we have rapport by nationality as well as by personal liking. The town itself is mostly Canadian. It is mayhap a whisper larger than Pittsburg and some of the houses are stone. There is even a chapel where Father Gibault — another Canadian — holds services when he is not in the forests bringing the faith to *les sauvages*. I have rented a roomy cabin to serve as a trading post. Justin and Luc even now rest their lazy bones in it. So what could be *en mal,* as you fear?"

"Nothing . . . nothing . . ." Abby's face cleared. "Let me help while you're in the Watauga. Some of your *voyageurs* could take me to Vincennes. I could help Justin and Luc. I might even find a house in which we could live."

It seemed to Marie Edward retreated within himself. He slowly rubbed his jaw, looked about the room as though seeing through the walls the long stretches of river flowing westward. He apparently wanted to sound judicious and thoughtful but Marie also thought of caution.

"I would not be easy in mind on the Watauga if you were out on the river. These are not normal times. Yankee fights British. There have been instances where English have attacked English first and only afterwards asked questions. That is true of the Yankees as well. How often have we heard lately of Indian raids and burnings?"

"All right," Abby surrendered. "If it would trouble you, I'll not go until you return."

"It will not be long, I promise."

In the next few days, Marie had much to do helping Abby with preparations for Edward's trip southward to the Cumberland. Clothing had to be mended, staple condiments gathered, patches cut for tamping powder and shot down rifle barrels. Henry seldom spent daylight hours in the house; neither did Edward. Both conferred with Dean as they hopefully planned for the great new trade area that promised to open for them.

Now and then Marie spent brief periods with the girls but her life momentarily became confined to the house, the warehouse and the village street. Quite often she encountered one or more of the Virginia militia soldiers, young men who spoke politely but covertly eyed her with appreciation and speculation. Marie loved their attention but hid it under a demure facade — downcast eyes and a low, soft voice.

Not two days after Edward's return and in the midst of preparations for the journey, Capt. Tatum Long himself knocked at the door. Though he was somewhat older, Marie thought the captain just as handsome and dashing as his men. Henry happened to be at the warehouse when Captain Long paid his visit but Edward was present.

Both men quickly studied one another, probing deeply below appearance and each liked what he saw. In less than five minutes they spoke as though they had known one another for years.

Long made an awkward, jerky bow to Abby as though he was not quite used to such formalities. He held his tricorn hat with its green and red cockade under his arm.

"Ma'am, a pleasure to talk to you again."

Abby smiled. "Indeed, sir, seeing that our only talk so far was half an hour of sharp questions in your office. I hope I convinced you I'm not a Connecticut Tory."

"That you did, ma'am." He flushed, then an edge of steel came into his voice. "Had you not, you'd be somewhere else than Fort Stanwix. Ah, but that business is well over with. I've come to meet your husband."

Edward grinned. "Fearful I'd be another Tory?"

"Yes . . . until I could put my eyes on you and size you up. Your name's too well known along the river and throughout the whole country not to be checked and tallied at first chance. I'd say you're French, though the name don't sound much like it. Canadian?"

In a quick exchange of questions and answers, Edward told enough of his life to satisfy the captain. It ended when the militia officer extended his hand. "You ain't a danger to us, Mr. Forny. Fact is, we need your services and goods here as much as any other place, maybe more. You have the freedom of Fort Stanwix."

"*Merci à Dieu!* It would be a problem if I'm banned from my home, my wife and my business."

"Not the way I've heard. You could establish yourself anywhere along the river like you're doing at Vincennes in the Ouabache country."

"Just business, Captain, and the small British garrison at Fort Sackville means only pence and sous in my pocket. Also peltry, of course, gathered by the Piankeshaw, Miami, Kickapoo and such."

"I understand. You try to be neutral." Long gave Edward a long, probing look, then said, "That could be of advantage here if we always knew what happens at Vincennes."

Edward's jaw hardened. "I am not an informant, Captain. That would not be neutral. I value the trust people put in me. If I inform on Captain Busseron, how do you know I will not inform on you? *Pas de tout!* You can't know. I do not lower my self-regard to become spy and lick-spittle."

Long's face turned beet red. Then he drew himself up. "My apologies. I know that. But I am under strict orders to test every river man I meet for such work. I look somewhere else . . . gladly."

"Eh, see that you do."

"Depend upon it, sir. I hope we can forget the miserable business."

Marie glanced at Abby who, with a slight move of her head, indicated the door. Marie understood and slipped into the street. At first she thought of going to Carrie Ryan's but the impulse hardly more than registered than it died. Instead, she strolled around the line of cabins and entered upon a well known path. The realization startled her. This was the way she had gone to meet Ike Ilam. She had not seen him since Edward's return. He would be sure to know of that event and probably had not bothered to wander into the woods — certainly not to expect her.

Marie's memories stirred warm sensations. She could almost feel Ike's fingers pulling the tight, folded cloth below her breasts and she could see his eyes, suddenly aflame, admiring the soft white globes they rested upon. She could feel his fingers' light touch upon her nipples and the sensation she had when they tightened and protruded.

She cast a quick look about. No one saw her. She swiftly walked along the rear of the cabins and then struck out toward the woods, angling toward the Allegheny. The forest swallowed her in a few moments. Once within the trees she paused and looked back. Reassured, she pushed further into the forest. She finally came to the place where Ike had met her and, as she knew it would be, he was nowhere about. No reason why he should, she dully reminded herself. How many times might he have come this way of late and waited to no purpose?

Marie looked slowly about. Yes, they had stood right over there near that sycamore when he had unbuttoned her blouse. She raised her hands to her bosom and cupped her breasts as Ike had done. She lightly manipulated her nipples. They became taut. She felt a minuscule tingle, nothing at all like the overpowering sensation of those memorable minutes under the tree.

"Well, now, look here!"

She whipped about and gasped, hardly believing her eyes. Ike Ilam stood but a few yards away, hands on his hips, a crooked smile on his worldly, lean face.

"Ike!" she breathed. "I didn't know you would be anywhere about —"

"Oh, come on, little'n! Ye musta seen me walking along the river in plain view of your house."

"But I didn't! I wasn't anywhere near the window where I could see you. My father and Captain Long were talking — and Mother, too."

"Hey, now! All the high muckities, eh? But ye still had time to glimpse me a-strolling by. Ye musta been watching for me . . . and hoping, maybe?"

She started to protest, then knew that alghough Ike had the wrong of it in one sense, in another he was right. What else but memories of him, his kisses and his touch had brought her out here? Her shoulders made a small movement, acknowledging his understanding. His face lighted and he made a low, laughing sound of triumph.

He took slow steps toward her and she read anticipation in every move. The thought of panic touched her but vanished in the same instant. Her eyes grew round, not at Ike's approach, but because of her recognition of the mighty drive within herself. She felt helpless before it.

Ike now stood very close and he smiled down into her eyes with mock concern. "Be ye touchy today 'bout your buttons and dress and such?"

He didn't expect an answer, his fingers already fumbling at her blouse. She flinched, then she stood passive, waiting. No, wanting! She had her next shock when he dropped his arm about her waist and began to lift her skirt at the back. At the same instant he lowered his head and his mouth fastened on one of her nipples. She could hardly breathe as his moist lips encircled her nipple and his tongue teased it. She could not think, overwhelmed by the roiling flood of desires sweeping through her. His hand touched her bare leg just at the knee, moved higher in a continuing caress until he touched her buttock, cupping it as he had her breast.

Her arms had circled him and now her fingers taloned into his chest. He abruptly jerked her close and she felt a hard object punch her groin. She knew what it was and tried to protest but her words became only gurgling mumbles as his mouth pressed fiercely on hers. His strong fingers encircled her wrist and forced her hand down. She felt his throbbing muscle through the thick cloth of his trousers. She tried to tear her hand away but he held it. His breath came in short, swift gusts. So did hers. She didn't know how it happened but her fingers slipped into his fly and she touched warm, pulsing flesh.

Ike made animal noises deep in his throat. He broke his tight hug. With a single sweep of hooked fingers he lifted her skirts in front, exposing her legs, startlingly white above her long black stockings. He pawed at the hairs between her legs, swung her about and tried to throw her to the ground.

"Damn . . . it! . . . lay down! . . . Get it in! . . . Jesus God! Do it!"

She never knew quite how it happened. Panic and fear gave her strength. She brought her arms up and, with an explosive bunching of muscles against his chest, sent him stumbling backward.

She whirled about and fled.

XII

Marie remained in the house the next few days, leaving only to do errands for Abby or to go to the warehouse to fetch Henry and Edward for meals. Each time she stepped out the door, she looked quickly around but never once saw Ike. Each time she breathed a prayer of gratitude.

She feared Ike . . . and now she feared herself. It took so very little to transform him from a handsome man with an acceptable amount of passion into a rutting beast. The fact that she was able to make him do it made Marie fearful of herself — that and the deeply hidden desire within herself to match his lust with hers. She had unleashed a fury within herself that had to be tamed before it destroyed her.

She did not want Edward and Henry to leave for the Watauga so she had to force herself to accompany Abby to the Monongahela landing to see them off on their long journey. The usual group of curious villagers looked on, their number increased by the Virginia militiamen and Captain Long. Her attention centered almost wholly on Edward and Henry, her brother a bit inflated by his moment of importance.

Suddenly, in the midst of the hubbub, she felt eyes boring into her. She looked around. Ike Ilam stood nearly within touching distance. The slight inclination of his head toward the Allegheny, hidden by the cabins of the village, asked a question. She half turned, presenting her back to him. He would understand her refusal. But some sort of traitorous entity within her clamored objection for the moment or two it took her to suppress it.

At last the single canoe shot out into the stream, Edward and Henry bent to the task of working against the river current. Marie remained close to Abby as they watched the torturous, slow progress of the bark craft until it rounded the first bend and disappeared. The group on the riverbank broke up, chattering and gossiping as everyone returned to the village.

Back home again, the door securely closed against Ike, Marie felt released from tension. Abby took a few steps toward the fireplace where the contents of cooking pots, suspended from heavy hooked arms, simmered over the flames. She stopped suddenly, threw off her shawl, and turned to a chair.

"D'ye mind seeing that nothing goes amiss?"

"Of course not, Mother."

Abby gave her a fleeting smile of thanks and sat down. Marie removed her own shawl, puzzled by Abby's action. She checked the pots, found everything progressing well, then also sat down. She looked around a room that suddenly seemed large, what with Edward and Henry absent. She didn't like the silence or Abby's vacant, distant stare. There should be voices, she thought, to keep Mother from worrying about their menfolk.

Abby abruptly broke the silence. "Did you notice any change in Edward?"

"In Father? No, was there?"

"I'm not sure. That's why I ask."

Marie reviewed the period of Edward's return. He had looked the same, tall and handsome as ever. He smiled and talked the same, everyone liking as well as respecting him. A girl never had a more wonderful father than she. Marie carefully eyed her mother, noting the deepened line in her forehead at the root of her nose.

"N-no." Then more certainly, "No, I could see no difference. Should I?"

Abby rested her head against the back of her chair and closed her eyes. After a moment, she spoke without opening them. "Did you notice he spoke little of Vincennes?"

"Mayhap he had little to tell. I mean, other than renting a warehouse. No trading as yet."

"Aye, that's true enough. But he's generally all agog about a new move like that — all French and bubbly."

Marie conceded. "Well, he really didn't do a lot of planning and we hardly know what the town looks like."

"That's what I mean. It's not like Edward."

Marie wondered if there was something she had completely missed. She felt like a dolt. But, damn it! She hadn't overlooked anything and she shouldn't feel foolish. She decided to meet the problem head on.

"Mother, you're talking in riddles. What is it?"

Abby's eyes flew open and she looked at her daughter with a startled expression. It vanished and her tone became apologetic. "I guess I have. Sorry, I didn't realize it."

"Then what's the trouble?"

Abby thoughtfully pursed her lips as she continued to study Marie. She came to a decision and spoke slowly, carefully.

"Will it be just between . . . us girls?"

Marie felt an inexplicable touch of fear but she answered, "Just between us."

"You're too young to have experienced it yet. No, maybe you're not. You do have boys sweet on you?"

Marie felt a moment of panic before she knew Abby did not speak of Ike. Others — like Ned Cooper, maybe. She nodded and it was enough to satisfy Abby.

"Well, then, have you ever had one of them making eyes at another girl while he soft-talked you into believing you're the only one he ever thinks about?"

Marie tried to digest the meaning of the question. Suddenly it crashed down into her mind with shattering impact. "Mother! You mean . . . Father? You can't. You really can't!"

Abby sighed. "I have to."

"But what proof? . . ."

"None — and that's the hell of it."

"But has he changed at night . . . when . . . in bed? You know what I mean."

"I know what you mean. It's the worst of all. Oh, Marie, honey. I hope you'll never have this thing to contend with when you grow up and are married."

"You can't tell . . . even then?"

"You think you can — and then you're as much in the dark as ever. If he's all ardent, heated up and bullyman, you wonder if it's really his conscience eating at him to

132

make amends. If he's tired, and he's just going through the motions, even though you know it, you still can't be sure. Maybe he's thinking you're not the woman the other one is. How do you unravel it?''

She fell silent. Marie was too shocked to ask another question. It was as though Abby had found rot in a foundation timber, or a crumbling of the solid stones that supported the whole structure of life.

Abby broke the silence. "Did you notice how anxious he's been to get to this Watauga country with Henry? Does he want to go somewhere safe from any chance question I might ask?"

"But he can't stay away forever, Mother."

"That's one of the advantages a wife has. That is, if her husband's not the kind of man to desert her. Edward isn't, whatever else he might be."

The revelation had come too unexpectedly and was much too overwhelming to be immediately understood. Marie's mind boiled and seethed like a dark storm cloud filled with thunder and lightning. She sought wildly for understanding and her thoughts fastened on the Wabash.

"Do ye mean there's someone in Vincennes?"

"There has to be." Abby's hands doubled into fists. "It's someone without a face or a shape or a name . . . like a ghost."

"How can ye fight it?"

"I don't know . . . just wait, I guess. I'd go to the Wabash but who do I look for? Is she a mature woman or one just out of maidenhood?"

"Not that young!"

"I've heard it said older men think a maiden can renew their ability and push away the years piling up on them. That's what scares them."

"Don't it scare a woman, too? I don't want to think of the time when I'll be old and ugly."

Abby smiled. "You won't ever be ugly. You have too much of Edward's fine features and spirit I guess you'd call it."

"What about my mother!" Marie demanded. "You'll always be pretty!"

Abby surprised Marie with a short, delighted laugh. "Will ye listen to the girl! She's a sweet-talker just like her father. But I love you for it."

Both women fell silent, Abby buried deep in her problem and Marie trying to sort out her tangled thoughts and emotions. She now had such a different picture of her father, one that made him almost a stranger. She didn't like it one little bit.

She also had a glimpse into the depths of Abby's love for her father. Not once had Abby so much as hinted at leaving him. She wanted only to discover the identity of the unknown rival and eliminate her. Would she even so much as accuse Edward of infidelity? Marie wondered. Oh, but she had to. She must!

As though the run of her own thoughts parallelled Marie's, Abby said, "Edward is French — pure French."

"I know." Marie's voice held something of a sneer as she said, "Minor nobility, isn't it? A baronet? Is this how the minor *nobility* acts!"

Abby sighed. "On occasion, yes, I'm afraid. You've never known why he left France for Canada and how I met him on the Allegeway?"

"I don't know about France and why he left, but all my life I've loved the story of your romance with him. It's exciting . . . like a storybook." Marie sobered. "But what about France?"

"He had an affair with a girl, only a bit older than you, who was the wife of a doddering old duke."

"What!"

Abby then told her of the *lettre de cachet* that had set the king's own cavalrymen on Edward's trail, of his escape aboard a ship out of Bordeaux bound for Canada. Marie had not heard that portion of the family history before and she did not know exactly how to consider it. In a way, it was a tale of dashing cavaliers and passionate lovers. Considered from another viewpoint, it spoke of lax morals in a decadent kingdom.

Abby made a deep sigh and shook her head. "Ah, but I've laid a burden on you. I shouldn't have."

"But you should, Mother. Someway, somehow, I would learn of it anyway. It's better to come from you."

"Mayhap. Anyway, it's done." She looked at the sunshine streaming in a window. "Why don't you get out into the day? It looks bright enough to chase away all the darkness we've talked about."

The moment she stepped out into the street, Marie knew Abby had the right of it. Not that she could dismiss the whole unsavory matter but she needed freedom from four walls. White, cottony clouds scudding in little clusters across a clear blue sky and a steady, gentle breeze made her breathe deeply. Walking seemed to help her thinking — Lord knew there was plenty of that to be done.

She hugged herself tightly as she walked, head down and eyes fixed on her moccasin toes, heedless of direction. Her mind moved round and round and round all the things she had learned, all the things that had shocked. Ah, but it would be many a day before she could get it all straight in her head.

Grass, weeds and wild flowers brushed her skirt as she moved along. She came to an old stump, cracked and weathered, marking the site of a tree that had been cut down in the early days when British soldiers first cleared the land to build the fort.

She sat down on it, moved about until she felt comfortable, then folded her hands on her lap, carefully watched her thumbs as she twirled them around each other. Her mind raced with thoughts, one following the other so swiftly that not one of them made a distinct impression.

Slowly, very slowly, an idea began to take form. It was more feeling than idea, a feeling that the talk with Abby had moved Marie out of true girlhood into something more mature, older, wiser. She wasn't at all sure she liked it, either.

For one thing, her uncertainty of yesterday did not exist today. The rules and admonitions she heard everywhere as to conduct were . . . what? . . . just older folk talk aimed to keep children in line. Idols and ideals must be of the same material — reins to be discarded when the right time came. When was that? Marie raised her head to look down the slope to the village, the log fort and the rivers. She really didn't see them as the answer came to her.

This was her time of discarding, of throwing off childhood and becoming a young woman. She didn't realize she lacked the necessary new code of maturity to substitute for the old. She only knew she was free of many restraints.

Edward had certainly discarded his long ago and far away in France, and if Abby's suspicions were true, recently in a Canadian town on the distant Wabash. Her body stiffened with a new and devastating thought. Abby had often spoken about herself and her years with the Onondaga Indians and Corn Dancer, her husband. Had there been other warriors? Was a marriage by heathen rites of the Iroquois a true marriage?

Another discard? Marie wondered, and then she thought of Henry. He was always out of the house and she knew he saw the village girls from time to time. Once or twice he had asked her about one or another of them. She began to feel mounting anger when she remembered how he had warned her against Ike Ilam. What right did he have? Purity? She laughed aloud and stood up.

She looked down at the distant village and fort, seeing it with different eyes. Why, everyone down there led a secret life, each had discards of childish — no, baby! — teachings. Only Marie Forny had been too stupid to realize it up to now!

She turned about so that she faced the rising slope of the hills. The waters of the Monongahela glittered and sparkled like scattered jewels in the sun and she could plainly see the trail leading to the Ilam house and the horse pens. Over to the left was the path she and Ike customarily used. Why not again?

She hurried off to the woods and the glade where they met. Ike was not about. She sought him, first in one area, then in another. She finally stopped, knowing he must have given up hope of meeting her. Her frustration added to her growing desire for him and a hardly recognized need to have revenge on all those who had misled her by admonitions, strictures, lectures.

She abandoned her aimless search and looked about, her lips compressed. She came to a decision and walked out of the forest, this time in a direction that would avoid the village and take her to the path along the Mononga-hela. Twice she faltered, knowing there could be no turning back from what she planned. She stood rigid and unmoving, fists clenched, chin out-thrust and then, more determined than ever, walked on.

The Ilam house stood before her when the path left its narrow woodland corridor. It was a squat building of logs, a high chimney and two small windows. Beyond it stood a stable and barn, also of logs, larger and far more impressive than the house. Marie saw high pole fences, broken by heavy, solid swing gates. They held surprisingly few horses until she remembered that Jep Ilam was out on a trading tour. She hardly had time for more than a single look when the front door of the house burst open and Ike jumped into the yard.

"Marie! My God, gal! I never thought to see ye here."

"I was up in the Allegeway woods where we usually meet."

"Hell, I stopped going there. I traipsed by your house a dozen times and ye didn't come. I figured ye tired of me."

"I didn't get tired of you, Ike. I just listened to the wrong talk. All their prim and proper teaching and scolding—"

"About me," he growled. "I ain't good enough to be with their kind. That's it, huh?" He laughed. "But now ye know better. Ye know what ye want."

"That's right, I know."

He swung her around and almost dragged her to the cabin. His face contorted with rage and his voice choked with passion. "Well, ye come right on in. This time you 'n' me will do what we've both wanted all along, won't we?"

She stumbled into the room on his arm and he impatiently righted her. She saw a nearly bare room. One piece of furniture seemed enormous, all out of proportion to the benches and tables. It was a wooden bedstead, the stained mattress almost hidden beneath ancient blankets and soiled patchwork quilts. The mattress rested on a web of thick ropes crisscrossing the wooden frame.

Ike swept the bed clothing to the floor, leaving the mattress fully exposed. He turned to her and the eagerness in his eyes changed to blazing anger.

"Ain't ye going to shed that damn dress! Git ye naked girl, like I be in a minute. Here, let me help ye strip down to bare hide."

He almost tore the buttons from her blouse and ripped her skirt in his eagerness. Now Marie began to feel fright but Ike moved too fast and too intently for her to deter him. She found herself flat on her back, staring up at him in dismay, aware of the stir of air along her naked buttocks and breasts, over her stomach.

Ike had been beyond her vision for a few moments but suddenly he stood beside the bed, looming over her. Her eyes instantly dropped to his groin and she gasped. The size of him! Were all men? . . .

He dropped atop her, knocking the breath from her lungs. His fingers fumbled with her, forcing her to part her legs and then clutching at her mound. She felt a second, larger, insistent finger insert itself. She sucked in her breath as it hit an obstruction she had not known was within her body. It struck again and then a knife-like shredding pain made her cry out.

A second later she felt him deep within her stomach. He filled her — filled her. She began to move in a ragged rhythm she could not control. Sheer instinct drove her on. Pain fled. She felt mounting ecstasy, a need to engulf and encircle him as he tried to fill her with plunging strokes.

Girlhood fled from Marie, never to return. She was older: wise, mature, fulfilled.

She writhed, moving with rhythm matching Ike's, clutching him, nails digging into his shoulder, her head thrown back. A new sensation became stronger, stronger . . . stronger and then shook her from head to foot. She beat at the mattress and screamed her delight aloud.

XIII

Edward began to understand the anger of the settlers hewing the trees and shaping the logs to form the high stockade wall of the fort they built. Daniel Boone sat quite still under the huge spreading oak in the forest but his was the stillness of the wild — the hunter and the hunted. Edward knew a snap of his finger would galvanize Boone into instant action as it would any animal. He would grab up his long rifle or snatch his tomahawk from his belt or slide his long, heavy bladed hunting knife from his scabbard and attack.

"They're new to these parts," Edward said, "while you've been hunting for years."

"I told 'em all that long afore they ast me to bring 'em out. They knowed it."

The man needed appeasing if Edward was to keep his promise to the settlers, so his first move was to make Boone accept him also as a wilderness wanderer. The man lived too much alone to have the normal responses men expected from one another. Edward shrugged and his face held an expression of disdain and disgust for the settlers.

"Eh, they are *enfants,* children — settlement and farm folk, not hunters like us."

Boone's cold eyes studied Edward from deep under shaggy brows. "You? I ain't heard of ye. I ain't seen sign of ye and I've traipsed all over this country from the Gap to the Big River down to the Salt Licks. Whar ye been huntin', if that ye do?"

"All along the Ohio. I've been on the Scioto, the Maumee, the Kentucky and the Licking." Edward's wide sweeping arm indicated the immensity of the country about them. "Maybe a million miles of woods, prairie — as many rivers and streams . . . and just two white men hunting in it! We're lucky to meet now. Hadn't it been for the party you brought from the Gap, likely we still wouldn't be talking face to face."

Boone grunted and Edward took it as a sound of grudging agreement. The hunter looked off beyond Edward down a glade between the giant trees. His thin lips moved as though he had tasted something bitter.

"I shoulda done it. Just crowding up good clean country. Couldn't stand all their yapping and barking and such. Had to git away."

"They said you just pointed to a stretch of open prairie land, said 'That's it' and left 'em standing."

"I only said I'd bring 'em to a good spot. I did. I've filled my word. I'm through."

"But you were to help them get established."

"Help 'em? Help 'em clutter up good, clean, empty land jus' as God made it! Look what that Harrod's doing

— building a second fort — cuttin' down trees and all. His hunters is out killin' game. They's fishing the river as ought to be left alone."

"You knew that would happen when you made your bargain, *mon ami*. So why did you do it?"

"For powder 'n' shot. For possibles. Now I got 'em, I don't need them spoilers and they don't need me." He noisily brought phlegm up into his throat and deliberately spat a huge gob of it just before Edward's feet.

"You . . . a long hunter! Hell, you ain't wet your britches yet in this country."

A hunting cougar could not have moved so fast with such an easy flow of muscles as Boone. He was on his feet and several yards away down the glade before Edward's shock passed and he could catch his voice.

"*Attendez!*" he called, realized he spoke French and called again, "Wait!"

Boone stopped, turned to glare at him. "No, be ye do the waitin' — clean 'til Judgment Day afore ye see me again."

He whipped about, took but three or four steps and was gone. It seemed as though the very trees had swallowed him. Edward called again, jumped after him. But Boone had vanished and Edward would never see him again.

Long before Edward returned to the open prairie, he heard the steady thud of axes and distant shouts warning of falling trees. Men clearing more forest from land that would eventually be scarred by plows, exposing rich dark clods that hoes would break up. He at last came out of the forest into the midst of steady and untiring activity.

The men with the axes were all too aware of the hatred of the Indian tribes. They counted this Kentucky country among their hunting and warring preserve. There could be no safety for anyone until high, stout walls of pointed posts formed a barricade and protection. The men had in mind particularly the women who, at the moment, worked at laundry and cooking along the near bank of the Kentucky River. Small children toddled, prattled and played about them. Older children helped with the tasks.

As Edward walked toward the center of the camp, men now and then looked up, using their shirts to wipe sweat from their faces, to speak a word, for the most part a question about Boone. Each barely heard Edward's answer before the axe blade glinted high in the sunshine and then chunked into a tree. Edward moved on.

He found Harrod talking to a stranger who must have appeared after Edward left the camp to find Boone. Harrod was a quiet man but just one look into his clear, direct blue eyes marked him as a courageous one, a leader who dreamed of opening virgin land to establish settlements and farms.

"Edward, what of Boone?"

"Eh, that one! Only the good God knows where he is by now. He says that since he has brought you and the company here, you can do what you please when you please. Ah, *oui,* and be damned to you, me, and all the rest of mankind."

Harrod nodded, not too upset. "I read him as that kind of person. But meet Col. George Rogers Clark — neighbor and friend of Thomas Jefferson over in Virginia."

"We're still in Virginia, sir," Clark said in a deep, resonant voice. "She claims all this Kentucky country. I'm here to survey it, once I take care of more pressing matters concerning my militia title."

The tall, muscular man had removed his wide-brimmed wilderness hat and at first all Edward could possibly see was his flaming red hair. It reminded Edward of a torch, the flames whipped by vagrant winds. Clark must once have had a fair skin splotched by freckles but the blazing suns of many summers had smoothed and darkened everything into an even tan, blending in the freckles so they were hardly discernible. He wore the wilderness long shirt, gathered at the waist by a wide belt bristling with pistol and hunting knife.

Harrod explained in a flat, disapproving tone, "He intends to war with the British taking a lot of my young men with him. Damn it, Clark, I need them!"

"You'll have 'em back — and soon enough to carry on your work. Besides, if we set the Britishers back, the Indians will lose a heap of courage that Tory whiskey and powder keep alive."

Edward asked, "Where will you fight them — along the Ohio?"

"Eventually, not right away. I think the first thing will be to isolate the posts at Cahokia and Kaskaskia that keep eyes on the Spanish around St. Louis. Then I have a mind to look at Vincennes. You know the place, sir?"

"Very well. I am setting up a second trading post there."

"Well, blast my eyes! We could be of good use to one another, sir — that is, if you're not a Tory."

"I am not. I am trader on the rivers, some would call me Canadian voyager. I am neutral. I will remain that way."

Clark took no umbrage, only grinned and Edward could not help his increased liking of the man. Clark linked his arm in Edward's and swung him around, away from Harrod. "Well, I travel Vincennes way and, be ye come along, we're company. Mayhap I can change your mind for ye."

"Not a chance. If you wish to spy out Vincennes, do it yourself."

"Two reasons I can't."

"*Vraiment?* And what would they be?"

"First, I am aiming for the falls of the Ohio and not the Wabash as yet. Second —" He jerked off his hat. "Did ye ever see a spy as well marked as me with all this red atop my noodle? I'd stand out like a chicken in a den of foxes. So . . . you're elected."

"You do not listen very well, Colonel. I will not act as spy for anyone at any time."

Harrod laughed harshly. "Mr. Forny, Clark is stubborn. If he does not have his will one way, he will have it another. I refused to strip my party of young bucks for this mad scheme of his. So he fires them up with insane promises of loot and derring-do. I lost them anyhow."

"The rest of you can get along very well." Clark turned his attention back to Edward. "In any case, travel with us, Mr. Forny. It'll be safer for you. Indians will think twice before jumping a party as large as ours, but a lone man — well . . ."

"When do you leave?"

"On the morrow." Clark grinned. "You'll be mighty welcome company and I promise no more arguments about using your eyes for me."

"Then I accept — and thank you. I'll bring my possibles to your campfire tonight."

In the days that followed, Edward sometimes wondered if there were not an unseen entity or force that shaped mens' lives. He had left Pittsburg ostensibly to take Henri into the Wataugas but he confessed to himself that he actually fled from Abby's presence. He knew beyond doubt she had no word of the events in Vincennes but yet . . . but yet . . . she knew something had happened there.

Ma foi! How she had welcomed him home. Their initial time alone had been like the first night of a honeymoon. He had thought little of Mathilde Rodare. A man was expected to make love to a woman when she threw herself at him. It was accepted. Of course, neither he nor his wife spoke of the matter. That was understood. How often Edward had known of this back in France or had been involved as the unmentioned third party in a marital triangle.

But there must be a sea change between Europe and the New World, particularly that of the thirteen colonies now fighting to become independent states forming a single nation. He had been slow to comprehend, he admitted now as he sometimes vainly sought sleep in the midst of George Clark's camp. Looking back on it, he could clearly mark the changes in Abby.

Eh, but he had thrown himself into the enjoyment of her still slender, loving body, her rhythm matching his own. But the ecstasies of that first night had never been fully experienced again. True, she loved him but more and more frequently as if she knew her husband was no longer fully her own possession. It was as though a thin gossamer curtain, so fine it could not be seen, had dropped between them.

Abby had always been enthusiastic and curious about his trading trips, questioning him as though she must belatedly share his experiences. She still questioned, but this time with a difference. She wanted to know about every person he had met in Vincennes, but this time he sensed she tried to find one of especial importance, one she must consider an enemy, a danger.

He had tried at first to dismiss the whole thing as an illusion of his senses. But why in the name of the God should he think that? No, it must have its source in Abby. Then he became aware that Marie unobtrusively watched him as though he slowly changed from her father into something of a stranger.

He reviewed his thoughts and ideas night after night, always arriving at the same conclusion. That which was merely a peccadillo in Europe could destroy a family along *La Belle Riviere*. He had in reality fled from an accusation he could not deny. He fled from Abby and everything of value to him. Fate, that unseen entity, had brought George Rogers Clark into Edward's life to lead him directly to the source of the trouble, to give him an opportunity to rectify his mistake. He must not let the chance slip away.

He reached his conclusion about three nights out of Harrod's budding settlement. With a sigh of relief and decision, Edward rolled tightly up in his blanket and fell asleep among his companions about the campfire.

Clark set a swift pace for his company of young adventurers and Edward, a former royal officer and soldier, gave him excellent marks for leadership. They came to the falls of the Ohio in record time, then turned westward without crossing the river. Time and again they came on trails of large Indian war parties, sure indication that the red British allies pillaged and burned the land at random and, almost certainly, at will. Edward would not allow himself to think of the number of homes burned, settlers murdered, scalps swinging from Indian belts. Hamilton, the hair buyer, would be paying out a veritable stream of bounties now.

Late one morning, they neared the mouth of the Wabash and Edward, river-wise, began searching the bank. He needed a canoe to cross the Ohio and he had excellent chances of finding a bark craft hidden in the bushes. He was even luckier than that. Within an hour, he and Clark strode around a riverbend to see a *voyageur* just on the point of pushing out into the stream.

Edward hailed the man, who grabbed up his long rifle before he began to listen. Rapid French whipped back and forth between Edward and the *voyageur*, who finally grinned widely.

"Of course, *mon ami*. I myself have business in Vincennes. Come along."

XIV

Marie lay with her blouse pulled down to her waist and her skirts above her hips. Ike had rolled off her and sat on the side of the bed with hanging head and his chest heaving. She could still feel him inside her, thrusting, hurting, yet building those rolling, heightening waves of emotion and desire almost too great to bear. She had a confused memory of crying out time and again, of saying words and sentences she could not recall with the exception of one phrase that rang over and over in her brain.

"Ram me, Ike! Oh, God! God! Ram me hard!"

An inner fire of shame burned her face. Had she actually said that? She must have acted and yelled like a slut. Ike moved slightly and she could look directly on his sprawled legs and a soapy, slick bit of exposed flesh. That small thing! Were those the oils of her body upon it?

She involuntarily looked down at herself, saw the same glistening stain along her bared inner thighs and small globules of it in her hair. Then her eyes widened as she saw a darker stain. Blood!

Ike stirred and she looked up, saw that he, too, stared at her spread legs. She snapped them together but his heavy hands fell on her thighs and he parted her legs. She struggled to escape his grasp.

"Ike! Please!"

"Bleedin'! By God, bleedin'. You was virgin. We — I got your cherry, didn't I?"

She clapped her cupped hands to her ears and closed her eyes as though that, too, would drown out his gloating voice. "Don't talk like that, Ike! Oh, please don't talk like that."

His wiry fingers circled her wrists and he forced down her hands. He leaned toward her, his face inches away. His smile was no longer that devil-may-care set of the mouth she had thought so romantic. It was a leering triumph.

"Oh, lackatee-day! Listen to the wench, would ye! The Fornys all high 'n' mighty, better'n anyone else! But this little Forny gal loves like a mink. Better'n a mink, by God!"

She jumped out of bed, took a step before her skirts tangled her and she fell sprawling. She heard Ike's laugh. It cut through her like a sword blade of burning shame. She grabbed up her clothing, jumped up and this time, unimpeded, raced out of the cabin. She heard Ike's yell to stop but she hurried on. The instinct of terrorized flight rather than any conscious thought made her race directly to the narrow path parallelling the Monongahela. She was instantly out of sight of the cabin as the underbrush whipped behind her.

Many yards into the wild tangle, she stopped. She listened, heard only a lessening whisper of the bushes immediately about her. She strained for even more distant sound, heard nothing. She plunged off the path into a jungle-like tangle whipping at her face, shoulders and body. But it concealed her. She stopped again.

She heard an angry shout, muffled by the intervening foliage. She held herself quite still even though no further sounds alarmed her. At last she slowly, carefully released her breath with the fear-lashed thought that even a little sigh would carry to Ike's ears. Two or three minutes later she knew she was quite alone and safe from him.

Only then she dropped her skirts to her ankles, bent and twisted to examine herself by sight and feel. The hairs between her legs felt bristly. Her inner thighs were dry and caked. The enormity of what she had done hit her with full force and she sobbed, bending double as she hugged herself. Could she ever face anyone again — ever?

She stepped out of the clothing about her ankles. Tears still blurring her vision, she slowly lowered herself to a seat on the ground, the green bushes high above her head. She rubbed the tears away with fingers and knuckles, so roughly that her cheeks and eyelids ached. That brought more tears but at last they dried away.

She examined her clothing, knowing it surely must bear the marks of her sin. She found no blood though she searched minutely. She did find one long strip of her skirt stiff and stained, filled with wrinkles beyond counting. There were dirt smears but, her brain beginning to function, she knew such soiling could always be explained. Every woman and girl in Pittsburg had them. Her attention returned to the long narrow, yellow stain. It could be washed out and never be seen . . . except that Abby

153

might very easily do the laundry. Mother would also be curious if she caught Marie scrubbing at the coarse petticoat.

Marie sat for long moments trying to solve the problem. She couldn't discard the garment without a sound reason. It would be too hard to replace. The solution came in a flash. She ripped out the ruined hem of the petticoat, leaving a ragged edge.

She dressed completely then, passed her hand through her hair to additionally tangle it. She rolled up the torn strip into a ball and looked about until she found what she wanted. She placed the damning strip deep into an old crack formed when some storm in the past had almost torn a tree limb from its trunk.

Making no sound, Marie moved with extreme caution to the river path down which she had fled. She paused before fully emerging from the tangled underbrush to scan the brush-lined river glade and listen.

Nothing broke the silence, everything so still she once thought she heard her own gasping breath. She finally ventured out, still ready to dart back to safety. She knew Ike had already passed and was quite certain he would not reappear, let alone linger in or near the village. He knew only too well what he had done and would be fearful of her denunciation.

Her lips curled in disgust. The dunce! Did he think she'd stand before all her neighbors and friends, point to him and say, "He raped me!"? He probably did, she answered her own scornful but fearful thought. He'd head directly for the Allegeway and the woods beyond. He'd make a huge circle back to the pens on the Monongahela, ride one of the horses off into the woods and remain out of sight until the storm had passed.

It took effort to bring her skittering mind to some sort of coherence. She must first take care of herself. That could be done if she brought off this last act. She again taloned her fingers in her hair and tugged hard on each side of her head. She glanced at her dress; the attached blouse was too smooth. She tore off another button, ripped a long tear down the left side. She took a deep breath, blanked her mind to everything but what must be done, screamed at the top of her voice and raced along the path toward the settlement.

The scream seemed to tear open an inner dam that held back all her emotions since Ike had first touched her, through the rape, the pain, the vivid ecstasies and the cold waves of fear. She raced on and on, screaming.

"Indians! Indians! They caught me! Indians!"

She broke from the woods and raced along the river. Her screams had all the effects of a cannonball exploding in the village. Cabin doors flew open and the streets lining both the Monongahela and the Allegheny near the fort filled with people. She continued her rush, head back, arms extended. She heard hoarse male voices, the higher-pitched cries of women. She suddenly slammed into a solid, muscular body. Arms whipped about her. A man's bellow sounded in her ear.

"Ye be safe! Marie, ye be safe!"

Her eyes flew open and she looked directly into Tatum Long's lean, hard face. "Be ye all right? Where'd they catch you? We'll have them dead and scalped before they get far."

She gulped. In her half-formed plan she had completely forgotten Captain Long and the Pennsylvania militia. Her brain functioned again. She flung her arm back to the woods. "Just two of 'em. I broke away afore they could harm me. They ran when I screamed."

Suddenly Abby stood at Marie's side. She literally jerked Marie free of Long's protecting arm, held her close. "Did they? . . ."

"No," Marie sobbed.

"They sure as hell tried," Long growled. "Tore her clothes into shreds. Look at her hair!" He roughly tugged Marie half about to face him. "Where'd they catch ye?"

"Along the river bank. I was just walking in the sun."

Long released her and whirled to the pressing crowd. "Get your rifles." He saw one of his men. "Call out the company. Full armed and ready. At the stockade gate in ten minutes or less."

The crowd instantly broke up, scattering to obey Long's commands. Abby held Marie tightly and made soothing sounds as she helped her toward the cabins. Though she walked with head hung low and leaned heavily on Abby's arm, Marie furtively eyed the activity streaming on every side around her. What a furor her story had kicked up. It frightened her but it was far too late to do anything but allow it to play itself out. Nothing would happen, of course. The mythical Indians would not be found and gradually the post would return to normal. But she silently vowed she would never again do anything remotely like this.

At last she stumbled through the door of her home and allowed Abby to lead her to a bedroom. She sank down on the bed with a grateful sigh, thankful that the walls now hid and protected her. But she heard muffled shouts and cries from out in the street and knew the excitement she had created continued.

Though safe now from the questions of her neighbors and friends, she could not avoid Abby's sharp, concerned questions. Marie turned up her skirt to show the long tear in the undergarment. There were also the small rips in her blouse. Abby made alarmed exclamations as she examined the garments and then asked Marie to strip off all her clothing. She minutely examined her daughter's body. Marie held her breath when Abby looked at her pubic hairs.

"My God! They must have truly raped you! The stain is there."

"One buck couldn't . . . contain himself . . . before he — That's when I broke away."

"Thank God you escaped. It's a miracle. But, here, put on this nightgown. You need rest and quiet, so sleep is what you're going to get."

"I can't sleep! Not now!"

"But you can snug down and know you're safe. I'll be here, so don't worry."

Marie knew there was nothing else she could do. She pulled the covers up to her chin, felt the warmth of the feather-stuffed mattress that billowed like clouds about her. She looked at the clear blue sky about the Allegheny. At long last, despite herself, she drifted into sleep. Her last, fuzzy thought puzzled her. Where had she heard something about "tangled webs" connected in some way with deception?

Nor did she ever have the true explanation of another consequence of her tale about Indians. Ike Ilam had managed to scramble into his trousers after she fled his cabin. He ran down the path after her, missed her and began a wide circle about Pitt to return home. He had almost completed the circuit but was well up on the wooded hillside when he saw her race out of the river path, free of the forest. He heard her screams but it came from such a distance he could distinguish no words. He saw the village erupt in an explosion, everyone racing to Marie. She made a motion back toward the Ilam pens and cabin.

His final sexual assault on Marie so filled his mind, it immediately jumped to a logical but wrong conclusion. Marie exposed his violent deed to the whole town! He had ruined the virgin daughter of the most influential family in Pittsburg. He not only faced their retribution but punishment from all the villagers.

He remained frozen, watching but a moment longer. Then he jumped back into the concealing trees and brush. Down below, everyone ran toward the cabins to the stockade but Ike knew they raced to gather up weapons. He'd be lucky if they used a knife or a gun on him. A hemp rope from a tree limb would be the most likely instrument of death.

He had no time to spare. He took off with the speed of a hunted deer, fairly clawing his way through an occasional tangle of brush beneath the trees. He came upon his home clearing from the rear. He paused but a fraction of a moment to listen but heard no alarming sounds.

He plunged into the house, grabbed up rifle, powder horn and shot pouch — nothing else. He whipped out into the yard by the horse pens. He thought he heard a distant, but ominous sound. It took but an instant to lower the bars of the nearest pen that, fortunately, held the last few beasts Paw had left. Ike did not need a saddle. He vaulted onto the bare back of one of the beasts, whipped his rifle barrel over the rump of the nearest horse. It bolted out of the gate Ike had opened and the rest followed in a mad rush. Ike clung to his mount, guiding it straight for the Monongahela.

Moments later, river water splashed against hoofs and

in another moment, the whole cavvy swam across the strong current. He heard a shout, risked a look over his shoulder and saw the armed men streaming along the trail.

Long shouted his warning once more. "Stop! Ilam! Stop! There's Indians loose. You'll run smack into 'em."

Ike did not hear above splashing water and equine snorts but kicked his heels into the horse's ribs and cursed it to greater effort. He expected shots to whistle about his head but none came. Thankful, he reached the far bank, kicked his horse and disappeared into the wooded hills.

No one at Pitt ever saw him again.

XV

The first part of Edward's journey, after he had crossed to the northern bank of the Ohio, was easy enough. The powerful current carried him and his canoe as lightly as a feather to the mouth of the Wabash. Once he turned into that stream, its current almost as strong as that of the Ohio, he knew he would be lucky to make any more than a mile a day paddling against it.

He pulled the bark boat to the western bank, unloaded his possibles then carried the light canoe on his back to the edge of the forest. He left it there, safe from the river's current but in plain sight of any chance traveller who might need it. He swung his pack to his back, hefted his long rifle and set out on foot for the town still miles to the north.

He immediately encountered unbroken wilderness but he knew only too well that it was not uninhabited. This was Indian hunting land and their wandering parties would constantly be looking for game or trouble, more than likely not caring much which they came across. That in itself posed a problem for he had to do hunting of his own and the sound of a rifle shot would carry for some distance. Red ears would be quick to pick it up and investigate. *Très bien* and so be it, he shrugged, dismissing a problem that could not be solved.

He remained close to the river for the most part, leaving it now and then to travel directly across the base of one of its many bends rather than wasting time and effort trudging the whole arc of the turn. On one long and nearly straight stretch of the river he saw a small moving speck far ahead. He instantly faded into the woods. The speck resolved itself into a long war canoe with four Shawnee paddlers. He watched them sweep by without seeing him but he cautiously remained out of sight until the canoe disappeared around a curve of the river just to the south.

At last he came out of the forest and saw the long, smooth landing before the town and saw the British flag atop the pole on Fort Sackville dominating Vincennes. His journey was over but the problem he had determined to solve still remained among those buildings.

He made a wide circuit and drifted into the town from the woods. Since he had no canoe, he need not be seen on the public landing, an advantage he appreciated. He had forgotten the sentries and had no more than flitted from one tree to another when a hoarse challenge pulled him up short.

"Halt! Who be ye? Speak up or ye get a ball."

Edward dropped his rifle and lifted his arms. He called, "Friend. You know me."

"Step clear and let's have a look at ye."

Edward stepped into plain sight, his arms still high. He

heard a muffled shout of alarm from within the post and wondered if he had inadvertently alarmed all of Vincennes. After long moments, the sentry called down.

"Ye be Forny, the French trader. Git your rifle and come in by the main gate. I'll send word down to the captain."

Edward made the circuit of the fort. Francois de Busseron and two of his men waited at the main gate. He stared at Edward, puzzled, and spoke in French.

"How is it you come like this, eh? You know you are welcome."

"I don't want it known as yet in the town that I am here, my friend."

De Busseron's brow cocked in a high bracket and then he smiled knowingly. "Ah, yes. Our good Madame Rodare."

"You know about? . . ."

"This is a village, *mon ami*. Not so much as a chipmunk stirs but we know it — all of us." He caught himself up and made a welcoming gesture. "But come in. I will have the good wife bring us wine."

Edward cast a searching look down the slope at the town. He saw people idling on the landing and more at work in their flower or vegetable gardens. There was no movement at the large house with the hollyhocks nor at the cabin he had rented.

Captain de Busseron apparently read his thoughts. "I doubt if you were heard down there. It usually takes a gunshot to arouse them."

"Certainly Justin and Luc seem sound asleep."

"They have enjoyed having little to do. It will be different now?"

He gestured Edward to the gate, then linked arm with

him and led the way to his personal cabin. Madame de Busseron filled the doorway and her face lighted with a smile when she saw Edward.

"Ah, you have been too long gone!" she called. "Welcome! Welcome!"

The three of them soon sat in comfortable chairs, wine glasses in hand. The de Busserons were starved for news along the Ohio. Edward told them all that he could recall about the movement of farmers, newcomers, rumors of the war far away in the east.

"It goes first one way and then another back there," he said. "But at Pitt, the Americans have sent a militia company. I find myself and my family under the banner of Virginia . . . they call it a state now."

De Busseron's face darkened as he worriedly pulled at his underlip. "We are still British. But the Virginians have built a fort — they call it Nolan — just south of the river, as we hear it. At least that land is claimed by the rebel colony." Then he laughed, flinging his hand up in a gesture of dismissal. "But claim all they wish, for that matter! Hamilton may be staying close to Detroit for the time being, but he will move out when it suits him."

"He could bottle himself up," Edward suggested.

"Not Colonel Hamilton. His Indians control the country. They hold the Yankee down while he makes up his mind when and where to move. I hear the rebels in York Colony around Niagara try to sieze the fort and the falls but Hamilton makes them pay too much in blood and gun powder. They'll give up before long and then we'll see redcoat soldiers along the Ohio once more. You can depend on it."

"*Allons y*, we talk of everything but Vincennes — and of little interest to me. Could you send someone to Justin and Luc to bring them up here without them knowing I am present?"

"Easily," Madame de Busseron instantly answered. "My Aspasie could take the message."

"*C'est entendure,*" Edward nodded in agreement.

The Negro girl was instructed and departed on her errand. Edward accepted more wine and for a time studied the village along the river bank. He thoughtfully tugged at his lower lip as he pictured the situation between Pittsburg and distant St. Louis. Until the Yankee and the British resolved their conflict this whole area would blaze with war. He could not see how Vincennes could avoid becoming embroiled in it. It was really the key to control of everything west of Pitt and south of Detroit. He would be foolish to move into the very heart of trouble but he could not cast off the strong urge to do exactly that. Besides, he had spoken too much about the move to Abby — before he had done business, on a distinctly different level, with Mathilde Rodare. No, he must move here. An Indian trader and trapper must keep far ahead of the advancing wave of farm and village settlement."

"Would there be another vacant cabin to rent?" he asked.

"No, Mathilde's was the last," Madame de Busseron answered.

The captain cut in with a wide sweep of his hand. "But there is plenty of vacant, unclaimed land, *mon ami*. You could build for yourself on the fringe of the town and still be near the landing. We have carpenters."

"*Ma foi!* That is it!"

"You are not happy with Mathilde's place?"

"Yes, but she could be too much around her own property, *n'est-ce pas?*"

"Yes, she could." Madame de Busseron placed her finger beside her nose and looked wise. "Besides, you have a wife, eh?"

"An item to be considered," Edward agreed.

"True, but could a place as small as Vincennes hold both women at the same time?"

"Ah, *qui sait!* We can only know by trying."

At that moment, Aspasie returned with Justin and Luc. When they saw Edward, their eyes rounded in surprise and they instantly lost their lazy, unconcerned postures. They whipped off their hats and bobbed their heads in deference.

"Monsieur Forny!" they exclaimed in chorus.

De Busseron suggested. "Take them to my office if you want privacy, *mon ami*."

Edward thanked him and soon sat behind the desk in the small room while Justin and Luc stood at attention before him. He immediately discovered that the two had not loafed all the time as the captain believed. They had made short expeditions down the Wabash with Tobacco's Son and had Piankeshaw peltry in the cabin to show for it. They had twice ventured out with Father Gibault; once upon the Wabash as far as a large, permanent Indian town named Ouitenon, and another time journeyed inland to contact hunting Shawnee. The Shawnee had little to offer.

"But Ouitenon is something else again," Luc vowed. "Even more fur and trade is to be had there than here. Our post should be at Ouitenon."

"Are French there?" Edward asked. "Houses?"

"Neither," Justin answered mornfully. His face cleared. "We could build cabins, monsieur."

Edward thought of what the captain had just suggested

in relation to Vincennes. The two before him might easily become carpenters of experience before the returned to Indian fur trade!

"I will first look at this Ouitenon myself if you are all this excited about it."

"*Mareveilleux!*" responded the two voices, again as one.

"But I have another thought on my mind — Madame Rodare."

The two exchanged glances and Justin asked very carefully, "What of her, monsieur?"

"Why — everything — you understand. What is she like? What have you learned of her? Has she been to the cabin — once? Many times? None at all? Has she many friends? Are they mostly women or men? Whatever you know or have heard."

They were reluctant and it took a great many more questions to start them talking. But at last he had enough of a picture and knowledge of her to give him increased confidence. He dismissed the pair.

"Return to the cabin. I'll see you there after dark. Say nothing of me, *vous comprenez?*"

"We understand," Luc answered, then eagerly asked, "Will you sup with us?"

"No — but breakfast in the morning, *mes amies*. For the now, *bonjour*."

He rejoined Captain de Busseron and his wife after the men departed. He explained Justin and Luc had been more active at business than any of them had thought but made a wry admission that they really could have bestirred themselves more.

"And they will, now that I'm back." He hesitated a second and then, recalling what Madame had hinted, realized there was no point in trying to hide anything.

"What can you tell me of Mathilde Rodare?"

"Much . . . or little," Madame shrugged. "Which would you like?"

"Much, I think. For instance, am I right in believing she is seldom long without a man?"

"Ho! That way!" de Busseron laughed. "You, my friend, may so truly believe. Twice I have come very near using an authority of office I have never invoked — to rid the town or the province of degraded, profligate inhabitants."

"As bad as that!"

"Not really, but if the women of the town become too upset with her, they lose the edge of anger when I mention it. They feel their men are safer."

"And Madame Rodare?"

"Just a suspicion of fear of me does wonders to control her."

"And it would also do it for me."

"But you do not have the governor's power."

"As his good friend, I have his ear."

"That you do . . . that you do. Nor would the governor deny it."

Edward slapped his hands on his knees and arose. "In that case, *à bientot*."

"Goodbye for the moment?"

"A word with Mathilde Rodare, *s'il vous plait*."

He took plenty of time strolling down the path to the village, turning over in his mind the idea de Busseron had given him. He found no fault with it by the time he came to the path leading to his rented cabin and Mathilde's house. He made no attempt at concealment and half expected her to appear in her open doorway. But she did not and he stopped directly before the house. Still no sign of her.

"Ah, *pourqois pas?*" he asked himself. Indeed, why not. He strolled to the hollyhock-shaded doorway and knocked. No reply. Once more he could look directly down the long hall, almost like peering in a telescope, through the open rear door into the vegetable garden beyond. He did not see her so he knocked more sharply and also called her name. A hall door opened and she stepped out of a side room. She instantly saw him. He was surprised to see alarm sweep her face. She swiftly erased it but remained at the door, her hand on the knob.

"Edouard! You surprise me."

"*Ma foi,* I believe I do."

He walked down the hall toward her. She leaned against the door instead of coming to meet him. He stood close to her, smiling, but he saw only alarm in her expression.

"Mathilde, you have no kiss for an old and very dear friend?"

"Of course." She leaned forward, her lips brushing his cheek.

Expecting the move, he made a slight twist as he bent to her. His shoulder struck her arm as his hand covered hers on the knob. The door slightly opened before she retrieved the knob. He had only a second's glimpse of a heavy chair, a man's trousers neatly folded over the back. She instantly closed the door with a slight thud of wood on wood.

He deliberately raised his voice so that it would carry into the room. "I have interrupted. You have company." She shook her head and, still talking loudly, he said, "I'll have only a word with you. Perhaps in the parlor?"

He jerked her hand from the knob but made no attempt to open the door. He led her across the hallway into her parlor. For the first step or two she resisted but, somewhat allayed, she did not fight him. They entered the room and Edward closed the door behind them with a bang that must have echoed through the house. He waved to a chair.

"*S'assyez vous.* Your friend, whoever he is, will be quite safe from discovery. It is just you and I who have business together."

She dropped into the chair, rubbed her wrist and glared defiantly. "What business?"

"Preparing for the immediate future, *ma cherie*. That is to say, what will and will not be done?"

"*Peste!* I go my own way, make my own decisions."

He smiled as he took another chair and lifted a finger. "*Un moment, s'il vous plait.* When I return, there is one decision you will not make for yourself. We decide that one here and now."

"Indeed! And what may that be?"

"*Attend,* Mathilde. Pay close attention. I am moving my business here from Pittsburg. It is further out in Indian country, far ahead of large settlement, and there are other reasons that do not concern you."

She tossed her head and her lips curled. "None of your reasons concern me." Then she softened, deliberately leaning forward to expose the soft, white mounds of her breasts and the warm shadow between them. Edward fought the tightening in his groin. Madness, the way a man's body lay beyond the control of his mind.

"Edouard," she whispered in a little girl voice. "Wait a little, *mon cher*. Come back tonight, eh? Then there'll be time for us to talk." Her lashes lowered, then lifted slowly. "You can't know how it's been without you."

Edward swallowed hard and crossed his legs. "This won't take long to say, Mathilde. When I come back to Vincennes I'll be bringing my wife and daughter with me."

She shrugged. "*Oui. Ta femme.* I guessed as much. Some frazzled little backwoods frump, no doubt. And very proper — ah, but aren't they always?" She chuckled and tossed her head. "*Ne t'en fais pas!* Don't worry, *mon etalon.* Mathilde is most discreet. I will say nothing. But you and I, there is no reason we cannot continue as before, *eh bien?* Surely she cannot offer you what I can." She glanced slyly down at her own splendid, creamy bosom.

God help me, Edward thought, trying to conjure up a mental picture of Abby. "There'll be no more of that, Mathilde. It must be over between us. *Fini!* You understand?"

She was looking down at her folded hands. Edward thought he saw the gleam of a tear on her cheek, but that meant little. Some women could cry at will, and he suspected that Mathilde was one of them. Very slowly she raised her eyes. Her smile was a vixen's smile now. "I could make trouble, you know," she said softly. "Mathilde Rodare is known as a woman of . . . integrity. No one would doubt my word, *cher,* especially when it is the truth."

Edward glared at her. His desire had given way to a simmering anger, and he was grateful for it. "You could indeed," he said coldly. "But what would be the point in it? It would only damage your own reputation — to say nothing of what it would do to Abby."

"Abby. Abigail." Her lips curled around the syllables. "I might have guessed that would be her name. Breasts like withered cucumbers, no doubt, and a thin little purse of a mouth! She probably smells of bear grease and lye soap!" Mathilde's eyes half closed, like a cat's. "Ah, I hate her already! Edward—" Her voice softened. She leaned toward him, the soft, lovely twin globes almost spilling from her blouse. "Edward, *mon cher,* your love would be more than enough to buy my silence." She reached for his hand, lifted it, placed his fingers along the warm cleft of her bosom. "And only now and then, *amour.* Only when you want something with a bit of spice in it, eh?"

Edward remembered the trousers folded over the back of the chair in the next room. "I have only one question," he said, slowly and deliberately withdrawing his hand. "*Je tu demande,* Mathilde, is your silence enough to buy my love? I'm afraid, *ma belle,* the answer is no."

"*Peste!*" She jerked away from him with a hiss. "I have no more to say to you, then! Bring her to Vincennes! Your wife, your frumpy, little Abigail! Just see what happens then, *mon etalon!* My dark stallion!"

"I know precisely what will happen, Mathilde. Open your pretty mouth and you'll be bundled out of Vincennes before you can blink. Captain de Busseron's orders! I have his word on it!" Edward forced himself to smile. "And now, *ma cherie,* I believe you have a customer—*pardon*—a visitor waiting for you. He must be most impatient."

She flew out of the chair. "*Brute! Cochon!*" She spat the words into his face. "Go, then! You think you have won, eh? You and your dumpy little Abigail! *Attend,* Edouard! You have wiped your muddy boots on Mathilde Rodare! And Mathilde does not forget!"

Edward slipped out the door, her whispered curses still ringing in his ears. *Ma foi,* but he was lucky to have escaped with his skin! He had hoped Mathilde would be understanding. He should have known better! Roused, she was like an angry she-bear.

He could only hope she was bluffing. How could she afford to leave Vincennes? How could she leave her property? He had her, Edward told himself. She would not have been so furious if she'd not seen that. Mathilde would make no trouble, he assured himself as he strode down the road toward the river.

Yet something in her eyes, some wild, animal fury he had glimpsed there, continued to haunt him. He shivered. With Abby in Vincennes, he would not sleep well. Not with Mathilde around.

XVI

The war seemed very far away to Marie. She sat in her father's long canoe, her back straight as an Indian princess's, and watched the glistening water of the Ohio slide past the sharp prow. The current was swift here. Edward, seated a few feet in front of her, used his paddle only to guide the slender craft. His muscles rippled beneath the weathered buckskin.

It seemed they had been gliding forever along *La Belle Riviere*. The sound of the water echoed in Marie's head. Even at night when they made camp on the shore, it splashed and gurgled in her dreams. Marie had lost track of the days that had passed since they'd left Fort Pitt, but she did not regret a one of them. Pitt was behind her. If she never saw the place again, it would be none too soon. Vincennes, and a new life, lay ahead. She was determined not to look back.

Edward Forny had returned to Pitt at the end of June

and set himself at once to preparing his family for the move. The cabin had been let to Dean Smith, who would stay behind and manage the business there. Most of the furniture had been disposed of as well. Only the barest essentials—clothing, food, pots, pans, dishes and a few treasures like Abby's prized spinning wheel could be taken in the canoes.

Marie still remembered the look on her father's face when Abby had told him the story of the Indian rape. Edward had clasped his daughter close, his whole body trembling with emotion. *"Ma fille,"* he had whispered, lifting her chin and gazing into her eyes. "So young. So very young for such a thing to happen. *Merci le bon Dieu* you're alive!" Marie had squirmed inside, trapped by those earnest eyes. What if he'd known the truth? *Le bon Dieu,* indeed! He'd probably have killed Ike Ilam, and who knows what he'd have done to her!

But all that was behind her, Marie reminded herself. She would never see Ike again, nor did she want to. She sighed as she watched the green banks slip past. She had left her girlhood in Pitt. Her body had awakened to new drives, new forces so strong that they shook her whole being. Ike's loving (Loving? Could it be called that? No, surely not with Ike. There'd been no more loving in it than in the mating of two wild dogs.) had roused a demon in her, a demon that would not be still. At night she lay feverish under her blankets, touching herself where Ike had touched her, frustrated by the emptiness of the tingling her own fingers could stir up. Sometimes the urge was so strong in her that she wanted to yowl like a cougar in heat.

"Soigneux, Ned!" Edward called out. "Watch that rock, it's a sharp one!"

"I see it!" Ned Cooper's voice rang from the stern of the long canoe as he moved his paddle with surprising skill. Ned himself was the biggest surprise of all, Marie reflected. Though he hadn't been gone to Philadelphia more than a few weeks, he had come back changed. He seemed taller somehow. His chest and arms had filled out, and his jaw had acquired a determined set to it. The boy who had scrambled with his friends playing stickball in the mud was gone. The serious young man who had taken his place was a stranger to Marie. A most disconcerting stranger.

With Henry off to the Watauga country, Edward had found himself in need of a new assistant. Ned Cooper was a natural choice. Ned could read and write and do sums, and he had proven himself capable and responsible in helping his own father. Absalom Cooper had let his son go, grateful for the chance the lad would have to better his lot and see something of the world. Absalom had long been aware of Ned's growing restlessness in Pitt, Marie had heard him telling Edward. Young Ned would do well to learn the trading business.

Marie did not glance back at Ned, though she knew that he looked almost as handsome as her father in the new buckskins Edward had given him. He had paid her little mind since his return from the east. It was clear enough that he no longer thought of her as his sweetheart. No doubt he'd heard about the alleged Indian attack on her. Maybe it bothered him that she wasn't pure any more. Well, fie on Ned, Marie thought, with a toss of her dark curls. There'd be plenty of boys in Vincennes! She'd show him!

The current was getting faster. Marie heard Abby gasp behind her as the canoe dipped and righted itself. Justin and Luc shot past them a few yards away in the other boat, dexterously plying their paddles. The bundled essentials of the Forny household were piled between them. Luc cupped his hand to his mouth and shouted something in French, his voice all but lost above the sound of the river.

"What did he say?" Abby called to her husband, strain showing in her voice.

"The falls," Edward answered clamly, giving her a smiling glance back over his shoulder. "Just a few minutes ahead of us. Don't worry, *ma belle,* I have passed this way many times. There is a safe passage for those who know it." He waved to Justin and Luc.

"Our things could get all wet," Abby protested. "Don't you think it would be safer to portage around them?"

He gave her a wink. "Is this Strong Woman of the Onondaga talking? To portage would take all day! We can cover the same distance by river in no time. Trust me!"

Marie glanced back at her mother, then forward at her father's back. She had felt the tension between them from the moment of Edward's return to Pitt. Abby had seemed more withdrawn, more cautious than she had ever been before. Edward's usual gaiety was forced, strained. The move to Vincennes, which should have been a joyous prospect, was overshadowed by the thought of the unknown woman that waited there. Had he been with her again? Marie wondered. Had the two of them done what she and Ike had done on that filthy mattress in the cabin? Marie shuddered. The thought of it almost made her ill. Her father. Her dear, good father.

"Are you all right, Marie?" Abby's voice was sharp with concern.

"Yes, Mother." Marie ran a hand through her fluttering curls. She wondered if Ned was watching her. Well, let him watch! What was it to her?

"Hold onto the gunnels! Hold on tight!" Her mother's words ended in a little gasp as the canoe skirted a large, square boulder, white water frothing around it. Ahead of them, Marie could hear the tumbling roar of the rapids.

"Hold it steady, Ned," Edward's voice crackled above the sound. "Just do what I do. If that gets too much for you, just pull in your paddle and hang on. I can do it alone if I must. *Compris?*"

"Aye," Ned answered quietly. "I understand, sir." Marie risked a glance at him. Ned's face was slightly pale beneath his tan. His lips were set. Their eyes met for just the flicker of a moment before he turned his full attention back to the paddle.

The other canoe, with Justin and Luc, raced along beside them. The two *courieurs* were laughing loudly, nervously, as they guided the long craft through the foaming water. "I'll go first. You follow! *Eh, bien?*" He swung the canoe sharply to the right, surging ahead toward the narrow channel that led safely through the rapids. The thunder of the falls was frighteningly near. Marie gripped the gunnels of the canoe until her knuckles whitened.

"Now!" Edward's paddle swung into the white water. The current took them, lifting the great canoe like a toy. Marie felt the snowy spray wash over her. She cried out.

"*Courage!*" Edward's laughing voice boomed above the rumble of the falls. "It's nothing, my beauties!"

Through the strings of her wet hair, Marie saw the passage ahead, between two great, black rocks. Her father was making for it, Justin and Luc shouting encouragement behind them.

Marie held her breath. The water poured between the two rocks. The passage was so narrow that she could have touched both sides of it at once if she'd held out her arms. She heard Abby gasp as they dropped into the dizzying whiteness. The sound of the falls roared in her ears, filling everything.

She closed her eyes as she heard Abby's scream. This is the end, she thought. But no, the canoe was not falling. It was shooting ahead, down, down through the stinging spray. Yards to the left she glimpsed the sheer drop of the falls, but Edward had found a side channel, where the slope was not so steep. Breathlessly they careened along, skimming rocks, drenched by the icy mist of the water.

Edward shouted something to Ned as they splashed into the seething caldron at the foot of the falls. The canoe bobbed wildly, spinning about in the eddies. "Stroke, Ned," he shouted. "Stroke for your life!" The two of them paddled furiously. The slim craft righted itself and surged out of the roiling water into another side channel.

Marie's father grinned back at them. "*Voila!* The worst is over. It's nothing from here! You'll see. There's a spot about a mile downstream where we can stop and dry off."

Marie gazed at him wonderingly. She had never seen her father quite like this before, so reckless, so gay. Maybe there were two Edward Fornys, she thought. One was the sober, responsible father she knew. And the other—perhaps she was seeing him now for the first time. Maybe it was this other Edward Forny who'd tumbled with the young aristocratic ladies of France, who'd bedded some unknown woman in Vincennes. Maybe this was the real Edward, she thought, and the other one, the one she thought she knew so well, was only something he put on like a cloak during the time he spent with his family.

She looked back at her mother. Abby was pale and dripping, her lips pressed tightly together, whether with fear or rage Marie could not tell. But Abigail Brewster Forny would have something to say to her husband when they pulled the canoe onto the bank. That was for sure.

Ned had lost his hat, and his buckskins were soaked, but he managed to return Edward's grin as he leaned into the paddle. The current was still rough. It took all their efforts to keep the canoe on course and off the rocks. The triumphant whoops of Justin and Luc from behind told them that the other canoe had shot the passage safely. Edward seemed to relax a bit.

But the danger was by no means over. The channel was narrow. The water gushed through it with terrifying speed. The green shore flashed past Marie's eyes. She clung to the gunnels, shifting as best she could to balance her weight in the canoe.

She was looking down when she heard her father's shout of alarm. Instantly her eyes darted ahead. What she saw made her stomach lurch with sudden fear. Some forty yards downstream a dead tree had somehow washed into the channel and was wedged between the banks. The fragile canoe was hurtling toward it. There was no way to stop or turn aside. There was scarcely time to scream as the prow of the canoe crunched into the splintering branches. Marie felt herself flying forward. Her skirt caught on a jagged limb. She reached out and clasped the trunk of the tree, clinging frantically as the foaming current washed over her. She glimpsed her father in the water, hanging onto the bow of the canoe. Abby was still inside the boat. Marie could not see Ned.

The tree had been jarred loose by the impact of the canoe. With a shudder it began to move downstream. *"Tenez bon*, Marie! *Hold on!"* She heard her father's shout before the tree dipped and the water closed over her head.

Marie fought her way to the surface, gasping for air. The tree bucked and pitched. Its broken limbs were like daggers, jabbing at her face and body, but she held on, sobbing with the effort.

Suddenly there was a head beside hers in the water, a face, and two strong arms, supporting her against the tree. It was Ned, holding her. His voice penetrated the roaring in her ears. "Ride behind it, Marie! Get the tree ahead of us!" She let him move her, let herself float in the circle of his arms while he shifted their position.

It was easier trailing behind the tree, though they still had to be careful of the sharp, pounding rocks. The current carried them until the land began to level off again. The river slowed and calmed to become once more the Ohio that Marie had always known. When the tree carried them past a sand bar, Marie and Ned let go and swam to shore, side by side, her stroke matching his. Gasping, they heaved themselves up onto the bank.

For a moment Marie could only lie there in the long, soft grass, her eyes shut, her heart pounding. She was alive. She was safe. The sound of the falls was far away now, like distant thunder.

She opened her eyes. Ned had raised himself up on one elbow and was looking down at her. His face was disturbingly close. Why had she never noticed what blue, blue eyes he had?

The summer grass was long and tall, like a green curtain around them. Marie could hear Ned's breath coming fast and deep as he leaned over her. Then his mouth came down on hers. She felt his lips, warm, strong, moving. The familiar stirring welled up inside her. She moaned and encircled his neck with her arms. "Marie!" He kissed her again, less gently this time. His tongue darted into the hollow of her mouth, in and out. Marie felt the wild, frantic tingling all the way down into her legs. Was Ned feeling it, too? What was it like to be a boy? she wondered. Could it be more exciting than being a girl?

With a little whimper she rolled onto her side so that he could hold her against the length of his body. *Tonnerre!* She had made it happen again! She could feel him through her skirt, the tight straining against his wet buckskins. It excited her, this new power she had over young men!

But she was no fool, Marie reminded herself. Not after Ike Ilam. Once she had thrown herself away like a common slut. But the new Marie was wiser. She knew all about boys now, and she knew when to stop. Oh, but she had been so frightened in the water. She was wet and cold, and Ned's body was so warm and exciting. She would enjoy him just a moment more, she promised herself. Then she would laugh and jump away from him. She'd show Ned Cooper she wasn't an easy mark like some girls!

Ned had stopped kissing her. He sat up, his face suddenly grave. "Ye ben't mine for the taking, Marie," he said softly. "I'll not be one to use ye badly, now. Besides, they'll be lookin' for us in the boats. We'd best stand up so they can see us." He scrambled to his feet, almost too hastily.

Marie let him help her up. Her clothes felt sticky and wrinkled. Sand clung to her legs and she'd lost her moccasins. Worse, Ned Cooper had bested her. *She* had planned to be the one to pull away. *She* had expected to leave him panting for more of her. "*Peste!*" she muttered under her breath. She'd show him yet!

The twin canoes swung into sight around the bend of the river. Her father and mother were in one of them, Justin and Luc in the other. Marie danced up and down and waved her arms. She heard her father's shout as the two canoes made for shore.

Ned stood beside her as they waited. She felt his eyes on her, but she tossed her hair, fluffing it with her fingers to dry it, and would not look at him again. He had humiliated her!

She shook her skirt. Her blood was still racing. She could feel it as she felt the tingle of her lips where Ned had kissed her, and the delicious prickling all up and down her body where he had held her close.

The first canoe touched the bank. Abby was out of it almost before her husband. Then she was up the bank, holding her daughter tight in her arms. She was trembling.

"How could you do it?" She turned on Edward as he came toward them. "How could you risk all our lives like that, just to save a few hours of portage?" Marie stared at her. She had never heard her mother speak to her father like that before. Abby drew herself up, quivering with anger. "Are you *that* anxious to get back to Vincennes?" she hissed.

Edward frowned at her, then looked away. "We'll camp here," he said, his voice masking whatever he felt. "It's early, but we'll need the sun to dry things out. Ned, can you get us some wood for the fire while the rest of us unload the canoes?"

Ned moved to obey him without a word. Marie patted her mother's shoulder. "It's all right," she whispered. "Nobody was hurt, and nothing was lost." Strange, but for a moment she almost felt older than Abby.

"Help me with the quilts, Marie," Abby said. "We'll need to get them in the sun right away if they're to be dry before dark."

By the time the wet clothes and bedding had been spread out on the grass, Abby was more like her old self again. She even smiled at the good-natured teasing that went on between Justin and Luc. "Ned's a mite long with the wood," she commented as she wiped the water from her big iron cooking pot. "Mayhap you'd best go and give him a hand with it."

Marie dawdled with the shirt she was arranging on a low bush. "Seems like you're always pushin' me after Ned," she said slowly.

"He did jump into the water after you."

"There was no call for him to do that. I could've saved myself just as well."

"Maybe. But he ought to be properly thanked anyway." Abby glanced up at her daughter, her sharp eyes probing. "That is, unless you've done it already."

"I thanked him well enough." Marie fluffed her damp skirt. What had passed between her and Ned was her own private concern. Yet, the way Abby was looking at her, it could be that she'd guessed.

Marie wandered about the camp, hands behind her back. Her father was busy repairing the weakened canoe where it had struck the tree. Justin and Luc had gone off to kill some game for sup.

185

She found herself looking down at the flattened spot in the long grass where Ned had kissed her. How had it felt? She closed her eyes and tried to bring the feeling back. His tongue—Ike had done the same thing, so that part had come as no surprise. Suddenly she stiffened as a new thought struck her like a thunderbolt. Ike had been around plenty of girls. He'd made no secret of that. But where had Ned learned to kiss like that? She couldn't quite believe that boys were born knowing such things. Girls certainly weren't.

She had begun to pace, consternation furrowing her brow and thrusting out her lower lip. What was it Ned had said to her? *You ben't mine for the taking, Marie. I'll not be one to use you badly.* . . . Marie whacked her fist against her skirt. How had he known about what would surely have followed their kissing if they hadn't stopped? How would he have known, unless—she put her hands to her hot face—unless some girl somewhere had taught him?

Could it have been Carrie or one of the other girls back in Pitt? Marie didn't think so. Why, she'd never even seen Ned speak to any girl except herself. He'd been almost shy around girls, right up to the time he and his father had left for Philadelphia.

It had to have been in Philadelphia! Marie found herself striding furiously in the direction Ned had gone. The more she thought about it, the more convinced she became that she was right. Ned Cooper had become a man in the East, the same way she'd become a woman back in Pittsburg!

Marie felt her eyes stinging as she strode between the trees. She thought of her father. Were all men the same? She'd been shocked at the idea of Edward Forny's faithlessness. But Ned! He'd been hers, hers alone! She wiped an angry tear from her cheek.

The sound of Ned's ax rang out ahead of her. She glimpsed him through the trees and hurried toward him, anger boiling up in her.

Ned had taken off his shirt. His lean muscles rippled as he swung the ax above his head. Then he lowered it when he saw Marie standing at the edge of the clearing. His throat moved as he swallowed.

"I came to help you with the wood," Marie said, her eyes narrowing.

"Thank 'e, Marie. I'm almost finished. I can carry it all, but I'd be pleasured to have you walk back to camp with me."

Such pretty talk! Where had he learned it? Marie felt herself seething as she bent to gather up the chips for kindling. She felt Ned's eyes on her. He cleared his throat uneasily, but did not speak. Her hands moved faster and faster as she picked up the little pieces of wood. Her anger boiled and tumbled like the river. Suddenly she stood up.

"Where'd you learn to kiss like that, Ned Cooper? Who taught you, some little slut back in Philadelphia?"

He leaned on the handle of the ax. His face was unreadable. "No girl who knows what she's about would ask that kind of question, Marie Forny."

Marie sucked in her breath. His answer was almost an admission of guilt! Oh, she hated him!

Ned shouldered the ax and bent to pick up the pile of firelogs he'd cut. "You kissed me back, you know. And any fellow would have knowed it wasn't the first time for you. D'you see *me* askin' who it was taught *you* how to kiss? Sure as you're born, it wasn't them Indians!"

"Oh!" Marie dropped the chips with a clatter. She'd have slapped his face if he'd been standing closer. "Oh!" She gathered up her skirt for flight. "I hate you, Ned Cooper! Don't you ever come near me again!"

She ran from him, her bare feet flying, her breath coming in sharp little gasps. She did not stop running until she had reached the river.

XVII

The summer sun dappled the dark surface of the Wabash. Edward put his back into each stroke of the paddle. The trip down the Ohio had been easy enough except for the falls, but now their progress had to be made upstream. He and Justin and Luc were well accustomed to it, but poor Ned had been so sore for the first few days that the pain in his shoulders and arms had kept him awake at night. Abby had rubbed liniment onto the boy's aching limbs. Even that had helped only a little.

But time had strengthened him. Edward glanced back over his shoulder and grinned his encouragement to the young man. Ned was doing well now. The long journey had left him as strong and sun-browned as a true *voyageur*. Edward congratulated himself on his choice of Ned as an assistant. Now, if the magic would only happen between Ned and Marie, then all would be well. Marie would soon be old enough to marry, and what better choice could she make?

But Edward's daughter puzzled him. From the beginning of the voyage she had been cool toward the young man, which was surprising enough. Since the crossing of the falls, however, when she should have been bubbling with gratitude for Ned's daring rescue, she had scarcely spoken to him.

When Edward had taken Marie aside to scold her for her manners, she had tossed her curls. "Did you bring Ned along for you or for me?" she'd asked saucily. "If you brought him along for me, you may as well send him back!"

Je n'y comprends rien. Edward shrugged his shoulders. His little Marie was becoming a woman. And even after so many years of experience there were times when he did not understand women at all. They were hot one minute and cold the next. A man never knew what might be going on in a woman's head, even when he'd lived with her for more than sixteen years!

Abby had been unusually quiet during the voyage. Except for that one brief outburst at the falls she'd said nothing to indicate that she'd guessed about Mathilde. But she *had* guessed. Edward was certain of that much. Now it only remained to be seen what would happen when they reached Vincennes.

Edward glanced swiftly back at her where she sat in the canoe, between Marie and Ned. There was no one like his Abby. She was beautiful this morning, with the sun dancing on her hair and the ends of her light, lacy shawl fluttering over her shoulders. She had taken extra care in washing and dressing this morning, Edward reflected. That was natural, with Vincennes lying only a few short miles upriver. Abby would want to look her best for the landing, especially if her unknown rival was waiting on the riverbank to size her up!

"Tonnerre!" Edward cursed softly under his breath. He'd scarcely been alone with his wife since they'd left Pitt. In one night, he told himself, he could have convinced Abby that she had nothing to fear from a woman like Mathilde! But the days had been long and tiresome. At night, for safety's sake, the small party had slept all in one place, next to the canoes. There'd been no chance to get Abby off alone, under the stars. At least in Vincennes they would have their own cabin, with their own private bed in it.

Once more he found himself wondering if he'd done the right thing in bringing Justin and Luc back to Pitt to help with the moving of his family. They might have been put to better use in Vincennes, building the new quarters he'd planned along the riverbank. The men he'd hired in Vincennes to do the job had promised to have the big cabin finished by the time Edward arrived with his family, but one could never be sure about strangers.

He'd needed Justin and Luc with him, however. One canoe had not been sufficient to move the Forny household and he'd needed men who could handle the second craft. The two *courieurs* had also provided an extra measure of protection. Edward had wanted the assurance of their ready long rifles in the event of an Indian attack. Strange, they'd not caught even a glimpse of Indians during the entire voyage. The river was peaceful. Almost too peaceful, Edward mused uneasily.

Justin and Luc had gone ahead. Their joyful whooping from around the next bend told Edward that Vincennes had been sighted.

"D'ici peu!" Edward called back over his shoulder.

"Vincennes! You'll be seeing it in a moment!"

He heard the excited stirring behind him. "Will you show us our new house, Father?" Marie asked him eagerly.

"In good time," Edward laughed nervously. For better or for worse, the long journey was almost over.

As they rounded the bend he was surprised to see Luc and Justin waiting for him, holding their craft steady against the current. "Look!" Justin gestured wildly in the direction of the distant fort. "The flag!"

Edward shaded his eyes and stared into the blue distance. He could just make out the high staff that rose above Fort Sackville, a dot of color fluttering at its tip. *"Ma foi!"* he breathed. "Closer!" He could not believe what his eyes had seen.

"What is it, Edward?" He heard Abby's soft voice for the first time in more than an hour.

"The flag! Can you make it out from here?"

Ned's shout almost made the canoe jump. "By thunder, it's a Virginia flag! The Union Jack's gone! Look at it, green and red! The fort's fallen to the Yankees!"

"Allons y!" Edward leaned into his paddle. "Come on, let's go!" The canoe shot forward as Ned dug his own paddle into the water. The boy's excitement surprised Edward a little. Most of the residents of Fort Pitt had been neutral in the conflict between British and Yankee. Could it be that young Ned had picked up some sympathy for the rebellion in Philadelphia?

The town below the fort took shape as they came closer. They could see people clustered on the landing. "The new house, Father!" Marie reminded him. "You said it was on the river."

"Ah, oui—" In the excitement, Edward had almost

forgotten. His eyes scanned the bank for the little inlet where he'd ordered the cabin built. *"Peste,"* he muttered as he spotted it at last. The structure was no more than half completed. Logs were piled on the shore. The unfinished walls rose to the height of a man's shoulders.

"Oh." He heard Abby's little murmur of disappointment. She was up to the added hardship of living without a roof, Edward knew. Still, he had wanted to surprise her with the size and roominess of the new cabin. He was determined it would be the finest home she had ever lived in.

"Those cursed carpenters!" he muttered. "A plague on them!"

"I'll help you finish it, sir," Ned put in. "Don't worry, Mistress Forny, we'll have it done in no time, even the new furniture. My pa taught me a few things."

Oui, he's a good lad, Edward thought as they headed toward the landing. Some of the people in the crowd that waited for them looked familiar. He could easily make out the black soutane of Father Gibault. But there were strangers, too, lean, hard-looking men in buckskins, resting their arms on the barrels of their long Kentucky rifles. Edward's eyes darted anxiously along the bank. No, he assured himself with an audible sigh of relief. Mathilde Rodare was nowhere in sight.

"Edward! Edward Forny!" The priest's voice rang out joyfully across the water. "Welcome!"

The canoe glided into the landing. Edward was the first to leap ashore, almost into the arms of the waiting Father Gibault. "What's happened?" he asked the priest breathlessly. "The flag, you—*Vraiment, je n'y comprends rien!*"

The dark priest beamed. "It's all Colonel Clark's

doing—"

"Clark?" Edward blinked. "You mean George Rogers Clark?" It had been some time since he'd even thought of the sinewy, red-headed surveyor from Virginia. And a colonel! *Ma foi,* how swiftly things could happen! It made one dizzy!

"The very one." Father Gibault cocked his head with amusement. "He and his men took Cahokia and Kaskaskia over on the Mississippi without firing a shot. And Vincennes soon followed! Come . . . come, *mon ami,* let's get your family ashore. Ah—your wife, I see. And your young daughter. And is this your son?" He nodded toward Ned, who was helping a rather disdainful Marie out of the canoe.

"My assistant. I've a son about Ned's age, but he's gone to the Watauga to look into the trade thereabouts for me."

The priest's sharp, birdlike eyes lingered on Marie and Ned. "But perhaps, my friend, you may yet find a son in that young man, *eh bien?* A charming pair."

"Yes, perhaps . . ." Edward's mind was on other things. "But tell me what happened. Where's Busseron? And where's Clark? Is he here?" Edward paused to help Abby out of the canoe and to instruct Luc and Justin. Then, with his wife beside him and Marie and Ned behind, he started up the path to the town. The priest kept pace with them, smiling at Edward's bewilderment.

"One thing at a time," Gibault said. "Patience, *mes amis.* I will explain in due time. Colonel Clark and his men marched on Kaskaskia early last month. They took our little garrison by complete surprise, and frightened the townspeople out of their wits—but as I say, not a shot was fired. A most amazing man, Colonel Clark. You know him, you say?"

"We traveled together last spring. But what about Vincennes? Tell me!"

"Ah—I'm coming to that. Cahokia, as I said, surrendered next, in much the same manner as Kaskaskia. There was no *resistance*. The townspeople are French like us for the most part, you see. They've no special love for the British. And when your Colonel Clark announced to them that France and America had formed a new alliance against England—"

"What?" Ned had been doing his best to keep still, but at the priest's words he sprang forward. "France and America, you say? By all thunder!" His face broke into a broad grin. "Took the fight right out of 'em, did it? Must've been old Ben Franklin's doin'!"

"In that you may be quite right, my young friend," Gibault continued calmly. "In any case, Cahokia and Kaskaskia are now quite firmly in the hands of the *Bostonnais*, as we call them. As for Vincennes—" He glanced up at the lanky frontiersman who had fallen into step beside them.

"It wuz Father Gibault took on Vincennes," the stranger announced, taking up the story without an invitation. He was a long-jawed fellow with a week's growth of beard on his chin, dressed in worn buckskins and a bedraggled coonskin cap. His long rifle balanced easily on one swinging hand.

The priest cleared his throat. "Captain Helm, you're speaking to the Forny family, newly arrived from Fort Pitt. My friends—" he encompassed the little group with his eyes. "This is Capt. Leonard Helm, the new commander of Fort Sackville."

"How do," drawled the captain with a slight bow in

the direction of the ladies. *Mon Dieu,* Edward thought, a *commandant* who smells like a stable! What next in this world gone mad?

"Like I say," Helm continued his train of thought without waiting for a formal reply. "It wuz Father Gibault took on Vincennes, all by hisself! Sashayed up here from Kaskaskia pretty as you please, with Cunnel Clark's letters in his hand. By the time he was done sweet talkin' them Frenchies here, why there wuz nothin' fer the rest of us t' do 'cept march int' the fort and run up the good ol' Virginny flag!"

"You!" Edward gazed at the slender priest in astonishemnt, his awe of the man growing. "Pere Gibault, I'd never have expected to scratch your skin and find a . . . a Yankee!"

Gibault smiled. "Then, my friend, you underestimate Colonel Clark's powers of persuasion. The man is astounding, and his troops, few as they may be, would follow him to the death."

"But what about Captain de Busseron? Surely he wasn't—"

"Shot?" Helm directed a dollop of tobacco juice toward the riverbank. "Hell, no."

"Your friend Captain de Busseron was in charge of the fort," Gibault explained. "Once he saw the futility of holding out against the *Bostonnais,* he most wisely surrendered his sword. Have no fear for him or his good lady. No harm has come to them, and they have the liberty of the fort and the town." The priest rubbed his chin in satisfaction. "Now that Busseron has accepted the idea of the American and French alliance, he actually seems delighted with it."

"I'm not surprised at that," Edward laughed. "Whatever Captain de Busseron's allegiance, he's a Frenchman first of all. I suspect he'd grown tired of licking English boots. *Non?*"

"You're right, I'm sure," Gibault nodded. "And what about you, *mon ami?*"

"I wish only to trade, and to live here in peace with my family," Edward replied, brushing away the image of Mathilde Rodare that had flashed into his mind as he'd spoken the words, *live in peace. Tonnerre!* He had more to fear from that black-haired witch than from the whole Yankee army!

They moved up the narrow road from the landing to the town. Ned was engaged in earnest, animated conversation with the Yankee commander. Edward felt a warning twinge in his mind. Was young Ned already leaning too strongly in the direction of the revolutionary cause? And would those all-too-obvious sympathies bode well for the Forny business, or for Marie?

" 'Twern't no need fer Cunnel Clark even t' be here," Helm was saying. "Why, any redcoat so much as hears 'is name tucks tail an' runs like a possum!"

Gibault raised on black eyebrow. "May I caution you, my good commander, not to underestimate the British. Your Colonel Clark has yet to meet an English soldier in battle. At Cahokia and Kaskaskia, as at Vincennes, there was little more than the local militia to contend with, and being French they were not unsympathetic to his cause. When Hamilton at Detroit gets word of what's happened here, that's when Colonel Clark will have his hands full, I fear."

"Hamilton, the hair buyer?" Helm spat contemptuously into a patch of thistles. "Let 'im come! That there's what Cunnel Clark really wants anyhow. The hair buyer's scalp hangin' at 'is belt, by jingo! We're all of us just itchin' t' march all the way t' Detroit an' catch the bast— pardon me, ladies—catch Hamilton in 'is bed!''

"Excusez-moi," Edward put in, "but am I to understand that Colonel Clark did not even come to Vincennes?"

"That's correct," said Gibault. "He's at Kaskaskia, holding council with some of the Indian tribes. If he can get them to stop selling white scalps to Henry Hamilton, maybe the Yankess will have a chance to hold this country!"

Ned gave a low whistle of admiration. "Clark! By thunder, what I wouldn't give to meet up with that man!"

They were approaching the main part of town, and were moving in the direction of the fort and Captain de Busseron's house. Edward found himself glancing nervously up and down the streets. He expected at any moment to see the tall, shapely form of Mathilde Rodare bearing down upon them. There was no guessing what Mathilde might do now that Busseron had lost his authority. There was no one to keep her in check now. The threat that Edward had against her no longer existed. The woman was free to wreak havoc upon his reputation and his marriage.

Other women passed them on the narrow street. Edward knew that Abby was inspecting each of them with her eyes, one by one. She was already on the lookout for her rival. But these women were plain for the most part. Wilderness life had not been kind to them. They were care-worn and sunburned, their dresses faded from washing, their hands roughened by hard work. In physical beauty, none of them approached Mathilde Rodare.

Now they were nearing Mathilde's house, on their left.

Edward glanced at it out of the corner of his eye. The hollyhocks were taller now, the frilly blooms lovely in their delicate shades of pink, white and lavender. The door of the house was closed.

"Father! Mother! Oh, just look!" It was Marie's voice that stopped them before Mathilde's low picket fence. "Oh, I never saw flowers like that afore! Did you ever see anything so pretty?" She reached over the fence and touched a pink petal.

Through a sense of worry that bordered on panic, Edward felt a stab or regret that this child of his had known so little beauty in her life. He remembered the gardens of his native Gascony, the lilacs and roses. Marie had never even seen a real rose in Fort Pitt, or worn a silk dress, or danced at a ball. Such a pity—

The door of the house swung open, slowly like the rising of the curtain on a stage, and Mathilde Rodare stepped out. She glided down the walk toward them, her ebony hair piled high on her head. She was dressed in a creamy blouse, edged with lace and cut low to show the tops of those splendid breasts. A blue skirt of rich French damask clung to her small waist and swirled gracefully about her legs as she moved. She was smiling.

Mon Dieu, Edward thought, feeling drops of sweat pop out on his forehead. What was the bitch up to?

"You like the flowers, *ma fille?*" She twinkled at Marie, her charm flowing thick as molasses. "Here, *cherie,* I make you a small gift." Deftly she twisted one of the long stems until it snapped off. Then she handed Marie the spike of deep pink flowers. "Enjoy them, pretty child. Alas, these do not keep, not even when you put them in water. An hour or two and they lose their beauty. It is so sad." She tilted her head artfully and flashed a burning glance in Edward's direction. "But then so many things are like that, *non?* Even love. It must be enjoyed while it blooms. Remember that always, *ma belle,* and remember that it was Mathilde Rodare who told you."

As Marie murmured her thanks, Mathilde raised her long, black lashes and seemed to see the rest of the group for the first time. "Ah, it is you, Monsieur Forny! And you have brought your family this time! *Que c'est charmant!*" Her eyes whipped over Abby's face and figure.

"Madame Rodare," Edward tried to keep the irony out of his voice. "May I present my wife Abby, my daughter Marie, and my assistant, Ned Cooper."

"Madame." Abby inclined her head, a bit jerkily, Edward thought. He felt her beside him, tense as a bowstring. Yes, she knew, he told himself gloomily. How could anyone look at Mathilde and not know she was the one?

"Pleased t' meet you, ma'am." Ned bowed slightly.

"*Enchanté!*" Mathilde's gaze moved like a caress from Ned's tousled hair to his moccasins. "So strong for one so young," she murmured in a voice that Edward knew only too well. *Ma foi!* Casting eyes at a mere boy like Ned! Was there no limit to what the creature could think of?

"*Commandant* . . . Pere Gibault . . ." She smiled dazzlingly and nodded in the direction of Helm and the priest. "Excuse me, *s'il vous plait.* I have biscuits in the oven, and they will burn. Such a pleasure to meet all of you!" She looked directly at Abby, her eyes laughing. "We will be such good friends, you and I and your lovely daughter, *eh bien?*"

"I hope so, madame." Abby's voice was tight and

cold. Her eyes followed the movement of Mathilde's hips as she swayed back along the walk toward her front stoop.

Edward exhaled as they moved on up the street. Ned chatting with Leonard Helm, Abby marching along in grim silence. Mathilde was playing with him, he realized. She was toying with him and his, the way a cat toys with a mouse. She was in no hurry. Revenge prolonged is revenge sweetened, he reminded himself, and shivered.

A frisky breeze swept up the hillside, fluttering the fort's new red and green flag atop its tall staff. Behind him, Edward thought he heard Mathilde's mocking laughter, light as the rustle of leaves. But then again maybe it was only the wind or the river.

XVIII

Marie posed before Madame de Busseron's long, oval bedroom mirror, her hands on her hips. Except for her own rippling reflection in ponds and rivers, she had never before seen all of herself at one time. The only mirror in the Forny household had been the small, uneven one on the wall of her room and the pretty rosewood-backed looking glass her father had given her mother. But this one! This great, gilt-framed wonder! She spun slowly in front of it, making her hair fly and her gray and black skirt stand out. If her mother and Madame de Busseron were not in the next room, she thought, it would be exciting to take off her dress and see herself naked from head to toe.

She tilted her head and smiled at her reflection. "Well, now, Mistress Forny," she said, in a gruff voice that was her best imitation of a boy's. "And how be ye likin' Vincennes after your first day?"

Then she tossed her hair and laughed. "Why, I be likin' it just fine! Right nice of you to ask me!" Marie hugged herself. She could not remember when she had been so excited.

With their cabin by the river still unfinished, Captain and Madame de Busseron had offered the shelter of their house to the Forny family for a few nights. Abby and Edward were to have the spare bedroom. Marie would share Aspasie's room, sleeping on a pallet, and Ned would bunk in the new warehouse with Justin and Luc. *Voila!* One worry out of the way! Abby and Cecile de Busseron had liked each other on sight. They were in the sitting room now, sipping tea out of little china cups that were almost as thin as eggshells. Marie had never seen anything so fine. She had drunk her own tea with great care, afraid that the pressure of her own lips and fingers would be enough to shatter the delicate porcelain.

And the furniture! Madame de Busseron, Marie had learned, had brought it all the way from Quebec, and some of it had even been made in France! She fingered the brocade cushion of a low dressing stool and sighed. Once she had thought that Ned's father, Absalom Cooper, made the finest furniture in the world. But oh, what a small and dreary world Fort Pitt had been!

Three little crystal bottles sat on Madame de Busseron's dressing table, the amber liquid inside showing through the exquisitely faceted glass. Marie glanced cautiously about before she lifted one of the stoppers. Perfume! She inhaled it giddily. One or two of the girls back at Pitt had known about perfume, but Marie had never seen it, or smelled it. She filled her whole body with the fragrance. It was as if the aroma of a thousand flowers had been squeezed into that one little bottle!

Guiltily she replaced the stopper. She had no right to meddle in someone else's things. But the lure of the remaining bottles was too much for her. She picked up the second and carefully twisted the stopper loose. This one was spicier than the first. Its fragrance tickled her nose.

The last bottle was the smallest of the three. Marie sniffed at the opening and raised her eyebrows. The aroma was strange, almost like the way her finger smelled when she touched herself between her legs, but a prettier, sweeter scent. This, Marie speculated, was surely what a woman would use if she wanted to get a man excited about her. Maybe that was how Madame de Busseron had gotten the captain to marry her.

Marie giggled to herself at the thought of it. Then she closed up the third bottle, proud of herself for not having given in to the temptation to put a dab of the stuff behind her ears. The right kind of perfume could drive a man out of his mind—was it Carrie who had said that? Carrie, who seemed to know everything. Marie sighed. She knew plenty herself now. She could probably teach Carrie a thing or two. But those days were behind her, she reminded herself as she put the pretty little bottle back on the dresser with the others. In any case, she'd not yet decided *which* man she wanted to drive out of his mind!

As she drifted back toward the sitting room, Marie heard the hushed voices of her mother and Cecile de Busseron. They were discussing something in low, serious tones. Marie did not mean to eavesdrop, but she'd been taught not to come bursting into a room when grownups were talking. There was nothing to do, really, but stand in the hall and wait.

"But, such a woman!" Cecile's voice quivered with contempt. "There's one in every town, you know! This one is prettier than most, but other than that there's no difference. All she wants is a man in her bed—almost any man!"

"Even another woman's husband?" Marie had never heard her mother sound so bitter. "Edward has a will of his own, Cecile. She could hardly have chased him down and raped him!"

"My dear, your Edward's a man. And what's worse, he's French." Cecile's tongue clicked sharply. "Besides, you don't know her. You've never seen the way she goes after a man. And with that body! *Ouf!* No man with anything left between his legs could resist her!"

"Then what chance do I have against such a one-woman army?" Abby asked sardonically. "You're French. You tell me."

Marie heard the impatient little *clink* of Cecile's cup as she put down her tea. "Abby! Abby, my dear, dear fool! Don't you see? He doesn't love her! A man doesn't love a woman like that one, even if he goes to bed with her!"

"Then, you mean I should do nothing at all? I should just forgive him and forget what happened?"

"Is that so unwise?" Cecile let her breath out with a dainty little *pouf*. "Listen to me, Abby. When Edward returned the second time to Vincennes, after he'd been home with his family, he came in by a back trail, just so she wouldn't know he'd arrived! In so many words, he told my husband he was bringing you here, that he wanted a way to make sure she left him alone! How could you not forgive such a man as your Edward?"

Abby did not answer, and Marie wondered if she was crying. Marie was close to tears herself. How could her father have caused his wife so much hurt? She felt a rising hatred for the unknown woman who'd pulled him down.

206

The town slut, if Cecile de Busseron was to be believed. Marie wondered how long it would be before she met the woman, and what she would do. What would she say to her?

She heard the rustle of skirts and the musical clatter of cups and saucers as Abby and Cecile stood up. They were moving toward the bedroom. Marie scooted swiftly down the hall, so that they wouldn't know she'd been listening.

They came into sight, the two of them. Cecile was still talking, but she had changed the subject. "Is that your best dress?" she was asking Abby.

"I'm afraid so. Not that Edward isn't a good provider, but there wasn't much call for fancy clothes in Fort Pitt. It's as good as what anybody had there."

"Well—" Cecile cocked her head like a plump little bird. "My dears—you too, Marie. Come here. Both of you could provide me with a great deal of fun. There's not much to do here in Vincennes—" She encircled both Abby and Marie with her arms.

"When I was a little girl," she said, her eyes twinkling, "my favorite pastime was dressing my dolls. I never quite grew out of it! You can see that by the way I dress Aspasie." Her bright eyes darted from Marie to Abby. "Would you be my dolls for the afternoon? Would you let me dress you for dinner tonight? You're slimmer than I am, Abby, but I've a lovely gown that can be taken in to fit you. And as for you, Marie, Aspasie's just your size. I've a brand new dress that I was just finishing for her. It would be perfect on you. Yes?"

Oh, please, Mother, let her do it!" Marie felt her emotions dancing up and down. "It'd be so much fun!"

Abby sighed. No, she'd not been crying, Marie decided, but she looked very tired. "All right," she smiled wearily. "Just for you two overgrown children, I'll say yes."

"*Magnifique!*" Cecile clapped her hands. "Let's get started!"

Edward was hungry. The day had been a long one, but at least it had been productive. Working with Justin, Luc and Ned, they'd gotten the walls of the cabin finished to the top and had begun laying the upper floor. Edward was proud of its size, but even this place wouldn't be their home forever, he'd promised himself. If they stayed in Vincennes long enough, he would build Abby a house of stone, the finest in the town.

He had thrown himself into the work with the fury of a driven man, Mathilde's laughter still ringing in his mind. *Demme!* He wanted to wring her neck! With Busseron out of her way, she had the power to do anything she wanted. He could expect trouble. Her hard, bold eyes had told him that much. And the way she'd looked at Marie had made him feel cold all over. He'd have expected her to wreak her vengeance directly on him, or perhaps try to wound him through Abby. But Marie! To win over a naive girl with such charm, only, surely, to hurt or destroy her—he had never expected Mathilde to stoop so low!

He trudged up the path with Ned beside him. The boy did not question it when Edward went out of his way to avoid Mathilde's house. She'd been making eyes at Ned, too, he reminded himself. *Le bon Dieu,* what was the woman thinking?

He would have to lay everything before Abby, Edward told himself, groaning inwardly at the thought of it. There was no other way. He himself would be at Vincennes only long enough to get his family settled in the new cabin, a matter of a few weeks. Then he would be off to the Watauga to see how Henry was managing. Abby would be left alone to deal with whatever scheme Mathilde might concoct. It would be foolhardy not to leave her forewarned and thoroughly forearmed.

His confession would hurt her. But, then, he reminded himself, it was almost a certainty that Abby already knew and had even identified Mathilde as the woman. Maybe talking about the affair would clear the air between them. Maybe it would at last tear away the tension and mistrust that had hung between them for so many weeks, thickening the way a cobweb does when it gathers dust and dirt.

But it would not be easy, Edward told himself as he and Ned wound their way up the rough street that led to the Busseron house. Ned had been silent, too, lost in his own thoughts. Edward wondered if the boy was homesick, or perhaps preoccupied with the recent turn of events in Vincennes. "Get ready for a treat tonight, Ned," he declared, trying to dispel the gloomy quiet that had crept over them both. "I know from experience that Madame de Busseron sets a fine table!"

"Be a nice change from river food, all right," Ned agreed, flashing him a tired grin. "Jerky an' rabbit an' johnnycake do get a mite old after a few days. A man gets hungry for bread an' taters an' gravy an' such."

"And what do you think of Vincennes by now, eh?"

Ned whistled. "Nothin' like I expected! Clear out here on the edge of nowhere like this. Nothin' around it 'ceptin' Indians—but it's a real town. Rock houses, flower gardens an' all! Why, it's more of a town than Pitt, though it's nothin' like Philadelphia. I like it here, sir. 'Ceptin' when I miss my ma and pa."

Edward patted the lean, young shoulder. "*Ne vous inquietez pas!* Don't worry. That's only natural. But what about Marie? I was hoping you two would get along. She needs a friend here, and so do you."

Edward waited for an answer, but Ned only shrugged and looked away as they mounted the front porch. Something had gone wrong between Marie and Ned. Edward was sure of it now.

They washed on the porch, splashing water from a copper basin onto their faces, hands and arms, scrubbing their palms and nails with Cecile de Busseron's fragrant soap and drying them on the smooth linen towels that Aspasie had laid out for them. A pity there was no time to bathe and change, Edward thought. It would be pleasant to sit down to a dinner with the ladies in clean clothes.

The dining room was just off the kitchen. Aspasie ushered them inside. Captain Busseron was seated alone at the table in his shirtsleeves.

"Are we early?" Edward asked, glancing around.

"I'm early. You're on time. The ladies are late. Some fool scheme my wife has cooked up, no doubt. She's been very secretive." The captain looked older than Edward remembered from a few weeks back. The enforced idleness after the loss of his command would weigh heavily on him. And even more pressing would be the fear of what his superiors in Detroit would do once they found out what had happened here.

"*Asseyez-vous.*" He swept his arm out to indicate the chairs. "Anywhere. We shall wait." A bottle of claret sat beside his plate. Drops of clear red trickled down the inside of his empty glass. "You'll have some with me?"

"Only a little before dinner. Enough to sharpen the appetite."

Aspasie bustled in to serve them, her pretty olive face glowing with some hidden surprise as she poured three fingers of wine into Edward and Ned's long-stemmed goblets.

Edward leaned back in his chair, swirling the red wine lightly in his glass as he savored its bouquet, the way he'd done so many times long ago in France. "It does not go well with you, eh, Captain?"

"Alas—" Busseron fidgeted with his long, waxed moustache. "I am a professional soldier, my friend. Now I find myself not only in disgrace, but unemployed."

"The Yankees could always use a good fightin' man," Ned put in boldly. "Why not talk t' Cap'n Helm 'bout it? You bein' French an' all, sir, I can't help but think you'd be welcome."

"Perhaps." Busseron smiled at Ned's earnestness. "But Captain Helm and those of his kind don't exactly strike me as being well paid. One has to live, you know. And when one has a wife who is accustomed to living in a certain style—" His eyes roamed over the well-laid table, set with china, crystal and pewter. He shrugged.

"Cap'n Helm told me he and his men are gettin' paid in land," Ned argued. "Three hundred acres apiece, once Clark's done with his fightin'. Three hundred acres of prime land!"

"*Oui*, my young friend. A most attractive offer. But I'm a soldier, now a woodsman or a farmer, and Cecile's a city woman. Even Vincennes is a dreary place for her." Busseron cleared his throat and poured himself another glass of claret. Edward feared that he would be quite drunk by the time the meal was served. His speech had already begun to slur. But who could blame the poor fellow?

Edward studied Captain de Busseron over the edge of his glass. "I suspect there's another reason as well, *vraiment, mon capitan?*"

Busseron nodded glumly. "Call it honor, *mes amis*. Call it prudence if you like. Or call it cowardice if you see it as such. It would not be difficult for me to be sympathetic toward the cause of the *Bostonnais*. But the truth of the matter is, there is no way that Captain Helm, or even Colonel Clark himself, can hold Fort Sackville against a British assault. It's only a matter of time before Colonel Hamilton—"

"The hair buyer!" Ned snorted, and Edward motioned for him to be still.

"So he is called by some, I believe," Busseron said with a little grimace. "Whatever his title, he has only to march down from Detroit with sufficient force, and Vincennes will be British once more."

"And you?" Edward's voice was full of sympathy for the poor wretch. He could not admire Busseron's lack of conviction, but it was hard not to feel sorry for the man.

"If I can be proven to have demonstrated one iota of sympathy for the *Bostonnais*, I will no doubt be marched to the wall and shot." Busseron swallowed the wine in his glass in one gulp.

Ned leaned forward in his chair. "But I'm not so sure ye be right about the redcoats, Cap'n. Not if Clark can win the Indians to his side. Cap'n Helm, he told me there ain't no way the British could hold this territory without the Indians to do their fightin' for 'em."

"Perhaps, my young friend." The captain sunk into his chair and stared morosely into his empty glass.

At that moment, Madame de Busseron came rustling into the dining room, her pretty, plump face flushed with anticipation. "Sit up gentlemen!" she chirped. "Monsieur Forny, your ladies will be joining us in a moment."

She twirled over to her husband's chair and very gently took the glass from his fingers. Edward caught the flicker of dismayed concern in her eyes as she brushed his cheek with her hand. "Smile, my dearest. We will eat now. Then you will feel better," she whispered in French. Then she turned to the doorway with a heraldic flourish of her hand.

Arm in arm, Abby and Marie glided into the dining room.

Edward caught his breath. What was this? He stared at his wife and daughter as if he had never seen them before.

Marie's gown was of the finest muslin in a shade of deep rose pink, its neck and sleeves edged with wide bands of cream-colored cotton lace. It clung flawlessly to her budding young figure, outlining the pert breasts, the tiny waist. Her skirt stood out like a bell, and as she walked, Edward could hear the dainty swish of petticoats. Her dark curls had been piled high on top of her head, except for one rich lock that fell alongside her neck to coil itself into the hollow of her lovely throat. Beside him, Edward heard Ned Cooper swallow hard, and he felt his own throat tighten. He had always known his little girl was beautiful, but tonight she was like a rose come to life. She was radiant.

The scrape of Captain de Busseron's chair on the floor startled him. Edward stood, as Ned and the captain did, bumping his knee on the leg of the table. It hurt. He reached down to rub it. As he glanced up, his eyes met Abby's.

He had saved her for last, Edward realized. His eyes had taken in Marie first because he wanted to take his time with Abby. She was his, and she was a queen.

Abby's gown was a luscious pale green that brought

out the flecks of emerald in her dark eyes and the warm glow of her skin. The fabric itself was light as fairy tale gossamer. Silk, Edward decided. Real Chinese silk.

There was no lace on the dress. But the bodice was so exquisitely tucked and ruffled that none was needed. Madame de Busseron bent low to whisper in Edward's ear. "My first love, when I was young, was a seaman. It was he who brought me that bolt of green silk, and I took it to the best *modiste* in all Quebec! So perfectly was the gown made that with only small changes it has stayed in fashion all these years. Look at her, Monsieur, is there any woman in the world so beautiful as your wife?"

Edward could not speak. Abby floated toward him, her hair piled high like Marie's. Madame had pasted a tiny black heart, a beauty patch, on her cheek in just the right spot to call attention to her eyes, and had wound pale green ribbons in her hair. But it was not the dress or the coiffure that made Edward's heart stop. It was Abby.

She was not smiling. What woman could smile after what she had been through that day? But there was a softness about her face. The tension and hardness that had been there these past few weeks was gone. She glowed quietly, like the flame of a candle.

Edward held out the chair next to his. She glided into it, Strong Woman of the Onondaga, the woman who had stolen away from Fort Pitt alone, dressed as an Indian at the height of Pontiac's siege, the woman who could paddle a canoe and handle a Kentucky rifle as well as many men. How lovely she was. He sat down beside her. Hidden by the edge of the tablecloth, her hand crept into his. Edward felt his heart swell inside his chest. Nothing, no one, not even Mathilde Rodare, had power against a love like this!

He glanced at her out of the corner of his eye as they bowed their heads for grace. *Tonight,* he thought.

Marie sat alone on the porch, her hands still damp from helping Aspasie with the dishes. She had dried them on her apron, and then taken the apron off and hung it on the porch rail. She wanted the pink dress to show. She wanted to sit there in the twilight, knowing that she looked prettier than she had ever looked in her life.

The day was almost at an end. Soon the dress would come off, her hair would come down, and she would be just plain Marie once more. But she had felt like a princess tonight! She wanted to keep that feeling just a little longer.

She heard a board creak behind her and she knew it was Ned. The grownups had probably sent him out here to keep her company. Marie sat very straight and pretended not to notice him. But she remembered the way he had gazed at her when she'd walked into the dining room. She'd liked it, Ned looking at her that way. But she wouldn't let on. Not after the way he'd talked to her that day on the river!

"Evenin', Marie." He sat down beside her, his hands on his knees.

"Evenin'," Marie replied with a little toss of her head. If he thought he could cozy up to her just because she looked beautiful, she'd show him a thing or two!

"That's a right pretty dress."

"Thank you." She felt her heart speed up at his words. But she wouldn't let him know it.

"Been a right pretty day, too," he said companionably.

"It has. And Vincennes is a right nice place, too. Should be plenty of fellows about to keep a girl company.'' Oh, had she really said that? Marie hugged herself with peevish delight. She was being just awful, and it felt so good!

Ned cleared his throat. "Marie, I been wantin' a chance to say I was sorry for what I said t' you back on the river. I had no call t' talk to you like that."

Marie stared off into the distance at the rising moon. It was going to be full tonight. She did not answer Ned.

"My bringin' up what them Indians done. I had no call t' do that. I shoulda been horsewhipped for it. Don't know what got into me."

Marie shrugged her shoulders, feeling the bounce and tickle of the curl that hung so prettily down one side of her neck. She would make him suffer, she thought. He deserved it.

Ned swallowed. His hands clenched and unclenched on his knees. "That girl in Philadelphia. There was one. I won't lie 'bout it. But she wasn't as pretty as you. An' she wasn't as good. I kissed her a few times an' we did some talkin'. But that was all. I swear it."

"Doesn't matter what you did, Ned Cooper. It's all the same to me."

Ned took a deep breath. "I reckon you're still mad, Marie. Well, you got a right t' be. I've said my piece, and I won't say no more, 'ceptin' one thing."

"What's that?" Marie wanted to look at him. But no, that would spoil things, she decided. She'd just get all soft inside and she'd say she was sorry, too, and then it would be over and done with. And she wasn't ready to let that happen yet. Ned had hurt her feelings too much for that.

"I always thought you was the nicest, and the prettiest girl in Fort Pitt," he said. "An' I still do. An' now that

I've said my piece I'll be goin'."

His words made Marie feel warm inside. Why was she like this, hating Ned Cooper one minute and liking him the next? Well, no matter, she would give him another minute or two to suffer. Then she would turn and look at him and smile. When he saw her smiling, in that beautiful pink dress, with her hair piled on top of her head, he would just melt. He would be her slave!

She waited, counting the seconds, wondering how her hair looked with the moonlight shining on it. She waited just long enough. Then she turned, a fetching little smile on her face.

Ned was gone.

The moon hung low above the fort on the hill, silhouetting the empty flagstaff. The Wabash flowed silently below the town, its ripples reflecting the golden light. Only the musical chirp of crickets, the distant yap of a dog, and the occasional twitter of a sleepy bird disturbed the nighttime stillness.

Abby and Edward had stayed up late, sipping wine and chatting with the Busserons. Arm in arm they entered the bedroom, Edward pausing to fasten the latch behind him.

"Unbutton me, please," Abby turned her back to him.

"Very well." Edward started at the topmost silk-covered button, working downward, disengaging each tiny loop. "A beautiful dress," he said.

"Cecile offered to give it to me. She says she's getting too plump to wear it any longer."

"And did you accept it?" He kissed the back of her bare neck. She was trembling.

"No, though it is lovely. I've never worn anything like it."

"You didn't want to be beholden to her?"

"Maybe that was part of it, Edward. But that wasn't all. Tonight was like a game. It was fun, but it was only make believe. What would I do with a dress like this? Dance at a royal ball?" She laughed.

"Abby—" His hands had worked their way down to her waist. "Do you ever wish for a different life? Did you ever want to live in the East, to dress like this every day, you and Marie, to have servants and go to balls and the theatre, eh?"

"You lived like that in France, didn't you? Do you miss it?"

He thought for a few seconds. "*Non*. It's strange, but I don't miss it at all. This is my life now. I like it."

"Then I like it too. And how can I miss what I've never seen. The city's a dirty place, I've heard tell. I like the new, clean country. I like the rivers. I like—" She caught her breath. Edward's hands had loosened the hem of her camisole and slipped inside, up and around, to cup her breasts. She gave a little moan.

Edward felt the heat pulsing down into his body. Should he take her now, while the magic was upon them? No, he decided, it wouldn't be fair to her. Not while the lie of Mathilde still hung between them. "We have to talk," he said, moving his hands back to the last of the buttons.

"Do we?" Abby slipped the dress over her head and laid it on a chair. "Is there anything I don't already know, or haven't guessed?"

Edward drew her softly into his arms. She came without any resistance. His hands stole up to her hair and began to pluck out the pins and the green silk ribbons. "Forgive me, Abby," he murmured. "I was a fool. A weak, crazy fool."

"A French fool. A man fool. I'll kill you if you ever do it again." The face she raised to him was smiling. He jerked her up to him and kissed her, his mouth crushing, hurting.

"Abby—" No, Edward told himself, he could not wait any longer. Somehow her camisole was gone, then her petticoat. She was naked in his arms. He was kissing her face, murmuring little half-words against her eyes and cheeks and lips. One arm clasped her tight. The other fumbled hastily with the waist of his trousers. He felt her hands helping him, freeing him.

Somehow they made it to the bed. Was she laughing or weeping? They flung the covers aside and he took her, in a wild, hot, joyous tumble. The barriers between them were gone. The mistrust had fled. He was all hers, and she knew it. She devoured him with her giving, their ecstasy mounting higher and higher until the whole world seemed to burst. Edward felt himself cry out. Then all his strength left him.

Abby lay against his chest, quietly sobbing. He felt her tears on his skin. "Cry, *amour*," he whispered into her hair. "Cry it all out." He held her tenderly, resting, his body still joined with hers. Never again, Edward Forny promised himself. As I live and breathe, never, ever again.

XIX

Marie stood on the landing and gazed at the ripple of white foam that trailed behind her father's departing canoe. Gone again. It seemed that he never stayed home long enough. This time he was headed south to the Watauga country where Henry had gone.

Marie fought back a wave of envy for her brother as the big canoe rounded the distant bend and vanished. Why was it always the menfolk who went off and had adventures? Why did it always have to be the women who stayed behind to scrub and wash and cook and spin? She kicked a rock into the river with the toe of her moccasin. The splash made pretty silver rings on the water.

Abby sighed, as she always did when she'd just lost sight of her husband. "There's carding to be done," she said cheerfully. "Come on. Let's keep busy so that we won't miss your father so much."

They strode up the path together, walking swiftly, as

women learn to do when they have little time to waste. Abby hummed softly to herself, swinging her arm lightly against her skirt.

"You act happier today than you did the last time Father went away," Marie commented.

"Do I?" Abby kept on humming.

"I'm thinkin' I know why, too," Marie continued boldly. "Last time he was going to Vincennes. This time *we* be in Vincennes."

"There's much more to it than all that, Marie."

"You been happy for weeks. Did you find out that Father hadn't done what you thought he had?" Marie had noticed the change in Abby and Edward. They'd acted almost like newlyweds lately, she thought. And the only explanation she could figure out was that both her mother and Madame de Busseron had been wrong about Edward. There'd been no other woman after all. The whole thing had been a big mistake, she decided. "Is that so, Mother?" she asked when Abby didn't answer her the first time.

They were walking through the lower part of Vincennes now, past the smithy and the tavern. A few Buckskin-clad Yankee soldiers moved along the street, wary-eyed as always, their rifles slung from their shoulders. One of them, a young, homely one, looked at Marie. She tossed her head and pretended not to have seen him.

Abby had not answered her. "Mother?" she persisted. Abby glanced at her.

"Well, Mother, did he, or didn't he?"

"He did, Marie. We'll talk about it at home, not here on the street. All right, honey?"

"All right." Marie walked along quietly after that.

There was no figuring out grownups. She only knew that at her mother's words she felt strange and aching inside.

The new cabin was roomy and cheerful, with fresh curtains over the windows, and Abby's new, braided rugs on the floor. Marie sat beside her mother's spinning wheel. Energetically she worked the flat, stiff wire carding brushed against each other until the wad of wool was combed and ready to be spun. Then she took another wad from the sack and began again. It was slow work, but she liked it better than sweeping or scrubbing.

Marie remembered Fort Pitt and the way the girls there had always congregated at Carrie Ryan's house to card wool. She remembered the talk, and she missed it. There were not so many girls her age in Vincennes, and what few there were were French. Besides, life was different here. People seemed to depend less on each other than they had at Fort Pitt. Marie found that she was spending much of her free time with her mother. It was surprising, she thought, that a mother could be so much like a friend.

Abby did not hurry over her spinning. With only Marie to card the wool, there was never enough of it to keep her working fast. Her slim, sun-browned hands were deft and graceful.

"You were going to tell me about Father," said Marie. They'd been talking about other things, but she'd had it in her mind all the time.

"There's not much to tell. He was sorry. I forgave him, and now it's in the past. I promised myself I'd forget about it, and you're to forget about it, too. After today, Marie, you're never to mention it again. Do you understand?"

Marie worked the brushes more slowly. "But how did it happen?" she asked. "How did he meet her? How did they . . ." she trailed off, not even knowing the word for what her father had done.

"I didn't ask him."

"You didn't even make him tell you?"

"Marie, a wife's better off not knowing some things. The telling of it would only cause hurt. Remember that. You'll be married yourself someday. There's no promise that the same thing won't happen to you."

"But didn't he even tell you who she was?"

"There was no need for that." Abby glanced up sharply. Something in her eyes told Marie that it would do no good to ask about the woman's identity. Still, there was so much she didn't understand.

"But when somebody hurts you like that, how can you just . . . just . . ."

"I believe it's called forgiveness, Marie."

Marie took a deep, indignant breath. "Well! You can forgive Father if you want, I guess. But I'd never forgive anybody that done it to me! That's for sure!"

"Keep thinking like that, dear, and one day you might be drinking your own poison. Hate can make you old before your time, Marie. I hope to heaven you never have to make the choice I did, but if you do, remember what I just told you. Forgiving can feel mighty good."

"Maybe." Marie went on with her carding, thinking of Ned. Anger made the stiff, flat brushes move faster. She hadn't seen much of Ned in the past few weeks. He'd been busy helping her father, and he slept at the new warehouse with Luc and Justin. When the Fornys invited him to supper, Marie kept her eyes sulkily on her plate, or laughed and chatted with everybody except Ned. If he cared much about it, he certainly hadn't told her.

Anyway, there were other boys in Vincennes. And

there were soldiers, too. The Yankee soldiers were few in number, and most of them looked as old as Marie's father. They probably had wives and children back in Virginia. Even the two or three younger ones weren't much to look at. But some of the French militiamen were not so bad. Marie had not spoken to any of them, but they looked at her. When she walked up the street to the Busseron house to see Cecile or Aspasie, she felt their eyes on her back. It was a feeling she liked.

Besides, she'd found another friend in Vincennes. Not a boy at all, but almost as fascinating in a different way. Two or three times a week, when her mother thought she was running errands or walking by the river, she had been at Mathilde Rodare's house. And Mathilde was like nobody she had ever met.

Marie wasn't exactly sure why she hadn't told her mother about going to Mathilde's. Abby didn't seem to like the woman, though Marie couldn't imagine why. There was nobody nicer or friendlier than Mathilde Rodare. Maybe the reason Marie hadn't told her mother about the visits was because Mathilde was teaching her things—things she'd always wanted to know about boys, about how to dress and how to flirt. Maybe Abby wouldn't like her learning those things, Marie reasoned. But one thing was certain, she wanted to learn them!

"My hands are getting tired," she complained. "Don't you have something different for me to do?"

Abby slowed the motion of the wheel. "There's the preserves," she said. "I promised a little jar of them to Cecile. Would you like to take it to her?"

"Can I stay and visit a spell?" Marie asked, thinking not of Madame de Busseron, but of Mathilde, whose house was on the way.

225

"Not too long, all right? We need to get back to the wool after you've had a rest." Abby patted her arm. "I'll get the preserves."

Just the week before they had stripped the ripe blackberries from the bushes that grew out behind the warehouse. Marie and her mother had spent the afternoon making the precious preserves in Abby's smallest copper kettle. There'd been six jars when they'd finished, each one sealed with hardened wax. Edward had taken two with him. Of the rest, one was for Cecile, and the other three would be kept on a shelf in the new pantry.

With the jar tucked into a basket, Marie set out up the hill. Once she was out of her mother's sight, she walked swiftly. If she could shorten the time of her errand, she could visit with Mathilde on the way back, and Abby would be none the wiser.

The day was filled with sunlight, but the fall air was chilly. Marie pulled the knitted shawl tighter about her shoulders. The hills were beautiful, she thought, with red oak and yellow maple covering the slopes in fiery clumps. Leaves drifted to the surface of the river, bright, floating specks on the cold, dark water. A flock of geese flew overhead, an elongated V against the blue sky. When she strained her ears, Marie could hear them.

Someone was coming out of the tavern. It was one of the Yankees, recognizable blocks away because of the tattered buckskins he wore. There was a woman on his arm. Nancy Jukes, the tavern-owner's daughter, half French on her mother's side. Marie had never met her, but she knew all about her. Aspasie had told her. Nancy was a pretty girl, with yellow hair and a turned-up nose. But no decent woman would keep company with her because she worked in her father's tavern. Aspasie had heard somebody say that Nancy Jukes could down a tankard of ale just like a man. What was worse, it was whispered that for a few coins she'd let any fellow spend the night in her bed.

Nancy was laughing. Her hair hung loose like straw, and the breeze blew strands of it into her face. The buckskin-clad Yankee brushed them away and kissed the end of her nose. A gust of wind whipped her homespun skirt so high that it showed her knees. Nancy did nothing to hold it down.

Marie walked past them with her head high. She'd have no truck with the likes of Nancy Jukes. Why, Nancy was nothing but a slut. Marie strode on up the street, then suddenly stopped as if lightning had hit her. Slowly she turned around and stared at Nancy's retreating back.

There's one in every town, Cecile had said. And Nancy had to be the one who'd caused Edward Forny to be untrue to his wife. Who else could it have been? The hussy! Marie stood there quaking with indignation. Her father and that . . . that . . .

Marie stomped her foot, spun back around in the direction she was headed, and marched away. She wouldn't let Nancy spoil her plans today. There wasn't time. But one day she'd get even, she promised herself. She'd make Nancy Jukes pay for all the hurt to her mother and herself. Why, if it hadn't been for what her father had done, Marie lashed her anger as she hurried along, she wouldn't have gone out to Ike's place on that awful day. Even what had happened with Ike was Nancy's fault!

At the Busseron house, Marie gave the preserves to Cecile. Aspasie had gone up to the fort to deliver a message for the captain. "I'll go and see if I can find her," Marie lied. "We can walk back together." There, she assured herself. She was covered in case her mother asked Cecile how long she had stayed at the house. She would only have to claim she'd gone looking for Aspasie and had not found the girl.

Marie headed off in the direction of the fort, then circled back around in the direction of Mathilde's house. No one saw her enter through the garden gate, skip up to the back door, and knock.

The door opened, and Mathilde stood there, tall and beautiful and soft-looking. She smiled. "Marie! What a pleasure. You're ready for another lesson, and so soon, *eh bien?*"

"If you got time. My mother will be 'spectin' me back afore long."

"Your mother, she does not know you come here, *oui?*"

"I never tell her a thing."

"*Bon!* She might not understand. Come in, *enfant*. Today we will continue with the fan, eh?" Mathilde drew Marie inside and closed the door. "It is better this way, your mother not knowing. Some women . . ." she shrugged. "They are jealous of their daughters. Jealous, almost like with their husbands. Foolish, *non?* But if she knew, she might not let you come."

"Well, I'll not be telling her," Marie said.

Mathilde smiled and ran one hand up Marie's arm. "Come, then. *Venez*. The bedroom, child."

Marie sat on the dressing stool before Mathilde's oval mirror, a black lace fan held awkwardly in one hand. "Now, flutter it, like so. . ." Mathilde leaned over her shoulder and watched as Marie made the lace edge of the fan tremble beneath her eyes. Oh, if only those silly girls from Fort Pitt could see her now!

"Now, you close it, *cherie*, and you open it very slowly. . . . Ah, more slowly still, with the head tilted, *un tout petit peu*, and the eyes—ah, *magnifique! Perfection!*" Mathilde clapped her hands, leaned forward and kissed Marie on the corner of her mouth. "The fan, it is a way to get a man's attention, *oui?* It has its own language, and you can learn to speak it, *ma cher*. Now, how much time can you stay?"

"A little while longer." Abby had told her she could visit at the Busseron house, Marie reasoned.

"*Bon. . . bon. . .*" Mathilde took Marie's rough little hands in her long, soft ones and pulled her to her feet. "Then today, we begin the most important lesson of all." Her blue eyes traveled up and down Marie's body. "You are so young, *enfant*. Tell Mathilde, have you ever been with a man?"

"Been with? . . ." Yes, Marie knew what she meant. But she had never told anyone about Ike Ilam. She could not put what had happened into words, not even for Mathilde Rodare.

"Ah, I thought not," Mathilde chirped. "You don't even know what it means. *Ecoutez-moi*, Marie. One day soon you will marry. For a pretty girl like you, very soon, I think. You must know what to do when your husband takes you to bed. If you do not please him—" Mathilde's eyes narrowed between their coal black lashes—"If you have not *learned* how to please him, then he will go out and find a woman who can give him what he wants."

Marie quivered. Was that what had happened with her mother and father? Hadn't Abby ever learned the right way to please Edward? No, she vowed, she would never let that happen to her. With Ike Ilam she had been scared and stupid. She would not be scared and stupid on her wedding night!

"Show me, then," she said, her voice shaking a little.

Mathilde licked her lips. They were very red. "The bed," she commanded swiftly. "Lie down, child."

Marie did as she was told. Madame Rodare's bed was covered with a blue quilt, the fabric very soft. Mathilde lay down next to her and raised up on one elbow. Marie could see the quick pulsing of her white throat. "I show you first what a man will do to you," she murmured. "Lie still."

Marie closed her eyes. She felt Mathilde's hand move up the front of her blouse, skillfully freeing the buttons. Then, a gentle tugging on the band that circled her breasts. "Ah, such pretty ones," Mathilde breathed. "*Oui*, some man will be very lucky. . .very lucky." Her fingers circled the soft mounds. "Don't tremble so. You must learn not to be afraid when he does this, *eh bien?*" Mathilde's hands caressed her in round, silky motions. "Pretend that I am a man, *ma cher*. . . your husband—" She laughed softly. "Or your lover. . ."

Marie felt the murmured words as flutters of Mathilde's lips against her nipples. She caught her breath as that full, red mouth drew them inside, the tongue licking, circling. Marie felt something tighten in the pit of her stomach. It was not a good feeling, but she could not move. She heard herself moaning softly.

"Now, this. . ." Mathilde's hand slid down Marie's legs, rubbing them through her skirt. "*Non*, don't tremble so. It is only Mathilde. She is only teaching you." A little at a time she began to lift Marie's skirt. "*Oui*. . . and he will touch you here, like this. And you will like it. . . ."

Marie felt the satiny hand slide up the inside of her

thigh. She gasped as Mathilde's fingers found her, parted her and began to move in tiny circles. She felt a tightening inside her that was almost pain. Even Ike had not done this. The pressure of Mathilde's fingers sent waves of delicious shock down into her legs, up into her body. She was dimly aware that she was moving her hips, her voice making little sounds that she could not control. Something in the back of her mind cried out that this was very wrong, but she could not stop.

Mathilde was breathing hard. She jerked up her own skirt and pulled one of Marie's hands down between her legs. "Do it!" she commanded in a rasping voice. "Do it to me!"

The feeling rising up in Marie was ugly, but it was stronger than her will. It was as if she had moved out of her own body, and Mathilde now possessed both of them. "No. . ." she whimpered, but it was a feeble protest. She was not strong enough to break free of Mathilde's spell. She began to move her hand.

A sharp rap on the front door echoed down the hallway. *"Peste!"* Mathilde raised up and brushed her hair out of her eyes. The knock came again, louder and more insistent this time. With another muttered curse, Mathilde slid off the bed.

"Wait," she whispered, brushing Marie's cheek with her hand. "I will find out who it is and send them away. *Attendez ici*. Mathilde will be swift, eh?"

She hurried out of the room, smoothing down her hair. Marie pulled her legs together and lay there, quivering in hot and cold waves. She felt the tears welling up into her eyes. From the parlor she heard the gruff voice of a man.

Run, some sixth sense whispered inside her head. Marie listened to it. In the next instant she was struggling to her feet, buttoning her blouse. With her heart pounding, she slipped out into the hall and stole out the back door. Then she was running, out the garden gate, down the path, her skirts flying.

Marie slowed her steps as she saw people on the landing below her. They would be curious if they saw her tearing down the hill like that. But she could not slow the frantic drumming of her heart. The sound filled her ears. It was all she could hear.

Nothing happened, she told herself. Not the way it had with Ike. But for some reason she could not fully understand, Marie felt even dirtier than she had after Ike Ilam had finished with her. She wanted to jump into the cold river and let it flow all over her. She wanted to take a bar of lye soap and scrub her skin till it burned.

Mathilde was only teaching me, she reasoned with herself again. But no, she had been a fool but she was not that stupid. For Mathilde Rodare it had been more than a lesson. But Marie had never even imagined that a woman could. . .could. . .Marie shuddered as if she had stepped on something dead. It was all she could do to keep from breaking into a panic again. She was dimly aware that her legs were carrying her someplace. She was running to someone, and she did not even understand who or why until she caught sight of her father's warehouse through the trees.

She burst in through the open door. Ned Cooper was alone, counting and grading the pelts that were stacked on low benches. He looked up, surprised to see her.

"Ned!" She stumbled into his arms. "Oh, hold on to me, Ned!" Marie buried her face against his shirt and clung there, trembling and sobbing. She was safe! It could all come out now, all the fright, all the awful, twisted, guilty feelings in her.

"Marie, what's the matter? Is somebody after you?"

She shook her head, feeling his hand in her hair. "Not now. Oh, just hold on to me! Hold on tight, Ned!" She was dizzy with relief. It was all right now. How strong he was.

"Are you hurt?" His arms tightened around her. "Marie, if anybody's gone and done anything t' hurt you, so help me, I'll—"

"No. No, it's all right now," she whispered. "I was only scared. I'm not scared anymore. Not with you here." She felt his chest swell as he drew in his breath. His heart was loud in her ear.

"Can't you tell me 'bout it?" he asked softly.

"Not now. Don't ask me now. But it's all right, Ned. It was just a scare. Just hold me till I stop shakin'."

How warm he was, and how clean. Marie closed her eyes and felt him lifting her face with one hand. He kissed her very gently, not like he had the first time. It was a tender kiss, a loving kiss. She lifted her arms to his neck and kissed him back the same way. The feeling was so sweet and so good that she almost wanted to cry again.

"I'd best be walkin' you back home," he said, his voice just a little shaky. "Anybody see you come in here, there might be talk if you stay. I wouldn't want that. Not 'bout you and me."

"Come on, then." She gave him her hand and they strolled out into the autumn sunlight. People would see them like this, walking hand in hand, she thought. People would say they were sweethearts, she and Ned, and that would be just fine. Once she thought she had loved him, when she was young and silly. Now, all at once, Marie *knew* she loved him, and it was a feeling like she'd never had before.

Maybe this is *really* what it's like to grow up, she told herself, loving somebody so much that you know you'd die for him if you had to.

She squeezed Ned's hand and held on tight. She felt giddy and wonderful. The awful thing that had happened at Mathilde Rodare's house seemed far away now. She was safe with Ned. She would not think about it again.

But when she glanced up the hill and saw the whitewashed house there, Mathilde's house, the old, icy fear stole over her once more. She gripped Ned's hand harder than ever.

XX

Cecile de Busseron thrust yet another log into the already roaring fire. She kept her house too warm, Marie reflected, edging her chair backward away from the heat. Even though snowflakes were flying outside in the icy December air, piling into the corners of the glass window panes, that was no excuse to keep the place like an oven! Marie put down the long scarf she was knitting as a Christmas present for Ned and fanned herself with one hand.

"Ah, forgive me! You are too hot!" Cecile glanced at her. "I freeze in winter! My bones shiver when I look outside, and I must have a big fire to warm them. Here, trade me places. Take this chair by the window, and I will take yours. Better?"

"Yes, thank you." Marie slipped gratefully into the high-backed rocker. A tiny current of fresh, cold air drifted in through a crack above the sill. Marie drew it into her lungs, looking forward to the long walk through the swirling snow that would come later when she stole down to the warehouse to see Ned.

She held the scarf up, inspecting the stitches with critical eyes. How wonderful it would have been if she'd had the dye to make it a beautiful indigo blue, to match Ned's eyes. As it was, the scarf would be nothing but the light natural buff color of the wool, though Marie had managed to stain enough of the strands with berry juice to make a thin, dark red stripe at each end.

Abby's own fingers flew as she worked on a pair of stockings. Her rapid movements were charged by anxiety, Marie knew. Edward was overdue. He had planned to be back in Vincennes well before the end of November, and there'd been no word from him.

Cecile clicked her tongue. "There, Abby. I know you're worried. But Edward—*mon Dieu,* I never saw a man more able to take care of himself. He's just been delayed, I'm sure. He'll be home soon. All that long face will have been for nothing, you'll see." She glanced over at her own husband who dozed uneasily in his chair. Marie wondered if Cecile envied Abby for her handsome, fearless mate. Captain Busseron had put on weight in the long weeks of inactivity. Now that rumors of a British invasion from the north were flying like the snow, his nature had deteriorated into nervous grumbling.

"The poor dear," Cecile clasped her hands for a moment, then picked up her embroidery. "He can't sleep at night. He only sleeps like that, in little snatches. He doesn't know what Hamilton will do to him, but Lord knows it won't be a medal on his chest."

"The weather's closing in. If Hamilton comes at all, surely it won't be till spring." It was Abby's turn to be the comforter now.

"Hamilton's coming. I can feel it. The whole town can feel it, Abby, and if you'd lived here longer you'd be able to feel it, too." Cecile glanced out of the window as if she expected to see a whole regiment of Redcoats marching up the street. "Didn't you hear? Captain Helm sent out scouts five days ago. They didn't come back."

"Indians?" Abby spoke softly.

"The tribes around here are friendly. Tobacco's Son, the Grand Door, has seen to that. If it *was* Indians"—Cecile's plump, white hands fluttered—"they'd have to have been sent by Hamilton. Either it was Hamilton's Indians or Hamilton himself. He's close by. I can feel it. I only wish Pere Gibault was still here!"

"You've met Hamilton. What's he like?" Abby questioned.

"Oh, such a gentleman!" Cecile's lip curled with disdain. "All polish and fine manners. But those eyes of his can undress a woman where she stands. *Sur ma parole!* You don't turn your back on Henry Hamilton! I got that advice from a major's widow at Detroit. She'd evidently been in a position to know."

"And as a soldier?"

"As a soldier, his reputation's spotless, *cherie*. Cecile looked up and smiled as Aspasie glided into the room with a pot of tea and three china cups on a tray. "*Très bien!* Just as I was dying for a cup of something hot!"

Marie had been waiting for an excuse to extricate herself. "Is it all right if I don't have tea?" she asked her mother. "Ned'll be gettin' through down at the warehouse soon."

"Ah, to be young!" sighed Cecile. "Not a care, eh? Let her go, Abby. She's had enough of this old lady talk for the day!"

"Very well," said Abby. "But you're to be home in an hour, Marie. No dawdling."

Wrapped in her woolen cloak and hood, Marie almost danced down the hill. Snow stung her face deliciously with its cold touch, and sparkled in her hair. Yes, she admitted to herself, she was worried about her father, too. But he'd been delayed before. And this time of early winter when the rivers seemed to alternately freeze and flood was the worst of all. He'd be back soon, she assured herself. Surely he'd at least be back for Christmas.

Even Cecile's gloomy predictions about the British did not concern her heavily today, though she did feel sorry for poor Captain de Busseron. British or Yankee, what did it really matter? The Forny family was neutral. They'd come to Vincennes expecting to live in a British-controlled settlement, only to find upon their arrival that the Yankees had taken the town. It had made no difference. Not to them. Why should it matter whose flag flew about the fort?

Besides, how could she feel unhappy about anything when Ned would be waiting for her at the warehouse? They would talk about the trading business and Ned's own plans for his part in it. They would talk about each other, about their feelings, about the things that had happened to each of them that day. And maybe, if they found themselves alone, he would pull her into the shelter of a tree. She would come willingly, and he would kiss her until she ached and quivered all the way down to her toes.

She passed Mathilde's house on the other side of the street. Marie had not gone back since the day she had run from Mathilde's bed, out the back door and through the garden. She still thought about what had happened there, although with time she found herself thinking of it less and less. For a while she had been afraid, but Mathilde had not bothered her. How could she? If such shocking conduct were to become known in the town, Mathilde would not have one friend left in Vincennes.

Sometimes they passed one another on the street. When they did, the back of Marie's neck would prickle with dread. But Mathilde would only look at her, her blue eyes shifting subtly to one side. Sometimes she would smile, but that was all. Marie never smiled back.

She could see the warehouse now, through the bare trees. Marie broke into a light, eager run, her fur-lined moccasins flying over the snow-dusted ground.

"Ned?" Yes, he was alone, as he usually was since Luc and Justin had left for the East. Marie ran to him and flung herself into his arms. His lips were warm on her cold face. He pulled her tight against him and kissed her until she felt her blood running hot, until his own breathing came in deep gasps and she could feel his hardness through her skirt.

"Marie, we'd better stop," he whispered.

Why? she almost asked. There was nothing she'd ever wanted in her life the way she wanted Ned. When she reminded herself that the one boy she'd given herself to was Ike Ilam, not Ned, she almost wanted to die! It was almost as if she still belonged to Ike, and the only way she could blot out the memory was to have Ned the same way.

But Marie knew better than to argue. Little by little she let herself move apart from him. Ned thought she was so good. He didn't want to do anything that would hurt her. Marie shivered. What would Ned think of her if he knew about Ike?

"Did you hear?" she asked him as he locked the warehouse door. "The Busserons think Hamilton's close by. The scouts that Cap'n Helm sent out five days ago didn't come back. Cecile thinks Hamilton caught 'em. Or Hamilton's Indians."

"I heard. That's all I've thought about all day long." Ned pocketed the key and took Marie's hand. "By God, Marie, I don't know what t' do. Somebody ought t' get word to Clark down at Kaskaskia. I even thought about goin' myself."

"No!" Marie cried out. "Father left you here to take care of me and Mother and the business! With Justin and Luc gone—"

"I know." Ned's hand tightened around hers. "That was the only thing what kept me from sneakin' off downriver today. If'n I did, and somethin' was to happen to you or your ma, how could I face Edward Forny?"

"That's right," said Marie. "Besides, it's no concern of ours if old Henry Hamilton gets his fort back, is it? Long as we can trade on the river, we can be friends with everybody!"

Ned made a little strangled sound. "Oh, Lord, Marie, we been talkin' for weeks now! Ain't you listened to nothin' I said?"

"You favor the Yankees some, I guess. Reckon it was Philadelphia put that into your head. But that's all right. Don't make much difference out here."

"Marie, it makes all the difference there is! I could talk to you all day 'bout what the British done t' this country. I could talk myself blue in the face 'bout what men like Patrick Henry an' Thomas Jefferson an' John Adams are sayin'!" He gazed down at her with pain written all over his face. "But maybe it wouldn't do no good."

The last words stung. Marie opened her mouth to protest, but before she could utter a word, a frantic shout from somewhere up in the town silenced her into shock.

"British! Three miles off! Whole army of 'em, and Injuns too! Headed this way!"

"Come on!" Ned jerked her hand. Marie raced behind him, up into the town where people were rushing about like ants whose nest had just been kicked open.

"Who saw them? What's happening here?" Ned seized the arm of one of the French militiamen.

"Somebody from upriver. They—" His voice was lost in the roar of a single cannon shot from the hilltop. It was the signal for the militia to assemble at the fort. Ned released the arm of the soldier, then gaped incredulously when the man turned and hurried off in the other direction.

"Wait a minute!" Ned caught his sleeve again and spun the fellow around. "You mean you ain't goin' to the fort?"

"*Mon Dieu,* you think I am crazy? Nobody is going. Nobody wants to commit suicide, monsieur. Now, if you will let go of me—" He jerked roughly away, leaving Ned standing there with his mouth open.

"Come on," Marie tugged at his hand. "We got to find my mother."

But Ned's eyes were fixed on the fort. "Cap'n Helm an' his Yankees might be all alone up there," he muttered. "Well, by thunder, I'll show 'em there be 'least one man in Vincennes who ain't scared to stand up!" He turned swiftly to Marie. "Run to the Busseron house. Your ma's bound to be waitin' there. You'll be safe."

"No!" Marie protested, realizing what he was about to do. "No, Ned! It ain't our fight. Stay out of it! You'll

241

only get—"

He glanced back at her for an instant. "You be wrong, Marie. It's my fight." Then he was off, running up the hill toward the fort.

"Ned!" she screamed after him. But he was already beyond the sound of her voice. Marie wheeled and fled in the direction of Captain de Busseron's house.

The Union Jack fluttered and snapped in the wind above Fort Sackville, hidden now and again by clouds of flying snow. The residents of Vincennes, assembled on the green before the open gate of the fort, gazed up at it. Some of them shrugged. A few of them spat. But most of them, including Marie, were greatly relieved that Hamilton's victory had been accomplished without the firing of a single shot.

Indians, Shawnee most of them, milled about the fringes of the crowd, who eyed them nervously. There were far too many of them, and the red-handled, British-issued knives thrust into their belts seemed perilously ready. They comprised the bulk of Hamilton's force, and who could say how much control the British commander really had over them?

With no more than half a dozen men left to defend the ramshackle fort against hundreds of British regulars and Indians, Captain Helm had made the only prudent decision possible. He had surrendered his command. The grizzled captain stood beside the gate now, tears freezing in his beard as Col. Henry Hamilton, resplendent in his scarlet unifrom, white wig and high, black, cockaded hat, read the terms of a new oath of allegiance which all were to sign. A priest, this one a stranger, stood by with a gilded crucifix, to be kissed as a pledge to keep the oath.

"Should we sign it?" Marie gripped her mother's arm.

It was cold, standing in the open as they were. The wind whipped at their cloaks and skirts. She could see Ned when she stretched on tiptoe, standing off to one side of Helm, in the small cluster of men who'd surrendered when the fort had fallen.

"What would your father tell us to do?" Abby glanced down at her daughter.

"Father wouldn't want trouble. He'd tell us to sign." Marie whispered her answer and saw her mother nod in approval.

"Aye. We'll sign. But I'll not be kissing that yellow cross!" Abby said. "Come on, let's get into the line."

Marie felt Ned's eyes on them as they moved over to join the long column of people that were forming up before the table on which quills and ink had been laid out. Ned would understand, she thought. What could they do except sign?

The line moved slowly. Marie shivered and rubbed her arms. Most of the French militiamen who had served under Helm and deserted when the British menace drew near, were waiting to sign like everyone else. Cecile de Busseron wrote her name with a shaking hand, then knelt to kiss the crucifix. Her husband, who had clad himself hastily in his best dress uniform, followed her.

"My good captain!" Hamilton's voice oozed sarcasm. He was a slender man of medium height, his swarthy skin, dark eyes and heavy black brows contrasting with his white powdered wig. "Stand up. *Stand up!*"

Captain de Busseron, who had been kneeling before the priest, rose to his feet, his hands clenching and unclenching nervously. His wife hovered behind him.

"And what have you to say for yourself?" Hamilton looked him up and down, eyes glittering with anger.

"We leave you in charge of one of our most vital positions, and you give it away! Taking a toy from a child would have been more difficult than taking this fort from a man like you! Now, what have you to say? Tell me?"

Busseron drew himself to ramrod straightness. "I had little choice in the matter, sir," he answered with as much dignity as possible. "Once that meddling heretic Gibault informed the people that France was now allied with the *Bostonnais,* what could I do?"

"But *you*—you are an officer serving under His Britannic Majesty!" Hamilton thundered. "Is that not so?"

"It is indeed, sir. But I had no support. The militia deserted me, just as they deserted Captain Helm today. I did the only thing I could. I surrendered under honorable terms and retired to my quarters."

"A likely story!" Hamilton slapped Busseron sharply across the face. "French coward! Yankee bootlicker!" He struck him twice more. Cecile had covered her eyes with her hands and appeared to be weeping with fright.

"Beggin' your pardon, Cunnel sir." It was Helm who had stepped forward, his ratty buckskins an almost comical contrast to Hamilton's splendid crimson uniform. "I ain't one t' meddle in no family squabble, now, but seems t' me you're makin' a mistake 'bout the cap'n here. He ain't licked no Yankee boots, leastwise shore as hell not mine. He be tellin' the truth."

Hamilton turned to Helm, his eyes like granite. "He's given you no help? No information?"

"Not a twaddle." Helm spat into the dry grass. "That wuz part o' the surrender terms, that he wouldn't hafta. Otherwise, the cap'n there woulda died fightin'. Swear it on a stack o' Bibles, Cunnel!"

Hamilton let out his breath and the rage seemed to

drain from him. "Very well," he sighed. "I'll call you no traitor, Captain de Busseron. But by heaven I challenge any man here to dispute the evidence that you're an imcompetent bungler! I just thank the good Lord you're not an Englishman!" The dark eyes snapped. "I do need someone in charge who knows the town and the people, however, and there's no one available except you. Consider yourself restored to temporary duty, Captain, at least till we can find a suitable replacement."

"Thank you, sir." Busseron saluted smartly, though his knees were obviously watery with relief. Cecile, almost swooning, had been helped to a seat on a log by one of the officers.

The line moved forward. With a gruff bark of dismissal, Hamilton turned his attention elsewhere. Captain de Busseron, his wife clinging to his arm, drifted away from the center of the crowd. He looked in Marie and Abby's direction, but his eyes did not appear to see them. His face was twisted with shame at the tongue lashing and physical abuse to which he'd just been publicly subjected. Mute with sympathy, Marie watched him. The captain was a good man, she told herself. He'd done the best he could. He certainly hadn't deserved to be degraded in front of the whole town!

The children in the line whimpered with the cold. The snow came and went in gusts. Marie and her mother had reached the table. "I'll sign," said Abby. "But I'm not of your religion. I'll not kiss that cross, and neither will my daughter."

"Very well," the priest murmured. "Sign. Just sign."

Marie gripped the quill in her numb fingers and penned her name below her mother's. It was done. She felt safer now. But when she raised up she saw Ned's eyes watching her. There was a hurt in them, a hurt she could see and feel.

As Marie walked away with Abby, she glanced back and realized for the first time that Mathilde Rodare had been just a few spaces behind them in the line. Mathilde's sea blue eyes met hers for an instant, and Mathilde smiled. She was dressed in a black cloak trimmed with rich brown sable that made her skin look very white and creamy. The cold had heightened the color in her cheeks, and her hair had been carefully arranged to form little curls about her face.

She stood before Hamilton and said something in a low voice, something that Marie could not hear. The British colonel's eyes narrowed as they moved expertly from her head to her feet. *Those eyes can undress a woman where she stands!* Cecile's words came back to Marie as she watched them.

Mathilde bent low to sign the oath of allegiance. As she reached for a quill the front of her cloak fell open, revealing for just an instant the lovely, rounded curves of her breasts. "Ah, *excusez-moi!*" she laughed softly and pulled her cloak back into place. Her eyes met Hamilton's again, dark lashes lowering against her cheeks, then slowly, artfully lifting.

Nancy Jukes, the tavern-owner's daughter had been shoved into the line by her father. "No!" she protested in a loud whisper. "I ain't signin'! I give my word on it, I ain't signin'!"

"Bring the wench here!" Hamilton ordered sharply. Two soldiers seized her arms and half-dragged her across the green to where he stood. Marie watched, her heart swelling with bitter anticpation. Now that slut will get what's coming to her, she thought.

Hamilton's eyes bored into the trembling girl, so sharp they seemed to penetrate not only her clothes but her flesh and bones. "You say you're not of a mind to sign the Oath of Allegiance to His Majesty?" he asked in a delicate voice that dripped sarcasm.

Nancy stood very straight, her unkempt yellow hair hanging down her back. "I ain't signin'," she said, thrusting out her chin. "I seen the right of what the Yankees done when they come here. I swore in the church I'd be a true Yankee, and by God I ain't signin'!"

A ripple of sound swept over the crowd, a little murmur of admiration for Nancy's spunk. Most of the town had sworn a similar oath of loyalty to the Yankees before Father Gibault. But with the British back in command the easiest course of action, it seemed, was to forget about it and roll with the tide.

Hamilton's granite gaze swept over the crowd. "Any others here of a similar mind? You may as well make it known now."

The crowd waited in breathless silence. Then there was a rustle as four or five men stepped forward. Marie recognized two of them—a storekeeper named Le Gras, and the slender, dark-haired younger brother of Father Gibault. They lined up at Nancy's side.

Captain Busseron, who had faded back into the crowd, his eyes on the ground, suddenly squared his shoulders, smiled grimly and strode back toward the spot where Hamilton and his officers stood. "You may strike my name from the oath and wipe my kiss from the cross, Colonel," his voice rang out boldly as he moved into place beside the other rebels. "I've been a toady to you British long enough! I'm ready to be a man again!"

With a little cry, Cecile broke free of the crowd and ran

to him. "Mine, too!" She hurled the words at Hamilton. "Strike my name as well, Colonel, and do your worst! I stand with my husband!"

A muscle twitched in Henry Hamilton's swarthy cheek. It was clear he had expected nothing like this. "Anyone else?" he asked gruffly. "Is anyone else fool enough to show himself a rebel?"

Marie's hand went to her throat as Ned Cooper stepped from the cluster of men who'd been taken when the fort surrendered. "No!" Her mouth screamed the word, but no sound came out.

"I ain't no soldier," Ned stared at Hamilton. "I didn't get no chance t' fight you proper-like. But by thunder I can stand here an' spit in your eye an' tell you that all the devils in hell couldn't make me sign!" He took his place beside Cecile.

"No!" Marie whispered the word frantically, wanting to run to him, to shake him, to drag him back into the shelter of the crowd. "Ned, no! Not you!"

Abby took her arm gently. "Hush, Marie. He can't hear you. Ned's made his choice. Let him stand up for his beliefs like a man."

Marie turned, buried her face in her mother's cloak and began to sob. "Lord," Abby murmured, holding her daughter close, "I wish Edward was here!"

XXI

Edward cursed the weather as he tied up his canoe at the Kaskaskia landing. It had delayed him at every turn, the sleet, the wind, the floating ice, the long days when no one could travel. He was weeks overdue, and he knew that Abby would be worried.

He had left Henry in the new settlement at the French Licks, busily throwing up a log cabin for himself and his new bride, Sara. He had listened with a lump in his throat to Henry's account of the ceremony that had made the two youngsters man and wife. If only he and Abby and Marie could have been there.

But they'd approve, no doubt of that, Edward told himself, a vision of the sweet, golden-haired Sara spinning itself in his mind. If he could have ordered a girl created especially for his son, he could not have done better than Sara. There'd be grandchildren soon. A little shiver went through him at the thought of it. Could it really be that he'd lived that long?

He secured the canoe and gave a boy a coin to watch it while he went to look for lodging. Kaskaskia was new to him. He'd come by this way because bad weather had closed off the Ohio. Besides, he'd wanted to see the town and to get news of the war from his friend George Rogers Clark, who was said to be here.

The afternoon was chilly, the sky overcast with gray, scudding clouds. Dirty snow crunched under Edward's moccasins, slowly melting. This weather was the worst of all, Edward thought, glancing up at the uncertain sky. A storm could strike without warning, bringing rain, sleet or snow, more water than the frozen ground could absorb. That was when the rivers flooded, rising over their banks to spread in the lowlands like lakes. And the lakes were treacherous, full of snags and strange currents that could do frightening things to a canoe.

Edward looked about as he walked up the street. Kaskaskia surprised him. It was bigger than Vincennes, its streets laid out in neat squares. A solid stone church stood on one corner. The houses and shops looked clean and prosperous, even on this gloomy day.

The orange glow of firelight through the windows of a small inn caught his eye. Long days had passed since he'd had a warming drink or a friendly conversation. Eagerly he swung open the door and stepped inside.

The place was dim and warm, lighted inside only by the fire that crackled in the smoke-blackened fireplace. A lone man, young and slender, sat at one of the roughhewn tables.

"If I may join you—?" Edward pulled out a chair.

"Don't mind if ye do." An easy grin spread over the young man's long-jawed face. "Joe Bowman's the name.

Cap'n Bowman when I'm on duty, which I ain't right now.''

"Edward Forny." They shook hands. "A captain, you say? Under Colonel Clark?"

"Aye. You know George?"

"*Oui*. We traveled together last year. I was hoping to find him here in Kaskaskia."

"Y' don't say! Well, he be here. I can take ye to him after ye've had the time t' warm your gullet. The rum ain't too bad here." He gave Edward a sly wink. "But that ain't exactly why I come."

Out of the corner of his eye, Edward caught sight of a pretty little barmaid in a white apron. Her hair, a deep auburn, hung down her back in a long, thick braid. *"Bien entendu,"* Edward murmured with a knowing smile. "I understand perfectly, *mon ami*."

"Trouble is," said Bowman, "she don't speak no English. And I don't speak no French. Can't do nothin' 'cept look at her."

"And that's not enough?" Edward chuckled over the pewter mug the girl had handed him. She had white skin, fetchingly sprinkled with tiny, golden freckles. He looked up and managed to catch her eyes with his. "Mademoiselle, my friend here says that he would like very much to know you," he said to her in French.

Her pert face flushed slightly. "I, too," she murmured. "He comes here often, and he smiles at me, but when one cannot speak—" She shrugged.

"What time do you finish your work this evening? Perhaps he might come and walk home with you. Yes?" Edward took a swallow of the rum. It burned pleasantly all the way down his throat.

"Perhaps." She lowered her eyes demurely. "I finish

at nine o' clock. If he is here—" A voice from the kitchen interrupted her. "Yes, I'm coming!" She flitted away with a swish of her skirt.

"It is all settled," Edward informed Joe Bowman with a smile. "Tonight at nine o'clock. But, my friend, I warn you, if you find your lack of French a problem then, there is no help for you."

Bowman grinned and drained his mug. "George ought t' be in his headquarters up the street. I'd be right pleased t' take ye to him."

"*Merci.*" Edward paid for the drink and followed Bowman out the door, the image of the pretty little barmaid still warm in his mind. He'd been too long away from Abby, he told himself, feeling the familiar surge of woman-hunger well up in him. He'd be out of Kaskaskia at dawn tomorrow, ready to head back down the Mississippi, then brave the Ohio and the Wabash. Vincennes seemed far away by that route, although it was not such a long distance as the crow flies. Maybe he'd ask Clark about the advisability of stowing the canoe and taking the overland way. Abby could be in his arms in less than a week. He smiled to himself at the thought of what was to come.

George Rogers Clark rose out of his chair, grinning with delight. "Edward Forny! I'll be damned!" He clasped Edward on the arm with one powerful hand. "What brings you to Kaskaskia?"

"In a manner of speaking, I'm on my way home." Edward took the chair that one of Clark's aides offered him. The young colonel's hair was as fiery as ever, his grip as strong. He was dressed in the blue uniform of the Continental Army.

"Home?" Clark leaned forward in his chair. "Does

that mean you've moved your family to Vincennes?" His eyes narrowed with concern. Watching them, Edward felt a sudden chill of foreboding.

"*Oui*. We arrived there just after your Captain Helm had taken command. Is something wrong?"

Clark's muscular shoulders rose and fell. "To be honest with you, Forny, I don't know. But it's been too quiet up there. Nearly a month's gone by since I last heard from Leonard Helm, and that's not like him at all. Something's not right up there! I can feel it!"

"Hamilton?" It was Edward who spoke the dreaded name.

"Maybe." Clark stood up and began to pace. "Hamilton, or maybe his butcherin' Indians— Sorry, Forny, I shouldn't have said that."

"The fort is not even worthy of the name, you know. I inspected it once with Busseron. It's falling apart. The timbers are rotten and full of gaps. There's a well inside, but it's no good anymore. In a major attack, there'd be no way to hold out for more than a few days." Edward's voice was grim. He felt as if a heavy weight were pressing down on him.

"So I've been told. Two weeks ago I sent Vigo—"

"You mean Francisco Vigo? The trader?" Edward had never met Vigo, but the man's name was well known all along the Mississippi and its tributaries.

"That's right. Vigo's on our side. You can't imagine what he's given—"

"And he's not yet returned?" Edward asked anxiously.

"Not yet. But he's a Spanish citizen. The British would be foolish to harm him with relations so touchy between England and Spain."

"But an Indian sees no Spanish citizen. An Indian hunting scalps for the Hair Buyer would see only a white man," Edward reasoned gloomily.

"Lord in heaven, what Vigo's loss would cost us—" Clark slammed a heavy fist on the corner of the desk. "When were you last in Vincennes, Forny?"

"I left in October. All was well then." Edward studied his friend with grave eyes. "I'm going to Vincennes myself, you know. The devil in person couldn't stop me. I'd be more than willing to let you know—"

"You?" Clark raised one russet eyebrow. "Remember last year when I asked you to scout for me? You refused, if I remember right."

Edward shrugged. "What can I say? My family is in Vincennes. I'm as concerned as you are."

Clark turned his back and stared out the window. "You know, it won't be easy, Forny. If Hamilton's got the fort, he'll have Vincennes surrounded. You may not even get through. And getting word back to me might be nigh on impossible. If it weren't, Helm would have found a way to do it." He turned back to Edward with a gentler look on his rugged face. "You've got a place to spend the night?"

"*Mais oui*. There's an inn—"

"I know the place. It's got bedbugs, I'm told. No, there's a spare room in the house where I'm staying. Get your gear and you can bunk there. That way we can talk tonight and you'll not be having to go out in the weather." Clark glanced out of the window again. "Looks like another storm brewin' tonight."

"*Merci*. That's a good idea. I won't keep you now, but I appreciate the room. The house—?"

"It's the big, whitewashed one up the street. You may

as well put your things in there now. You'll be welcome, and I'll see you at supper."

"Again, *merci*." Edward shook Clark's hand again, amazed at the strength in that big, sun-bronzed fist.

Then he went out again into the strangely warm wind, and headed down the street to the landing to get his clothes and bedding out of the canoe.

Specks of sleet had begun to dot the air. The Mississippi was swollen with gray-brown water, and the Wabash, Edward knew, would be worse. The lowlands on the west side of the river could be flooded for miles. He cursed under his breath, his chest tight with worry.

There was a crowd on the landing. Edward hurried his steps and arrived in time to see a long pirogue pull up to the shore. There were two men in it. Both of them were strangers, one small, dark and wiry, a typical French *courieur* in weathered buckskins. The other man caught Edward's eye at once. He was a stocky fellow, almost as broad as he was tall, and solid, with a great barrel of a chest. His square face was singularly pleasant, his clothes, of fine, imported wool, expensively made. Clearly he was no ordinary man. As Edward leaped forward to help drag the pirogue ashore, he realized that he was looking at Francisco Vigo.

"I thank you, friend, whoever you are. You've saved me from wet feet." Vigo climbed out of the boat, surprisingly agile for his size and weight. His deep voice carried an Italian lilt, for although he was a Spanish citizen in the New World, Edward knew that he had come originally from Sardinia.

"My name is Forny." Edward extended his hand. "And there is no one on the river who would not recognize you, Monsieur Vigo."

"Colonel Clark. He is here?" Vigo's huge hand smothered Edward's for an instant. The small, deep-set eyes flickered with anxiety.

"*Mais oui!* I spoke with him not more than ten minutes ago. He was most concerned about you. Come with me. I'll take you to him."

They hurried back up the street, Vigo puffing slightly as he kept pace with Edward's long strides.

"And what news of Vincennes?" Edward dared to ask him. "My family is there. I have been most worried—"

"The news from Vincennes is not good. However, it must be first for the ears of Colonel Clark." Vigo glanced at Edward, his eyes softening. "But you need have little fear for your family. As I understand it, no citizen of Vincennes had been harmed."

"Thank you." Edward felt some of the weight lift from him, though not all of it.

George Rogers Clark had seen them coming. "Vigo!" He raced down the front steps. In the next instant he and the trader were hugging each other like two huge bears. "By all heaven, Vigo, I've not been able to sleep nights since you left!"

"And you'll not be sleeping tonight either, friend. Not after you've heard what I have to say."

"Hamilton?"

Vigo nodded. "We'd best go inside."

"Aye. I suppose so." Clark glanced at Edward. "You can come in too, Forny. You're as concerned as anybody."

"Hamilton's got Vincennes, I take it." They had settled themselves into chairs and an aide had brought Vigo a glass of sherry. Clark leaned forward against the edge of his desk.

"That's right. Took it last month without a shot. When he marched on the town with two hundred regulars and twice that many Indians, your poor friend Helm had few options, especially when the French militia deserted him."

"Leonard's all right?"

"He is. He has the run of the fort, a bit like a pet dog. Gets along famously with our friend Hamilton. But then Helm's no fool. He'll bide his time while he must, but whatever can be done, he'll do it. I saw his eyes."

Clark's massive shoulders lifted and fell as he sighed. "The size of Hamilton's force?"

"Most of the Indians have gone, which is just as well for Hamilton. You don't keep that many of those red devils penned up in a place like Vincennes without all hell breaking loose sooner or later. But the regulars are there. And the French militia, whatever they're worth. They drift with the prevailing wind, it seems."

"The stockade?" Clark stared thoughtfully at a fly on the ceiling.

Vigo scratched his ample chin. "You heard how it was before. A half dozen boys with slingshots could have knocked it over. But Hamilton's been rebuilding it. The timbers have been reinforced, the blockhouses strengthened. They've got new cannon on the walls, and Hamilton's even had a well dug. In short, friend, Sackville is now a fort worthy of the name."

"Aye, just as I feared." Clark fingered the quill on his desk. Edward could almost see his mind working, weighing, speculating.

"You knew it might happen," Vigo said softly.

"Aye. I knew. I had no choice but to gamble in the

hope that we could get enough reinforcements to hold the place before Hamilton got there." Clark's fist slammed down hard on the corner of the desk. "Damn it all! To hold an area this size when you've got less than two hundred men you can count on—" Then he looked at Vigo and his eyes warmed with affection. "But you, friend, you risked your life for us. How did you fare?"

Vigo's deep-throated laugh shook his belly. "Not badly! We let ourselves get captured. They hauled us before Hamilton, and when I professed my neutrality as a Spanish citizen, he didn't dare lay a hand on me. Hamilton let me go free on my word of honor that I'd go straight on to St. Louis without stopping here at Kaskaskia to report to you."

"Your word of honor?" Clark's brow lifted. "And you broke that, even for me?"

Vigo roared with laughter. "But no! Francisco Vigo breaks his word for no man! I beached the pirogue in St. Louis, got out, drank a glass of good Madeira on the landing, pissed, and came right back downriver to Kaskaskia. Forgive the delay, but honor is honor!"

Clark was laughing too, but his eyes were red with emotion. "My friend. My dear, good friend. So help me, if Hamilton had harmed you I'd have had the bastard's guts for garters before the week was out!" He straightened in his chair. "Well, there's nothing to do but get the fort back. Tell me, Vigo, I know it's my scalp Hamilton really wants. Did you get wind of his plans to march on Kaskaskia and Cahokia?"

"He intends to, of that much I'm sure. But he had a devil of a time getting down from Detroit, with half the rivers flooded and the other half frozen. He told me that himself. I think it's safe to say he'll hole up in Vincennes till spring. He knows you can't move on him until then either, not with this weather and the condition of the rivers—"

"We can't?" Clark's eyes were suddenly wide and hard, like a wolf's. Edward felt his own breath catch.

"But it would be madness!" Vigo rose out of his chair and leaned over the desk. "The snow! The ice! And you've got no troops to speak of. Besides, I've seen the Wabash. It's like an ocean, for miles west of Vincennes!" The chair creaked as Vigo sat back down, hard. "Wait till spring. You'll have reinforcements by then. The country will be passable—"

"And Henry Hamilton will be expecting me. He's not expecting me now."

"Pah! Let it wait, George! Hamilton's not going anywhere. He's as warm and cozy as a skunk in its den. Why, the *bastardo*'s even found himself a woman in Vincennes! And, my soul, what a woman! A French goddess!"

Edward felt the hair prickle on the back of his neck. "You saw her?" he asked casually.

"Saw her!" Vigo chuckled. "When she leaned over me to pour the brandy, I saw all the way to her navel! The kind of creature a man dreams of. Tall, with hair as black as night and skin like white china. Blue eyes. And haunches like a prize Flemish mare's! With *that* warming his bed, a man would be a fool to—" Vigo suddenly blanched and looked askance at Edward. "By God, Forny, she's not your wife, is she?"

"*Non.*" Edward managed a smile. "No, Vigo, she's not my wife." He kept the smile on his face, but he had felt the cold chill of danger creep down his back. Mathilde. Mathilde in Hamilton's bed, and likely with all his influence at her command. There would be nothing she could not do to Abby, to Marie.

He had to get back to Vincennes.

XXII

Marie was awakened in the night by a sharp rapping on the door of the cabin. She sat up and rubbed her eyes, wondering if she had dreamed the sound. Then it came again, louder and even more insistent than before.

"Mother?" Marie slipped out from between the blankets. The wooden floor was rough and cold under her bare feet.

"Mother?" The rapping sound came a third time. Marie pattered down the stairs and saw her mother moving toward the door, a lighted candle in one hand and Edward's old pistol in the other.

"Who is it?" Abby stood with one hand on the latch. "Edward?" Her voice was full of hope. Oh, thought Marie, if only it could be her father!

"Open in the name of the king!" The gruff voice rasped from the other side of the door. "Open, or we've orders to force our way in!"

"Very well," Abby's voice and hands shook as she slid back the bolt. Marie crouched on the stairs, shivering with cold and fright.

A British sergeant stepped across the threshold, accompanied by two red-coated privates, their muskets at ready. "Mistress Forny? Mistress Abigail Forny?"

"Aye." Abby faced them boldly, her eyes huge in the candlelight, her chestnut hair drifting about her face. Only the flame of the candle, shaking like the hand that held it, betrayed her fear.

The sergeant drew a rolled-up paper from under his arm. "We have here an order for your arrest, signed by Colonel Hamilton."

Marie pressed her hand to her mouth to hold back a cry of terror. She blinked her eyes. Maybe she was dreaming, for the scene taking place below her was like something out of a nightmare.

"Might I ask on what charges?" Abby spoke calmly.

"You stand accused of spying, madam. Spying for the Yankee rebels." With one gloved hand, the sergeant took Abby's pistol by its barrel and passed it to one of the soldiers. Abby, almost limp with shock, scarcely seemed to notice.

"Might I ask who's doing the accusing?" she whispered.

"You may not. You'll find out in due time. For the present, madam, you are ordered to come with us to the fort."

"I'll not go!" Abby drew herself up. "It's a lie! I signed the pledge. Go and look, my name's on it."

"That we know," growled the sergeant, "though any number of witnesses could testify that you did not kiss the cross."

"But—" Abby's protest was a disbelieving whisper. "That alone couldn't—"

"Not that alone, I assure you. But the presence of your name on the pledge will not save you, madam. Quite the contrary. Those who openly refused to sign are regarded as mere enemies. One who signs and then betrays the crown is a traitor, as you are."

"It's a lie!" Abby gasped. "I won't leave this house!"

The sergeant nodded to his two companions. They moved in closer, muskets raised. "My orders are to take you by force if necessary, madam," he said coldly.

Marie saw a shudder pass through her mother's body. "May I have time to dress?" Abby said in a low, lifeless voice.

"Be quick, then. And no tricks."

"Mother!" Marie ran down to her as Abby mounted the stairs. "No, Mother! They can't take you!"

"Hush, Marie. Come and help me. Keep away from them." Abby encircled her daughter with her arm and drew her swiftly up the stairs with her.

"We don't have much time," Abby spoke in a terse whisper as she dressed, an armed soldier just outside the door. "Keep yourself safe, Marie, that's the most important thing. This accusation is false, and somehow we must find a way to prove it. Somebody wants to harm us."

"But who? Who could hate *you*?"

"That we must learn," Abby replied, her eyes flickering in the candlelight as if she knew more than she was telling. "But you may be next. You can't stay here, Marie. Go to the Busserons. Cecile and Francois—"

The soldier rapped on the door. "Your time's up, ma'am. The sergeant says to come right away."

"I'm coming," Abby called out, fastening her dress and reaching for her warm cloak. She paused at the door and held out her arms to Marie. "Keep safe, my dearest. Do that much for your mother. We'll see this through. Don't be scared." She clasped her daughter close, the tightness of her arms almost hurting. "Go to Ned," she whispered. "He'd die to keep you—"

The latch rattled on the door. "Ma'am, I've orders to shoot if—"

"There, I'm coming—" Abby opened the door and stepped out into the hallway, her head high.

"Mother—" Marie wanted to fling herself between her mother and the soldiers, to fight them, hit them with anything, but a sharp look from Abby's eyes silenced her. There was nothing she could do. She stood on the stairs, watching in mute horror as the three redcoats marched her mother out the door and into the black night.

The door closed behind them. Marie flung herself against it, weeping wildly and helplessly. She was alone, truly alone for the first time in her life. Her mother was a prisoner, and if Abby Forny could not be proven innocent of spying, she was doomed. Everybody knew what the British did to spies.

Marie sank to the floor, her tear-streaked face still pressed against the rough wood. Crying wouldn't help. She had to be calm. She had to think.

Who was in a position to help her? Almost no one. Ned, the Busserons, and the others who had refused to sign the petition were at liberty in the town. By the rules of honorable surrender, they had committed no crime. But they were kept under close surveillance by the British. They could not make a move that would not be duly noted and reported to Colonel Hamilton.

Keep safe, Abby had told her daughter. Go to Cecile. Go to Ned. But that would only worsen her own situation, and theirs, in British eyes. She would be seen as having joined the rebels, and since she had also signed that cursed pledge, she might well be charged with treason herself. Ned and the Busserons, on the other hand, might be placed in even greater danger if they were found to be sheltering the daughter of an accused spy.

Marie buried her face in her hands, quivering with dread. She had to do something. She had to find someone, someone who had the ear of Colonel Hamilton, someone who might be willing to help her. . . . Suddenly the answer struck like a thunderbolt.

Mathilde Rodare.

In a town like Vincennes, it was no secret that Mathilde had become the colonel's mistress. She strutted back and forth between the fort and her house, swathed in a beautiful red cloak lined with otter pelts that Hamilton had given her. And it was not uncommon to see the colonel's big, gray stallion tied up at her gatepost at any hour of the day or night. She even presided as hostess when he entertained guests at the fort. It was well known that Hamilton had a wife back at Detroit. But if Cecile de Busseron had been right in what she said about him, he had never taken his marriage vows very seriously.

Marie stood up and pressed her fingers against her throbbing temples. She had to think clearly. Her mother's life might well depend on it.

She had not spoken to Mathilde in many weeks, Marie reminded herself, not since that day when— She shivered at the memory of it. But Mathilde had not been unfriendly to her. She had even smiled when they passed on the street, although Marie had not returned that smile.

She would go to Mathilde as soon as it was light, Marie resolved. She would plead, beg, offer anything she had if Mathilde would speak to Colonel Hamilton about her mother. Who could say what Mathilde's price might be? Marie felt the gooseflesh rise on her arms as she tried to imagine it. Hang the price! Marie twisted her hands till they ached. She would pay it. She had to save Abby.

The next morning Marie washed and dressed by first light. Her eyes were red from crying and sleeplessness. They stung in the icy morning air as she walked up the street toward Mathilde's house, wrapped in her long, brown cloak. The town was already stirring. Wisps of gray smoke crept from the chimneys of the houses to spread and hang low over the rooftops. The ring of an ax echoed from somewhere down by the river. Two of Hamilton's Shawnee braves wandered up the street, still scratching themselves sleepily under their blankets. The Indians were a common sight since Hamilton had come to Vincennes, although most of them had gone. They strode boldly about the town, their red-handled scalp-knives gleaming at their belts, an ever-present reminder of what could happen if the colonel chose to unleash them on his enemies.

When Marie looked back down the street she could see the landing through the bare trees. What a frightening, strange thing it was, this river the Indians called the Ouabache. It was no longer a river, but a wide, shallow sea, stretching westward to the horizon. Here and there, small hills rose out of the flooded lowlands to stick out of the water as islands. Trees thrust up out of the rippling current like drowning hands.

The morning cannon shot from Fort Sackville echoed over the town and across the water. Marie jumped. Even familiar sounds made her uneasy this morning.

An Indian canoe came gliding into sight from upriver, a large craft with four people in it. Curious, Marie watched as it touched the bank. A squat-looking brave in a ragged blanket leaped out to drag it ashore. Marie could see the other people in the canoe more clearly now. One was a woman, her hair hanging down over her breasts in two long, black braids. One of the others was not an Indian at all, Marie realized as he swung his long legs over the side of the canoe and stood stretching on the bank. He was dressed in buckskins and a fur cap. His dark hair and beard were long and unkempt. Marie shuddered. She'd heard of such men and seen a few. They were renegades, white men living, hunting and fighting with the Indians, foul creatures, most of them. With a final shiver of revulsion, Marie turned away and hurried on up the street to Mathilde's house.

The colonel was not there, although he had clearly been there, and recently. Marie smiled bitterly as she noticed the fresh horse droppings beside Mathilde's gatepost, still steaming in the cold morning air. With luck she would find Mathilde Rodare awake and at home.

Mathilde answered Marie's timid knock at once. She was still dressed in her lace-trimmed wrapper, but her hair had been brushed. It hung like a black silk curtain around her shoulders. The smell of ham and biscuits drifted out through the open doorway. Evidently Mathilde had just given the colonel his breakfast and sent him on his way back to the fort.

The blue eyes looked Marie up and down, bold and free of surprise. Slowly the red lips smiled. "Marie! *Quelle plaisr.* Come in, child. Mathilde has missed you." She swung the door open wide and ushered Marie inside with a sweep of her hand. "You ran away that day. *Méchant enfant!* And you did not come back." She closed the door behind them. "But now you come. You are ready for another lesson, *eh bien?*"

Marie shook her head. She stood in Mathilde's parlor, her cloak clutched about her, feeling like a fly that has just walked into a spider's web. "I—I come to ask a favor," she stammered. "A big favor. Oh, you just got to help me!"

"Cherie!" Marie felt Mathilde's hand slide up her arm. "What is wrong? Your eyes—you have been weeping!"

"My mother! Colonel Hamilton had her arrested last night." Marie's voice broke with the strain. "Somebody accused her of spying."

"Your mother? *Ah oui,* Abigail. That plain, little woman." The blue eyes narrowed. "*Mon Dieu,* a spy? *C'est possible?*"

"She's not a spy. She signed the pledge, and she hadn't done anything. But they got her locked up in the fort. And they hang spies. I heard that once."

"Mais oui, I believe you are right. But to hang a woman! *Terrible!"*

"You got to help me!" Marie clenched her hands. "Nobody else can help like you can."

"I?" Mathilde touched her throat. "What can Mathilde do, storm the fort?" Her eyes were wide with mock innocence.

Marie sucked in her breath. "You can talk to Colonel Hamilton. You can ask him to let her go. He'll listen to you."

"To me?" Mathilde swished her hair. "And you think Henry Hamilton comes to me to listen? *Cherie,* he comes to me for one reason only."

Mathilde laughed lightly, and Marie realized that the woman was playing with her. She had the power to help Abby, but she also had her price. Soon she would name it.

"Tell me what you want," Marie pleaded. "I'll give you anything I can get from my father's warehouse. Furs, cloth, ribbons, anything you want."

"You hurt me, child. You think Mathilde Rodare would ask to be paid?" She patted Marie's shoulder, her hand lingering. "*Non,* do not fear, I will help you. I will talk with Henry, and for that I ask nothing. I do it only because I am your friend, *eh bien?*"

"You'll talk to him?" Marie clasped her hand. "And he'll listen to you?"

Mathilde shrugged. "Who can say? Sometimes a man listens to a woman. Sometimes he does not. But I will help your poor mother if I can." She let go of Marie's hands and circled her with slow steps. Her eyes were like hard, blue stones. "My poor Marie, so frightened, so tired. Do not fear, *enfant.* Surely your mother will be safe."

The room was warm. Marie felt faint with relief. Her head was swimming. "Mind if I sit down?" she asked.

Mathilde took her hand. "Lie down instead, poor child. Sleep in my bed, and when you are rested I will cook you something for breakfast." She was leading Marie into the bedroom. The soft, white sheets beckoned invitingly as she turned back the covers.

"Rest awhile," she murmured. "No more worry, eh?"

"Thank you." Marie sank gratefully into the bed. She had not slept since her mother's arrest. Fear and worry had drained the strength from her, and finally, the relief of knowing she had an ally in Mathilde had opened the floodgates of exhaustion. It was all right now. Mathilde would help her. She could rest.

"*Tiens.* I will rub your back to help you sleep." Marie felt Mathilde's weight beside her on the bed, the long, smooth hands loosening her blouse. "Turn over, *ma cher,* you cannot sleep in your clothes. Mathilde will help you."

At Mathilde's touch on her bare skin, Marie's eyes opened wide. It was happening again. She moaned softly as her buttons came loose and her skirt slipped away. Yes, she told her spinning mind, she had known all along that this was the price Mathilde would exact from her. She would not run away this time, and Mathilde knew it. She would stay, and let herself be dragged down to whatever depths the woman wanted to drag her. She would be Mathilde's toy, passive, pliant and willing. It was the only chance she had of saving her mother.

Mathilde slid under the covers beside her. "I like a man," she murmured, her breath hot in Marie's ear. "Men are strong. Men are powerful and exciting, *non?* But now and then, a change is nice . . . a change to someone small and soft and trembling, like you." Her laughter stirred Marie's hair. "It is lesson time again, *cherie,* and this time Mathilde will teach you a lesson you will remember forever."

Marie closed her eyes tightly and clenched her teeth as Mathilde's hands slid over her breasts. She wanted to claw the woman's face. She wanted to leap from the bed and run to Ned as fast as her legs could carry her. She wanted to feel safe and loved in his arms once more. But no, she would not run. She would not fight. She would stay.

"Ah, let me look at you." Mathilde pulled back the covers and studied Marie's body from where she lay, her eyes glittering. "Such a little beauty! Such lovely, golden skin. . .almost like your father's. *Magnifique!*"

Marie's eyes flew open. What had Mathilde just said? "My father? You and my father?" Her voice quivered as she sat up.

Mathilde lay back on the pillow and laughed until her whole body shook. "*Quelle enfant!* You did not know?"

"My father! My father and you!" Marie was white with shock. All this time, and she hadn't realized it. She'd thought Nancy was the woman. How could she have been such a fool?

Mathilde shook her hair, still laughing. "Your father! What a stallion! And so passionate! *Mais oui!* If I could tell you the things that man did to his Mathilde—"

Marie was on her feet now, the sheet clutched around her body. She stared at Mathilde through a red haze of fury. How could anybody be so loathsome? "Shut your mouth!" she hissed. "You—you aren't fit to say my father's name! You aren't fit to live!"

Mathilde sat up, a ghastly smile on her beautiful face. "Poor little fool. And Mathilde is not fit to speak your mother's name either? Not even into the ear of *Monsieur le Colonel?*"

Marie's heart sank like a piece of lead. And then she suddenly knew that nothing she had said to Mathilde would make any difference. It all made sense now. She picked up her clothes and began to pull them on, swiftly and angrily.

"It doesn't matter," she said. "You wouldn't help my mother anyway. You wouldn't help her because you're the one who got her arrested and locked up in the first place. You hated my father because he didn't want you anymore. And when you saw that you couldn't hurt him for it, you tried to hurt my mother and me. You tried to turn me into an animal, just like you are! You be worse than an animal! Animals don't do what you do!''

"And where are you going, *ma petite?*" Mathilde stretched her arms above her head and yawned like a cat. She had ugly teeth, from the inside. They were rotten, Marie thought, just like the rest of her was rotten inside that beautiful body. "You think you can save your mother without Mathilde? Poor little Abigail Forny. How sad, that proud neck. A rope does not leave a pretty mark, *vraiment?*"

Mathilde laughed. Marie ran from her laughter. She ran out of the front door, slamming it behind her. Down the front walk she flew, out the gate and into the street. Her lungs gulped the cold, clean air.

She had to find Ned. Maybe he couldn't do anything to help, but Marie's burden of fear was so heavy that she could not carry it alone. She had to talk to him, to tell him she had been wrong about so many things, to feel his arms around her.

Since the day of the pledge signing he had spent a good deal of time at the Busseron house. She would go there, Marie resolved. Even if she did not find Ned, who but the captain and Cecile could help her think of a way to save Abby?

She turned her steps swiftly up the road toward their house, almost running, her eyes on the ground. So it was that she did not see the small group of people clustered in front of the tavern until she had nearly run into them.

The four who'd landed in the canoe earlier that morning, the renegade, the squaw and the two braves, stood arguing with one of the British privates. The renegade, whose back was turned toward Marie, had a bloodstained leather bag over his arm. He kept pointing to it and gesturing with one long, skinny hand.

"I know Colonel Hamilton usually pays for those things," the scarlet-coated private was arguing with him. "But, Lord, you mustn't bring 'em right into town with you. It's different in Detroit. The people are used to things like that. But here in Vincennes we don't want people nervous, understand?"

"I don't understand nothin'. Just tell me where I can find his highness the hair-buyer an' I'll be off." The renegade's twangy voice caught Marie's attention. It was almost as if she'd heard it before. But the man was clearly a stranger. His dark hair curled into his eyes and hung down over his shoulders in greasy strings. His beard, seen from the side, was thick and matted. Still he looked young. He was tall and very thin. The squaw stood close to him, her small eyes fierce and possessive. His woman, Marie decided. The two braves, Kickapoo, probably, judging by their dress, looked enough like her to be her brothers.

"By hell, we come all the way from up north with these here scalps," the renegade protested. "An' we ain't leavin' till we gets our pay for 'em!" He held the bag open. The private looked gingerly inside.

"My God, you took all those?" he asked, eyeing the man with amazement.

"Me? Hell, no. These two bucks, they got some of 'em. And their friends got the rest. Me, I don't take no scalps, less'n I have to. Only help sell 'em for a split o' the proceeds, y' see."

The young redcoat shuddered visibly. "All right. The colonel's in the fort. Get on up there. But keep that bloody bag under cover. The next time you've got scalps, man, take them to Detroit!"

"Thankee!" The renegade chuckled. As he swung around to go, his eye caught sight of Marie standing a few yards away in the street. He stared at her, blinking.

"By damn! By hot, bloody damn! If it ain't Marie Forny!"

Marie gasped. Under the greasy, unkempt hair, behind the matted beard, the face that grinned down at her was Ike Ilam's.

XXIII

Marie reached through the bars of the cell and gripped her mother's hands. "I ran," she said in a choked voice. "When I saw it was Ike, I just turned 'round and ran!"

"You're sure it was Ike?"

"It was him. He knew me."

In the past ten minutes of the quarter hour allowed for visiting the prisoners, Marie had made an open confession to her mother. The full truth about Ike Ilam, the alleged Indian attack, and Mathilde Rodare had all come tumbling out. "You don't know how good it feels to have somebody know it all," she whispered tearfully.

"Growing up is harder for some than for others," Abby soothed. "I reckon you've had a harder time of it than most. You're learning, Marie. And you're growing into a woman."

"I swore I'd never think 'bout Ike again. It was hard not to think 'bout him, but I tried. I almost had him licked, Mother. Then he came back."

"Ned doesn't know?"

Marie shook her head. "I don't see Ned much now that he's with the Yankees. Maybe—" She caught her breath— "Maybe he doesn't love me anymore."

"He's only trying to protect you. I know Ned. He wouldn't want you hurt because of what he believes."

"If only I knew that for sure!" Marie held Abby's hands tighter. Under the rules of the fort, prisoners were allowed two short visits a week. This was the first time Marie had seen her mother since the night of the arrest, now three days past. Abby's cell was small and dingy. Mice poked in and out of the straw that covered the floor. A foul-smelling wooden bucket sat in the far corner. No provision had been made for the kind of privacy a decent woman should have.

"Have they hurt you?" Marie asked softly, trying to keep the tears out of her voice.

"No. And they feed me all right. I just wish—" Abby struggled with her composure— "I just wish there was some word from your father!"

"He's been late afore. He'll come. But what about you? Do you know if they'll give you a trial?"

Abby smiled bitterly. "There won't be any trial. There isn't any evidence. That Rodare creature wasn't smart enough to fix any up. Under British law they can't hang me without a trial. But they can keep me waiting here for a long, long time."

"Captain Busseron's trying to figure out a way to get you out of here—"

"Hush! Somebody might hear you! Tell the captain that I'm quite well. I don't want to be free at the peril of somebody's life. There'll be time, Marie."

The guard was strolling their way, his eyes on his pocket watch. Marie knew their time was almost up.

"Take care," Abby squeezed her hands. "Don't fret for me. Worry about yourself. You understand, honey?"

"Aye." Marie pressed her mother's hand to her cheek. The guard was already tapping her shoulder. "I'll be back soon."

Marie walked out through the fort. The place had changed since the first time she'd seen it. Hamilton had repaired and reinforced the walls. The old dry well had been cleaned out and deepened so that it once more flowed with water. And the guns seemed to be everywhere, their blue-black barrels gleaming in the morning sun. Henry Hamilton himself was out inspecting the parapets, a resplendent figure in his spotless uniform and white-powdered wig. Marie wondered if he'd really paid Ike for the scalps he'd brought.

She glanced warily about her, a swiftly-growing habit. Ike, to her dismay, had not yet left Vincennes. She had seen him several times, strolling up the street with his squaw behind him. Always he smiled at her and tipped his filthy coonskin cap in a mockery of fine manners. Sometimes he even spoke: "How-de-do, Mistress Forny! Fine day! Must say you be better dressed 'n when I saw ye last in Pitt!"

Marie never answered Ike, but her blood boiled with rage and shame every time she saw him. She felt fear as well, like ice, deep in her bones. She had caused Ike to leave Pitt. He had every reason to hate her. And he seemed to be biding his time, playing on her nerves, waiting for a chance to take his revenge.

As Marie walked toward the gate she passed the tall form of the Indian chief named Tobacco's Son, the one known as the Grand Door of the Wabash. Marie had seen him many times before, for the Piankeshaw village was not far from Vincennes, and the chief had become a great friend of the American captain, Leonard Helm. Now that Helm was a prisoner, Tobacco's Son came to the fort every day, declaring to the British that as Helm's brother he would be their prisoner, too. They made an odd pair, the grizzled, tobacco-spitting Helm and the stately, middle-aged chief who followed him about the fort like a shadow, every day, for as long as he was allowed to remain.

Marie saw Helm now, ambling out from behind Hamilton's quarters. On an impulse she stood beside the Piankeshaw chief and waited as Helm crossed the compound.

"Mistress Forny," Helm tipped his cap to Marie and raised his palm in greeting to Tobacco's Son. "Bin t' see your ma, I reckon, little lady. Damned shame, lockin' up a fine woman like that."

"Cap'n Helm, my mother isn't a spy. She didn't do nothing."

"Hush, gal, I know that. Ain't nobody in their right mind would believe she had."

"Then what can we do? How can we get her out of here?"

"Ain't no easy way, that be for sure. But she be safe where she's at for the time bein', so don't ye go frettin' yourself none. Best we jest bide our time. Cunnel George Rogers Clark ain't one t' leave things sit when they ain't right. One o' these days, little gal, you'll look out through them trees, and there he'll be, a-comin' up the hill with a whole army. Nothin' stops ol' George. You'll see."

Marie reached for his rough hand and held it between hers. "Will you see to my mother, Cap'n? Will you make sure she gets enough to eat? And the soldiers—"

"Hush, gal. I already be seein' t' your ma. She be fine. An' if any redcoat so much as touches one hair of her head, he'll have me t' reckon with! No need fer you t' fret none."

"I'm much obliged." Marie released his hand. "Thank you, Cap'n."

"No frettin' now. Remember." Helm winked reassuringly, then he strolled off in the direction of the well, the Piankeshaw chief following.

Marie's step was lighter as she passed through the gate of the fort. At least Abby was all right, and Leonard Helm had promised to watch out for her. There was time, at least, to work out some kind of plan to free her.

Marie remembered what Helm had said about George Rogers Clark. When she looked out through the trees at the vast sheet of water that the Wabash had become, she found herself wishing fervently for the sight of Yankee canoes, a whole fleet of them, bringing Clark's troops to storm the town. By heaven, she thought, she could almost take a musket and blow Henry Hamilton's head off herself!

"Well, I'll be," she whispered out loud. She was becoming a Yankee herself. Almost as much of a Yankee as Ned. It was her war now.

The sudden urge to see Ned, to tell him all about her new feelings, almost swept her away. She wanted to run down the hill, to run to wherever Ned was, and throw her arms around him.

It was then she saw the slender, dark form of Aspasie coming up the street toward her. The girl caught sight of her and hurried her steps.

Aspasie was almost out of breath by the time she reached Marie. "Monsieur Ned," she whispered in her birdlike voice. "He wishes you to come at once."

"Where?" Marie felt her heart beating faster. This was like a wish coming true, Ned wanting to see her just when she was thinking about him.

"The warehouse of your father. By the river. He is waiting." Aspasie chirped her message, then flitted off in the direction of her mistress's house. "Hurry!" She glanced back over her shoulder and was gone.

Marie almost ran down to the warehouse, her cloak flying out behind her. Ned would be there. Everything would be all right now. Even the day was going to be beautiful, the sky clear and blue and cold, the flooded river crusted with a thin frosting of ice that glittered in the sunlight.

She could see the warehouse through the trees. Ned was waiting, dressed in his buckskins and the same kind of fur-lined coat that Edward Forny wore in cold weather. Marie waved to him as she hurried down the hill.

"Ned!" She ran toward him, but the expression in his eyes stopped her short.

"What's the matter?" she asked, suddenly fearful.

Ned looked down at the ground. "You been to see your ma? Is she all right?"

"Yes—" Marie gazed at him. He could not meet her eyes. "What be the matter, Ned?"

He kicked at a loose piece of crusted snow with a moccasined foot. "Marie, we got to talk. I got to ask you somethin'."

Marie waited for him to continue, a feeling of blackness hanging over her like a storm cloud.

"I ain't got no right to ask you this," he said slowly. "If you don't want to tell me 'bout it, that be fine. But I got to know."

"What is it?" Marie whispered.

"I saw Ike Ilam today," he said, and her heart sank. "He be renegade now, travelin' with a squaw and her two brothers."

"Aye. I saw him, too. I know," Marie admitted.

"Marie, he be sayin' things. Things 'bout you an' him. Awful things that a proper man wouldn't say 'bout no girl, even if they be true."

Now it was Marie who stood with her eyes on the snow. She could not look at Ned. She wished the ground would crack open and swallow her up.

"You don't have to explain less'n you want to," Ned continued in a low voice. "Just answer yes or no, an' I won't ask you no more. Marie, you been with him?"

"You be too good for me, Ned." Marie uttered, turning away from him. It was done now. She'd lost Ned forever.

"Then it be true?" Ned waited.

A harsh laugh shattered the stillness. "Hell, yes, it be true, all of it! Just ask 'er!" The snow crunched as Ike Ilam stepped around the corner of the warehouse. "Just ask 'er, Cooper. Ask 'er how Ike Ilam got 'er cherry! Ask 'er how she just laid there on 'er back an' opened up them purty white legs, just as willin' as ye please!" He cackled with laughter. "Go on, Cooper! Ask 'er how she liked it! Ask 'er what she yelled when we wuz a-doin' it!" His voice went high in imitation of a girl's. " 'Oh, ram me, Ike! Ram me hard!' That be what she hollered! An that be the truth, don't it, Marie Forny!"

Marie pressed her hands against her face. With a sound

that was part sob, part gasp, part scream, she spun away and began to run around the warehouse where Ike had come from, toward the river.

She had it in her mind to run into the water, where she would surely drown or freeze. But her eyes were blinded by tears. She could not see where she was going. She ran headlong into something soft and solid, a buckskin-covered body that smelled of smoke and rancid grease. Strong hands grasped her arms. She blinked her eyes hard and realized that she was looking up into the face of one of Ike's Indian companions.

The Indian dragged her roughly back around the corner of the warehouse where Ike stood facing Ned. The other brave and the squaw, who would have been pretty except for a pair of small, hard, squinting eyes, followed them.

"Hold 'er!" Ike growled at the Indian. "Now, Miss hoity-toity Forny, ye can watch whiles I make hash out o' yer sweetie here. Then he can watch an' see how well ye likes it this time!" He laughed through his beard. "I be bettern' before. Got me a good teacher, I did!" He jerked his head toward the squaw and winked lewdly.

"Come on, Cooper!" Ike moved toward Ned, dancing lightly on the balls of his feet. "That little gal of ours moves like a mink! Or maybe ye already done found it out like I did!"

Ned rushed him, his fists and body propelled more by rage than by judgment. Ike sidestepped skillfully. Ned's punch barely grazed his jaw. Ike turned expertly and landed a hard jab to Ned's midsection. The blow almost knocked Ned flat, but the shock of it cooled his blind rage and brought him back to reality.

He backed off, giving himself time to regain his balance and catch the breath Ike had knocked out of him.

Slowly, cautiously now, the two of them circled each other while the buck held Marie by the arms and the other two Indians watched.

Marie's eyes were on Ned. He was not as tall as Ike, though he was more solidly built. Ike, however, was clearly the more experienced fighter of the two. And Ike wouldn't fight fair. Marie knew that. Out of the corner of her eye she saw the one Kickapoo brave fingering the red handle of his knife. Henry Hamilton had given out knives like that as gifts to the Indians. That knife, she knew, had been used, and the brown-skinned devil would not hesitate to use it on Ned. Marie was suddenly wild with fear for him.

"Don't fight him, Ned," she cried out, trying to twist away from the Indian's steel-like grasp. "I ain't worth it!"

Ned did not answer her. All his attention was focused on Ike as he crouched and circled, his fists ready.

"Go on away, Ned," Marie cried desperately. "It all be true, what Ike said! An' it be Ike I want!" She struggled frantically to break loose. "Ike, don't fight him. Let him go! I'll do anything! I'll go away with you—"

Ike grinned. "Oh, lackety day, just listen to her now! Wantin' it agin! You be gettin' it good, Marie Forny, soon's I finish with yer hot-headed friend!"

Ned made his move then, diving in with a sharp punch to Ike's chin. Ike wheeled and staggered, then regained his footing and retaliated with a blow that glanced off Ned's shoulder.

Then they flew together like two roosters, punching, swinging, rolling in the dirty snow. Marie watched helplessly while the one brave held her, the other toyed with his knife, and the squaw whooped encouragement.

There was blood on Ned's face, and Ike's left eye had begun to puff. He grunted as the force of Ned's body crunched into his belly. His hand caught a wad of Ned's hair and he jerked hard, swinging Ned's head up so that he could get another punch at his face. Then in one swift, startling movement, Ned shifted under him. Ike spun in the air and slammed into the snow on his back. In a flash Ned was on top of him, pinning him down, his fists pounding into Ike's face.

Ike twisted in the bloody snow. His eyes were wild under the shaggy mop of dark hair. "Help me!" he gasped at the Indian. "Damn you all to hell, get him off me!"

Marie screamed as the red-handled knife flashed. In another instant the brave had Ned's arm pinioned behind his back, the knife at his throat.

Ike scooted backward in the snow and sat up, a leering grin on his battered face.

"Kill?" The Indian pressed the sharp edge of the knife blade against Ned's jugular vein.

Ike laughed as he stood up. "Not yet. Later, mebbe. Fer now, ye just hold 'im. Over there, with the knife, just like you got 'im. Now fer you, Mistress Forny. Ol' Crow Feather there, he got a mighty jumpy hand. Ye do just like I tell ye, or that hand just might jump the wrong way!" He nodded at the Indian who held Marie. "Let 'er go!"

Marie twisted loose and fell into the snow at Ike's feet. "Ike, don't hurt him," she begged. "Ain't nothin' I won't do if you just let him go."

"Stand up." Ike's eyes glittered in their puffy slits. "Now, Mistress high and mighty Forny, ye can give me a kiss!" He pulled Marie to her feet. His arms jerked her hard against him and his swollen lips ground onto hers.

She tasted grease, and blood. "Aw, hell, that hurts good!" He kissed her again, hands ranging over her body this time, reaching down to clasp her buttocks through her skirt. He held her there like that, moving his body up and down until Marie could feel him almost bursting against her. "Unbutton yer blouse," he growled. "Lemme see them tits agin!"

"Don't do it, Marie." Ned stood with Crow Feather's knife at his throat. His face was pale.

"Do it!" Ike rasped. "Do it, or by hell ye'll be lickin' yer friend's blood up off the snow!"

Marie slipped each button out of its hole, her cold-numbed hands shaking. When she had reached her waist, Ike grasped the cloth band that covered her breasts and jerked it loose.

"There they be, Cooper. Have a look! Y' ever see such purty li'l tits?" He turned Marie in Ned's direction. "Just look! Cold they be. Just lookit the way them nips is all scrunched up. Like li'l berries!" He laughed and pinched one with his hand. Ned strained against the knife. "Keerful, Cooper. Ye don't rile ol' Crow Feather if ye know what be good for ye!"

Marie stood shivering with cold and humiliation. Her arms crept up to cross over her breasts, hiding them. She felt hot tears of shame forming in her eyes, cooling on her cheeks.

"Put that there cloak on the ground," Ike ordered. "Ain't no featherbed, but it'll have t' do, I reckon. Go on! Be ye quick 'bout it!"

Marie untied her cloak at the neck and let it slide to the snow. Ike kicked it with his foot to spread it out. "Now," Ike grinned through his beard. "Get ye down on yer back, Marie Forny. Get ye down and get yer skirt up

285

and yer legs out, and ye begs for it! Beg, damn ye, or I turn Crow Feather loose on yer friend. Crow Feather, he can carve a body up real purty!"

Ned groaned. "No, Marie! Don't do it, no matter what! I'd sooner let the devil kill me!" He jerked to one side. Crow Feather pressed the knife tighter. A thin, red line appeared on Ned's throat.

"Please, Ike—" Marie was sobbing now.

"Get ye down! You and yer high-falutin' family! Thought Ike Ilam weren't good enough fer ye, eh? Thought I be dirt! *Get ye down!* He flung Marie roughly onto the cloak, knelt down, and jerked up her skirt. "Aw, that be better now. All right, let's hear ye beg fer it, Marie Forny! *Beg!*"

"Please Ike," Marie's head twisted back and forth in her anguish. "Let us go. Don't—"

Ike's sharp slap cut off her words. "I said *beg* fer it!" He fumbled with the flap of his breeches with cold, swollen hands. It fell loose at last, and he crouched over her, exposed and ready. Out of the corner of her eye, Marie glimpsed Ned struggling against the knife and Crow Feather's arm-twisting grasp.

"Ilam, you bastard," Ned rasped, "fight me like a man! Kill me if ye want, but don't shame her that way! Ye do an' so help me, I'll kill you someday! I'll kill you, an' ye'll know it's me, and ye'll know why!"

Ike ignored him. "You beg fer it, Mistress Forny. Open up them legs an' beg me t' stick it in ye! That's what I want t' hear!"

Marie closed her eyes and set her mouth. "Go on," she muttered. "Get it over with! But let him go, Ike!"

"That ain't beggin! Tell me how much ye want it! Tell me!"

"Ike, please—" Marie lay rigid beneath him. With a snort of exasperation he jerked her legs apart. She felt his blunt, hot probing—

"No!" With a desperate lunge, Ned crashed an elbow into the big Indian's gut. Crow Feather grunted and doubled over, but he did not loose his hold on Ned's arm. Snapping him painfully back around to face him, the Indian raised his red-handled knife. Marie heard herself screaming. Then a sudden shot rang out.

Crow Feather staggered and dropped the knife, then fell to his knees in the snow, clutching at his bleeding shoulder. In a flash Ned was at Marie's side, shoving the startled Ike backward, lifting her up in his arms.

Capt. Francois de Busseron stood at the edge of the clearing, a smoking pistol in his hand. Just behind him, a flint-tipped arrow in his bow, was the tall Piankeshaw chief, Tobacco's Son.

"The sound of that shot should bring half of Vincennes down here on the run," the captain said calmly. "And even if it doesn't, monsieur, my friend here can have an arrow in you before you can try any tricks. Ned, you get yourself and Marie behind us."

Ned had pulled Marie to her feet and flung his coat around her. She ran with him across the clearing to where the captain and the chief stood side by side.

"How. . .how did you—?" Marie gasped.

"How did we know you were in trouble?" The captain reloaded his pistol while Tobacco's Son held Ike and the three Indians at bay with his bow and arrow. "It was Aspasie. Curious little creature that she is, she followed you, Marie. When she saw that you two might be in danger, she ran back to get help. The chief here was coming out of the fort just as we passed." He pointed the loaded pistol in Ike's direction.

"As for you and your friend, monsieur, raping a young girl is a crime under any flag. You ought to be damned thankful I got here in time to save you from it. Show your face in Vincennes, any of you, and I report you to the authorities myself. Now, *allez!* Get going, and don't come back!" He glanced contemptuously at Crow Feather, who was standing now, his teeth clenched in pain. "Your friend will live, I think. Pity. I should have aimed lower."

Ike turned to go. "I won't be forgettin' this, Cooper. You watch out fer me, an' you too, Mistress Forny. Some day Ike Ilam'll be right behind ye, and then ye'll be sorry." He spat on the ground.

They moved off in a line, the four of them, going down toward the landing where they had left the canoe. Only the squaw, who was the last to leave, turned to look back. The look she flashed Marie was one of pure animal hatred.

It was over. Marie buried her face in her hands. Her whole body was quivering violently, but strangely there were no more tears. She could not even make them come.

She was safe. Ned was safe. But she had lost him, that much was sure. He knew everything now, how she had gone to Ike, how she'd let Ike do what he wanted, even what she'd yelled as the craziness swept over her. Ned had always thought she was so special. Well, he knew better now. Ike Ilam had seen to that.

"Marie." She heard Ned's gentle voice behind her. "Marie, be you hurt?"

Marie could not look at him. She turned her back and walked away. After a moment Captain de Busseron followed her.

"You're all right, Marie?" he asked, moving to her side.

"Aye. He didn't harm me."

"Good. I'm glad of that, because we have another problem to deal with, and we may have to move fast."

Something in the gravity of his voice struck Marie. She turned to him, her eyes wide with concern. "My mother. . ."

"I'd meant to speak to you before you left the house this morning. Your mother doesn't know this, Marie, but we have it on good authority from someone inside the fort that Hamilton is planning to bring her to trial."

Marie suddenly felt weak. "And if she's made out to be guilty?"

There was anguish in the good captain's eyes. "I won't lie to you, Marie," he said. "If your mother's found guilty, there's a good chance she'll be sentenced to hang."

XXIV

Edward Forny stood in the ranks that had formed up before the Church of the Immaculate Conception in Kaskaskia and wondered if he had lost his mind like the rest of them. To march nearly one hundred seventy miles in the dead of winter over a flooded, frozen landscape, and then to take Vincennes from the British with a force of less than two hundred men—it was madness, he concluded. But he was here. Like everyone else in this pathetic little army, he had fallen under the spell of George Rogers Clark.

At first Edward had been determined to set out for Vincennes alone. His family needed him, and he was anxious about their safety. "But what can you do for them, Forny?" Clark had argued with him. One man by himself—you'd be damned lucky even to get through, with Hamilton's scalp-hunting Indians prowling the woods. And what would you accomplish even if you succeeded?

One man alone. You'd be no better off than the rest of those poor devils that Hamilton's got under his thumb. March with us. A man like you would be worth ten of the regular militia!"

So Edward had stayed, cursing the inevitable delays that sprang up. Even now, while Father Gibault blessed and absolved the little army, he shifted his feet impatiently, anxious to begin the march. A sense of urgency tugged at him, as it had constantly in the frustrating days that had just passed. He had to get to Vincennes. In some very desperate way, he sensed he was needed there.

George Rogers Clark stood beside the slender priest, a towering figure in his blue Continental Army uniform. His hair blazed like a torch. A long saber hung at his belt. Before the priest's blessing, he had delivered a thundering oration that stirred his men to a frenzy of wild whooping and cheering. The man should have been a general, Edward thought. He should have ridden his dappled stallion at the head of an army of ten thousand men, for he was worthy of it. He had the genius and fire of an Alexander. But this—Edward glanced around him and sighed. This ragtag little troop was all the army Clark had. About half the men had come west with Clark from Virginia and Kentucky. Still dressed in their buckskins, they were tough, hard and trail-wise. Their devotion to Clark was total. The rest of the force consisted of volunteers from Cahokia, Kaskaskia, and the surrounding countryside. They were little more than farmers, most of them, their strength and loyalty still untried.

A number of men had been sent on ahead by river, aboard a large galley, the *Willing*, well-equipped with guns and commanded by a Captain Rogers, who was Clark's cousin. The *Willing* was to move on Vincennes after the beginning of the surprise attack by land, to provide support and firepower. But the river route, down the Mississippi, up the Ohio and the Wabash, was long and difficult. With timing so critical, Edward could not help feeling that the big boat's arrival could not be counted upon in time for the attack.

Father Gibault stood on a raised platform, intoning in his rich Latin the final phrases of the blessing. Edward crossed himself with the others, something he had not done in years. He had left the church behind him in France. His busy life in America had given him precious little time for religion. But today Edward had the sense of having come full circle. The blessing was welcome. All of them would need it.

Clark nodded at last to the lively young boy he had recruited as a drummer. The lad raised his sticks and began a rousing tattoo that stiffened the spines of all who listened. Then, at a sharp command, they were off.

The people of Kaskaskia lined the street, cheering, waving and weeping. Mothers held their babies up for what might be the last sight of their fathers. The pretty, red-haired girl who worked in the tavern broke loose from the crowd, flung herself into Joe Bowman's arms, and kissed him lingeringly on the mouth. Edward smiled to himself. It appeared that language had been no barrier between those two after all.

The day was crisp, but not cold. The sun shone out through the clouds. The soft, steady drip of melting snow filled the air like a gentle counterpoint to the beating of the drum. The date was February fifth, and an early thaw was upon the land. Edward scowled down at the mud that was already sticking to his moccasins and wished for frozen ground. A biting cold would be less of a danger than this cursed thaw. The rivers would be swollen, spreading in great sheets across the lowlands. And whatever other powers Clark might have, he could not walk on water.

Edward shifted his shoulders to even the weight of his pack. Two, more likely three weeks of marching lay ahead of them, nights of sleeping on soggy ground, meals consisting of whatever they could hunt, find, or steal. "Madness!" he muttered under his breath. *"Folie!"* Here was Edward Forny, trudging off on a near-suicidal mission to help fight a war in which he had never meant to become involved. Once he had thought that remaining neutral was the answer to everything. He was a trader, not a soldier or politician. What a joke life had played on him!

One of the men started up a song to the rhythm of the drum. Soon the entire company had joined in, swinging their arms in time.

> *Here I sit on Buttermilk Hill*
> *Who could blame me cry my fill.*
> *And ev'ry tear would turn a mill;*
> *Johnny's gone for a soldier.*
> *Shoolie, shoolie, shoolit, too.*
> *Shoolie, sacaracca biba libba boo.*
> *If I should die for Sally Bobolink, come*
>   *bibba libba boo sa ro ra*

They marched only three miles that day, ferried across the Kaskaskia River, and made their camp on a wooded rise. Half a dozen men took the horses hunting and came back loaded with deer, rabbits and grouse. That night they ate their fill, laughing and singing around the campfires until the moon was high.

"*Ma foi,* you'd think they were on a picnic," Edward remarked to Clark as he passed the colonel's camping place.

Clark sucked at his pipe. "Give them their fun, Forny. Let them feast and act like boys while they can. It's no picnic they'll be having in the days to come. I know it. You know it. And I've a feeling they know it too."

A week later, after slogging endless miles in mud and water up to their ankles, they faced their first major obstacle. A branch of the Wabash lay before them, spread in a gray, tree-dotted sheet across the valley. Clark stood on a hill and gazed down on it, scratching the red stubble on his chin. "How deep you reckon it to be, Forny?"

Edward shrugged as he strained his eyes to see the distant blur of land across the water. "If we had a boat, maybe we could find a ford."

"A boat? We'll build one!" Clark declared, and within minutes the men were busy felling a tall, stout tree to be hollowed out into a pirogue. "They ought to be done tomorrow," Clark said, taking Edward aside. "Forny, pick your men and take the boat out, with some long poles. Find the channel and mark it if you can. Then get us a look at the territory on the other side. I don't need to tell you to look for some spot of land where we can rest. If there be none. . ." Clark paused and stared out through the trees at the wide, gloomy stretch of water. The ring of axes echoed behind him. The sky was clouding up. They'd had rain the day before, and there was not a man who was not soaked to the skin. "If there be no land 'twixt here and the far shore, then we'll be in the water all night."

Edward felt more in his own element the next day as he paddled the pirogue through the flooded woods, though the wind was cold, and his clothes felt as if they would never be dry again. Behind him in the boat, the two Kentuckians who'd come with him tested the depth of the water with long poles. In most places it was at least waist deep. The main river channel ran close to the west bank, where the troops were camped. Edward swiftly concluded that it would be possible to ferry the men across it a few at a time in the pirogue and deposit them on the other side, where the water was maybe three feet deep. They would have to wade the rest of the way.

By early afternoon they had found a small, brush-covered island. Edward breathed his thanks as they marked the route by cutting blazes on the trees. Some of the men were already sick. They would not be able to stand a day and a night in the icy water.

With the islands marked, they paddled the boat swiftly across the lowlands to a wooded ridge. From there, Edward calculated, it might be possible to see the condition of the valley of the Wabash. "Bring back a good report," Clark had instructed him earlier that day. "No matter how bleak it looks out there, I must have something to encourage the men. They must not lose hope."

Edward remembered those words as he mounted the ridge. At least they had found the island, he reminded himself. That alone would serve as an encouragement. But if he could report that the Wabash Valley was passable, that there was some kind of easy route to Vincennes, then he could return with good news to Clark and the little band of men.

Through the trees he caught the gleam of winter sun on the surface of water. He hurried forward until the woods parted and he could see all the way to the horizon.

He stopped short. The distant Wabash was one vast

lake that covered the land with its cold, gray water for miles, almost as far as Edward's eyes could see. Somewhere on the other side lay Vincennes.

They crossed the first stretch of water the next day, the troops laughing and singing to keep up their courage as they pushed out into the flood. The sick men rode in the pirogue. The little drummer boy balanced himself bellydown on his floating drum and paddled along like a dog. Edward kept his rifle and powder high. The water swirled around his waist as he moved forward, so cold that after a few minutes his feet and legs were completely numb. It took all his will power just to keep them moving.

Clark splashed along just ahead of him, his head a red beacon to the men who followed him. "Only a little way more," he shouted back over his shoulder. "Take good advantage, men, there's not a one of us who doesn't need a good bath today!"

Joe Bowman, Clark's second in command, seemed to be everywhere at once. He moved among the men, encouraging the weary, speeding up the stragglers. Edward's respect for the young man grew by the hour as they trudged along through the icy current.

Miraculously they had reached the island by evening, still in high spirits. The men built roaring fires and roasted what was left of the previous day's meat. Some of them stripped and made a pitiful effort to dry their clothes. Most of them did not bother. They stretched out on the damp ground and fell into exhausted sleep.

"Forny—" The harsh whisper cut through Edward's slumber like a knife. He opened his eyes to find Clark's massive silhouette looming above him in the moonlight. He sat up.

"Come with me, down by the river where we can talk

without the men hearing us." Clark straightened to his full height and moved off, silent as a shadow. Edward had joined him at the water's edge a moment later.

"What do you think, Forny?" Clark stared out at the silvery flood. "We've come this far, and you've already given me your report on what's ahead. But what do you really think?"

Edward shivered in the damp cold. His clothes crackled with frost when he moved. "It's flooded most of the way from here," he said. "You got only a taste of it today. After tomorrow it's going to be worse. There'll be no promise of land to rest on at night. And there's no food. The game's all gone to higher country or drowned. We didn't see so much as a squirrel yesterday. How are our supplies?"

"Gone." Clark shook his head.

"It's not a pleasant way to die, *mon colonel.*"

"By damn, Forny, we can't even think of that! I can't let a one of those lads think we won't make it, or they'll all give up! It's not death we're marching to, man, it's Hamilton the Hair-buyer! It's Hamilton I've got to dangle in front of them like a carrot on a stick, not food, not rest! If they've nothing else to march on, they'll march on hate and glory!"

Edward studied Clark's face in the moonlight, the high, stony planes of his cheekbones, the well-formed nose and the heavy, thrusting jaw that gave his features an air of total determination. I am looking at one of the greatest heroes this country will ever know, he thought. Either that, or I am looking at a madman!

Hour by hour the days ground on, one, then two. The men moved without thinking now, slogging blindly ahead, one step, then another, through the swirling, icy water. Edward was one of the strongest. Yet even he had begun to wonder each morning if he would end the day lying dead in the flooded river. The cold and the agony of movement drained the strength of the men, and there was no food to replace it. They moved on, their bodies consuming their own flesh.

Twice the day before, Edward had taken the pirogue and paddled up and down in a wandering course that failed to find land or any other sign of life. They had spent that night in the water, moving like sleepwalkers through the blackness, their minds and bodies dead to everything but hunger and pain. Even the hardened veterans who had been with Clark were almost too weary to speak. As for the volunteers, they were in a state of total despair. Many of them were ill. They staggered through the water, supported by the stronger men or riding by turns in the pirogue.

On the morning of the second day without food, a large number of them collapsed on the thin ridge of land where they'd spent a cold, rainy night, refusing to move.

"They cain't go 'nother step," Joe Bowman reported to his commander. "They're sayin' it'll kill 'em to try."

Clark's face darkened like a storm cloud. He had spent the days marching at the head of his men while his horse carried supplies. He was as weary as any of them. "By all heaven, they'll die for sure if they stay here! Bowman, Forny, take your rifles and herd the poor devils into the water!" His eyes narrowed. "Shoot any man who hangs back!"

Edward, who had already waded into the stream, dragged his legs back onto the land again. His rifle felt so heavy that it was all he could do to hold it steady. "On your feet!" Bowman barked at the men who clustered on the shore. "On your feet, you sluggards. Last man in the water gits a bullet through his head!"

Muttering, the men struggled to their feet. *Mon Dieu*, Edward thought, what if I have to shoot someone? He followed Bowman's example, walking from one man to another, shouting rough words of encouragement, prodding their backsides with the butt of his rifle. *"Allons-y!"* He forced himself to laugh. "Let's go! It's a fine day for a bath, eh?"

"Bath!" Bowman grinned, his face as gaunt as a skull. "We be goin' duck huntin'! And the name of the duck be Hamilton the Hair-buyer! Git ye goin'!" He prodded the last of the men into the water and they were off again.

Step by agonizing step they dragged themselves through icy water that swirled as deep as their armpits, or even the chins of the shorter men. Toward midday it began to rain. The downpour closed around the little party like a gloomy curtain. The men were already completely soaked by the river, but the rain seemed to penetrate their very spirits with its cold wetness. Hunger gnawed at their insides. One of the Kaskaskia volunteers, a stooped, wiry little man, began to whimper softly with each step. The sound mingled with the steady drizzle of the rain.

"By heaven, what's this, a funeral procession?" George Rogers Clark broke his stride to shout back at them. "Here, Sergeant DeWit!" He beckoned to a tall, husky Virginian, an affable fellow who was a great favorite with the men. "Take our drummer boy here up on your shoulders—aye, like that. And here's the drum. Now, we'll make a parade of it, lads. Forward, to the drum!"

The crisp tattoo of the *charge* echoed above the rain as the boy drummed with a fury. The exhausted marchers raised their heads and moved forward. Joe Bowman began to sing, the words keeping rhythm with the drumbeats.

*Oh, my name was William Kidd, as I sailed, as
   I sailed.*
My name was William Kidd as I sailed.
*My name was William Kidd, God's laws I did
   forbid,*
And most wickedly I did, as I sailed, as I sailed.

The men took up the song, half-heartedly at first, then with a rousing enthusiasm that almost brought tears to Edward's eyes. He did not know the song himself, but he sang along as best he could. When Bowman began again, substituting Henry Hamilton's name for the infamous Kidd's, the exhausted soldiers almost shouted out the words.

By nightfall they had lost even the strength to sing. They staggered along through the blinding rain, falling from one foot to the other. There was no food and no place to rest. They could only continue on, step by step, following the sound of the drum in the darkness. It was that or lie down and die in the water.

The night was half gone when Edward, who was helping Bowman mind the stragglers, heard a shout up ahead. "Land! Thank God, land!"

The men surged forward. The land proved to be nothing more than a tiny, bare knoll, emerging just inches above the line of the water. By the time they had all pulled themselves onto it, collapsing where they stood, there was barely enough room for all the men to lie down. But at least it was land. They laid their heads on the soaked ground and slept the sleep of dead men.

Edward dreamed of Abby's face. She was reaching for him through a strange, blue mist. He caught her hands and let her pull him up to her. She was warm and soft and fragrant. Her loose hair twisted around him. Her clothes seemed to float away, and then they were both naked, tumbling ecstatically among the soft clouds. She laughed, and suddenly he realized that it was not Abby in his arms, but Mathilde Rodare. With hands as powerful as a man's, she seized him and thrust him inside her body, moaning and twisting like some devil witch. He fought her, but she was too strong for him. He felt his own passion mounting as she jerked back and forth. He could not control himself. . . .

Something seemed to burst in Edward's head with a loud bang as the dream vanished. Edward opened his eyes. It was dawn. The rain had stopped. The other men were stirring, muttering with excitement.

There had been a noise, he remembered, forcing his starved mind to concentrate. Yes, it had awakened him, that loud but distant bang. It must have awakened the others, too. What was it?

Then, as Edward rubbed his eyes and stretched himself awake, he suddenly knew.

It was the morning gun at Fort Sackville. They were within hearing distance of Vincennes.

XXV

The trial of Abigail Forny was held inside Fort Sackville, with Henry Hamilton presiding as judge. It was not until the following day that the verdict became known in Vincennes. Enough evidence had been produced to find Abby guilty as charged. Hamilton had condemned her to be hanged, the sentence to be carried out in three days' time.

It was Leonard Helm who guided the near hysterical Marie into a quiet corner of the fort compound and explained to her the details of the trial. "It wuz a sham!" he said. " 'Tweren't a man there but what didn't know the whole thing was one big lie from start t' finish!' "

Marie gripped Helm's arm for support. She had heard the news in the street, as she was heading up to the fort to visit her mother. "But there wasn't no proof," she whispered unbelievingly. "How could they have proof when she didn't do a thing?"

"They brung in two witnesses. One wuz a young feller, some scalp-sellin' renegade what claimed to have known 'er back in Pitt. Said she'd been a Yankee all along, he did."

"Ike Ilam!" Marie shook her head in despair. "He hates us enough to say anything. But I thought he'd gone away from Vincennes."

"It wuz Hamilton hisself give 'im permission t' stay." Helm scratched his ear. "T'other witness wuz that black-haired doxy o' Hamilton's. That Mathilde. Lord, it wuz the devil hisself put that woman t'gether, I swear!"

"What did Madame Rodare say?"

"That one. She claimed she saw your ma sneak down t' the river one night an' give sumpin' t' some feller what wuz waitin' there in a canoe. Swore to it, she did."

"Lies!" Marie shuddered. "Ike and Mathilde hate our family. But I don't understand Hamilton. He didn't even know my mother. I know he listens to Mathilde, but would he hang a woman just to please her?" Marie struggled to control her voice.

Helm chewed his tobacco thoughtfully. "Way I figger it, Hamilton wants a sort of goat. He wants somebody he can punish jest t' scare the others, so's they know he won't put up with no foolin' 'round with the Yankees. Your ma, she jest got the bad luck t' be that somebody."

Marie choked back a sob of despair. "Cap'n Helm, can't ye do anything? We got to save her!"

"I'm a-thinkin' on it, little gal. If there be a way, by God, we'll find it. Meanwhile, you'd best pray some miracle'll happen in time t' save your ma!"

Marie thanked him and hurried on to the low building where the prisoners were kept. A red-coated guard met her at the door. He was young, with a pimpled face and a shock of straight, blond hair. "Here to see your mum, are you?" He greeted her with a leering grin. "She be in there all right. But she won't be much longer. They be a-buildin' the gallows already."

Marie pushed past him, ignoring his laughter. She found Abby sitting quietly in her cell, her skirt spread around her in the straw.

"Mother!" She ran to the bars and thrust her hands between them. "Oh, Mother—"

Abby looked up. Her face was pale but composed. Calmly she rose to her feet, moved to the bars and took Marie's hands in her own. Her eyes scanned Marie's face. "You know, don't you?"

"I know. But we'll get you out. We'll find a way."

Abby shook her head. "I don't want anybody risking harm on my account, Marie. My life's not worth any more than anybody else's."

"But they're—"

"I know. They're building the gallows. I've been listening to the sound of hammers and saws all morning." She turned her face away, and Marie caught the flash of anger in her eyes. "That Rodare woman! To take an oath and then lie like a strumpet—"

"And Ike! How could anybody hate us so much?"

Abby looked into her daughter's eyes. "Marie, if I'm taken. . .and if your father doesn't come back, promise me you'll leave this place as soon as you can. You and Ned—he'll take care of you. Go to the Watauga and find Henry. I—I'd like it, knowing that my children will be together."

"Stop it," Marie whispered. "You sound like it was all over. We be going to get you out! We won't give up till you're free!"

305

There was no hope in Abby's eyes, only resignation. "Promise me," she insisted again.

"I can promise you that I'll go away, an' that I'll try to find Henry. But Ned and me. . .that was done with once he found out about Ike."

"Did Ned say so?"

"He didn't have to."

"Have you talked about it? Have you told him you were sorry?"

"Wouldn't do much good." Marie shook her head. Even being around Ned had become hurtful. She could not meet his eyes when he looked at her. How could he even think about her now, without remembering the things Ike had said.

"Father will come." Marie changed the subject. "It ben't too late to give up hope."

"I hope not, Marie." Abby squeezed her daughter's hand. "But I have to prepare myself if the worst happens. I can't face it if I don't have certain things resolved in my mind. Things like you."

"Don't give up!" Marie kissed her mother's hands. The yellow-haired guard was coming over to take her away. She did not like him. "I'll be back tomorrow," she said quickly. "Don't fret. We'll think of something."

After Marie had left the fort, she ran all the way to the Busseron house, where she'd stayed since Ike Ilam's attack on her and Ned. She burst into the house. "They're going to hang my mother! We got to help her—"

"We know." Cecile put both arms around her. "Aspasie's been to town. She just told us."

"*Ne vous inquietez pas,*" the captain soothed. "Don't worry. We'll keep it from happening no matter what we have to do. De Gras and the others are with us. We'll save

306

her if we have to blow up the fort to do it."

"Blow up the fort?" Marie's eyes widened.

Cecile flashed her husband a cautioning look. "She doesn't know, Francois. Perhaps it's best not to tell her. It would only put her in danger—" She spoke in rapid French, but Marie caught enough of it to understand.

The captain shook his head. "It could be, my dear, that she already suspects." He turned to Marie and spoke gently, in English. "You signed the pledge, child—"

"So did you," Marie answered. "By now I reckon my signing don't mean any more than yours did."

"Then you consider yourself one of us?"

"Aye." Marie spoke the word in a whisper, but it was true. Even though Ned was no longer hers, she had joined his cause heart and soul. She was as much a Yankee as any of them.

Captain Busseron leaned toward her. "Then I will let you in on one of our secrets." He ran a finger along one curl of his waxed moustache. "If you were to roll back the rug and pry up the floor planks of this house, you could find the entire space filled in with kegs of black powder and enough bars of lead to make rifle balls for an army!"

"But how—?" Marie caught her breath in amazement.

"De Gras had it. But he knew his store would be one of the first places to be searched. He and Ned and I spent a very long winter's night carrying it from his place to ours, hiding it, and nailing down the floor again. We've been saving it for Colonel Clark, whenever the day comes that he wants to retake Vincennes."

"It'll come." Ned had walked into the room, his cheeks still red from the cold outside. "And when it does, we'll be ready t' help." He walked over to warm himself at the fire. He still spent his nights at the warehouse to safeguard Edward's trade goods, but he often took his meals with the Busserons. Frequently he brought them pheasants, turkeys and rabbits that he'd shot in the woods outside the town. Today he had two wild ducks slung over his shoulder in a string bag.

"Ah, *magnifique*, Ned! They'll make a fine dinner!" Cecile gave him a nod of thanks. "Take them in the kitchen and give them to Aspasie, *s'il vous plait.*"

Marie felt Ned's eyes on her just before he turned to leave the room. She stared down at her hands, as she almost always did when he was there. They had not spoken alone since that awful day at the warehouse. She dreaded what he might say to her if they did.

He returned a moment later, without the ducks, and realized for the first time that something was wrong. "What is it?" He stared at the three troubled faces, Marie's, Cecile's and the captain's.

"You haven't heard yet?" Cecile asked.

"I been huntin' since first light. What is it?"

"It's my mother," Marie said softly. "Hamilton sentenced her to hang."

"When?" Ned's face was pale.

"Three days from now."

"But we're going to save her," the captain put in hastily. "We can't even think in any other way. That's why I mentioned the powder—"

"We could distract them somehow." Ned sat down on the edge of the raised hearth. "We might start a blaze somewhere, maybe blow up somethin' under the wall. Then we could try an' get her out."

"But, *mon Dieu*, the risks!" Captain Busseron had begun to sweat. "Hamilton would hang us all. He'd have reason enough. And he'd know about the powder, then, even if we only used a little of it. He wouldn't stop looking till he found the rest. Why, I'd blow up this house before I let him get his hands on it!"

"There's Tobacco's Son." Marie groped for another idea. "Would he help us?"

Captain Busseron sighed. "Maybe. But his village is very near Vincennes. Hamilton could take terrible revenge on his tribe if he chose to. The chief is our friend, but would he risk the lives of his own people for the life of one white woman? Could we even ask him to?"

Cecile took a deep breath. "I know how much that powder and lead could mean to Colonel Clark," she said slowly. "But it's not worth Abby's life. We could offer it to Hamilton in exchange for her freedom."

"That might work." The captain shook his head. "But the powder's safe now only because Hamilton doesn't know it exists. Once he learns about it, we won't be able to keep him from finding it. He won't need to bargain in order to take it by force."

Ned tossed a stray chip of wood into the fire. "There be Clark," he said.

"We could never get to him in time to save her." The captain's shoulders slumped. "Kaskaskia's a good two weeks from here. To get there and back—"

"Suppose he ain't in Kaskaskia. Suppose he be on his way here right now?"

"*C'est impossible!* Look at the river!"

"Cap'n Helm told me there ain't nothin' stops him." Ned stared into the flames. "Or maybe there be somebody else out there. Maybe Marie's pa. Somebody. I'm willin' to go out there an' look if need be."

"Ned, it's hopeless!" Cecile threw up her hands. "Hamilton has us all watched. The town's patrolled, and the river. There are Indians in the woods. And what would you find out there?"

"I don't rightly know. But there ain't nobody here can help. I got t' do something. Mistress Forny, she be like my own ma almost." His blue eyes met Marie's for an instant. She saw no contempt or anger in them, only concern. Love swept over her like a sweet, warm wave. There was nobody like Ned.

"I could go tonight," he said. "The Redcoats know I sleep at the warehouse. I could hole up there till after midnight, then sneak off down the river by canoe."

"We got no canoe," Marie said. "The Redcoats guard the landing so's nobody can steal one and get away. You know that."

"We got one, Marie. It be a little one. Your pa left it in the warehouse. When the Redcoats come, I hid it under the furs and blankets."

"You'll be risking your life, Ned." The captain twisted his moustache nervously. "And you may well be risking it for nothing."

"Or maybe for somethin'. I got to try." Ned took a deep breath, his eyes on Marie. "I might not come back in time."

The captain nodded. "I understand. If you haven't brought help in three days, we use the powder. Then God help us all."

Marie lay awake on her pallet and listened to the sound of Aspasie's low, even breathing. The moonlight shone in the window, making a square pattern on the floor. A dog howled somewhere off in the distance.

Ned had left after supper to go on down to the warehouse, as he usually did. British eyes watched the Busseron house closely. It was important, Marie knew, to make sure that everything appeared to be normal. Later on, after the moon had passed the peak of the sky, he would launch the little canoe and set off downriver. With good luck, he would not be seen or missed until he was well out of reach of Vincennes.

The escape would be a dangerous one. Hamilton's Indians prowled the woods, always on the lookout for scalps. The river itself was treacherous in flood, and a storm could swamp a small canoe like Ned's. Anything could happen.

Marie sat up in bed, her eyes wide with fear. She had let Ned go with little more than a simple goodbye. She'd had no time alone with him, no real chance to tell him how much she loved him, or to explain what a fool she'd been about Ike Ilam. Even if he never forgave her, she wanted him to know. If he did not come back he would never know. He could die, she realized to her horror, with things still unsettled between them.

Trembling in the cool darkness, Marie slipped out of bed. She pulled on her long black stockings and her shoes, her dress and her cloak. She had to see Ned one more time. She had to talk to him, even if it meant making a ninny out of herself. Whatever happened, she could not let him go without at least trying to set things right.

The door creaked softly as Marie stole out onto the porch. Were any hidden eyes watching? she wondered. Did the British have their spies out, even in the middle of the night? Well, no matter. They would only see a girl sneaking out to meet her sweetheart. That was nothing so unusual.

A light snow was falling, the flakes dry, fine and small. Marie felt the icy coolness on her face as she ran. Stars shone brightly among the drifting clouds, blotted out on the horizon by the dark bulk of the fort. She hurried down the street toward the river, her heart pounding.

She knocked timidly on the warehouse door, her knuckles aching with cold. In a moment she heard Ned stirring.

"Who be it?" His voice came softly through the door.

"Marie."

He opened the door just wide enough to pull her inside, then closed and locked it again. "Be ye daft, Marie, out in the night alone like this?"

"I had to come. I had to talk to you before you went away."

"Come on then. Ye be half frozen." A single candle burned in one corner of the warehouse, beside his bed. There was no other source of heat or light. He guided her toward it.

"Here, you be shivering." His bed consisted of a pile of straw covered with buffalo robes. For warmth he had chose a great, shaggy, dark brown bear pelt. He seated Marie on the bed and wrapped her in the pelt, which was still warm from his own body. Marie snuggled into it.

"Better?" Ned pulled a keg of nails close to the bed and sat down on it.

"Aye," Marie whispered, though her teeth were still chattering. "You'll be goin' soon?"

"In an hour or so. When I be sure it's quiet out there."

"Ned, what if somethin' happens? What if you don't come back?"

"Hush, Marie. We don't even want t' think 'bout that." The candlelight flickered on the strong planes on his face. How handsome he looked, his hair still tousled from the bed. Marie wanted to reach out and smooth it with her fingers.

"I had to talk to you," she said softly. "I know you don't feel the same 'bout me anymore, but I wanted you to understand 'bout what happened with Ike back in Pitt. There weren't no Indians, Ned, only him. An' I done it of my own free will. I wasn't forced."

"Then Ike spoke true?" Marie could scarcely hear Ned's voice.

"Aye. All of it. I was a fool, Ned. I didn't know much about boys. Ike'd been after me, an' I stayed away from him for a spell. Then one day something hurt me inside. I went a little crazy, I reckon. That was when it happened. There weren't no love in it, Ned. There weren't. . . nothing at all. No more than when two dogs. . ." Her voice began to quiver. "It was. . .just. . .awful!"

"Things happen, Marie. We make mistakes. All of us do." Ned's voice was very gentle.

She was weeping now. "But you. . .that day with Ike an' the Indians. . .You were ready t' let yourself get killed t' keep Ike from doin' it again! Oh, Ned, I wasn't worth it!"

He shook his head. "You were willin' t' go through it all over again just t' keep me from gettin' hurt. That makes you worth a lot, Marie."

They sat and looked at each other for a long, silent moment. Then Ned's hand reached out toward her. Their fingers touched, then clasped.

"Marie—" He was beside her, his arms crushing her close, his mouth almost gulping her kisses. She felt her tears mixing with his as they sank into the softness of the buffalo robe, whispering each other's names.

Ned had forgiven her. Something began to sing inside Marie's head, a sweet and tender song that grew and grew until her whole body tingled with happiness. *Forgiving can feel mighty good*. . .Marie remembered her mother's words. Yes, forgiving did feel good. As for being forgiven—oh, it was heaven!

Was it Ned's hands or her own that pulled loose the buttons of her dress and slipped it down off her hips? Marie did not know, any more than she knew whose hands tore away Ned's shirt and parted the flap of his trousers. She was only aware of the delicious warmth of his bare flesh against her own, of the sweet, musky smell of him, and the salty taste of his skin.

The candle flickered and went out. In the darkness there was no sound except the wild rush of their breathing as Ned's hands and lips moved over her body. Marie could not think. She could only feel. She could only give herself up to the rippling, heaving rhythm of his muscles and to her own need for him. She heard him gasp with wonder as he came into her. Then the frenzy seized them both, and there was no more thought or reason. There was nothing but a wild, mad exploding of the whole world. Marie heard herself cry out again and again until at last she lay limp and trembling in Ned's arms.

He held her for a time, gently stroking and kissing her. Neither of them could speak. There was nothing that needed to be put into words.

At last, when their pulses had slowed and the darkness had become real once more, he drew softly away from her. "It's time, Marie," he whispered. "I got to be well on my way afore first light."

"No. . ." she protested with a little moan.

"Aye. It's got to be done." He was already into his clothes. "Be careful goin' back. Wait a bit after I'm gone, but don't delay too long. It wouldn't do for you t' be seen."

"Take care, Ned." She heard the sound of his arms sliding into the sleeves of his coat. "Come back. . . ."

"Aye, I'll come back." He bent over and kissed her. "And as soon as I do, we be gettin' married, you an' me. We be doin' it right."

Then he was gone. Marie heard the dragging of the little canoe across the floor, followed by the opening and closing of the warehouse door. She lay alone in the darkness.

"Come back," she whispered. "Oh, come back safe, Ned."

XXVI

The cold, gray water had all but paralyzed Edward from the chest down. He and his comrades moved forward, step by step, drawn now by something beyond mere human will as they followed the broad back and flag-red hair of George Rogers Clark.

Someone had killed a scrawny doe the day before. It was not much meat, one deer divided among one hundred seventy men, but it had been enough to keep them alive for another day. Now they were hungry again. They kept moving only to stay alive.

The men had taken heart when they'd heard the morning gun from Fort Sackville. But it was amazing how far the sound of a cannon shot could travel in the dead of winter. For two days they had marched in the direction of the sound and they had yet to reach Vincennes.

Some of the men were beginning to see things in the branches of the bare trees, twisted faces and snake-like forms. Edward himself sometimes fancied that he heard Mathilde's laughter in the ripple of the river. The sound reminded him that Abby and Marie could be in great danger. Maybe he would arrive too late to save them. Maybe he would not arrive at all.

They no longer sang or marched to the beat of the drum. They moved as silently as possible. If discovered, they could be picked off like ducks in the water. And they were close to Vincennes now. The loudness of the cannon that morning had assured them of that.

Edward glanced around him. The men were hideously pale, most of them, like bearded ghosts. He brushed the gritty stubble on his own chin and realized that those faces were mirrors of how his own must look.

It was midday. The sun was a thin blur of light through the gloomy clouds. Flakes of snow blew through the air, melting on the water. Edward kept a sharp lookout up and down the river. The sight of a canoe or any other craft could mean friends, food, or the gravest danger.

Joe Bowman was scouting ahead of the troops today, armed with a long stick to feel the bottom. The young man had been a wonder, Edward reflected. He was constantly alert and cheerful, his strength nearly a match for his commander's. He moved through the water now, probing the bottom, peering ahead through the drowned trees. Suddenly he stiffened like a hunting dog and gave a low whistle. In an instant, every man had his rifle ready. There was no place to hide, and they were too cold and weary to run. If the enemy had found them, they would stand and fight.

A small birchbark canoe appeared around the bend. Only one person was in it, a broad-shouldered young man who appeared to be searching for something. By the time he came near enough to see the waterlogged little army, there were at least fifty Kentucky rifles aimed at his heart.

"Stay where you are, lad." Clark's voice rang out across the water. "No tricks, and you won't be harmed. That's better. Now, closer. Slowly. You're a dead man if you try to get away."

The canoe moved closer, and suddenly Edward recognized the young man. "Ned! Ned Cooper!" he called out, sloshing his way to the front of the ranks.

"Mister Forny!" The canoe shot forward and a moment later the two of them were clasping hands with a vigor that almost tipped Ned into the water. "I found you! God be thanked, Mister Forny, I found you!"

The canoe was surrounded now, by a circle of curious men. "Ned, may I present Colonel George Rogers Clark." Edward nodded toward the gaunt, hollow-eyed, red-haired giant who had led them so many agonizing miles. Ned's eyes were round with awe.

"And do you know how close we be to dry ground, lad?" Clark's voice was hoarse with the cold.

"That way. Not far." Ned pointed with his arm. "You be maybe three or four miles downstream from Vincennes, but you'll be havin' to cross the main river channel to get to it. Won't be easy, sir."

"You've seen patrols? Indians?"

"Not a one, sir. Hamilton ain't expectin' company, I reckon." Ned grinned.

"What about canoes? Is there someplace where we could get any? They'd be a great help in crossing the main channel." Clark glanced back at his exhausted men. "Lord knows, they'll not be makin' it any other way."

"There be two, sir. Down by an old sugar camp yonder. They be old, and they might leak—"

"Never mind, can you get them?"

"Aye, if they'll float."

"Then go, lad! We'll be behind you!"

The crossing was made at last, with the help of the canoes, the pirogue, and a few makeshift rafts fashioned of floating logs. The men staggered up onto the shore and into the woods, their clothes heavy with the weight of water. Many of them were too weak to stand, without the river to buoy them up. They collapsed on the bank, blue with cold and fatigue. The stronger men held the weaker ones between them, walking them up and down to keep them warm.

It was only then that Edward had the chance to speak to Ned alone. "What news do you have of Abby and Marie?" he asked anxiously.

As swiftly as possible, Ned told him everything, about Mathilde, about Abby's arrest, her shameful trial and her sentence.

"When?" Edward felt his chest tighten with dread.

"Tomorrow morning. We got to hurry. Cap'n Busseron's got powder an' lead stashed away under the floor of his house. If there be no other way t' save Mistress Forny, they plan t' use some of it to blow a part of the fort, in hopes they can get her out when the ruckus starts."

Edward swallowed hard. "But, *mon Dieu*, the risk! Hamilton could kill them all, and Abby, too!"

"Aye. And he'd know they had the powder. We got to get there by tomorrow mornin'. Ain't no other way that's bound to work."

"Come on!" Edward seized Ned's arm. "You've got to tell this to Colonel Clark!"

Clark listened solemnly to Ned's story. "You're right," he said. "Of course, you're right. We've got to take the town tonight and be ready to march on the fort at dawn. We can't wait for the *Willing* to get here. But look at these men! By heaven, they're starving! Some of them won't live to make it to Vincennes. We've got to have time to hunt for food!"

Almost as if in answer to Clark's needs, a large Indian canoe rounded the bend of the river. In it were an old man and some squaws. When forced ashore, the canoe was found to contain a quarter of buffalo meat, some dried corn, and several kettles for cooking. In no time the food was simmering away over the crackling fires. For so many men, the share was not much. But it was enough to fortify body and spirit for the last, desperate leg of the march to Vincennes.

"If I may make a suggestion," Edward said quickly to Clark as they dried their steaming backsides at one of the fires. "We're evidently not expected in Vincennes. Surprise is the one thing on our side. But if Hamilton sees the size and condition of our force, he'll laugh in our faces."

"Exactly what I was thinking," Clark agreed. "We'll have to spread out, and use enough of that blessed powder and shot to make the Hair-buyer think he's fighting the whole Continental Army!" He turned to Ned. "What about the people in the town, lad? Will they welcome us back, or will they stand with Hamilton?"

"Don't fret on that score, sir." Ned spread his hands before the fire. Seeing him, dry and well-fed, Edward realized for the first time just how pathetic and near death Clark's little troop appeared. "They've come t' hate the bastard, sir. Ain't a one of 'em what won't give ye welcome."

"Good. . .good. I'll draft a letter then. To the people of Vincennes." Clark had begun to pace up and down, the vigor back in his step once more. "I'll warn them we're coming—an with a sizeable force, eh? I'll tell them to stay in their houses and not a one will be harmed! Can you carry that letter back to Vincennes tonight, lad, after the fort's locked up? We'll be in position and ready to attack before daybreak."

"Aye. It'll pleasure me greatly to do it!" said Ned.

"I could go with him," Edward put in quickly. "I live in Vincennes. There's no need for anybody to suspect I came with you."

Clark scratched the reb stubble on his chin while he thought about the idea. At last he shook his head. "You can't see yourself, Forny. Anyone who caught sight of you would know you hadn't come upriver the easy way, by boat; and they'd know you'd never have crossed that flooded bottomland alone. I know you're concerned about your wife, but I can't risk it. If the British got one look at you, they'd know something was up, and they'd be ready for us. Trust me, Forny. The hanging's set for daybreak. We'll be there in time to save your wife."

Edward sighed his agreement. Clark was right. "But *ma foi,* what would Abby be going through tonight, with her execution set for dawn? And what would happen if something went wrong, and they didn't arrive in time to save her? Edward shivered. How would he live through this night?

Marie had been allowed to spend one last night inside the fort with her mother. She had passed the long hours crouched outside the cell, clasping Abby's hands through the bars as she whispered encouragement.

"It's not over yet, Mother. Ned'll be back with help.

And if he don't get through in time—" Marie refused to think of the possibility that he would not get through at all. "Then, the captain and the others, they got something else planned. You'll see."

Abby only squeezed her daughter's hands. "Marie, I want to be able to hope. But I must be prepared to accept my own dying. The fort is well-guarded. There's so little chance—"

"No, Mother. Don't even say it!"

"I got to say it, Marie. Evil things happen. Fairy tales and wishes don't always come true. It's something you learn as you grow up." She was silent for a long moment. Marie could hear the sound of her breathing in the darkness. "Hanging doesn't take long, they say."

"Stop it!" Marie bit back a surge of tears. "There be somethin' else, Mother. Ned and me. We be gettin' married, soon as he gets back—leastwise, soon as we can find a parson."

"You're both so young," Abby spoke softly, but there was a note of joy in her voice. "But I'm glad. I'm right glad for it, Marie. He'll make you a good husband."

Marie leaned against the bars of the cell. "Mother," she whispered, "there be somethin' else. It happened the night Ned went away. It was afterwards we decided to get married. Ned says he wants to make things right."

Marie felt the understanding pressure of her mother's hand. "Are you sorry, Marie? Do you wish you'd waited?"

"In a way... Maybe if nothing had happened with Ike, it would have been easier to wait. But I think I had to know how it could be with somebody you love. Oh, Mother, it weren't anything like with Ike!" Marie sat there trembling, Abby's fingers stroking her damp cheek.

"Mother, did you and Father—?"

Abby took a deep breath. "Aye, Marie," she said at last. "We did. You know your father. But we made it right afterwards, just like you and Ned want to do. And it's been right ever since."

Marie squeezed Abby's hand. "I want to be just like you," she said. "I want to be as wise and as good and as brave as you are some day." She felt the tears flowing out. She could not stop them.

"Hush, dearest. You'll be wiser and better and braver. You're learning, Marie. You're growing up."

Marie gazed at her mother and thought of the gunpowder, and the men who were preparing even now to sacrifice their cause, and even their lives to save Abigail Forny. By the time the sky grayed with the first light of dawn, Captain Busseron and the others would have the powder charges in place. If nothing intervened to stop the hanging, the fort wall would be blown at the critical moment, and they would rush in through the breach. Marie licked her lips nervously. Yes, it would be even riskier than she had thought. She could see it now, a foolhardy scheme, set up against impossible odds. Some of them, if not all of them, would be killed.

Her thoughts were interrupted by the tramp of military boots on the wooden floor. "One side, Mistress Forny, we come to take your mum to the hangin'," the yellow-haired private spoke.

"No!" Marie cried. "It isn't time. Sunup's more'n an hour off!"

"Colonel Hamilton's orders. There's rumors of a rescue plot afoot. He doesn't want any trouble. So hang 'er now, he says!" He shoved the struggling Marie to one side and opened the cell.

"No! You can't—" Marie tried to claw at him, but the other guards seized her. "You can't! Not now!"

"It doesn't make any difference," Abby walked calmly out of the cell. "Go now, dearest. Don't stay for this—"

"No! I won't leave you!" Marie followed her mother and the red-coated guards out into the compound where the finished gallows rose against the waning moon. Her head was spinning frantically. No, it was too early. Captain Busseron and the others would not be ready. And Abby was marching toward the gallows. Now, now would be the time to save her. But Henry Hamilton had bested them all. There was nothing to be done.

The drummer beat out his somber cadence as Abby's wrists were bound behind her. A small crowd had assembled in the compound to watch the hanging. Marie caught a glimpse of Ike Ilam lounging against the wall of the stockade, torchlight illuminating the leering grin on his face. His Indian cohorts lurked behind him. Mathilde Rodare, in her sable-lined cloak, stood in the doorway of Hamilton's quarters, her head thrown back in smiling triumph as Abby mounted the first step of the gallows.

"No!" Marie tried to run toward her, but the soldiers held her back with their rough hands. She twisted and fought. Abby mounted the second step, a musket point at her back.

Where was Captain Busseron? Where was the powder? Maybe by some miracle they'd come early. Maybe they'd hear the drum roll. Marie's eyes searched the torchlit walls frantically. The sentries walked their posts along the parapets, silhouettes against the sky. There were six steps in all, then the platform where the noose dangled, waiting. Marie closed her eyes. "Please. . .

please. . ." she prayed, her lips moving silently.

Four steps, five. . .Out of the corner of her eye Marie could see Mathilde. She was gripping the edge of the doorway, her hands ranging nervously up and down the length of the smooth-worn frame. She was no longer smiling. Abby mounted the sixth step and walked slowly out onto the platform with its treacherously hinged trap door. Hamilton himself waited there like a bridegroom, the hangman beside him.

The drumbeat ruffled and ceased. "Have you any last words to say, Mistress Forny?" the colonel's voice rang out in the still air.

Abby shook her head. Her eyes swept over the crowd and fixed on Mathilde's face for a moment, then came to rest more lingeringly on Marie. "I'm ready," she said in a clear voice.

The hangman, a grizzled sergeant, slipped a black hood over Abby's face. His fingers seemed to be shaking. "Maybe he never hanged a woman afore," someone behind Marie whispered.

He looped the noose over Abby's head, adjusted the knot snugly, just behind her right ear. At a nod from Hamilton the drum roll began again.

"Non!" The shrill scream tore itself from the throat of Mathilde Rodare as she lunged out of the doorway, raced across the compound and flung herself, sobbing violently, at the foot of the gallows steps. *"Non! Par mon âme,* I won't have her death on my head! I won't burn in hell for it! I lied! By all the saints in heaven, I gave false testimony!" She pounded on the steps with her clenched fists. Her hair had come loose, to swirl around her face like a madwoman's. "I never thought you would really kill a woman, Henry. . . ." she wept. "I. . .never

thought you would do it! Oh, God save me, don't hang her!"

Hamilton's outraged gaze darted from Mathilde's to Abby. "Release her!" He growled the order at the hangman. The man quickly lifted the noose from Abby's neck and pulled away the hood that hid her face. Abby stood blinking in the light, her eyes wide with disbelief.

"You are free to go, Mistress Forny," Hamilton said icily. Then he turned to the lieutenant who had commanded the morning's operation. "Dismiss them all to their duties," he snapped. "This little farce is over for the time—"

The sharp *crack* of a rifle shot split the air, cutting off Hamilton's words in midsentence. A sentry on the wall reeled and collapsed on the parapet. The compound below erupted into a melee of running and shouting men.

Bullets whined through the air like wasps. "It's the Yankees!" someone shouted. "They've taken the town! Must be a thousand of 'em out there!"

"Get under cover!" Hamilton bawled from his place on the gallows platform. "Lock those Forny women up! Both of—" He fell to one side as a rifle ball whizzed past his ear, then scrambled down from the platform. "Man the cannon!"

One of the prison guards had rounded up Abby and Marie, and now he herded them back toward the guardhouse with his rifle. "It's both of ye under lock an' key, ladies. Can't have no Yankees runnin' loose inside the fort. We got trouble enough outside."

Just as they were being shoved in through the doorway, Marie caught a glimpse of the fort gates swinging open far enough to expose the muzzle of the fort's largest cannon. The soldier who fired it off caught a bullet in the ribs and fell, writhing, into the mud. The big gun spat flame, smoke and shot, the ball slamming into the side of a rock house that stood in its path. By the time the gates swung closed, two more British soldiers had fallen wounded.

Marie and Abby were shoved into the guardhouse. Their captor, scrambling for his own musket which he'd left inside, did not bother to lock the cell. "Stay put if ye be smart," he cautioned them before he ran back outside to join his comrades at the wall.

From somewhere outside, Marie heard an exultant whoop and realized it was Leonard Helm. "By damn! I'll be a pickled possum, if it ain't ol' George, come back, jest like I said—" The rest of his words were drowned out by the sound of cannon fire. Abby and Marie flattened themselves on the floor, clinging to each other for courage and comfort.

XXVII

Edward Forny thrust the hickory ramrod into the blue-black octagonal barrel of his rifle and prayed harder than he had ever prayed in his life. The hanging had been scheduled for dawn, but Hamilton, the devil, had beaten the sun by at least an hour.

The drum roll had come before Clark's men were fully in position. There'd been some delays, a problem of a key gun not in position. The order to fire had come too slowly. Edward, hearing the drum roll stop, had fired the first shot, the one that brought the sentry down. But had the shot come in time?

He cursed the slowness of the light as he poured the black powder from the horn into the flintlock pan and made ready to shoot again. He cursed Henry Hamilton and Mathilde Rodare, and the fool militia who'd caused the delay. If he found Abby dead when he entered the fort—

"I couldn't find Marie, sir," Ned wriggled up to the breastwork from somewhere behind the lines. "She must be inside the fort."

"Then God help her," Edward muttered, aiming for a small chink between the logs where the flash of a torch and a red coat showed through. "God help us all, Ned."

Fort Sackville was entirely surrounded by Clark's men. Though they were few in number, the stores of powder and lead that De Gras and Captain Busseron had saved for them were enough to keep the air humming with bullets. So well were they dug in behind mounds of earth, brush and rubble that they were almost invisible to the defenders of the fort. Henry Hamilton would have every reason to believe that the attacking army was a huge one.

The residents of Vincennes had welcomed them gladly. The women of the town were even preparing a big breakfast in the square before the church, where the famished men could come a few at a time and eat their fill.

Edward stretched out on his belly, his long rifle propped on a heavy fallen tree. He aimed and fired in cold, unhurried anger. Silence the gunfire from the fort, those were the orders. There was to be no more killing than absolutely necessary. Most of the rounds whistled harmlessly over the walls, but any Redcoat or militiaman who stuck his head up to fire was in danger of getting a bullet between the eyes. And Clark's Virginians were astounding marksmen. Any one of them could squint over the sights, squeeze the trigger with a powder-blackened finger, and send a rifle ball singing through the smallest chink in the logs of the fort wall. Often as not, there was a yelp of pain as the tiny chunk of hot lead struck home.

So close were the attackers to the fort that bawled

taunts and insults, flung back and forth from one side to the other, could be heard above the sound of the guns. "Stick yer arse up there, Redcoat, I'll blow it off! . . . What be the color o' yer scalp, Henry Hamilton? I'll buy it meself! . . .There! Take that, ye bastards! An' take that fer my maw an' my sister what yer bloody Injuns kilt last year!"

Edward filled his pan with powder, capped the horn, and fired a shot at the parapet that sent a British gunner diving for cover. He functioned almost without thought, his only aim to see this ordeal through and find his wife and daughter safe inside the fort. His mind tried to blot out the picture of Abby's limp body dangling from the gallows. He had seen hangings in France. It was not a pretty death. Edward fought to keep himself from shaking as he rammed the barrel again. *Mon Dieu,* he thought, if I do not find Abby and Marie alive in that fort, I will go as mad as a rabid dog. He filled the flintlock pan once more and shifted himself back into firing position. He would kill Hamilton himself, he resolved, and would probably kill Mathilde Rodare as well. They could hang him after that. It would no longer matter whether he lived or died.

He rested his cheek on the stock of the rifle for a moment, his eyes squeezing shut in anguish. It had been his fault, all of it. If he had not let Mathilde lure him into bed in the first place, there would have been no need to extricate himself from a prickly situation, and there would have been no need to make her angry. If Abby had been hanged, it was for his own crime, Edward realized to his horror. And if Marie died because she was in the fort, then that, too, was his own doing. His eyes, reddened by weariness and emotion, focused on a blur of movement atop the wall. He squeezed the trigger, felt the recoil slam into his shoulder. The pain was welcome.

The firing continued on through the night and into the next day. By now a good part of the townsmen had joined in the battle under the leadership of De Gras and Busseron. Tobacco's Son, too, had come from his village to offer Clark the assistance of one hundred braves, an offer which the American colonel politely declined. If any of Hamilton's Indian allies were to attack, there was a very real danger that the friendly Piankeshaws could be shot as enemies by mistake.

That afternoon, the first exchange of notes took place between Clark and Hamilton, the American demanding complete surrender, the Englishman stalling for time in the hope of getting reinforcements. Clark read Hamilton's reply and shook his head. At his signal, the barrage on the fort began once more.

Vincennes had taken on an air of almost savage festivity. The battlers on the breastworks made up songs to the whine of the bullets and yowled for Hamilton's scalp. The women of the town baked bread and cooked hot soup that the fighters gorged down in their brief rest periods. The air was alive with the smell of powder and the zing of gunshots.

Edward was off duty that evening when Tobacco's Son brought in six of Hamilton's Shawnee braves, their arms tightly bound with buckskin thongs. "We caught them on their way to the Hair-buyer!" The tall chief grunted his satisfaction. "Look!" He held up a beaded leather bag. "This we took from their leader!" He loosened the drawstring and shook the bag until the contents tumbled out onto the ground at Clark's feet.

There were scalps, six or seven of them in shades of

blond, red and brown. One of them, the fairest, clearly the fine, soft hair of a child. Two of the others were very long and had probably come from women.

Edward stared at them, the blood-matted hair, the little wads of dried flesh at the end. He had never seen white scalps before. The sight sickened him, but he could not take his eyes away.

Clark dismissed the Piankeshaw chief with his thanks, then looked the prisoners up and down, his eyes burning with hot fury. "Lock these murderers up!" he rasped. "We'll deal with them tomorrow!"

"What are you going to do with them?" a pale, young lieutenant asked him.

"Do with them? Why, Mister Fuller, we're going to execute them! There be a good number of men among us who've lost kinfolk to the scalp hunters. We'll let those of them who've a mind to have away at them!" He glared briefly toward the fort. "Maybe that'll curdle our friend Hamilton's porridge!"

The next day dawned startingly clear. The clouds had fled, leaving the pale, cold sun hanging against a winter sky. Clark cleared an area in the meadow, just out of range of the British guns, but close enough to be easily watched through a field glass. The men of Vincennes turned out in full force for the spectacle, though most of the women were absent.

Edward stood near the fringe of the crowd, with Ned Cooper beside him. He knew what they were about to see, and his flesh crawled at the thought of it. "*Allez-vous*, Ned. There's no reason for you to stay and see this."

"Orders of Colonel Clark." Ned drew himself up and remained in his place.

The six captives, stripped to their breechcloths and moccasins, were marched onto the field at rifle-point and forced to kneel on the frozen mud. Then the six who had been chosen from among Clark's men, those who bore the greatest bitterness against the Indians, moved into line, each carrying a sharp, steel British-issued tomahawk, captured with the Indians themselves. Shuffling, their eyes downcast, they took their places, each beside one of the captive Shawnee braves.

Clark shaded his eyes and peered across the open space toward the fort. Yes, he nodded his satisfaction, the Hairbuyer was on the parapet, watching through a field glass. "Proceed," he said, his voice cold and lifeless.

The first man gripped the hair of his captive and raised the tomahawk. Edward knew the fellow. He'd lost his entire family to the Shawnee two winters ago when he was out trapping. The brave had begun his death chant in a wailing, jerking voice that silenced abruptly as the tomahawk crashed into his skull. Blood spurted upward as the brave shuddered and slid to the ground. He lay there in the red pool of his own gore, eyes and mouth gaping like a fish's. The frontiersman who had killed him kicked at the still-twitching body, then turned and walked away. At the edge of the field he suddenly doubled over as if he'd been punched, and burst into great, heaving, uncontrolled sobs.

One by one the captives died, some less mercifully than others. One of the Indians required a second, then a third, then an incredible fourth smashing blow from the tomahawk before he stopped thrashing. Others were dispatched swiftly, a single, clean, savage blow ending their death songs. Some of the men who did the killing wept at the bitter memory of their own lost loved ones. One cursed. The others bit their lips in pale silence as they swung the cruel weapons downward.

At last it was done, and the six corpses lay alone, their blood freezing slowly into ice on the ground. Edward had watched the execution without a word. Ned had stayed at his side, uttering little, choking gasps each time a tomahawk fell home. Edward laid a hand on the boy's shoulder and they walked from the field together.

The firing resumed later that morning. The same afternoon, Clark sent another note to Hamilton. Edward was with him when Hamilton's answer was returned.

"Damned stubborn fool!" Clark crumpled the white paper in his fist. "Wants a three-day truce, does he? I'll show him a truce!" He sat down at his desk, jerked a quill out of its inkwell, and wrote a reply with slashing strokes. "Give this to him," he thundered to an aide. "Then double the fire on the fort. Pour it on, lads!" He suddenly turned toward Edward and stared at him as if he were seeing him clearly for the first time in days. "Lord, Forny, how long's it been since you've slept? You look like a ghost!"

"Two nights and a day, not counting today." Edward shrugged. "No longer than yourself."

"Damn it, man, I'm not shooting. Didn't I order every man to sleep at least half the time he's not on the line?"

"*Mon colonel*, I—"

"Never mind. I know you're worried about your wife and daughter. Who wouldn't be? But you'd be damned lucky to see to hit the side of the fort with those bleary eyes of yours! When's your duty?"

"In four hours—"

"Then get some sleep! That's an order, Forny!"

Clark was right, Edward mused as he made his way

down to his own warehouse on the bank and unlocked the door. He was so tired that the bare trees swam in wavy lines before his eyes. As a fighting man, he was of no use to anyone in such condition.

He closed the door behind him and found his way to the bed of straw and pelts that Ned Cooper had made for himself in the corner. He was so sleepy that he almost fell into it. By the time he had pulled the bearskin up to his shoulders, his mind was already drifting away.

He was walking through a cold, white mist, between trees that appeared to be made of human bones. In the distance he could see Fort Sackville, silent now, the guns stilled and the Virginia flag hanging limp at the top of the staff.

The gates of the fort swung open by themselves, and Edward moved through them, the mist of his dream swirling about his legs as he walked forward.

The fort was empty except for a towering gallows that stood in the center of the compound. Edward's eyes traveled slowly upward to a slender form in a gray cloak that dangled from a rope, the feet tracing little circles in the air. He saw the white, strangled face. It was Abby.

As he gazed up at her in horror, he became aware of a slight movement from a figure huddled at the foot of the gallows. The figure stirred, then uncoiled and rose. It was Mathilde Rodare. Her hair was floating loose on the mist; her eyes and cheeks were very red, and she was laughing, except that no sound came from her mouth. There was no sound anywhere. She floated toward him, her beautiful face twisted with that silent laughter. Edward felt a murderous rage well up in him. She must have seen it in his eyes, for she suddenly turned and fled from him, stumbling over her flowing skirt. Two long bounds and he caught her. One hand seized her long, black hair and jerked it upward. She hung there, her mouth working in soundless screams.

Suddenly there was a steel tomahawk in Edward's free hand. George Rogers Clark had given it to him, he realized. Mathilde was his prisoner. She had killed his wife. It was his right to execute her. It was his duty.

He pulled her hair tight. Slowly he lifted the tomahawk, high above his head. He held it poised. Then he brought it down with all his strength—

Edward Forny opened his eyes. His body was soaked with sweat, his muscles were still twitching. *Ma foi!* He sat up and buried his face in his trembling hands. What was a man to do when sleep was more exhausting than being awake? He stumbled to the door of the warehouse, opened it wide, and let the icy air shock him into alertness. The sun had moved a considerable distance across the sky. He had, he realized, been asleep for several hours. Edward cursed and rubbed the long black stubble of his beard. He'd probably missed the change of duty on the firing lines. Well, there was nothing to do but hurry. He ran a hand through his tousled hair, retrieved his rifle from beside the bed, locked the warehouse door behind him and set off up the bank.

By the time he had gone a few steps, Edward had noticed that there was no sound of firing from the direction of the fort. He paused and listened to make sure. Maybe Clark and Hamilton had agreed to a truce after all. He quickened his steps.

Suddenly he became aware of a movement ahead of him in the trees, a fluttering flash of color, too big to be a bird. An Indian perhaps— He lifted his rifle, which he always kept loaded and ready for use. He could hear footsteps coming toward him now, light and quick through the wet leaves.

"Edouard!" Mathilde Rodare burst into the clearing. She stopped short when she saw him, her hand at her throat.

"Mathilde." The cold calmness in Edward's own voice amazed him. He stood and looked at her, the gun still held in readiness. She was wrapped in a sable-lined cloak that might have once been elegant, but was now dirty and torn. Her hair drifted in loose tangles, almost the way it had in his dream. But it was her face that truly startled him. A long, blue-black bruise lay across one cheek, running from her eye to her chin. One side of her upper lip was swollen and flaked with dried blood. Her eyes were wide open and staring, an animal's wildness flashing in their blue depths.

"*He* did it to me!" she hissed. "Henry Hamilton, that great, fine gentleman! He hit me with his boot! *Le bâtard!* He didn't even have the decency to use his fist!"

"Mathilde—" Edward spoke softly, for she looked as if she might bolt and run at any moment. "You were with Hamilton? You were in the fort?"

"I was!" She tossed her black hair. "And I stayed long enough to see the *diable crasseux* made prisoner! Strike me, will he? I hope your Colonel Clark strings him up by his—"

"You mean the fort's surrendered? The fighting's over?"

"*Mais oui!* Of course it is," she snapped. "Where have you been, eh?" Her expression softened. "Edouard, *mon cher,* if I had known you'd come back to Vincennes—" She glided closer to him. Even with her bruised face and disheveled hair she was beautiful, he thought. She was as beautiful and as deadly as one of the little ribbon-striped snakes that lived in the swamps and bayous beyond New Orleans.

Edward tightened his grip on the rifle. She paused. "You would shoot me, *mon etalon?* You would shoot Mathilde?"

"Where is my wife?" he said, his voice suddenly harsh with strain.

"Your wife? Your Ab-i-gail?" Her face wore an expression of doll-like innocence.

"It was your testimony that sentenced her to hang, you black-haired witch!"

She began to laugh then, and her laughter was that of a person who is not right in the head. "So I did! So I did, my fine stallion! I told you, no man wipes his boots on Mathilde Rodare, did I not?"

"Where is my wife? Where is my daughter? If you've harmed them, you and your red-coated—Why, I'll—" Maddened beyond reason, Edward had flung down his rifle, crossed the clearing in three long strides, and seized Mathilde roughly by the shoulders. "Where are they? Tell me!"

She only laughed, wildly and senselessly as he shook her back and forth.

"Where are they, Mathilde? Tell me, or, so help me, I'll kill you with my own hands!" Edward felt the blood boiling up in him, with a rage as near to madness as anything he had ever known.

She laughed again. "They're dead," she said, spitting out the words. "Both of them. Your Abigail hanged; your daughter raped by the soldiers until she—ah, but you should have seen it, Edouard. Such a sight one does not easily forget! All that blood—" Her laughter filled Edward's ears. It was a dream, he tried to tell himself. In a moment, if he shook himself, he would wake up, still on the bed in the warehouse.

Without power to will otherwise, Edward felt his hands move to her throat and tighten. He could not stop what was happening.

"Edouard. . ." She was no longer laughing. "No, Edouard. I lied. I wanted to hurt you. . .*Non,* Edouard, you're strangling—"

It was almost as if Edward could not hear her at all. All his grief and fury were concentrated in the tightening ring of his fingers around her throat. She began to choke, and he could not stop—

"Edward!" The voice stunned him like a bullet.

"Edward! Oh, Edward!" Abby stood at the edge of the clearing alive and beautiful. Yes, he was dreaming. He was sure of it now, for this scene made no more sense than a dream.

His hands went limp. Mathilde slumped to the ground at his feet. He had no strength to move. He could only stand there as Abby ran to him and flung herself into his arms. She was real and solid and warm. Slowly Edward's reason returned. He tasted the salty tears on her face. Real. "And Marie?" he whispered hoarsely.

"She's fine. They just let us out of the fort. Somebody told her Ned had come back. She went to look for him."

"The hanging—?" Edward searched her face with his eyes.

"It almost happened." Abby glanced down at Mathilde who was coughing and moaning on the ground. "She wouldn't let them do it, Edward. She confessed that she'd lied about me."

Mathilde rolled over and sat up, her eyes still glazed

with madness. "And Henry Hamilton didn't like that! The monster! He beat me for making such a fool of him!" She began to giggle, softly, senselessly. "He locked me in a closet, and he said he was going to kill me when the fighting was done! Three days in that closet! No food. No water. Not even a bucket!"

Edward gazed down at her. The hate was gone from him. In its place there was only pity. "*Pourquoi*, Mathilde? Why did you tell me such a horrible lie?"

Mathilde pushed the tangled hair out of her face. She shrugged. "*Pourquoi pas?* I was hurt. I wanted to hurt somebody else. I wanted to make you feel the way I feel." She cleared her throat and spat on the ground. "And I didn't care what you did to me! I wouldn't have cared if you'd killed me, *mon etalon*." The blue eyes, devilish now, glanced up at Abby. "He's all man, your Edouard. *Quelle homme! Non?*" Slowly, wickedly, the swollen mouth grinned.

"You're ill, Madame Rodare," Abby said in a gentle voice. "Let us take you back to the fort. There's a doctor there."

"*Non!* Not the fort. Never!" Her eyes had gone wild again. She struggled to her feet, clutching her skirts up around her legs.

"Mathilde—" Edward took a step toward her. She jumped backward like a deer.

"Ha! You think you can catch me! You think you can lock me up again! You'll never catch Mathilde. She is too smart for you, monsieur! No one catches Mathilde!" She spun out of Edward's reach, laughing. Then she was off through the trees in a flash of tattered scarlet and sable, her bare legs flying.

"Mathilde!" Edward shouted after her. "Come back

here, you fool!''

But she was already out of earshot, and there was nothing left of her but the echo of her maddened laughter on the wind.

Marie mingled with the crowd that thronged outside the gate of the fort. The cannons boomed in joyful salute as the Union Jack quivered its way down the staff, and the Virginia flag rose to take its place. She saw Leonard Helm dancing a jig, a mug of whiskey in his fist. Tobacco's Son had come with his band of Piankeshaw braves to join in the celebration. Clark's tiny army had assembled itself as a body for the first time in the presence of the sputtering Henry Hamilton, who blanched with humiliation when he realized he had given up Fort Sackville to a force of less than two hundred ragged men.

Marie and her mother had been released immediately after the surrender, tired, hungry and dirty, but otherwise unharmed. Abby, as soon as she'd learned that Edward was in Vincennes, had gone to look for him.

"Ned Cooper? Is he here?" Marie had asked the first Yankee soldier she met.

"Young Ned? Aye, lass. He be hereabouts, though I've not seen 'im since the surrender."

"Thank you." Marie hurried on, so eager for the sight of Ned that she bounced with each step. Her eyes darted among the jubilant crowd. Ned had to be looking for her, too. She would find him soon. Then everything would be perfect.

But Ned was not to be found in the vicinity of the fort. After asking for him again and again, Marie decided that she would have to look someplace else. Maybe Ned was with the Busserons, or down at the warehouse, waiting, knowing she would come. Maybe he was with Edward. Maybe Abby had found them both.

The Busseron house was closer. She would look there first. Marie set out almost at a run, her cloak flying behind her in the chilly breeze. She did not feel the cold. She was alive. She was safe, and in just moments she would be with Ned. She could almost feel his arms closing around her, his strong, sweet mouth pressing onto hers.

She mounted the steps of the Busseron house and knocked anxiously on the door. No one was home, not even Aspasie. Puzzled and dejected, she turned away from the door and walked slowly down the steps. Maybe somebody was out in back, she thought. She would take a moment to check. Then she would try the warehouse.

The Busserons were not gardeners. The bushes grew close to the back of the house, with only enough of a clearing for a woodshed and clothesline area.

Marie came around the corner of the house. The small back area was empty. Cecile's freshly-washed petticoats fluttered back and forth on the clothesline, crackling with frost. A slate gray junco scolded from the low branch of a hickory. A side of bacon hung from a hook under the roof of the open woodshed.

Nothing seemed amiss. Yet Marie felt her spine prickle as she looked around. Something in her sensed danger.

But this was foolish. No one was there. There was no use in staying to look around. She turned to go back around the house. Just then something caught her eye. She turned, then sucked in her breath with alarm.

Something—no, someone—was lying under the bushes, only a pair of well-worn moccasins and buckskin-clad legs showing. It was a man. It was Ned Cooper.

She ran toward him with a little cry. She could see his face now. There was a bloody welt just below the hairline. His eyes were closed. He was not moving.

"Ned!" She flung herself down beside him. He was so still. She felt for his pulse. Yes, it was there, faint but steady on the inside of his wrist. But he was unconscious.

"Ned—" She stroked his face, trying to wake him. Panic began to tighten its icy grip on her. Someone had done this to Ned. Someone who hated him.

Marie heard the twig snap behind her, but she did not even have time to look around before a pair of muscular arms seized her from behind and hauled her to her feet. A hand clapped tightly over her mouth.

She kicked and struggled, dimly aware that the arms holding her were brown, and that the blended smell of wood smoke, grease and wet buckskin was an Indian smell. She knew then who had her.

Ike Ilam stepped out of the bushes, a hideous grin on his face. "Well, now, Mistress Forny. We got yer sweetie, we did. Now I'm gonna take ye so far away that ye'll never find yer way back home agin! An' on the way, Mistress High an' Mighty, ol' Ike, he'll be teachin' ye what a real man be like! Ye liked it once, Marie Forny! Ye'll be likin' it agin!" He laughed as the squaw and the other brave moved out of the bushes to stand beside him.

On the ground at his feet, Ned Cooper moaned and stirred. Ike looked down at him, his face twisted with pure hatred. He jerked his head toward the brave who stood at his side.

"Kill 'im!" he said.

XXVIII

"No!" The word exploded out of Marie as the brave jerked the red-handled knife out of his belt. Her nails taloned into the hand of the Indian who held her, drawing blood. He yelped with the unexpected pain. His arms loosened just enough for Marie to tear herself free and fling her body down across Ned's. "He'll have t' kill me first!" she hissed, locking her arms around Ned's neck. Ned moaned incoherently. Ike grinned through his beard. "Aye, an' he just might, if'n I tell him." He circled Marie at a leisurely pace, looking at her from this angle and that, laughing at her fear. "But that be too easy. Got t' be some better way t' have a little fun."

Marie looked up at him, her mind groping for any way to save Ned. "I know what you want, Ike. Let him go, an' you can have it. I'll go any place with you. Any place at all. An' I won't fight you."

"Ye won't, eh?" Ike squatted down beside her. One

hand reached out and snaked up under her skirt. Marie gasped as his cold fingers moved up her thigh and clasped the curve of her rump.

"Wal, I'll be damned!" Ike glanced down at his swelling crotch and pulled his hand away. "Bustin' my britches already! Flyin' Swan there—" He jerked his head toward the Indian woman. "She be better'n nothin on a cold night, but every now an' agin I gits a hankerin fer a white woman! Ye'd suit me right fine, Mistress Forny. But what's t' keep me from killin' her highfalutin' friend there and takin' ye anyway?"

"Touch him, Ike Ilam, an' I kill myself first chance get—an' you too if I get the chance. I'll jump into the river an' drown afore I'll come with you! But you let Ned alone an' you got me willin'."

Ike stood up and scratched at his greasy beard. "I be of a mind t' bargain," he said at last. "Besides, this ain't a safe place t' kill a body. Ye'll come willin' now. Ye promise me, Marie Forny?"

"Aye," Marie whispered between her teeth. She was sweating with fear and sudden relief. The cold made her damp body shiver.

"Git ye up, then. We'll tie ol' Cooper there so's he can't foller us if'n he wakes up." He reached for Marie's arm and jerked her to her feet. She stood where she was, shaking beneath her cloak while one of the Indians bound Ned's wrists and ankles with rawhide thongs. Just as the brave was pulling the last knot tight, Ned's eyelids fluttered and opened.

"Marie—" He blinked in disbelief as he saw her standing beside Ike.

"Tell 'im!" Ike rasped. "Tell 'im you're goin' with me. Tell 'im you're goin' willin'."

"Ned—" Marie ached to go to him. "I'm goin' away with Ike. It be him I want. It always was. I just didn't know it till now." She stood still and let Ike slide his arm around her waist.

"Marie, you can't—" Ned was still groggy. He shook his head to clear his vision.

"She be mine now, Cooper!" Ike spat on the ground. "She ain't never gonna be yours no more. An' when ye go t' bed at night, ye just remember it's Ike Ilam got 'er betwixt his blankets, fillin' 'er full better'n you ever done." He walked over to where Ned lay, straddled his body, then slowly, deliberately lifted a moccasined heel and drove it down hard into Ned's groin. Ned doubled up with the pain.

"I'll kill you, Ilam," he muttered. "I'll. . .kill you for this. . . ." Then his eyes closed as he lapsed back into unconsciousness.

"C'mon!" Ike jerked Marie's arm. "We be a fur piece away by the time somebody finds 'im."

Marie followed him, biting back her tears and her terror. She had to keep her head. Somehow the chance would come to get away. She would have to be ready.

The streets and the landing were deserted. Marie's heart sank. She had hoped to see someone, anyone, to whom she could cry out for help. Ike would have no choice but to run then. He could not very well go back and finish off Ned. But they passed no one. Everybody in the town of Vincennes, it seemed, was up at the fort celebrating.

The big canoe was waiting on shore. Ike helped Marie climb into it, then followed, taking the middle seat for himself and putting her in front of him. Flying Swan slipped ahead to the foremost seat, with the two braves, once they had launched the canoe, swinging into the stern. The canoe was crowded. It rode low in the water. But with two men paddling, it moved swiftly upstream. Soon they had disappeared around the bend, and Vincennes was lost from sight.

The afternoon deepened as the heavily-laden canoe glided north, past the bleakness of bare trees and frozen shores. The Wabash was broad and sluggish with flood. Gray water reflected gray sky. The men paddled in shifts, two working, one resting. Marie sat with her hands in her lap, staring ahead at Flying Swan's rigid spine.

From time to time the Indian woman would look to one side or the other, enabling Marie to study her face in profile. She had broad, flat features, a wide mouth, and small, sharp eyes like a weasel's. In the rare moments when she glanced back at Marie, those eyes blazed with hatred.

She had been Ike's woman. What was she thinking now? Marie wondered as she let her eyes trace the length of the single long braid that ran down Flying Swan's back. How would she react to Ike's taking another woman, and a white woman at that? Would she be submissive and accept the situation? Or was her dark mind already seething with some murderous plan?

Marie decided to make a small test. Turning in the canoe, she looked back at Ike and forced her face into a smile. "Will we be landin' soon?" she asked in a loud flirtatious tone whose meaning no one could have mistaken.

"Why? Ye gettin' anxious t' have me?" Ike grinned. The poisonous glance that Flying Swan shot back at them told Marie as much as she wanted to know.

"Oh—" Marie looked down at her hands. "It's jus

that I—well, I didn't have time t' get ready afore we got in the canoe. It's been a long time, an' a girl can get a mite uncomfortable."

Ike guffawed. "Y' mean ye got t' go t' the bushes? Hell, why didn't ye say so? This ain't no place fer fine manners, Mistress Forny!" He motioned to the Indian paddlers and the canoe glided toward shore.

They stepped out onto the bank, Marie gingerly walking the tingles out of her legs. "Gals over thataway!" Ike pointed toward a heavy clump of willow. "Watch 'er!" he hissed at Flying Swan. "She be a tricky one!"

Marie squatted in the willows, carefully holding up her skirts. Flying Swan faced her at arms length, also squatting. Both of them were completely hidden from the men. Flying Swan glared at Marie for an instant, then lowered her gaze to the ground in front of her.

"Flying Swan," Marie whispered.

The woman raised her hard, black eyes.

"Can you understand me? You understand?"

Flying Swan nodded cautiously.

"You let me go. You stay here. I go away. I won't bother you no more. Yes?"

Slowly Flying Swan nodded. Marie, with her heart pounding, edged away from her, toward the other side of the willow clump. She was taking a big risk, she knew, for she would be missed in moments. But it was just possible she would not have any other chance to escape. She hugged the ground as she snaked her way between the tightly-growing willow clumps. A few feet more, and she would be clear of them.

"What the devil be goin' on in there?" Ike's impatient voice rang out behind her. "Ye gals gonna take all day? We gotta git movin'."

Flying Swan retorted with a few disgruntled phrases in her own language. Ike stood there at the edge of the willow patch, fuming and muttering impatiently. Marie could hear him above the sound of her own breathing as she crawled forward over the frosty ground. If she could just make the river, she thought, she could follow the bank south. Surely it would only be a matter of time before someone came upriver searching for her—

A rabbit squealed in alarm and shot from its hiding place, bounding off through the dry leaves. Marie swallowed her heart. Yes, Ike had heard. He gave a shout, and a moment later one of the braves had seized Marie by the arms and was dragging her back to where he stood.

"So ye'd go willin' would ye, ye lyin' bitch!" he sneered. "Well, willin' or not, here ye be. This'll fix ye!" He whipped out a leather thong and tied it around Marie's wrists, so tight that it cut off the circulation in her hands. "Any more tricks, Marie Forny, an' after I be finished with ye, ye'll go t' these two bucks. I already seen what they c'n do to a woman. They ain't exactly gentle, believe you me!"

Flying Swan had come out of the willows. Ike turned on her with towering rage. "Slut! Filthy, lyin' slut! Cross me, will ye?" He raised his hand and brought it down hard across the woman's face, again and again. Flying Swan took his abuse in tearful silence. Even her brothers did not move to help her. She was Ike's property. It was his right to do what he wished with her. By the time he'd finished, Flying Swan's face was beginning to swell, and her nose was trickling blood.

"Take a lesson, Marie Forny! Ain't nobody crosses Ike Ilam what don't pay for it!" Ike spun away and strode back down to the canoe. Flying Swan followed him, her body hunched over with pain and humiliation. One of the bucks lifted the bound Marie into the canoe. Ike climbed in behind her. In a moment the craft was launched and they were moving upstream again.

It had begun to snow, the flakes big and soft and fluffy. This kind of snow would fill up the woods before morning, Marie reminded herself unhappily. Escape would be twice as difficult through deep snow. She had no warm boots, no covering but her cloak, and even if she did get away, tracking her in the snow would be easy.

Flying Swan sat in front of her in the canoe, a huddled lump of misery. The woman would not help her again, Marie concluded. She feared Ike too much for that. Maybe she loved him, too. Marie had seen the jealousy blazing in those little black eyes. Poor Flying Swan.

Marie's wrists throbbed from the tightness of the buckskin Ike had used to bind them. Her hands had lost all feeling except an awful sense of puffiness. She pulled at the knots with her teeth. They only tightened, and she was rewarded for her efforts by Ike's laughter behind her.

"Ye ain't goin' t' get away that easy, Mistress Forny. An' come tonight, ye won't be wantin' to. Ike Ilam can promise ye that. I'll have ye down on your back so ye'll wonder what the hell ye was runnin' away from!"

Marie did not answer him. She put her hands back into her lap and sat still, thinking, groping, finding no answers. The sun sank toward the horizon, turning the sky and the water to flaming crimson as it hung low above the trees. Then, slowly, it dropped out of sight, and there was only darkness, only the ripple of paddles in the water and the sound of Ike's breathing behind her.

* * *

It was Aspasie who had found Ned behind the Busseron house, bound and only half-conscious. Edward and the captain had carried him inside and brought him fully around with smelling salts and a few swallows of brandy.

"Marie—" He sat bolt upright and struggled to get off the bed. "They got Marie! I got to—" He fell back, his head twisting on the pillows. "So dizzy. . ." he muttered.

"Where's Marie? Who's got her?" Edward leaned over him.

"Ike Ilam. Him and them three Kickapoos. They took her! We got to go after them—"

"Ne vous faites pas," Edward soothed, though his heart pounded with rage and fear. "Rest, boy. You've got a devil of a bump on the head. I wouldn't be surprised if your skull was cracked. Now, think, do you know which way they went?"

"They come in a canoe. I big one. But I didn't see them go."

"Then you don't know if they went upriver or down?" Abby sponged the welt at Ned's hairline with a damp cloth.

It was Edward who answered her. "Upstream, most likely. It makes more sense that the Kickapoos would head toward their own country. They'd be safer there."

"And didn't you say that Clark had a gunboat coming up from the Ohio?" Abby put in quickly.

"He did. The *Willing*. It ought to be here any day. They'd have a hard time getting past it if they went downriver." Edward was thinking hard now.

"If you will permit me to suggest it," Captain de Busseron interrupted, "I myself could head south at once by horse and warn the captain of the *Willing* to intercept

352

them if they've gone that way. Though I think you're right, my friend. It makes more sense that they'd go upriver. It may be they've got friends at Ouitenon."

"Do it, then! We've no time to waste!" Edward clasped his friend's hand. "You go downriver by horse. I go upriver by canoe. *Allons!* We leave at once, eh?"

Ned sat up, fighting off the waves of dizziness. "I'm comin' with you, sir. Wouldn't let you go after Marie without me!"

"Non!" Edward shook his head. "Don't even ask, boy. You belong in bed."

"Ain't nothin' can keep me here," Ned declared stubbornly. "Beggin' your pardon, sir, but if you don't take me, I'll get a canoe an' go by myself! You'll be needin' help anyway, and you know I can shoot."

Edward hesitated. Then Abby put a soft hand on his arm and beckoned him out into the hallway. "Let him go with you, Edward," she whispered. "They're in love. They want to get married. It's only fair."

"I see, and you know I approve, Abby. But *mon Dieu*, with that head! The boy could faint on me at the wrong time—"

"Maybe. But it's his right, Edward. You've got to take him. I'll bandage his head up good and tight, and send along plenty of possibles—"

Edward swept her into his arms and covered her warm lips with his. Her arms crept around him and they held each other close. He had so recently come home. Now he was going away again. "You win, *amour*. I'd get up off my deathbed to go after you. If he feels the same about our daughter, there's nothing to do but take him along!"

She clasped him fiercely. "Take care, Edward," she whispered. "Both of you take care. And bring her back safe!"

The big canoe glided into the shelter of the bank. The sky was black now, the snow materializing eerily out of the darkness. Marie was cold. She pulled her cloak about her as best she could with her bound hands as she waited for Ike to help her out of the canoe.

"Up with ye, Mistress Forny!" He steadied her, for she could not balance without the use of her arms. "Won't be long now afore we get a fire built, an' then ye can warm me up proper!" He took a short, braided rope out of the bottom of the canoe and looped it between her wrists, pulling it tight around the buckskin thongs that bound her. Marie gasped at the sudden pressure.

"Hurt, do it?" Ike grinned. "Well, that be what ye get fer tryin' t' run off! We'll be a-tyin' ye while we makes the fire so's ye won't try it agin!" He led her like a horse on a tether and tied the other end of the rope to a sturdy branch. Flying Swan was already gathering firewood, stumbling about in the light snow.

Ike struck his flint to the tinder, and soon the small campfire was flickering in the darkness. They had taken care to select a camp spot behind a high bank. The fire, Marie realized to her dismay, would be almost impossible to see from the river.

It was too dark to hunt. They supped on jerked meat and drank melted snow. Marie held the chunk Ike had given her between her numb fingers and gnawed on it like a dog attacking a bone. She was too frightened to be truly hungry, but she knew she had to eat. She would have to be strong if she wanted to survive.

Flying Swan squatted by the flames. Her face, gilded by firelight, was more swollen than ever. She chewed morosely on her meat staring blankly ahead of her as she ate. None of the others paid any attention to her.

Ike had gathered enough brush and dead limbs to make a rude lean-to at the foot of a massive old sycamore. The two bucks had rigged a simpler shelter on the other side of the clearing. Flying Swan, however, did not move from her place by the fire. She only crouched there, gazing into the flames, a lifeless expression on her face.

"Ain't no use stayin' up when a body can go t' bed," Ike said with a grin that showed the slivers of meat between his teeth. "Reckon I can let ye off the rope fer a spell, Mistress Forny, though I'll be tyin' ye up again afore I goes t' sleep. C'mon! I reckon this t' be the best night I done had in a possum's age." He pulled the rope loose from the tree limb and jerked Marie toward the lean-to.

"Please, Ike, loose my hands," she begged. "You got me tied so tight it hurts."

"Mebbe." He winked. "If'n ye pleasures me enough, Marie Forny. But not right yet. I be waitin' t' see how bad ye wants t' be cut loose. Show me."

With a brutal tug on the rope he pulled her after him into the lean-to, where he had brushed away the snow and spread a buffalo robe. "Get ye down," he grunted. "On yer back. It be too cold t' get naked, so's we'll have t' manage as best we can." He pushed her shoulders to the blanket. Marie was too weary and too frightened to resist him.

"Ike—" She tried one last plea. "Can't we wait? It's so cold. And the others, they can hear us. I feel so. . . funny 'bout it."

"Hell, they don't pay us no mind. They's just Injuns. They do it with ten of 'em sleepin' in one tepee." Ike knelt over her and loosened the front of his breeches. Marie could not look at him. She turned her head. Through the piled brush she could see the dancing orange firelight and the huddled silhouette of Flying Swan.

"No—" she gasped as he lifted her skirt and his cold palm slid up her leg. "No, Ike—"

He stopped her words with a kiss, his tongue thrusting deep into her mouth. His hand had found the warm moistness between her legs. His rough fingers separated the delicate folds that closed the entrance to her body. Helpless, Marie bit her lip and waited. He was breathing loudly now, making little moans in his throat. Marie felt the thick, hot press of him against her, the sudden, hurting thrust—

All at once the lean-to was ripped aside. The icy night air rushed over Marie's body. She screamed as she looked past Ike's shoulder and saw Flying Swan standing over them, one of the red-handled scalping knives in her upraised hand. Her swollen face was contorted with pain and wild rage.

Ike tensed and bellowed as she drove the knife down into his back. He rolled off Marie and in one swift motion his own knife was in his hand. His arm shot back and he flung it blindly. The steel blade sang through the air and caught Flying Swan squarely in the chest.

Flying Swan staggered backward and fell across the fire. Smoke billowed out from under her body, heavy and black with the odors of burning leather, hair and skin. But Flying Swan made no sound.

Ike had slumped to one side, where he lay clawing at the snow. A trickle of blood was forming in one corner of his mouth. Marie rolled away from him. The two bucks bolted out of their shelter, coughing as the smoke filled their lungs.

Marie scrambled to her feet. Now! her senses cried out. Run! Panic gave her swiftness as she darted across the little clearing and into the trees. Over the snow-slicked ground she ran, low branches whipping her face. She could not see her way. She could not feel for obstacles with her bound and benumbed hands. She could only run. Fear shot arrows of strength into her legs as she tore blindly through the dark woods. Her foot caught on a tangled tree root. She pitched forward and went sprawling onto the ground, sticks and pine needles jabbing her flesh. She struggled up and plunged on again.

Flying Swan was dead, Marie was sure, and Ike was dying. As soon as the two Kickapoo braves recovered their wits they would be after her. Swiftly she glanced back at her trail through the snow. They'd have no trouble tracking her now, not even in the dark. And the snow was letting up. Only a few dry-looking flakes were drifting out of the black sky. There would never be enough to cover her tracks.

On and on she ran. Somewhere off to her right she could hear the rippling sigh of the Wabash. She could not stray far from that sound. Not if she wanted to keep alive the hope of being found by searchers.

Marie's face was scratched and bleeding by now. Her legs ached and her sides throbbed with weariness. She tripped over a sharp rock and fell forward, wrenching her shoulder as she tried to break her fall with her bound hands. Her rib cage heaved with exhaustion. No matter how she tried, she could not get up.

She lay there on the snowy ground, her ears filled with the rush of her own breathing. Between gasps she tried to listen for the sound of Indian footsteps, the crackle of a twig, anything that would tell her the two Kickapoos were following her trail. Even when she held her breath, she could hear nothing.

Marie closed her eyes. She had to rest. Maybe they would not try to trail her until dawn. She licked at the snow to cool her burning throat. She could not even feel the coldness of the ground.

Marie could not be certain how long she lay there, but she opened her eyes some time later and realized that the clouds had gone and the stars had come out. The sky was beginning to gray above the eastern horizon. Soon it would be dawn.

She got to her feet. Her muscles were aching. Her hands were swollen and almost blue. She would go down to the river, Marie resolved. She could not survive alone. Her life depended upon her being found by rescuers.

A faint sound came to her ears—or perhaps it was more of a feeling than a sound: a whisper, the cry of a bird, the rustle of a leaf. But Marie knew that she was no longer alone. The two braves were coming after her.

XXIX

Edward and Ned had paddled upstream until it grew too dark to see the bank. Then they'd pulled the canoe into the trees, rolled up in their blankets and gone to sleep under it, the snow falling soft and cold around them.

But neither of them had slept well. Worry had made them both restless, and Ned's wound had given him a dull, drumming pain in his head. By the time the first faint streaks of dawn began to pale in the sky they had given up on sleep, risen, stretched their legs, and downed a hurried breakfast of cold johnnycake.

"Feeling any better?" Edward studied the young man with anxious eyes.

"A mite. It'll mend in time. Let's go."

The canoe glided out over the glassy water and moved into the current. Edward put the strength of his back into each stroke, his mind seeing nothing but Marie—Marie in danger, Marie hurt, raped, or dead. "We'll find her," he said out loud, striving to reassure not only Ned but himself. "We won't stop searching until we do."

"Aye." Ned leaned hard into his paddle. He had driven himself to exhaustion the night before. Edward was more than a little worried about him. "We shouldn't've stopped for the night. They be well ahead of us by now."

"*Non*. . ." Edward answered him thoughtfully. "The night was so black we could have passed them at a stone's throw and not seen them. We had no choice."

"Do you think. . ." Ned started the question, then let his voice trail off. There was no need for him to finish. Edward knew what was in his mind. There was no question about what Ike Ilam intended to do to Marie, or that by now he would have at least tried to carry out those intentions.

"*Oui*," Edward answered gently. "There is no use deluding ourselves, Ned. By now Ilam has likely done his worst."

"It don't matter." Ned dug the paddle into the water with a determination that was almost violent. "Long as we get her back alive. That be the only thing that matters now."

"You love her very much, don't you, son?" The last word slipped from Edward's mouth with a sense of complete naturalness.

"Aye. That I do."

"Then let's find her! *Allons-y!*" They flung themselves into their paddles, and the canoe shot forward like an arrow from a bow.

Marie was running for her life. Behind her she could hear the rustling of the underbrush as the two Indians came after her. They made no effort to conceal their pursuit now. It was only a matter of time and speed before they caught her. She could not even hope to outrace them.

She had tried to move over bare rock and through thick bushes to make her trail harder to follow. But it was all useless. That cursed, thin frosting of snow covered everything. Her footprints left a trail that a child could follow. She had even plunged into the edge of the river, hoping to hide her tracks the way a fox does. But it only slowed her down. And with the river's flooded condition and her own bound hands there was no way she could cross to the other side or try to float a log and get downstream. She would have to come out of the water on the same side as she had entered, and the Indians knew it.

She was exhausted by now. Her sides heaved. Her throat ached from the effort of breathing. He knee was gashed and bleeding where she'd slipped in the snow and fallen onto a sharp rock. Her hands were a swollen purple from the tightness of the thongs about her wrists.

Somewhere behind her, coming closer and closer, she could hear them yelping like wolves. Marie fought her way through the dense bushes along the riverbank. Why run? her weary mind screamed at her. It's hopeless! They'll catch you any minute!

At the river's edge she stopped. The pounding of her heart filled her head and her whole body as she stood with the gray-brown water rippling around her feet. Yes, why run? Marie asked herself again. The two Kickapoos would be upon her any minute, and when they caught her, she could expect. . .what? Rape, almost surely. Torture, and an awful death. She would have been better off if Ike Ilam had lived. Well, that was none of her doing, and neither was Flying Swan's death. But the two braves would blame her, and Flying Swan was their sister. They would enjoy their vengeance.

She had only a little strength and a little time left. She would use it to die, Marie resolved, stepping out into the water. She would wade out to where the swirling current covered all but her head. Then, when they were almost upon her, she would only have to move a little farther out. The river would take her. Better the Wabash than the Indians, she told herself as she waded deeper. The water was up to her knees now, and the elated whoops of the two braves were very near. Drowning was a merciful end, she'd been told. And with her bound hands there would be no struggle. The water would slide over her like a cool, dark blanket and she would sleep forever.

The river was up to Marie's chest when they burst out of the bushes and saw her. Shrieking, they splashed into the water. The one in the lead was swinging a steel tomahawk above his head. The other had his knife ready.

Marie moved into deeper water. *Now,* she told herself. There was no time to be lost. Her feet fumbled for the moss-covered stones. Fleeting visions of her father and mother, of her brother Henry, of Ned burst into her mind as she pushed herself out into the deep current. The water closed over her head as she kicked her feet to carry herself farther away from the Indians. She felt herself sinking. Yes, she had beaten them at last. She had cheated them out of the pleasure of her death. Marie felt the air escaping from her lungs, bubbling to the surface through her open mouth. There would be only a moment of struggle, a struggle she could not hope to win. Then it would be over.

Suddenly she was conscious of a movement beside her in the water, a groping hand, then a skull-wrenching jerk on her hair. An instant later her head broke water again. She coughed and sputtered. The life-giving air rushed into her lungs. She opened her eyes to find herself staring into the face of the Indian with the tomahawk. The Indian grinned. His fist tightened and twisted in Marie's hair, and he began to drag her toward the bank.

Ned and Edward had heard the cries of the Indians from beyond the bend of the river. Like devils they paddled, bursting around the bend just in time to see the Kickapoo jerk Marie out of the water.

The other brave waited, closer to shore. Edward raised the long rifle that he'd loaded earlier. Marie appeared to be helpless. She could drown, or be hit by mistake if he fired at this range on the Indian who had her. But he could improve the odds in her favor by picking off the other one. The braves, intent on Marie, had not yet seen them.

"Steady. . .hold it steady," he muttered to Ned, who was ripping into the water like a madman with his paddle. "Hold it. . . ." He took careful aim and slowly squeezed the trigger. The Indian staggered backward and fell with a noisy splash. He floated there, a flat circle of crimson spreading around him in the gray water.

The other Indian spun around and saw the canoe. Acting quickly, he moved behind Marie, so that her body would act as a shield against a second rifle shot from the canoe. Carefully he began to edge toward the bank.

Edward could see his daughter clearly now. She was conscious, but weak and paralyzed by fear. Could he trust her to break away and run if the chance came? Edward gazed at her and agonized over what to do next.

Ned's paddle sent the canoe racing forward, but the Indian would beat them to the shore with Marie. Maybe the red devil would drop her and run for his own life, Edward dared to hope. But then, he reminded himself, if the Kickapoo had intended to do that, he would more than likely have let her go in the water. And they were almost onto the bank now, the brave holding Marie by her hair and supporting her weight on one arm. It did not appear that Marie could even stand up under her own power.

Then Edward saw what the Indian intended to do. He was holding Marie only by her hair now as his free hand worked the red-handled knife out of his belt. His face was twisted with hatred and contempt. He would kill his prisoner at the risk of his own life before he would let her go free.

With a shrill cry of defiance, he raised the knife high above his head. Breathing a prayer, Edward whipped Ned's loaded gun to his shoulder and aimed at the one part of the brave that was not protected by the girl's body. He pulled the trigger; the lead ball sang through the air, and the knife flew from the Indian's hand. Blood spurted and trickled down his arm.

At that moment, Ned's body hurtled from the canoe. A few swift strokes and a powerful lunge brought him to the shore, and he flung himself at the Indian. "Run!" he yelled. "Run, Marie!"

"Run!" Edward echoed the shout, and he saw his daughter break loose from the savage's grasp, spin away and stagger up onto the bank. In a moment he had beached the canoe, leaped out of it and seized her in his arms.

Ned and the Indian thrashed and struggled in the water, the Kickapoo's wounded hand spreading a thin wash of red. But even wounded he was bigger, stronger, and a more experienced fighter than Ned. Marie screamed as the brave shoved Ned's head under the water and held him there. "Do something!" she gasped.

There was no time to reload either of the rifles. Edward seized the barrel of one and swung it like a club. The solid hickory stock crashed into the back of the Indian's head. He shuddered and collapsed face down in the water, releasing Ned, who bobbed sputtering to the surface. In the next moment, Marie was in his arms.

Edward waded into the river and hauled the brave out by an arm and a leg. The Kickapoo was unconscious from the blow, but still breathing, lightly and easily. The wounded hand trickled blood.

Marie gazed down at him and shuddered. "Kill him," she whispered, and buried her face against Ned's chest.

Edward gazed at her. "Kill him? Club him like a fish while he lies here helpless like this? Is that what you want, *ma fille?*"

Marie did not answer him. She only clung more tightly to Ned, sobbing deeply as he held her.

"Non," Edward shook his head. "The fight is over, my children, and we have won. Killing this man will only add one more evil to what has already passed. Showing mercy to him will begin a new time, a time of good, and he will live to remember how we spared him, *eh bien?*" Swiftly he knelt beside the brave, who was already beginning to moan softly. Just as swiftly, he ripped off the hem of his linsey shirt and tightly bound the wounded hand to stop the bleeding.

"Now—one of our blankets, Ned. *Rapidement!* He is waking up! He is wet, he will be cold." Edward took the woolen blanket from Ned, unfolded it and spread it over the Indian's body. "Now, *les filles,* let us be away!"

Edward had never seen a more magnificent sunset. He rested the paddle on the gunwales of the canoe and allowed the slim craft to float downstream by itself while he watched the sky turn from gold to amber, then to red and to deep violet as the fiery ball of the sun sank over the distant hills.

Ned and Marie lay sleeping like two children in the bottom of the canoe, both of them still damp and exhausted. The setting sun gilded their smooth young faces where they lay, sharing the same blanket, their arms flung loosely about each other. What beautiful sons and daughters they would have one day, he thought. They were young, almost too young, but Abby had told him what had happened. Yes, it was best that they marry as soon as possible, young or not. It was a good match, and they loved each other. *Pourquois pas?* Why not, indeed?

Vincennes lay less than an hour ahead. Abby would be waiting for them on the landing. They would celebrate Marie's return together. Then, when the cabin was quiet, they would light a single candle and Abby would lead him upstairs to their bedroom. Edward's face warmed as he thought of the great, soft bed, Abby's beckoning arms, and the sweet, splendid ripeness of her body. Such a night! He had had homecomings before, any number of them, but this one, he promised himself, would be the best one of all!

And what of tomorrow? Colonel Clark would likely be needing him for a time, until the new town government was organized and permanent systems of defense and communication were set up along the frontier. There would be Indian tribes to visit, peace pipes to smoke, treaties to sign. Maybe there would be need of a search party to go and look for poor, mad Mathilde.

As to the business—Edward glanced fondly down at Marie and Ned. He would make Ned a partner, he decided. That would be his wedding present to the young couple. Forny and Cooper. It had a fine ring to it!

His dynasty was already begun, Edward realized, with Henry and his fair-haired Sara in the South; Marie and her Ned here in the North. Someday their children, and their children's children, would be plying the trade of Forny and Cooper up and down a whole network of lakes and rivers, all along the frontier of this rambunctious young land! He would be old by then. A white-haired old man, with his Abby by his side, God willing. And that was fine. He wanted to live forever, to see it all. He wanted to live to be a hundred!

But as for tonight—Edward Forny laughed with pleasure as he dipped his paddle into the silvery water of the Wabash. As for tonight, he had never felt so young!

BESTSELLING ROMANCES BY JANELLE TAYLOR

SAVAGE ECSTASY (824, $3.50)
It was like lightning striking, the first time the Indian brave Gray Eagle looked into the eyes of the beautiful young settler Alisha. And from the moment he saw her, he knew that he must possess her—and make her his slave!

DEFIANT ECSTASY (931, $3.50)
When Gray Eagle returned to Fort Pierre's gates with his hundred warriors behind him, Alisha's heart skipped a beat: would Gray Eagle destroy her—or make his destiny her own?

FORBIDDEN ECSTASY (1014, $3.50)
Gray Eagle had promised Alisha his heart forever—nothing could keep him from her. But when Alisha woke to find her red-skinned lover gone, she felt abandoned and alone. Lost between two worlds, desperate and fearful of betrayal, Alisha hungered for the return of her FORBIDDEN ECSTASY.

BRAZEN ECSTASY (1133, $3.50)
When Alisha is swept down a raging river and out of her savage brave's life, Gray Eagle must rescue his love again. But Alisha has no memory of him at all. And as she fights to recall a past love, another white slave woman in their camp is fighting for Gray Eagle!

TENDER ECSTASY (1212, $3.75)
Bright Arrow is committed to kill every white he sees—until he sets his eyes on ravishing Rebecca. And fate demands that he capture her, torment her . . . and soar with her to the dizzying heights of TENDER ECSTASY!

Available wherever paperbacks are sold, or order direct from the Publisher. Send cover price plus 50¢ per copy for mailing and handling to Zebra Books, 475 Park Avenue South, New York, N.Y. 10016. DO NOT SEND CASH.